MW00884640

Candlelight Vigils: Book One: The Foundation is a work of fiction. All incidents and dialogue, and all characters, with the exception of some well-known historical figures, are the products of the author's imagination and are not to be construed as real. Where real-life historical figures appear, the situations, incidents, and dialogues concerning those persons are entirely fictional and are not intended to depict actual events or to change the entirely fictional nature of the work. In all other respects, any resemblance to persons living or dead is entirely coincidental. All trademarks, service marks, registered trademarks, and registered service marks are the property of their respective owners and are used herein for identification purposes only.

Candlelight Vigils: Book One: The Foundation
Copyright 2019 by Shayne Anthony Kelly
All rights reserved
ISBN: 9781709725838

1

Candlelight Vigils: Book One: The Foundation

A Novel

Shayne A. Kelly

Shayne A. Kelly
11-27-19

Chapter One

His eyes pierce like a lion stalking his prey, not through leaves in a humid jungle, but over his tangle of rusting steel abutted against rotten wood and concrete floors washed nightly to erase the horrid memories in this modern world.

Today, his hunting ground is within a Cali, Colombia disco, his quarry, is rummaging its way towards Don Pedro.

Don Pedro is encircled by his seated loyal compatriots drinking the most expensive brandy, smoking crack, and snorting cocaine. Cocaine delivered to the table by young 'wannabes,' who are dispatched to fill the recalcitrant orders, skeletons running to and from the renovated warehouse, their frail brown bodies functioning on pure chemicals, skeletons neither in this world or the afterlife. Hooked noses inherited from their Spanish conquerors and thrown to the street by their mothers, wearing only discarded emblazoned Nike and Fila t-shirts and shorts. Mothers no longer able to care for their children, because their fathers have left, been killed, or are in jail.

The wannabes obtained their name as they 'wanted to be' someone of stature in the organization. Viewed by the upper crust of Colombian society, including Don Pedro and his organizational members, as a mere nuisance, the world can be so cruel. The young wannabes retrieve the potent cocaine elixir from an adjacent dilapidated steel reinforced room dripping with water from the roof to the cement floor protected by a seemingly equal wannabe. However, this wannabe protecting the 'personal use' stash has received a field promotion as he possesses an AK-47.

The 'straw' owner of the disco, Paola, previously the real owner, allows the Don Pedro criminal incursion to occur. Paola the straw owner owns the bar in name only, but does not control the finances. After all, what choice does Paola have, death or abject poverty?

Before Paola's capitulation to the bar's straw owner, on a typical hot, humid afternoon, pale-faced men entered through the disco's opened door and approached Paola. Dark bluish-green rain clouds developed on the horizon pushing cool air inside. The men are cordial but firm in their demand that they now control the disco. However, they will allow Paola to continue to act as the owner, and he will be paid little for his troubles. The traffickers do their best to act like business people. The traffickers know they needed Paola's expertise in the day to day operation of the disco. After all, they are not willing to work. The traffickers do not divulge to Paola why they chose his bar, but reason dictates the disco will be a new meeting place for these traffickers' bosses.

Paola is familiar with this approach. After all, this is Colombia. So, Paola politely listens and asks for extra time to think about their proposition. Paola assesses the likely outcome. He delays in telling the men of his acceptance. His thoughts, in postponing his decision are many; he hopes that the criminals develop an interest in another location, rivals kill them, or they go missing. Paola ignores the traffickers' telephone calls to the bar. He works fewer hours at the bar, and as a result of his absence, his employees accept more responsibilities and work hours. He acts on the philosophy: out of sight out of mind.

Eventually, Paola hears a knock or more like a constant drumbeat at his front door residence. The noise rattles Paola waking him from his afternoon nap. Paola, enraged, leaps from the couch to his feet, hands clenched, head down, and walks with broad determined steps towards the front door. He prepares for a verbal altercation. He opens the door and his mind instantly flashes to a vision of his wife and kids cowering and shaking after being told by Paola of the extortion plot. His family immediately grasped the severity of the proposition. Why didn't he? With the door open, Paola views three emotionless men standing in the doorway. They do not bother turning their heads to meet Paola's gaze; they only move their eyes to stare at Paola. The men in the door do not speak and remain motionless. They are Don Pedro's assassins. He lost.

Paola ignored the first approach by Don Pedro's men, what a mistake. In that first proposition, the killers provide

Paola an opportunity to accept 'silver' (plata) for his disco but now, he faces the 'lead' (plomo). Consistent throughout the corrupt world, one has to choose between the 'silver or lead.' Pleas for police assistance is not an option.

Now, Paola dutifully stands erect, a white towel draped over his left arm awaiting instructions from Don Pedro's guest. Air conditioning vents throughout the disco sweat, blowing jets of intermittent cool air. The units clack as if requesting maintenance, aware the pleas will go unheeded. The disco was transformed, by Paola and his wife, from an abandoned vegetable warehouse constructed of corrugated steel with a semblance of a concrete floor. They hung long full white, light blue and canary yellow drapes from the roof's steel girders to steel fasteners bolted to the floor in the corners of the warehouse. More substantial curtains in horizontally curved fashion fall between the roof's steel girders. They installed a multicolored lighting system capable of accenting the drapes and the dance floor. Potted tropical plants are placed in the bar segmenting patrons' tables providing a sense of privacy.

The partying and cavorting with women continue for hours, as a DJ and musical bands wail from the evenings to the early mornings. After the parties, the drug lord, Don Pedro, and his compatriots/associates return to their city apartments accompanied by the beautiful 'working women.' Women entangle themselves in this mess as a possible tragic means out of poverty; others are products of human trafficking. Don Pedro's people treat the working women much the same as the young men wannabees.

Nobody is more relieved than Paola at the conclusion of the parties. On many occasions, Paola's white button-down cotton shirt is drenched in sweat sticking to his body, and he is left leaning on the bar, taking deep breaths. The party combatants are oblivious to the emotional stress placed by them on innocent civilians. Today, Don Pedro, his men and a woman arrive early in the afternoon and will wait at the disco until their game comes. To Paola, this early arrival could be his death.

On a typical weekend, these partygoers' make use of helicopters or drive in armed convoys to their fincas (ranches) outside the city limits, especially during festivals, Christmas Holidays, and Easter. During these events, the city is too dangerous for even Don Pedro and his like. Indiscriminate and directed killings combined with kidnappings in Colombia are almost on par with Venezuela.

Don Pedro, leader of the Cali Cartel, enjoys the title 'Lord' given to him by the press; he acquired the royal title by poisoning hundreds of thousands of his loyal subjects. How insane is that? Don Pedro blatantly abuses his subjects physically and mentally, hoards their cash, and uses his people as throwaway commodities. Poverty is a horrible life. However, so many of his subjects are still attracted to him. His serfs believe through time served, they will receive a small amount of Don Pedro's power and accompanying money. In turn, they give their undying loyalty to the 'Lord.' Their misery resembles the clanking of the disco air conditioner. Pleading for relief, from their miserable conditions consciously aware that if some form of aid does avail itself, it only will be temporary.

Don Pedro temporarily mused as a magazine article, authored by a Colombian National, estimates his self-worth on par to legitimate American and Chinese billionaires. The reader of the column could infer Don Pedro is also a legitimate businessman. Don Pedro plays the businessman role and wears the appropriate clothes. His tailored made suits separate him from the street urchins, but deep down, he recognizes he is only one mental step away from the animal kingdom. His thumbs are the only physical attributes that differentiate him from a majority of animals except for gorillas, chimps, apes and a few others. Losing a thumb will be a problem for all.

The recent magazine article is exceptionally detailed and accurate. Listed in the section are suspected 'front' businesses associated with Don Pedro's smuggling ventures, locations of residences and the name of a port city utilized by Don Pedro and his associates. Amusing, but dangerous to Don Pedro and the Cali Cartel. It is highly probable that the article's information, as described by the journalist, originated from elements within the Colombian government. More weekly articles detailing Don Pedro's expansive criminal organization follow. His enemy, the Medellin Cartel, in its continual bribes to government officials, called in a favor in acquiring the Colombians government Don Pedro investigative files. The file, in turn, loaned to the investigative reporter for publication. Public attention is terrible for his businesses. If the articles continue, the Colombian government officials he collaborates with will be forced to act against the Don Pedro organization.

Following the Cali and Medellin Cartel's wars that ended in 1993, Don Pedro over eight years slowly rebuilds the Cali Cartel as do members of the Medellin Cartel. Don Pedro's international bases suffered during the Cartel wars so he makes it a priority to strengthen these overseas operations.

Although, it appears to the 'common man' Don Pedro is untouchable, that belief is never further from the truth. Don Pedro is in effect a temporary contractor assigned to various government officials who take bribes from his organization. When Don Pedro becomes a liability, he is sure to be replaced. Moreover, it is during this forced transition that violence in the streets, bombings, random and targeted assassinations of law enforcement officials, and disappearances all increase in intensity. If Don Pedro is successfully replaced then low-keyed successors will emerge. However, facilitating corruption within the government remains. After his fall, the arrest of low-level government officials ensues, others are reassigned, resign or seek early retirement. Don Pedro's Cali Cartel congratulates its rival the Medellin Cartel for creating the recent periodical attacks.

For decades, the Colombian government stands at the forefront in the fight against the likes of the 'Don Pedros.' The Colombian government is the most effective fighting apparatus in combating the Cartels. Many brave Colombian soldiers and police give their loyalty and lives for their country and in effect the same to the United States. As odd as it appears, Don Pedro congratulates and has the most profound respect for the uncorrupted Colombian soldiers and police. At least, they stand for something. The world should commend the righteous Colombian soldiers and police for their sacrifices, but the corruption undercurrent which Don Pedro participates, continues to wash away some of their gains.

Don Pedro understands he is not unique. There are other 'Don Pedros' with operations in the BLT (Burma, Laos, Thailand) trafficking heroin, Afghanistan (heroin), Russia, the Philippines, Somalia, name a country in distress and the 'Don Pedros' exist. If killed he wishes it is a result of honest Colombian soldiers and police. Although his organization corrupts officers/soldiers and works in concert with corrupted government officials to achieve its goals, Don Pedro espouses no respect for the government officials, soldiers, and police who accept his organizations' bribes. Strangely, he longs for his own country's stability. Not cognizant that he is one facilitator in its instability. Don Pedro is a severely conflicted man. He wonders if a Colombian peacemaker will avail himself in the future. Rephrased, he hopes for a peacemaker.

The damning articles continue publication weekly. So, Don Pedro reaches out to his corrupt government officials and seeks advice in countering the ingenious Medellin Cartel threat. It is paramount that he gets out of the medias eye. His is now the face responsible for everything wrong in Colombia, poverty, violence, and corruption. It is Don Pedro's opinion that the articles have persuaded the general public of his guilt, and because of this, the Medellin Cartel will overtly attack the Cali Cartel in Colombia. The Colombian citizenry will attribute the increase violence initiated by the Medellin Cartel against the Cali Cartel to one person, Don Pedro. Executing the reporter will only exacerbate the issue.

The Medellin Cartel act as bees. It is in their nature to sting hurting their victims and killing themselves. The Medellin cannot let things go.

To redirect the impending violence, Don Pedro plans to move the battlefront. One government official provides a way to covertly disable the Medellin Cartel by instigating the war to a different geographic sphere, not in Colombia. The subjects capable of succeeding in such a plan are not palatable to Don Pedro. However, after multiple conversations, Don Pedro swallows his long-term hatred and prejudices of these individuals and accepts the corrupt government official's offer.

Don Pedro is sure of one thing about his government friends. They will do anything to protect their pilfering from the government coffers and acceptance of bribes. Don Pedro realizes his organization is merely a 'Sideshow.' Allowed to operate because of some of these government officials. His friends in the government might allow Don Pedro to dangle for a short time taking advantage of the deflection. However, they will not let Don Pedro absorb too much heat from the public. Alternatively, their enemies the Medellin Cartel and their contacts in the same government will threaten their aggrandizement. So, government officials supporting Don Pedro decide to protect Don Pedro for now.

Don Pedro is a product of his third world surroundings. His family sacrificed in his early years caring for and harvesting coffee beans on their little plot of fertile Colombian soil located in a valley surrounded by high mountains. The mountain tops typically covered by mist complete with thick groves of trees and expansive undergrowth.

The land belonged to the family for as long as his great-grandfather could remember. The land was acquired through a wager by his great grandfather from a feudal Spaniard.

At times, Don Pedro's grandfather, Enrique Jose Speranza-Gutierrez would assemble the family besides outside barbacoa, ignited on chilly nights, and tell stories of their ancestors.

All of Don Pedro's family shared in the work and built their farm sufficiently enough to sustain their needs. The family is poor but endure in turbulent times by literally clustering together, a defense mechanism for personal survival. New crops are planted yearly combined with the acquisitions of a few cattle, goats, and chickens. With the yearly purchases, Don Pedro's family continue to survive.

During a particularly revolutionary period, Communist rebels referred to as the FARC, an acronym for Communist Revolutionary Armed Forces, hurl themselves into Don Pedro's world. The Colombian authorities recently reasserted control of self-designated FARC controlled sections of the jungle. The FARC pillage and burn the family farm as well as others nearby. The FARC is sending a message to the remaining farmers and ranchers in the area. If you assist Colombian law enforcement authorities, your farm and ranch will be next.

Don Pedro is only four when he watches in horror as these horseback rebels brandishing automatic weapons trample his family. The flames overcome his father fighting the house fire set by the FARC rebels. Don Pedro, known as 'Little P' tries in vain to drag his father from the flames but only succeeds in cutting and burning his right hand, reducing his little finger to a stub. Thank God, it is not his thumb for everybody's sake. The smoke from the raging fires conceals Don Pedro from the marauders. He runs with his surviving relatives into the safety of the dense green wet jungle surrounding the family farm.

They are now refugees. The remnants of the now destitute family are forced to deliver 'Little P' to a nearby Catholic orphanage where he resides until he is seventeen years of age. The nuns are kind, and within his soul, he feels their genuine mercy but scarred. However, he will never forgive the animals that destroyed his family. His beautiful life and family devastated and for what, temporary occupancy of farmland and furtherance of a meaningless Communist ideology. He learns his future survival depends on his ability to attach to no one and to take preempted aggressive stances when needed. He is determined not to be placed into a defensive posture as he experienced while hiding in the jungle from the FARC. He will take the fight to his enemies. When provoked, his body involuntarily convulses to his snub finger, his nostrils will flare resembling a bull before a snort, and he appears to raise his back in anticipation of the hunt.

During this particular afternoon at Don Pedro's newly occupied disco, the potential victim is one of Don Pedro's narcotic transporters, Juan Federico Sanchez, a Mexican, but known to others in Colombia as The Mexican National or aka Mex Nat. One subject within Don Pedro's Colombian organization refers to Sanchez as, 'The Asshole.' In Mexico, Sanchez uses another alias.

Sanchez is principally responsible for some of Don Pedro's shipments of narcotics from the South Texas border known as 'the valley' to New York City. At times, Sanchez's employees take receipt of Don Pedro's narcotics from as far south as the Guatemalan border with Mexico. This area, the southern State of Chiapas, Mexico bordering with Guatemala, is a no man's land.

Sanchez never met Don Pedro. Sanchez is ordered to plead his case, a result of recent law enforcement narcotic seizures under Sanchez's responsibility. Sanchez will accept responsibility for the seizures. Sanchez, although ruthless in his small part of the Don Pedro organization, is aware he will meet his match.

The effects of alcohol and a recent snort of cocaine before departure on a non-stop flight from America to Colombia leave Sanchez in a stupor that evolves into a high state of paranoia. This flight from America, if missed, would seal his fate. A Cali subject identified as Flaco orders Sanchez to Colombia. Flaco is Don Pedro's 'spokesman.'

While sitting at the airport concourse bar before departure, Sanchez acknowledges who is in charge, Don Pedro. For years, Sanchez took advantage of Mexican Nationals, recent immigrants to America, and strung out Americans for the sole purpose of 'mulling,' transporting narcotics to their destinations in the United States. These individuals, the mules, knew little of Sanchez's organization and especially of Sanchez himself. Sanchez layers his links to the mules by delegating orders to a few subjects which in turn delegate the same to other nicknamed and or alias monikered Sanchez associates.

Moreover, it is these mid-level delegates who communicate with the lowly transporters, who physically smuggle the narcotics via various modes of transportation. These Sanchez associates, utilizing names of convenience contact the mule via prepaid cell phone and advise the same of the location and expected date of the initial 'pick up' of narcotics.

Following the receipt of the initial narcotics, the mules are ordered to travel north on a designated highway, road and or route. As the mules close on their 'offloading' destination, the mules are advised of the specific delivery site, on a street corner, a mall parking lot, residence or highway rest stop. The last-minute delivery notification shields the Sanchez organization in the event of a seizure by law enforcement under the control of the mule. They are careful only to expose the mule with information on one person, the trafficker instructing the mule to the first pickup.

The restricted notification limits the mule's ability to provide evidence against the recipients located at the mall parking lot, highway rest stop or truck stop. Sanchez's organization practices compartmentalization: each person is provided with information on a 'need to know' basis. Sanchez also refers to the mules as 'throwaways.' Because of this serious dispatch for travel 'down south,' he knows his role. To those in Colombia, he is a mule a throwaway.

Don Pedro does not reminisce of tales of grandeur at the disco, his known history speaks for itself. Don Pedro rises from the Cali Barrio on the outskirts of town, working as a cocaine waiter, to motorcycle assassin, to cocaine broker. Cocaine trafficker histories are similar. Don Pedro's offensive trait, deadly assaults, and luck propel him to the pinnacle of his criminal career. Don Pedro rises faster in the ranks and becomes the puppet master before Sanchez can do the same. The reason, Don Pedro possesses the geographic advantage as he resides at the source of supply.

Faced with the sudden travel to Cali, Sanchez thought of 'going on the run.' Little did Sanchez know that little old Paola, Don Pedro's disco straw owner thought the same when given the 'plata' proposal. Sanchez will never leave the narcotic trafficking world. Even with his limited knowledge of technology, the smuggling world is growing smaller. He cannot elude Don Pedro's assassins. Sanchez's only option is to get in good graces with his boss.

If he refuses to meet with Don Pedro, Sanchez is smart enough to know how it will go down. Assassins hired in Colombia by Don Pedro, cocaine and blood dripping from their shark-like brown teeth will dutifully comply 'to do

Sanchez in.' Don Pedro's spokesman, Flaco, might even volunteer to shoot Sanchez. Alternatively, Don Pedro might procure a local American 'made man' mafioso for the killing. Crime is transnational, and Don Pedro is the first to make appreciated advances in its use.

Sanchez remembers when he orchestrated the killing of three of his rivals at a Houston, Texas convenience store. Upon the termination of the subjects by his hired guns, Sanchez using a prepaid cell immediately notifies Flaco of his role in their deaths. Through this call, Sanchez expects Flaco to put in a good word to Don Pedro. Did he? Who knows? However, like everywhere else, all the past good deeds are forgotten when there is a detrimental effect on the bottom-line. The recent seizures affect the bottom line and could lead to more significant losses. Sanchez's lifespan is tenuous. Sanchez knows not to expect a simple pink slip. His slip will be dark red.

The public will not recover his body in an open place for all to view. So, the media cannot repeat its 'go to' scenario of a found murdered body, with no signs of robbery. The deceased is a result of a 'Drug Deal Gone Bad.' Is there a good drug deal? Every time he hears or reads about a drug deal gone bad; he shakes his head. The media leaves the viewers to believe the deceased is an economic failure. Never has the media jumped to the conclusion that the dead are responsible for the poisoning and the subsequent destruction of hundreds of souls.

Arriving by commercial air to the Cali, Colombia airport, Sanchez walks from the airport concourse without luggage. If he makes it back to the US, he will likely encounter US Customs as they tend to key on single passengers without luggage making use of one-way trips. Sanchez was not provided enough time to rent a family for cover.

Sanchez hails an independent taxi. His cab brightly colored with large swaths of red over yellow paint, its windows are in the down position and its air conditioner is not working. Sanchez sits on the deteriorating blue cloth, sticky to the touch. Will his would-be assassins kill him here in front of the airport? His head is on a swivel. He scans for threats.

Upon acceleration, the taxi cabs' exhaust creates a smoke screen temporarily disguising his exit from the airport. As the taxi is driven from the area the sounds of the airport: intercoms, vociferous passengers, vendors barking and visitors not realizing they are screaming to each other begin to disappear. With one last glance at the airport, Sanchez views amongst the carnival-like motion polite petite women and children of native Indian descent seated on the sidewalk with their arms extended begging for money. If the Indian women are not successful in relieving you of your small change, their small children are sent to finish the job.

It is Sanchez's responsibility to lose any potential police 'tails.' Don Pedro ordered his men not to retrieve Sanchez at the airport allowing Don Pedro latitude in his decision to meet today, tomorrow, or the next not a good start. Sanchez constantly scans for repetitive people memorizing their clothes and faces, cabs, cars anything that resembles a tail. The biggest threats are motorcycles occupied by two people, the driver and the assassin seated behind the driver. If the motorcyclists are not wearing vests with official government numbers inscribed on the back matching the motorcycle plate then he is as good as dead upon sighting them. Without notice, these assassins strike and retreat easily manipulating any traffic condition.

Sanchez changes taxis to divert numerous unscrupulous taxi drivers (halcons/falcons/hawks) employed as lookouts by rival narcotic organizations and the police. Besides observing patterns in traffic, vehicles, license plates, he concentrates on peoples' reactions upon seeing him, are they surprised, not interested, did they make a verbal or physical motion as he passes.

Sanchez directs the cab drivers to stop at random hotels and departments stores. He walks inside one door of a business and exits a separate entry. Sanchez walks the streets monitoring reflected images in store windows in an attempt to get a glimpse of any sign of a tail. If a tail is spotted, Sanchez knows not to react, but to continue his travels until he feels comfortable that the suspected or confirmed tail is no longer a threat. Sanchez walks in the opposite direction of one-way streets in an attempt to lose vehicle surveillance. He is forcing the suspected surveillance vehicles to drive away from him. This also enables Sanchez the ability to see the occupants exit the surveillance vehicles. If the occupants follow him on foot, there is a high probability they might be surveillance.

Time is on his side, and this counter-surveillance activity continues for approximately three hours. During this period, he receives a cryptic message to proceed to meet with Don Pedro. Sanchez randomly crosses the city from modern high-rise apartments, factories ultimately leading through streets paralleled by small stucco and concrete-walled shops and various residences painted in bright colors. Shared walls connect the structures. Sanchez walks past political posters plastered haphazardly on decayed painted cinder blocked walls. Signs placed over posters imploring one to vote for one political candidate or another.

The dull grey streets a result of years of discarded waste, some thrown by the residents and small food vendors into rusting black metal oil barrels serving as trash receptacles. Food vendor customers are seated or standing next to suspended wooden planks placed underneath trees that line the streets. Three to four customers at a time discuss politics, crime, and lack of employment. The vendors sweep their sidewalk area with a Clorox solution. Sanchez smelled this Clorox solution too many times in his life. A similar, more potent solution is used to dispose of his victims. He hails another taxi.

Entering the thickest part of a notoriously dangerous barrio, Sanchez realizes he is entirely alone. Sanchez directs the taxi driver to stop a few blocks from Don Pedro's lair. He is preventing the taxi driver in identifying Sanchez's ultimate destination. Sanchez's shaking hand throws an unknown amount of money to the cab driver and stands from the cab, the seat cushion sticks to his damp clothes. The taxi driver leaves the area miraculously entering the flow of traffic, through a chorus of car horns and rapidly fired brake lights set in motion with numerous self-appointed conductors replacing the conductor's baton with derogatory hand gestures, only to disappear into a menagerie of color and movement.

Sanchez walks to the disco warehouse and struggles to open the door as it is pressed closed from the pressure of the semi-cool air inside. Sanchez pulls hard to break the suction on the door. The heat and sweat from his body cause a fog to rise from his body as the warehouse semi-cool air hits his chest. Sanchez enters the warehouse inhaling the damp smell of urine, stale alcohol, and cigarette smoke. His eyes have trouble focusing. He observes no guards. He knows they are close. The inhabitants are comfortable in their surroundings. Someone pays the local authorities.

Sanchez has spoken with Flaco on the phone but never met him. He surmises Flaco is the tall, skinny, bald, brown-skinned individual the first to reach his stare. Flaco stands from the table and raises his glass in a proper salute directed to the esteemed patrons Don Pedro, Don Ochoa, Don Garcia-Garcia, Francesca Gutierrez and others. Major brokers and owners of several smuggled shipments from Colombia to the United States, Europe and with the aid of absolute corruption – Russia. Sanchez recognizes a few of

the other patrons but does not know their names. Sanchez
identifies Don Pedro from a photograph in a Colombian
paper he purchased at the Cali airport. The accompanying
article blames Don Pedro for the world's ills, crime, cancer,
poverty, so on and so forth. The paper folded in his back
pocket. The meeting conducted in a semi-public
environment is accepted as performing one's activities in
the most blatantly transparent manner deflects the curious,
the few suspecting good cops and aspiring criminals.

Sanchez remains still during the salutations, legs half
erect mumbling, wishing Don Pedro will choke on a fried
plantain from the basket at his table. Can he be so lucky to
have Don Pedro stroke out on some high-grade coke
brought to him by an unsuspecting coke waiter? The
cocaine switched by a Don Pedro rival. Don Pedro should
have a food taster maybe this is a good time to recommend
such a policy. He is still a wise ass.

Sanchez can make 'quick reads' of people. In float like
gestures, Flaco circles the esteemed guests. He looks like
Dracula. Dracul, Vlad the Impaler, but with diplomatic
skills matching that of Cardinal Armand Jean du Pleiss
Richelieu advisor to King Louis XIII. Cardinal Richelieu
was ruthless in his advice to King Louis XIII on how to
deal with the French citizenry. Sanchez concludes Flaco is
not one to misjudge. Back to the problem at hand. A
plausible recovery scenario is required to demonstrate
loyalty to Don Pedro as he is not willing to risk alienating
himself from the likes of the 'Flaco's' in the organization.

While traveling on the plane to Cali, to meet his maker,
Sanchez reviewed a list of tenable scenarios for the
'disappearances.' During this meeting, the word 'seizures' is
too harsh of a word. The word seizure spews of law
enforcement infiltration into the organization. Sanchez
examined the standard seizure checklist. What caused the
seizures? Did an Informant/Source exist in the
organization? Was this good investigative work; a simple

traffic stop? Sanchez will have to kill someone to make amends, but who? Was there a wiretap? Reacting to the seizures, Sanchez orders all phones changed, including e-mails and Skype. Sanchez will communicate via smoke signals or paper cups connected by string whatever it will take to get back and running. Sanchez plans to advise Don Pedro that he had a communication problem with a 'throwaway' and because of that, the throwaway zigged when he should have zagged and then smoked the zig-zag, and then the 'throwaway' asked for more money…yada…yada…yada.. Blah blah and now he and his cohorts are all locked up in jail. Sanchez will make it known he might have identified the problem.

The police are familiar with the smugglers' tactics, and the smugglers are familiar with police tactics. The smuggling routes have remained the same for decades — smuggling narcotics, weapons, money, air conditioning freon by car, truck, train, boat, and by the person. When a route is deemed successful, every invited smuggler floods the way with so much dope it is comical. Because of technology advances, submarines are now used to smuggle narcotics from Colombia with the help of Mother Russia.

A quick impassionate dismissive introduction by Flaco of Sanchez to Don Pedro immediately deteriorates into the primal ooze of life and death. In this chess game, Sanchez's a rook. Sanchez is not allowed to talk directly to Don Pedro unless spoken to by the same. So, the seated Sanchez directs his verbiage to Flaco.

Don Pedro's slicked-back black hair gleams with sharp detail. His predator's eyes bore into Sanchez cutting into his soul. For some reason, he feels that he must appear a schoolboy to these people. He is not naïve, but the economy slaps him in the face. These people lost money. Money has no soul. You either control it, or it manages you. Right now, the cash controls him. Sanchez focuses on Don Pedro's right hand and its stub little finger. The stub is twitching. Flaco sits next to Don Pedro and although not as powerful as Don Pedro is more dangerous for he desires Sanchez's death. Is Don Pedro considering the same?

In actuality, two loads of cocaine 'disappeared' were seized — the first seizure from a throwaway on a lonesome highway by Texas Highway Troopers. The second confiscated inside a New York City, New York residence resulting in the arrest of several subjects. A total of 75 kilograms of cocaine seized from the two law enforcement actions. The details of the seizures are inconsequential, and the amounts are not that great, but the seizures could have long-term consequences. All one had to do is watch the New York local news and see crooks dressed only in their underwear running from the police to conclude something, somewhere and or someone screwed up.

Sanchez cannot give the impression of debating the issue of 'seizures' or 'disappearances.' Sanchez's history of savagery and deception barely matches the esteemed participants in the inquisition. The seizures are dangerous. Could they be a prelude to more massive seizures in the future? That is what the esteemed guests want to know. Sanchez is in a precarious position. It is more fiscally sound to have him killed. His group can quickly rebuild itself.

Sanchez's distant poverty-stricken family whereabouts are known to Don Pedro's people. If Sanchez is not forthright in his communication with Don Pedro, Don Pedro's people will torture and kill them to obtain the truth from Sanchez. Summarily, Sanchez will be tortured and killed. Sanchez will compensate them for the losses.

The cost per kilogram of cocaine is approximately $1650.00 to $2000.00 a kilogram in Colombia for the participants at the table. Sanchez states he will pay for the damages at $8000.00 a kilogram and will begin to make payments in cash and turn over deeds of existing property, cars, stock, and other tangibles. $8000.00 is the worth of a kilogram of cocaine when it reaches Sanchez in Mexico from Guatemala. Sanchez pays for his life at $600,000.00 and waives transportation fees in a future shipment to offset the remainder of the balance. Sanchez appeals to their greed. The people at the table pull some of the strings. Don Pedro clips them. The amounts are not that much, but presently Sanchez does not possess significant amounts of cash.

Something bothers Sanchez. A person sits at the table during the negotiation. The stranger tries to remain innocuous and because of this draws greater scrutiny from Sanchez. Who is this mysterious person? Sanchez has never seen this person before. This person is out of place. Is the person, Colombian?

Sanchez readjusts his thoughts. When one chooses a life as Sanchez, one understands that you must go all the way, fully committed, or one will not succeed.

Following hours of self-induced anesthesia from many drinks inhaled at the table followed by Sanchez's nonstop dissertations, Don Pedro determines Sanchez is not stealing the dope or working with the police. Don Pedro makes it clear, one more mistake and Sanchez's corpse will be thrown into one of Don Pedro's freshwater fish farms in the Colombian mountains. Sanchez body will supplement the fishes' diet. One's position is temporary and to think that one is impervious to such transgressions is foolhardy. For a few days, Sanchez's death will be a focus of discussion only to be replaced by another more influential drug trafficker who succumbs to a more inventive economic death.

Don Pedro finishes with Sanchez. Don Pedro is satisfied with Sanchez's proposed financial arrangement. Fleetingly, Don Pedro waives his hand at Sanchez to leave. Don Pedro adjourns the meeting. Flaco floats into the shadows of the bar, maintaining a stare on Sanchez.

Sanchez stands from the table and makes a decent flexion to all participants. He walks toward the front door. Again, Sanchez spots the mystery person as he leans towards Don Pedro's left ear and speaks. Don Pedro affirmatively nods his head.

Sanchez dismisses inside the disco a pre-determined kidnap scenario and subsequent hit as amateurish. He walks past Paola with a white towel in his left-hand noticing Paola does not move. Paola's eyes track Sanchez's motion. He observes Sanchez's every step and appears to cringe at his every step. Readying himself to cover his ears with cupped hands anticipating the impending gunshot. Paola's reactions are similar to the childhood game; whereby, the teacher says, "Cover your eyes." "Faster!" "Cover your mouth!" "Cover your ears!"

All movement slows. A blur enters Sanchez's senses. He reaches the front of the bar while Don Pedro speaks with the stranger. Where is Flaco? Sweat pours from his forehead. There is an immediate need to urinate as an animal before a kill — his senses peak.

As he opens the front door, Sanchez is engulfed with the sights and smells of the city, the thick heavy exhaust from cars, bar be que, oppressive humidity, the excessive honking of cars horns, numerous pedestrians walk on the sidewalks, crisscrossing the streets, the talking, the car radios, the yelling. Sanchez observes young street urchins seated, some leaning on cars parallel parked next to the curb on both sides of the entrance of the disco. One urchin, wearing a soccer shirt bolts from his right towards him. The zydeco colors of the city are now more vibrant than ever. They are burning through his eyes directly into his frontal lobe. He is blinded and or thinks so. Is he shot? He is paralyzed and waits for the urchins to run towards him from the parked vehicles belching black smoke. Are they going to grab him and stuff him into the backseat of one of the cars? The emotions pass. The street urchins reposition their bodies on the cars, and the one wearing the soccer shirt slows to a walk passing in front of him. Sanchez is allowed to live but in need of lifetime intravenous injections of Pepto Bismal. He quickly hails a cab and slumps in the back seat of the cab. He inhales the sweaty, smoky, sex residue seat cushions. Comatose. He feebly instructs the cab driver to the airport.

Chapter Two

A bang on the front door and the subsequent entrance of Seamus O'Malley's neighbor announces another round of verbal judo. The topic is no doubt the water line break in front of O'Malley's residence. A hole in the ground with an accompanying geyser of water put the serenity of the middle-class neighborhood in a watery amiss.

"How did you do it?" asks John Jenkins, O'Malley's neighbor.

"It was not easy. I placed one hundred plus phone calls to the city all without a response. So, I called 911 and said while fishing in my front yard, I pulled on a pipe, and it began to leak gas," replies O'Malley. "They are out there repairing it right now; gas entered my house you know and all that."

"There's a gas smell all right. The police will get you for calling in false alarm report," warns Jenkins.

"Nope left a cane pole near the hole. What are they going to do? They'll think I'm crazy, and that will be the end of it," laughs O'Malley.

"What's up?"

"Nothing, just eating a bologna sandwich and watching T.V. I'm celebrating," answers O'Malley.

John is aware of being baited into a fight.

"Celebrating?"

"Yes, I'm celebrating America Week," O'Malley repeats with a sheepish grin.

"Never heard of it, but it sounds racist. What do you mean, what is America Week? Where is the designative hyphen for them? You know, Mexican-American." Jenkins retorts.

"I don't need a hyphen. I'm an American, and that's that. There is Baby Seal Week, Locust Week, Sensitivity Week, America is about celebrating its diverse ethnicity." O'Malley quirks hardly able to hold his laughter. Prodding the young Community College professor is easy.

"You don't like the distinctions of them whether it's Irish hyphen, Mexican hyphen, African American hyphen." Jenkins snaps.

"You got it backward you exploit by categorizing" ... "Oops, did you use the word 'them'? Mister, you are one word away from losing your job at that prestigious college. I have filed that comment in my memory banks. I will come out of the woodwork to dethrone you in the future unless the money is right. I'll wait to disclose your use of that word when you begin your political career, young internet Doctoral recipient." Seamus raises his hand, "Excuse me, but I have to digress to movie academia for a moment as a means to communicate with you, oh, cough, cough, on a level plain. Do you remember that Vietnam movie, Apocalypse Now?"

Jenkins looks at O'Malley as if he has three heads thinking this guy is random.

"Well, in the movie they say…the more they try to make it like home the less they succeeded. Something like that." Seamus waves his beer at Jenkins. "Well, polarization has now set in because of those silly hyphens. You can celebrate your culture, but we are all Americans. Those not in the trenches ignore or are not aware of the incubation of racial polarization. Hell, no one can answer one way or the other about a particular issue without someone chastising his or her perceived intentions."

"You're hopeless. You're a bigot."

"See, you lost the argument. You resorted to name calling. If attacked today and actual troops or terrorists make gains on American soil will the populace segregate on commonality?"

"Nope."

"Look at the former Yugoslavia, Christians versus Muslims. South Africa under white apartheid rule over the black majority, Zimbabwe black rule over white. White farms seized. Mexican Indians in Chiapas fighting for their rights, Brazilian Indians fighting with their government, Iraq dividing into Shiite south, Sunni center and a Kurdish North, the list goes on forever…. segregate on commonality. When the bow breaks, when the government breaks, people cluster to what is familiar and comforting. They seek security in levels, by attaching to a religion, then to a tribe and when everything breaks down to the family. Let me explain it this way. Prison has no 'rule of law'; it is in effect, lawless. When sent to prison, a prisoner seeks security with his/her own's race. It is that simple."

"You believe there will be conflict in the States and I say you are wrong, we are more educated, by far have a better quality of life and live in diverse regions throughout the entire country. We have assimilated. Moreover, if you believe America will separate based on commonality, then how will we divide race, color, origin, religion?" Jenkins slams back.

"I told you before guns and bullets, that's my investment strategy that's the commonality in my future conflict. You know until there are more interracial marriages creating kids that look like all, then and only then will everyone calm down. Fear of the unknown, fear of people with whom we have never had contact, fear of religion we do not understand until we open our brains this insanity will continue."

O'Malley first encountered raw, racial hatred when he was a police officer propelled into settling domestic disputes, securing shooting scenes, and arresting subjects. It was during these tense situations that he or more like the police department only controlled the ground where he stood, and that was questionable. The callers' vitriol was unjustifiably heaved, because of a lack of introspection at the responding officers; instead of towards the perpetrators. It was during these times that the 'rule of law' had to be restored by lowly police officers. After the persistent calls for service, O'Malley would ask is America breaking apart? This dark world is not known to the general populace. During these conflict resolutions, O'Malley had his first thoughts of polarization. Is he an alarmist?

However, occasionally without explanation would emerge from the chaos a person from the neighborhood who would attempt to induce reason into the madness, sometimes successfully. Because of these unidentified peacemakers, O'Malley decided years ago to do his small part to inhibit 'polarizations' slow creep. Learning from these brave peacemakers, O'Malley believes 'the slow creep' can recede through open civil discourse. He also realized that when citizens dialed 911, they were not inviting a police officer for lunch to sing songs. The citizens needed help. He recognized that as a police officer, one experienced more evil than good. So, one needed to consciously counterweigh the bad calls for service and relish the good ones during the shift.

O'Malley takes a sip of beer and smiles at his neighbor. Jenkins is right about US citizenry successful assimilation. He reminds himself that concrete without aggregate is useless. Assimilation makes America powerful, but of course, he reserves his acknowledgment until the next round of talks. O'Malley loves to 'wind up' Jenkins.

"What, you've lost it. Kids. Looking the same. Prison. We don't live in prison. You're over the edge."

O'Malley did not let it go, "just something to think about when civilization fractures. Remember the decline of the

Roman Empire, the result Dark Ages. Brother, we are entering the chasm."

"Yea, I see the chasm it is in your front yard. It has grown, gather your children and women!" Jenkins elevates his voice.

"Ah… that remark, insinuating that women need to be gathered and are helpless like children will not be tolerated in my castle…soldier." O'Malley laughs out loud, sloshing his beer with his right hand.

Jenkins relents he is successfully ambushed. He knows it is all in fun, but next weekend, he will make sure to research the next topic and initiate before O'Malley does. O'Malley must have recently read some anthropology book and is outwardly digesting its contents. Not a wrong way to pass time while sitting on his ass on all-night DEA surveillance. Jenkins decides in the future to choose the topic-legalization of narcotics. The Netherlands legalized marijuana. Ambushing Seamus will be easy. Jenkins remembers one day when O'Malley, a federal narcotics officer, returned from work. O'Malley walks to Jenkins house as if in a trance. O'Malley tells Jenkins that his supervisor said he needed to quit thinking on the job. That's probably why O'Malley always engages in these debates as he cannot at work.

"Hey, were you at the marijuana bust last night? The one I saw this morning on T.V.?" Jenkins asks while helping himself to a beer in the refrigerator.

"Nope, didn't even hear about it. Only the big bosses in the front office are privy to such pertinent information," a quick smirk, "they determine as to whether it is press conference worthy." O'Malley waves his hand towards the returning Jenkins. "Those press conferences are comical. You just saw one. The principal speaker holds on to the podium for dear life, the chosen ones stand in a concaved line behind the speaker. The principal speaks in a slow demonstrative deliberate manner, so soothing. The others fold their hands or grasp their wrist with one hand. The pious as if standing in church pray, the public does not get a whiff that this briefing is a bunch of crap, and the speakers are clueless." Seamus changes the television channel.

"Occasionally, they have to act like they are part of the decision-making process. Dissemination of information is not common practice. Dissemination of information would assist us in case development and provide linkages. However, that is common sense, and we don't use common sense. You know." O'Malley says in a low voice, "We are workers, we are merely the proletariat, we are not capable of comprehending such vaulted information."

"What?" Jenkins dumbstruck sits on a broken chair next to Seamus.

"I'll learn about it if somebody talks about it on an aside, maybe near the office snack bar. We don't exchange information between each other or with other agencies. People are secretive, territorial about their investigations."

"All right, whatever." Jenkins looks at the game on the television.

"It's a big world. We're only good for feel-good or bad news flashes. Narcotics are a threat, but so far, the United States economy absorbs the losses associated with narcotic crime. So, until the economy collapses, nobody cares. Terrorism is everything now, but how do you think the terrorists fund a portion of their operations, other than from Iran. I'm a prophet, John." O'Malley leans back in his chair.

"Very philosophical… yes, indeed."

"I thought so, so shut it down and listen to the game on the television. Celebrate America Week with me. Do you smell the gas?"

"I smell the love if that's what you mean? If I drink with you, will that make me an American?" Jenkins could not resist.

"It could."

"By drinking with you, do I give up my ancestral privileges?"

"Ancestral, one from whom a person descends, past tense," O'Malley remarks with a smile.

Jenkins nods and opens his beer. Without notice, the foam spills on the chair. He wipes his hand on a dirty pillow. They watch the game; the volume shakes the windows.

Suddenly, O'Malley has a déjà vu moment indicating this conversation already occurred. More significantly, he feels as though something tragic happened. It seems hundreds or thousands of miles away, an occurrence he assumes will affect his life. Powerless, no matter how one tries to control one's life, outside forces always impact one's life. The impact can be subtle, not realized or blatantly obtrusive never disclosing the linkage. Will this déjà vu moment or sixth sense affect him in a good or bad manner? Something is not right all. Is he experiencing fear, helplessness, anxiety? He needs to react but does not know how, where, or to whom. He sits motionless ignoring Jenkins, what is it? He shivers its serious. He slowly reemerges and engages his random thoughts and looks into his beer can.

Maybe, he'll win the lottery tonight and tell his boss that he will resign. Better yet, remain on the job become the village idiot, and watch management squirm in their chairs when mentioning his name. Too many beers and not enough sleep, he guesses.

John Jenkins possesses latitude in controlling his working hours, that sounds pretty good to O'Malley. As a federal narcotics officer, scheduling one's life is manageable. It requires the agent to remain proactive in the management of 'Sources' and undercover agents. Managing the case is one issue the other problem is the supervisors. It only takes one supervisor to ruin your life.

When threatened, management circles the wagons when a proletariat is bucking for admittance to Siberia. Management realizes if one supervisor falls, they will all fall like a row of dominoes resulting in the clowns running the circus, but will anyone realize there is a change in command? However, O'Malley is aware that the disenfranchised employee is a real pain in the abdomen of the Tagamet drinkers. Management can only transfer these employees so many times. It's a balancing act, and when one balances, nothing gets done, but the fulfillment of administrative procedures.

Occasionally, a spike of effort occurs with management support, and after the investigation, the sloths go back to sleep, and the case agents wish like holy hell that he/she will never have to endure such management induced insanity again. However, if the case and subsequent spin-off investigations are exciting and have a real impact, there is nothing administration can do to stop the effort. That is the world O'Malley enjoys. That sounds crazy, but the 'political' managers are preoccupied with future promotions and transfers to more desirable areas than remaining focused on case development. O'Malley transgresses.

"Do you plan on going to the bar-be-que tonight?" Jenkins interrupts O'Malley's whimsical thoughts through the televisions' roar.

"I sure am." The ability to do as one pleases is the most sacred privilege in America. O'Malley is a patriot; his views are open to honest debate by anyone at any time. Quality debate on real issues occurs only in times of real crisis. Americans devote their energies to production, service, and the accumulation of wealth. They don't have time to screw around with this philosophical stuff, and rightfully so. Their success and accumulation of wealth combined with their rich diversity, ideas, and action is the real threat to America's enemies.

Seamus genuinely enjoys working and communicating with everyone he encounters. He believes 'man' to be inherently good and that simplifies his life. He harbors no hidden agendas and crazy conspiracy theories. His biggest pet peeve is individuals who threaten others or are blatantly rude to others knowing that the recipient of the hatred will not reciprocate — taking advantage of the victim's belief in the rule of law. Seamus knows this as he and a majority of humanity have experienced it firsthand. Eventually, someone will react to the bully, and that will be the end of the bully. His bullies are the narcotic traffickers. Was he born to be one of 'Plato's' guardians or just interested in the hunt? Man, he is random today.

Despite the déjà vu, his life is great. O'Malley bought a small old house in a beautiful neighborhood. He has furnished it with stacked cinder blocks acting as legs for a door serving both as the living room and dining table. Accompanying the door table is an old couch that was dragged and carried by him throughout his college days. Complete with beer caps and bar food jammed between the cushions. One room is full of metal weights and the other a punching bag. The punching bag chain already destroyed the ceiling's drywall. His entire house is a man cave; he lives a simple existence.

Again, John interrupts O'Malley's internal discourse and states he is preparing to hire a new individual at work. In conducting a background check, he contacted the previous employer to ascertain the applicant's ability to be rehired and contacts a few references provided by the applicant. John never feels comfortable in the hiring process. He's concerned over the recent rashes of employees shooting their co-workers and managers. He would like to probe further into the applicant's background, but his hands are tied. When we hire someone, it is difficult to dismiss them if you think he/she is a mental case.

O'Malley nods his head and says, "We have the same problem."

"I thought you might enjoy that one. I got to go." Jenkins stands from the chair and walks to the refrigerator.

John enjoys these conversations. Next week, Seamus O'Malley will spew about US public education and its ties to Socialism. Discussions should be animated and should encompass various 'hot button' topics. John recognizes their animated joking is a thing of the past, especially in the office environment. This kind of 'no hold bars' concourse can only happen within a limited circle of friends. John admits to himself that he too has seen signs of the beginning of polarization. He knows he is not an alarmist. He interprets the polarization signs as cyclical. Presently, serious issues, discussions, and humor remain hidden in the catacombs for fear of reprisals and open discourse without retaliation have gone the way of the dinosaurs. The US is self-censuring itself doing more damage to Democracy than any Dictator. Who has the right to elect themselves to designate a 'line or level of acceptance' in free speech? Of course, the ones who yell the loudest.

O'Malley will take various stands, not even believing in some to get a rise out of John. Both know their opinions do not affect the world. 'The Big Picture.' 'The "BIG PICTURE.' Does it exist? O'Malley involuntarily shakes his head on how many times he heard that phrase at work. Where is it? Maybe, it will surface soon.

John returns to the living room with another beer.

"Hey, John. I hope you bring those baked beans again."

"I will. You know it's about the gas level. I was told to mow the yard before the Q. I needed some liquid carbohydrates; that is why I came over. I ran out over there. See you at the Q."

"Well, at least I am good for something. Sounds good."

John leaves the house carrying the cans of beer. Drinking beer not concerned about driving afterward is very relaxing.

Seamus changes the television channel and listens to Senator John "I vote for my own self-preservation" White. White, a member of the Senate Intelligence Committee, is asked by a reporter as to his thoughts related to Russia's past indiscriminate bombardments of Grozny, Chechnya.

White responds, "As you are all aware, Congress is returning from "recess.""

"Recess!" Seamus shouts at the television, "a bunch of school children."

A cough, "Uh hum, I plan to meet with my colleagues to discuss this matter."

"The Russian bombing occurred two years ago. Assassinations between Russian and Chechens continue to this day. What is your response to the killing of innocent Muslim citizens?" the reporter speaks unabated, "What further do you have to discuss with your colleagues? What recommendations will you provide to the present administration?"

"As I stated after I meet with my 'distinguished' colleagues, our uh…cough…our committee does not meet until the following week."

"So, you personally and or your committee members have not discussed this highly volatile situation? What have you been discussing besides this?"

"We are aware of the bombing allegations."

"We possess two separate videos of Russian military 'marked' jets bombing Grozny killing innocent Muslims," the reporter displays the videotapes. "The city was decimated. Have you addressed these transgressions with your Russian counterparts?"

"Well, your 'purported' videos which I have not seen 'possibly' depicting 'alleged' Russian jets. Bombing 'unidentified' landscapes, the origin of the videos 'highly questionable' and as you are aware will need 'vetting' to authenticate." The congressman is losing his cool and speaks in a condescending tone. A cough, "Uhm as you are aware, each side of the 'conflict' or should I say 'disagreement' tends to exaggerate their claims. I can't say it is a 'situation.' I'm sure you understand?" Senator White forces a smile on his face and says, "Why are you just now providing the tapes?"

"The tapes recently came in our possession. My office made copies of the videos, but we are willing to provide the originals for your review. Might I say 'vet'? People are dying while you fail to act."

"Nobody is delaying. We have procedures to follow. We are against any killing. I tell you right now. I am categorically against killing. Killing is horrible. Yes, very bad." His President Nixon like hands rise as he brays like a goat saying the word 'bad.' "We have compiled a plethora of data streaming from Chechnya. Of course, I cannot divulge how much we know. You know national security and all. You are behind the curve. We have greater access capable of producing a 'Big Picture' analysis not available to those without such access. Your tapes, if genuine, are singular in scope." The burning bush is now visible behind Moses the Senator. "Be assured." His voice bellows. "We got a good handle on what is happening over there." The Senator tires and provides his exit phrase. "Of course, we appreciate your interest in this matter." The Senator walks from the silenced reporter.

"You might want to view the videos. The families who provided the videos are livid of their abandonment. Your staff for authenticity can test the blood, DNA, and fingerprints on the videos. Alternatively, should I say the new 'tactical' word of the day, 'vet.'" The reporter is mad. "I suggest your people find more human Sources 'on the ground' as you lost two!"

"Ha, set that Jackass Senator up." O'Malley slaps his thigh. Oh, that reporter just lost access to future interviews. I am sure the reporter believes it was worth it — my kind of guy. Of course, the Senator does not know individual's Sources — no reason to go down that road as to why. At least, the reporter succeeds in ensuring that the Sources families will not be forgotten and evacuated immediately, if they are still alive — a small success but one none the less.

Chapter Three

"Settle down, the situation is under control!" the old man barks.

Both are seated, within reach of each other, in their respective solid natural timber constructed rocking chairs. A flame resembling a blow torch and heat escape the smoke-stained rock fireplace. The snapping of the fire and popping embers come close to igniting the bark on the chairs. Over sips of brandy, the men continue their animated conversation

"There is no way to settle down," the young man speaks slowly with a thick Eastern European accent. He remains in a methodical tone, "You, as well as myself, know that any operation is susceptible to unwanted incursions from various entities. Everyone ultimately has a price or a motive not to remain loyal to an activity. An Informant, a Source, can kill this deal. There is no reason to think that this operation is immune to history." He ends his remarks by lighting a Turkish cigarette sending whiffs of smoke cascading into the malodorous room. A reddish glow invades his rounded white and pinkish face.

"No need to lecture me in the ways of intelligence," the old man says. "This is not rocket science, nor is it unusual. My proposal is only a means of transportation to sell goods for the betterment of the country a patriotic endeavor. It's just that the one deal needs to happen first."

"To obtain hard currency for the country or yourself? I admit we are in an economic survival mode. I don't want to hear about patriotism from you," the young man steams. "The word, 'patriotism' clouds young minds during the time of war. Moreover, I am not that young, and we are not in a declared war with these people. However, I'm loyal to the objective, the spread of our country's ideology, and the disabling of our enemies in any way possible."

"You can live your life as is or be part of the team," the old man threatens.

"The team is not sanctioned by higher authorities."

"Not today, not yesterday, but in this environment, it does not hurt to have insurances if the political situation changes. It is a viable plan. I admit it's a risky operation. So close to our enemy. They might sanction it."

The older man's lower lip raises into his upper lip, forming a frown. He cocks his head upward and to the right. The older man's blues eyes meet the young man as he exhales cigarette smoke.

"You have seized too much authority. Someone will take the fall in the event the operation is exposed."

"Are you fully in?"

"I haven't decided yet. At this point, I am only monitoring the situation."

"The operation is in peril as long as one person knows too much and has no skin in the game..." The older man is interrupted in mid-sentence.

"Don't preach to me about operations. By that remark, you insinuate that I am in danger if I choose to detach."

"No, no, my friend, we have been through too much. It is for our relationship that I merely wanted to ingrain into you that you are important to this operation."

The young man's blood pressure spikes, the older man is an ugly ass. "I borrowed that line from you telling the same thing to that lady days before she's shot on your orders. We have been to the same schools. My value is only good as long as I appear to be an asset to you. We both know that," the young man fires back. His right knee bounces up and down, visibly releasing tension and almost spills brandy from his glass.

"Don't be so obstinate and naive," the old man says through a cloud of cigarette smoke.

"How do I know I will not be the one blamed if the operation is exposed or unsuccessful? It is highly likely that our enemies will target me as I will be the front man on this deal. I can live with that. Anyhow, there are no internal guarantees. Nothing is on paper."

"Such consternation, paranoia and I might say, lack of respect. Those are not characteristics of your training." The older man is now squinting through the cigarette fog enveloping the entire room. He casually rocks in his sturdy wooden chair. An intermittent rolling sound originating from the base of the wooden chair on the stone floor and an occasional crack in the fire resonate in the room.

"You taught me to be self-reliant," the young man holds his head low and speaks in a soft tone. He sits on the edge of the chair, leaning towards the older man.

"This is just another cycle of uncertainty in our government. In a functioning government, what we are discussing will never be considered, and the advocate branded a fool. Cycles, my friend, cycles, justify our actions at particular times. We need to exploit beneficial cycles existing today. We must hedge our bets. Just as an Initial Public Offering (IPO) opens on the New York Stock Exchange, the rush to clamor on board is infectious and creates an exponential windfall for all. It would be best if you, my friend, looked on this as insider information, privy to pertinent data before the IPO. Rewards abound for your loyalty. Embrace the opportunity. In a perfect world, the plan could be considered foolhardy, I admit it, but with proper planning and luck, the benefits outweigh the risk. I feel we possess the advantage of surprise, and I am confident in its success."

The plan is known to both. It is not necessary to review the proposal again. By not mentioning the details of the operational plan, both individuals are reduced to talk in riddles. To the outside world, the conversation is meaningless. They speak as if the room is not secure. It is a long dissertation, but the older man believes it needed to be said.

"As I said before we have a history," the older man continues, his whitish skin as rough as burlap, thick rolls of skin hanging from his massive forearms. His sixty-five years of age show more like seventy to eighty. A stubborn resolve always grows in the older man once he understands there is no other recourse. The younger man's tradecraft, mental skills, and vitality are instrumental in the success of the impending actions. The older man exhausts his persuasive powers. The younger man summarizes the overall operation and becomes convinced of the plan's veracity.

To end the older man's drumbeat, the younger man relents to his primal urge for the need for action. The younger man agrees to assist in the upcoming plans. He is aware of his expendability if this deteriorates. By being so direct with his comments to the older man, he was reinforcing to the older man that he will be working with a person who has a clue. The younger man's military training pulses through his body, he is now fully committed. He is determined to strike without notice, cautious at the same time. He has some regrets on the harmful impact on his future adversaries. Machinery, goods, money, and services will stream to the younger man through the older man's contacts.

It is going to be bloody — pity for the young man's adversaries, sympathy for the US agent. Paybacks are hell. His future actions place him close to the US agent.

However, it is a long shot. As soon as the younger man locates the agent, he'll take care of him hopefully during this operation. The younger man hopes this agent will stumble into this operation, allowing him the opportunity to take out the agent.

Chapter Four

Leaving Cali, Colombia Sanchez realizes his reparations to Don Pedro are too generous. He's aware of that now. However, during the Don Pedro meeting, Sanchez was prepared to imitate a disgraced Japanese Yakuza. Chop off a portion of his small finger and speak Japanese as penitence to Don Pedro. Making sure it was his right hand's little finger, just like Don Pedro's. How did Don Pedro injure his finger? As a result of this business, we all have physical and mental scars. Some people are just better at concealing them. Exposing weakness is not recommended.

It is time for Sanchez to send a meaningful message to Don Pedro. Departing the commercial aircraft from Colombia upon landing in Mexico, Sanchez grabs his cellular telephone from his pocket, with nostrils flaring, dials his subordinate, Jose's telephone number. Jose is no doubt, relaxing on a Cancun, Mexico beach. Sanchez will flame if Jose's cellphone is off.

Now, not in the presence of Don Pedro, the 'disappeared' loads are acknowledged as to what they are, 'seized' loads of narcotics. The first seizure occurs in Texas just north of the Mexican border taken by Texas Highway Troopers, Storm Troopers more like it. To Sanchez, this seizure is not a random act. Especially, as it occurs before the New York seizure, it is obvious the Troopers wanted to confirm the existence of narcotics secreted in the first vehicle. Corroborating Source information. Why conduct surveillance the entire distance to New York if you are not satisfied, the next car contains drugs.

The Mexican Federal Police Officer (Mex Fed/Federale) based in Nuevo Laredo, Mexico is complicit in these seizures, whether guilty or not. Sanchez discovers the 'Mex Fed' is receiving 'payoffs' from a competing narcotic smuggling organization for the protection of their loads from the northern Mexican border into the southern United States. The Mex Fed is playing all sides. His greed will be his downfall. Assassinating the Mex Fed will 'send the world down' on the northern side of the Mexican border, but Sanchez's confident he can endure the retaliatory onslaught.

Risky, will be Don Pedro's initial reaction to the targeted killing of the Mex Fed. Don Pedro will review the assassination's impact on Sanchez's compartmentalized smuggling. Hopefully, Don Pedro gleans Sanchez identified a 'leak' within the Sanchez organization, that being the Mex Fed. Sanchez believes Don Pedro will approve of the strike. Without facts only conjecture, Sanchez surmises Don Pedro has plans for him in the future. He asks himself what plans?

Orchestrating the killing of a Mex Fed Colonel sends a strong message that one means business in Mexico. Generally, United States (US) cops killed by subjects in the line of duty are a result of spontaneous actions. Pandora's box opens when a US police officer conducts a vehicle stop during 'routine patrol.' Sanchez even comprehends there is no such thing as 'routine patrol.' Who is in the car? Without the police officer's knowledge, the subjects recently committed a violent crime, are actively smuggling, possess existing or believed warrants for arrest or are 'high' on drugs and in some cases all of the above resulting in tragic circumstances. He realizes too that domestic disputes are as dangerous as car stops. At present, a majority of US police officers killed in the line of duty are a result of vehicle accidents and medical issues.

It is Sanchez's belief; US cops usually are not targeted by criminal organizations to remove the police because of their investigation into a criminal organization. That is the principal difference from Mexico. The murder of Mexican cops is because they violate a criminal 'contract,' refused to 'sign' an agreement with the 'winning' criminal group or the police officer is a good cop. Killing cops in Mexico benefit the criminal organization, not so in the United States. At present, a US cop killer's arrest is a high probability. If a subject murders a US cop on behalf of a criminal organization, the arrested subject will eventually provide information, to reduce his/her sentence, on the same criminal organization that hired them — bringing additional 'heat' on the criminal organization. At times, US law enforcement is slow to react to particular threats, but overall well organized and not to be underestimated. The US operates with the 'rule of law.' The Mexican judicial system is non-existent operating without the rule of law, and Sanchez takes advantage of Mexico's shortcomings.

Sanchez finally connects with Jose, his real name not necessary. Hell, Jose probably forgot his real name. If arrested in the United States, the name Jose gives to the first arresting officer will be associated with him for the rest of his life. He chuckles to himself. Sanchez tries to guess the name. What name would Jose give up? He loves food. He'll say (mi) my (appellido) last (nombre) name (es) is (pollo) chicken y mi (primer) my first name is (arroz) rice. His name will be Rice Chicken from then on. Jose enjoys screwing with authority. After all, Jose never experienced legitimate authority.

Answering the phone, Jose is surprised Sanchez escaped from Hell. Sanchez is stronger than he realizes. Sanchez lives up to his Mexican based nickname, El Gato Negro, the Black Cat. Without hesitation, Sanchez cryptically provides orders to Jose. Jose is to meet Sanchez at the 'ranch.' A sparsely populated privately owned ranch south of Matamoros, Mexico. The abandoned land serves as a temporary narcotic storehouse before the narcotics insertion into the United States. There, Sanchez will provide the remaining orders in person. Personal meetings eliminate electronic interdiction.

Sanchez always conducts conversations on the phone as if someone is listening. At times, he cryptically praises the same Colonel he is now going to murder. In the event, the Colonel's men are intercepting the conversation. As a test, Sanchez mentioned in a phone conversation with Jose a desire to meet a beautiful Mex Fed under the command of the Colonel. Two weeks later she approaches Sanchez in Matamoros. It is not a coincidence. The entire Mexican communication network is suspect.

Matamoras is a notorious outpost of smugglers located in the northeast quadrant of Mexico bordering with Brownsville, Texas to the north. Meeting here will not attract the attention of law enforcement officers. Matamoros tourism recovery mode continues a result of US press coverage detailing the narcotic/satanic killing by Mexicans of a young US tourist visiting during spring break. Calls to reduce narcotic smuggling and its causation of evil acts spread throughout the United States. The facilitating factor in the flow of smuggled narcotics into the US, as identified by the press was the forgotten disheveled porous border. Calls ensued of the need for a secure border. The construction of a wall wails throughout the US Congress. With the subsequent arrest of the satanic killers, once again the issue is shelved. Never did the Mexican government give the appearance to work so fast in solving the killing. The Mexican government officials recognize the arrests will end the calls for the construction of a wall.

Jose immediately travels by air from Cancun and is driven by an associate to the ranch. The associate leaves the area, and Jose meets with Sanchez. Sanchez provides a brief of the plan to kill the Mex Fed. Events transpire at high speed. In hectic periods, smugglers make mistakes. Geographically operating in an 'insurgency masquerading as a country, namely Mexico' problems are bound to happen. Sanchez did not rise to his status without an awareness of this particular political situation. An insurgency simply defined by Webster's is: a condition of revolt against the government, and Sanchez is merely determined/categorized as an insurgent- a person who revolts against civil authority. However, in reality, the line between this government and the insurgency is no longer definable.

Sanchez drives Jose from the ranch battling the stifling heat towards their Matamoros office. Cloudy yellowish dirt fills the air as cab drivers drive at breakneck speeds throughout the streets delivering tourist to and from the US southern border to the Mexican duty-free markets. Silently bouncing on the broken roads inhaling the clouds of dust, Sanchez reviews the Don Pedro meeting. You cannot relax in this business. There is no doubt that direct action is necessary. Something happens even if it is wrong.

Sanchez worries Don Pedro's men are waiting for him at his office. Again, paranoia develops his heart flutters as they close on the office. Both exit the vehicle. Sanchez enters the office, first. Jose is barely able to keep up with Sanchez's pace. Jose wonders if something is wrong. Sanchez surveys the office's interior. Quick scans of every crevice, under furniture and around walls. Where will the assassin or assassins strike? Sweat pours from Sanchez's forehead into his now stinging eyes, his hands shake during the search looking in vain for the killers. Sanchez races to his desk and underneath it retrieves his guns from an old sizeable heavy metal safe blowing a concaved depression in the thick office stucco wall. The remnants of the wall tumble to the floor.

Sanchez jumps similar to a cat maintaining the guns in each hand. Smoke fills the office. Jose drops to the ground and yells in Spanish. He's on all fours craning his head for potential threats. Who's shooting? The sound reverberates through the substantial room in waves similar to a thrown rock causing concentric circles on a lake. The windows bulge outwardly toward the dirty street. A few passing pedestrians hear the gunshot, crouch their bodies protecting their heads with their hands. The pedestrians simultaneously look towards the direction of the sound instinctively looking away in seconds. As if in unison, they discreetly cover their faces from the shot's origination, with one hand, and scuttle away like land crabs. No way are they going to get involved with that! The citizens in this city have been trained to differentiate the sound of gunfire from fireworks. They know it is a gunshot.

Sanchez says to himself and then to Jose, "We've got to settle down, this is crazy." He momentarily frowns and looks at the gun, well, at least it still works. He internally justifies the accidental discharge (AD) as bound to happen with the magnitude of its use. Sanchez selects one of the guns and gives it to Jose. He places the other weapon into the safe.

Following Sanchez's instructions, Jose employs the assassins. Jose and the assassins depart Matamoros in separate vehicles one containing two assassins and the other occupied solely by Jose. They drive west on Mexican Federal Highway 2 paralleling south of the Texas/Mexican border. The Black Cat remains in Matamoros. The assassins, initially on par with the Cali cocaine waiters, have received field promotions as they now possess AK-47s. Are they killing someone, moving dope, stealing dope, are they going to Boy's town? No, wrong direction for Boy's town. The assassins are left guessing.

Jose avoids providing a complete brief of the true nature of their services. Regardless, the assassins conclude the job is something of importance based on the money 'fronted' to them. A staggering amount of money, their pockets are exploding with paper. It's not like they use banks. Small talk and the smoking of crack cocaine, provided by Jose, consume the assassins time while en route to their destination Nuevo Laredo, Mexico.

Nuevo Laredo, a Mexican border town of considerable violence, is located south of the US bordering city Laredo, Texas. Mexico has exhausted its adjectives in describing the violence associated with narcotics. In contrast, the US has yet to drain its attributes for the word 'violence.' US extreme violence is still in its infancy. Presently, the US press fixates in discovering new and improved adjectives for the word 'offended/offense': outrage, disbelief, mad, irate, disgraceful, shocked, upsetting, unbelievable and everybody's favorite moral indignation. In time, the US media will need to consult a thesaurus to discover 'shocking' terms to describe the increase in US violence. It is Sanchez, the Black Cat's belief it will come soon.

The Sanchez plan demands that the assassins and Jose kill the Mex Fed Colonel and any additional occupants located at the Mex Fed's residence. They are eliminating all witnesses. Jose's primary job is to ascertain the Colonel's presence at the house and act when confirmed.

The assassins, without concern the Mexican Police/Military might stumble onto their activities, continue to smoke crack throughout the trip to Nuevo Laredo. If stopped by the police, the assassination target is not known to the assassins providing some comfort to Jose. When the team arrives on the outskirts of Nuevo Laredo, the killers will receive a thorough brief. If Jose encounters the police en route to Nuevo Laredo, he'll take his chances to escape instead of bribing the officials. If arrested and placed under temporary custody for possession of weapons, Jose cannot rely on the Colonel's assistance. The Colonel's men will ask, why is Jose carrying such firepower into the Colonel's area? The Colonel playing all sides might transfer Jose to his new criminal partners for torture, revealing the Black Cat's operations.

The assassins are fraternal twins: a boy and a girl who reside on the Matamoras streets. Both have permanent brown stained skin from the sun's rays combined with the accompanying city dirt. Due to a lack of adequate nutrition, they are short and skinny in stature. They never attended formal school. Street training makes them marketable in their particular field, robberies. One might first notice, a detachment to their surroundings, no direct eye contact initiates in the lifeless eyes. The consumption of drugs throughout their lives dull their conscience, causing the twins to react and act. The twin assassins move in a series of quick, short, jerks, sometimes mimicking the image of recoiling snakes. Instant gratification is the priority in their daily fight for survival. The twins live without hope from the regular bleak days and nights.

The twins occasionally obtain odd service jobs in Matamoras. They are robbing unsuspecting drunken American tourists at night. The Mexican police tolerate the twin's criminal activities, but they are becoming troublesome with recent upticks in their robberies. They are now violating the crime bell curve, the 'level of acceptance.' The twins, in their small part of the world, now threaten the economy, tourism. Tourists visiting Mexico expect a certain amount of security provided by the government not wanting to end up face down in a ditch. If the government security apparatus is unreliable, tourists spending will decrease.

An inhuman event in Acapulco, Mexico diverts attention from the twin's tourists assaults and robberies granting them a short shelf life. Narcotic traffickers battling for control of the ocean smuggling routes from Colombia to Acapulco leave 13 competitors heads inside a favorite Acapulco bar. In retaliation, the second impacted group hangs from public highway overpasses various tortured bodies of the first group with the customary accompanying banners describing we will kill everybody, our enemies, your momma, his momma, so on and so forth.

A similar threat to the tourist economy presented itself in Palestine and Israel. Reasonable people in this area eventually realized the economy fairs better when the tourists are not targets. In other words, leave the tourist buses alone whether they transit Israel proper, the West Bank and Gaza. Mexico learns from the Middle East 'tourists' detente. Nationalist talk and religious beliefs pale to tourists spending. US tourists in Mexico purchase leather goods, alcohol, and prescription drugs all at discount prices. Prescription drugs purchased in Matamoras by the 'Snow Birds' are illegal when transported into the States. These unsuspecting older tourists carrying cash are the twins' favorite target.

The assassins' cars are driven at a constant pace on the highway passing small older model trucks with manufactured horizontal metal and wooden slats exposing the heavily stacked fruits and vegetables. The road also comprises numerous long-haul tractor-trailers bellowing black smoke from high sulfur low-grade diesel. Tractor trailer drivers expect to wait in two-mile stop and go traffic from Nuevo Laredo into Laredo, Texas USA.

The cars slow, reaching the outskirts of Nuevo Laredo. The twin assassins' vehicle drives to the rear of Jose's vehicle. A slow wave of dust envelopes the cars originating from the trunks cascading over the hoods as if to disguise their movements. The vehicular headlights accent the swirling dirt. Jose gives the final instructions to the twins, the general location of the target, the assault plan, and the exit strategy. A crescent moon forces its light through the cumulus clouds. The city is eerily quiet.

The Mex Fed Colonel recently demanded delivery of Sanchez's organizational payments (mordida) to his residence. The Colonel is confident, brazen, and now quite lazy. Sanchez's payoffs to the Colonel ensure successful transport of narcotics, without Mexican police interdiction, through this designated corridor into the United States. The Colonel accepts cash for protection from anyone wanting to smuggle freon, cigarettes, terrorist or non-terrorist it does not matter. Lately, the Colonel's business spiked with Middle Eastern aliens arriving in Mexico from Cuba. Historically, travel to and from Mexico and Cuba is passport stamp free disguising a traveler's history, thus denying the US Border Patrol an investigative tool. That large floating aircraft carrier off the Florida coast is complicit in smuggling into the US from Mexico not to mention directing past Cuban flotillas into Florida.

Based on Jose's familiarity with the area, he instructs the assassins to follow in their vehicle. He gives the light signals to the killers. Jose will direct the assassins with his vehicle's brake lights and headlamps. Jose will tap his brakes designating the exact location for the twins to park just north of the Mex Feds residence out of the 'line of sight' of the Mex Fed/Colonel's front iron gate. There was no time to obtain cellular telephones or 'Walkie Talkies.' Jose does not tell the twins the identity of the target. The Colonel employs one guard at the residence, usually positioned at the front gate. Jose tried to convince Sanchez to delay, allowing Jose to stalk the Colonel, to learn his pattern of life. Assaulting any house or building is dangerous. He wants to kill the Colonel away from home. However, the Black Cat is adamant that the assault occurs tonight.

Jose well-schooled realizes only one drive by the residence is safe. More than one pass will raise the guard's suspicions. The street constructed of asphalt with concrete curbs is more extensive than a typical street allowing the current residents, the luxury of parking transport trucks in front of their houses. There are four streetlamps the length of the road curiously appearing to watch Jose's actions.

Jose drives slowly in the direction of the Colonel's residence tires crunching rocks on the asphalt. The acrid smell of the city permeates the interior a combination of raw sewage and stale alcohol mixed with freshly cooked frijoles. He will roll the car windows down after the initial pass as the guard may recognize him, and secondly, the windows need to be in the down position in the event he has to shoot unexpectedly. Shattered glass deposits in the eye and the reduced effectiveness of a bullet piercing the windows changing its trajectory are signs of an amateur, especially when one cannot fail. God, he hates sweating at night. Is there any relief from the wretched heat? His yellow shirt is buttoned down to his chest. A silver cross dangles from his neck. Before arriving at the target's location, Jose taps his brakes once designating the twins staging area.

Jose then approaches the Colonels' stucco constructed residence. The perimeter wall comprises half-moon stucco walls complete with vertical iron fencing. The vertical iron fencing fills the half-moon voids reaching each stucco column. The wall's entrance is secured by two black vertical iron gates similar to the half-moon fencing, except in an upside-down position from the fence gating forming a curve to the top of each iron gate. Jose taps his brakes twice identifying the Colonel's residence to the assassins. Hopefully, they are alert and don't leave with the money before conducting the hit.

Observed next to the main entrance gate inside the curtilage is a young security guard holding an AK-47 in his lap. The guard sits by the gate in a cheap rickety steel frame chair. The worn cushion pops up as he rises resembling a Doberman pincher to meet Jose' glare. Jose views the padlock securing the two sections on the entrance gate, a cheap one oh, this dirty little Colonel did not pay for a good lock. It is probably locked and unlocked by the guard from within the curtilage as the guard can reach through the iron fencing. Exterior lighting illuminates the Colonel's residence.

Jose sees the Colonel through an open window talking on a satellite phone, its antennae points towards the sky to maintain the link. Oh, the Black Cat is right, this Colonel has graduated and is working for another trafficker. We seldom communicate via satellite telephone. The satellite phone is an expensive, sophisticated communication device for smuggling random Middle East entries, the disadvantaged Central Americans and drugs. Man, we generally use a simple HF/VHF system with an antenna and a radio box. We paid for and installed a radio box at the Colonel's residence. Well, if we do not take him out now, he strikes at us first at the behest of his new associates, Jose rationalizes to himself.

In a southerly direction, Jose passes the residence without slowing and is careful to drive the total distance of the street out of the view of the young guard. Within a few minutes, Jose circles his vehicle at the end of the road out of view of the inquisitive guard. Before making the northern turn, he turns off the vehicle's headlights, the windows now in the down position. His engine remains running, so the guard becomes accustomed to the noise. The guard will hear the starting of an engine. Jose remains motionless and from his position observes the entrance to the Colonel's residence. The area remains quiet. Most of the Colonel's neighbors sleep, eventually to awake in the . morning and walk north across the Rio Grande for day employment in the United States.

Jose continues to sweat even though the air conditioner roars. His heart pounds. His hands tremble. He barely retrieves the now heavy gun from the back-seat floorboard. He struggles in placing the gun magazines into his empty pockets a knife strapped to his belt. He feels the urge to pee. He realizes that what he is about to do is not normal. Orders are orders. Who used that defense in the past?

If it resorts into a knife fight, Jose doubts as to whether he can go through with it. The knife pierces the skin, cartilage with the blade eventually hitting bone. The unfortunate victim is holding on to your body, begging for their life. He awakes at night haunted by the stabbing victims scared faces. To him, this business is abhorrent. The assassins are entirely calm, their weapons within reach.

Jose breathes deeply and tries to slow his heart rate. When he believes himself somewhat under control, Jose turns on the vehicle's headlights and positions his car for the assassins to view. Jose flashes his headlights as was pre-arranged to initiate the assault.

The boy assassin slowly with vehicular lights off drives from the opposite end of the street. Accelerates and turns the vehicle far left to maximize the width of the road and then careens right. Wheels squeal, straight through the gate, instantaneously snapping the small padlock, sending the right side of the iron gate crashing towards the same window Jose saw the Colonel and just missing the guard. Jose follows in his vehicle. The girl assassin, with her hair flowing, fires her weapon through the open passenger window. Her frail gazelle body moves from the car as it slows, and she races to meet the young guard head on. Both are firing point blank shots. A bullet hits the boy's calf. The girl dressed only in shorts and a small top inflicts fatal wounds to the guard. He's unaware until he involuntarily collapses next to the metal chair, his weapon bounces by his side.

A whirl of activity appears within the residence. Gunshots originate from at least three windows. What the hell Jose says to himself? The gate on the right-side lands in the Colonel's window and stops the progress of the assassin's car, which was to drive straight into the front door. The left gate fractures the solid front door, nonetheless. Occupants from the house continue the barrage of bullets. Jose and his crew return with a volley of their own. The boy staggers from the car cradling his rifle and throws his body into the front door sending it crashing to the entry tile. Jose follows the boy. The girl climbs over the right gate and enters the residence through the now abandoned open window similar to a cat coming for milk.

Bullets bounce off and through the assassin's vehicles seconds after the killers enter the residence. The reaction of the shooters from within the house is seconds behind the assault. The noise emanating from the weapons, not yet noticeable by the participants, scream for attention from the neighbors. Upon entering through the front door, a soldier not previously seen by Jose fires shots at the boy assassin hitting him directly in the chest. Thump! Bullet hits center mass, casing flies. Thump! Bullet hits center mass, casing flies. Thump! Bullet hits center mass, casing extracts. The boy's body turns to Jose his lips move slightly, and he crashes to the edge of the wooden door. His weapon falls onto tile sounding like broken glass exposing Jose to the soldier. The soldier adjusts his gun towards Jose. Immediately, the girl assassin fires within two feet of the soldier's head exploding the soldier's brains throughout the hallway and into a portion of the living room. A pinkish mist of brain matter, bone followed by a metal smell floats to the tile floor. The twin girl screams as she runs past her fallen comrade and the lifeless soldier through a hallway and into an accompanying bedroom where additional shots originated at the assault vehicles. Jose runs directly behind her.

She sprays bullets with such intensity into the bedroom they ricochet off the walls creating a blender of flesh-eating lead. Jose maintains control of the hallway no signs of the Colonel yet. Immediately, the firing ceases from within the bedroom. Gunpowder smoke from the bullets fills the room. Lying face down on the bed is what resembles the

Colonel's wife, her hair matted and sticky with blood and brain matter. Red liquid adorns the colorful sheets — one limb dangling from her body by a thin stretch of skin. The limb waves back and forth, eventually reaching the floor. Jose glances at the dead women. She was probably attractive in her youth. No doubt, the dead woman grabbed the closest weapon previously placed by each window and began to fire in the direction of the assault. She was just too slow to react but could have been lethal in her actions. Jose admires the dead lady 'muy fuerte.'

The Colonel bolts from an adjacent bedroom and into the hallway supposedly protected by Jose. Jose screws up. He momentarily became infatuated with the dead lady. The Colonel stumbles — bounces off the hallway wall. The Colonel retreats to the master bedroom, bullets, smoke, splinters, and pieces of mortar follow his route. He races to close and lock the thick pine door with a black metal latch. Jose concentrates his assault on the still opened door.

The Colonel screams unintelligibly and succeeds in closing and locking the heavy door. The neighborhood wakes from the noise. Jose needs to accelerate the assault. It is necessary to get out of the area in the event of an unexpected approach by a police officer. Jose instructs the girl to go outside the residence then towards the master bedroom windows to flank the Colonel. She steps from the dead woman's bedroom behind Jose into the hallway over her lifeless brother and exits the residence on the fallen, broken front door. The dead boy's expression was the same when he was alive.

While reloading her weapon, she creeps towards the master bedroom exterior windows. Jose retreats to the bedroom where the Colonel's wife lay, crouches, and throws a grenade towards the locked door. He and Sanchez always possess an excellent supply, after all this is Mexico. Jose covers his ears opens his mouth to reduce the percussion on his brain and lungs from the eventual explosion. He lays prone behind the bedroom's cement wall — the locked pine door splinters as a result of the grenade. Jose runs through the master bedroom doorway.

A doorway is commonly known as the 'fatal funnel.' He does not remain in the fatal funnel doorway as it will frame his body similar to a paper target, making it easier for the Colonel to shoot — no time for peaking around corners. Jose dives to the floor. He can feel the concussion of the Colonel's bullets as they cross overhead. The noise is maddening. He becomes more aware of his surroundings his tunnel vision disappears. Events slow. Unbelievable even to Jose, massive uninterrupted gunfire originating from the girl streaks from the exterior window into the master bedroom.

The Colonel lay hidden behind thick bed timbers woozy from the grenade blast and shrapnel. Jose smashes his body against the wall closest to the exterior window. The girl assassin drops to the ground behind a decorative garden rock reloads her weapon and waits for the Colonel's return fire. The Colonel reacts to the lull in the girl's onslaught. He stands and moves to address her; Jose shoots the Colonel in the back. The impact, of the bullets, causes the Colonel's chest to turn towards Jose involuntarily. Jose shoots the Colonel in his left raised hand, the raising of the hand a common defensive move by the dead. By hitting the Colonels' left hand, Jose demonstrates that he primarily shoots at the first thing that moves. Jose regains his composure shooting the Colonel in the chest. The Colonel slumps along the pockmarked stucco wall and crashes amongst the spent shells — the gun held in his right-hand lands into his lap. The clinging of spent metal shells reveals the end of the gun battle.

Jose administers a double tap to the Colonel's head. Due to the number of spent shells on the ground, he moves like a novice ice skater to the front door. Jose drags the boy's body towards his car, assisted by the girl. Without speaking, both place the body into Jose's vehicle trunk. Jose left his car engine running. It will be a challenge to keep it operating on the road. The tires are intact, but the body sustains significant damage.

They enter Jose's car. Jose slowly drives from the residence watching sporadic residential lights illuminate the length of the street in sequence as they move. The girl sits on the passenger front seat. She reloads her weapon as well as Jose's. A few residents walk outside only to hide in the shadows realizing they exited too early they do not intend on being 'follow up' victims. Jose glances at the lampposts on the Colonel's street.

They drive southeast from Nuevo Laredo passing a federal office and a nearby graveyard. Jose then drives east on Highway 2 by tall metal streetlamps resembling grotesque totem poles in their flight. Contorted ugly faces transcend the street lampposts to the lights. Jose stares in disbelief at the developments within the streetlamp's yellow rays. Jose suspects the four streetlamps on the Colonel's street observed, then impartially judged him for his evil act. The four lamps transmitted the message throughout the electrical system to each streetlamp on his route.

As he drives, bulbous white eyes with streaks of red emerge from the yellow lights and lock onto Jose's path. Yellow block-shaped teeth framed by dark residue expose themselves within the same lenses. The exposed teeth signal a threat, much like an animal to its foe. Passing each streetlamp, they glare at him in disdain as if shaking their heads. The original streetlamps on the Colonel's street he concludes are also responsible for illuminating the Colonel's neighbors' homes during the assault to protect the innocent families.

Jose increases the vehicle's speed to get away from the haunting streetlamps that are growing more violent as he drives. They sway like trees in a hurricane. Their eyes expose their hatred for him. The haunting streetlamps try to reach him. They are getting closer and closer, attempting to make physical contact. He is losing control. Air whistles loudly from the car as wind rips through the bullet holes in its exterior.

Jose glances at the girl on the passenger seat, and she disappears and reappears in the streetlamp shadows as he drives by each. He wipes his eyes. However, she continues to vanish and reappear. To him, she is not aware of the grotesque lampposts or the happenings to her body. He considers to ask if she is cognizant of her transformations, but the question will make him look foolish, weak. He must get away from this haunted place and the demon lampposts. He accelerates. The car rises from the road surface. It becomes dangerously unstable.

As Jose races south, houses, businesses, and the haunting streetlamps are less frequent. Jose encounters the last streetlamp before entering into the wilderness. A lone sentry keeping watch over the evil in the darkness Jose is to join. A bluish haze envelopes Jose's thought. Jose wonders what this particular streetlamp knows. Why does this lamp remain motionless? Is it going to warn him? Warn him about what? Was it satisfied he was leaving the area?

He exits the paved road and drives on a rocky dirt road the streetlamp seen in his rearview mirror. No vehicles are on the way, the car screams for maintenance. The red engine light engages. The water hose or water pump releases a white steam cloud smelling of rust. The girl is no longer disappearing. The girl wishes to retrieve the cash from her brother's body before they dispose of the car. Jose agrees. They are driving towards a pre-arranged location to obtain a replacement vehicle pre-deployed for their escape.

When they arrive at the drop-off point, Jose drives the now clanking vehicle next to the pre-deployed car; the

Black Cat emerges from behind a cluster of rocks a sling on his shoulder. Jose did not know the Black Cat would be present at this site. Others are supposed to dispose of the vehicles. Is the Black Cat going to take him out? Did something go wrong? Something he is not aware of? Was Sanchez, The Black Cat getting rid of all the witnesses? The lampposts knew this was going to happen. They want him dead. That's why the last one had not reacted as he passed. The girl could care less who the person is she never met him. She unbuckles her seat belt and prepares to exit the vehicle to retrieve the money from her brother's pocket.

Jose stops the car. The Black Cat pulls on the sling and holds the AK-47 that rested on his back. He raises the weapon. He fires through the windshield and into the passenger seat incrementally cutting the girl in half. Windshield glass fragments enter the Black Cats' clothes attacking him as if in retaliation slicing his arms and reaching to his face. A purple ooze immediately pulses from the girl's body. Her body heaves back and forth as the volley impacts her body. During this barrage, she manages to reach her weapon with an accompanying look of…. "I will see you in Hell." and "There will be payback." The girl is so incensed at the time of the first volley that her head remains erect with a permanent scowl on her face. The weapon remains clinched in her hands. The Black Cat hesitates to view the girl's facial reaction and feels as if he just lost one of his lives. More importantly, he is sure the next encounter will not go well for him. The Black Cat momentarily regains his senses but is permanently scarred by the girl. The girl's dark brown eyes cut through him and expose the weakness of his ambush. The Black Cat feels a chill through his body. Her open eyes follow his movements. Shaking, the Black Cat stumbles on the rocky terrain, his face pale. His is short of breath and feebly holds the weapon above his waistline.

Jose thrust himself out of the vehicle and remains on the ground beside the car. He crouches next to the engine block to maximize his cover and periodically conducts a quick peek at Sanchez. Jose's incensed that his weapon's strap snags on the girl's weapon's front site. Again, Sanchez fires into Jose's vehicle's back-seat, bullets exit the car into the ground. Sanchez is looking perplexed not realizing the boy's body already laid dead in the trunk not from his shots but others.

Jose waives his arms at Sanchez to stop the assault. Sanchez releases the grip on his weapon, and it hangs from its strap. Sanchez waves his right hand towards Jose in a demonstrative motion to calm down.

"Where is the boy?" Sanchez's voice cracks. His legs tremble at the thought the boy was left behind.

"He's in the trunk, dead." Jose looks through Sanchez's now translucent body. He rubs his eyes with his hands, trying to relieve himself of the visual.

"Get the money from them and let's leave."

Jose gathers the money from the brother and the sister. When he touches the girl's weapon, it burns his hand causing him to release it. Pure evil stares at Jose. The darkness blends with the night. It is shapeless undefinable, but it engulfs him physically and mentally. How does he see it? Such power. It does not strike. He is cognizant that this evil is more than capable of literally destroying him. However, it chooses not to act, making it even more powerful. He never encountered such power. He staggers from the vehicle. Exhausted, he shuffles towards Sanchez not concerned if Sanchez will 'light him up.'

"There can be no witnesses to this one," Sanchez remarks. Sanchez is aware that the assassins are without I.D. Both cars were bought months ago for smuggling. The vehicle registrations do not lead to them.

Somehow, Jose enters Sanchez's vehicle. Sanchez stops by the assassins' car. He throws a lit Molotov cocktail inside the vehicle containing the twins' bodies — an incendiary device developed by Russians at the behest of one of their leaders Vyacheslav Mikhailovich Molotov. The device is comprised of flammable liquid and spreads fire when the glass or container breaks. Molotov's were quite effective when thrown at the exterior ventilation of German tanks during the German assault on Stalingrad, Russia in WWII. The Molotov explodes in the assassins' vehicle eliminating the bulk of the evidence.

Jose involuntarily shakes. He hides it from Sanchez. Pure evil, pure evil he never experienced such a feeling. Sanchez's stomach knotting and tangling into hard rock opens the driver's car door and heaves. Blood and a whitish fluid burst from his mouth splashing on the rocky ground, some of which absorbs in the sand. Pressure builds in his frontal lobes. He almost faints. He hurls his upper body onto the driver's seat eyes forward staring endlessly into his savage future. He does not bother to wipe the vomit from his lips. He thinks he's under control. Never is he more wrong.

From the vehicle rear-view mirror, the flames from the assassins' car rage entirely out of control more than the Molotov and gasoline in the car's gas tank should have created. The flames snap at the rear of Sanchez's car. A roar blows towards their car and pushes the vehicle. Jose awakes from his thoughts and looks into the Black Cat's face and views a skeletal frame. He looks away. Wishes that the image will not manifest again. He turns to see the Black Cat's face. Sanchez's angular facial bones now have flesh. The vomit hangs from his lower lip. Sanchez turns the steering wheel and drives by the wreckage again. The girl's body immersed in flames is still upright staring intently at the Black Cat. The Black Cat views a white shadow of her face. He looks again. Is he seeing a cute young, innocent girl laughing? A cold touch hits the Black Cat's face.

Sanchez accelerates from the area. Rocks fly, from the tires, ricocheting on the rear metal wheel wells. Jose quietly observes the scenery, exposing its tall, weathered cactus each disappearing in the darkness as Sanchez drives. The plants fall by the wayside as if each is individually hacked down by Jose as he passes. Why didn't the lampposts act? Are they not strong enough? Alternatively, are they just gathering information and reporting, but to whom?

Chapter Five

"What!" Don Pedro yells. Flaco hovers for a hiding place. The bad news associated with the messenger. Flaco always provides the controversies and increasingly bad press related to Sanchez to Don Pedro, the leader of the Cali Cartel the reason Flaco has a problem with Sanchez, the Asshole.

"Sanchez killed the Mex Fed?" yells Don Pedro. His stub finger twitches. His left-hand presses down on his thick black oily hair. "Does he realize the intensity of the heat that will overwhelm the Mexican Northern border? Our load of cocaine in Guatemala needs to be held up. Secure that immediately! Make plans to use Rodriguez and ship to the US, via Miami, Florida."

"Si," Flaco replies. "Sanchez must have felt that this would make amends to you after your conversation with him."

"Flaco, get the man on the phone." Don Pedro continues to rub his stub of a finger. The numbness helps calm him and bring him back to rationality.

"Si, Senor."

Don Pedro initiates the conversation and relays the recent events as cryptically as he can and asks that a meeting is granted to assess the situation. The listener agrees. Within a few days, Mexican law enforcement will saturate the northern Mexican border.

The man with the Eastern European accent listens intently to Don Pedro's rendition of the recent Sanchez developments.

"Will he be able to withstand this onslaught?" the Eastern European asks.

"He must. We need to accelerate our plans," Don Pedro continues, "if viewed calmly and from a detached point of view, the movement of additional Mex Feds to the border could be beneficial to our operation. Provide me with new contact numbers, and I will arrange a meeting with Sanchez, the Black Cat."

The man with the Eastern European accent replies, "I will."

The parties terminate their conversation.

Following the conversation, Don Pedro approaches Flaco who in turn says, "Sanchez's people have already taken receipt of the narcotics from Guatemala." Flaco is simmering more lousy news delivered by him to Don Pedro.

"All right, we'll see what the great Sanchez can do now. Flaco, is he still making payments on the last load?"

"Yes."

"Well, let's play it out," Don Pedro says. Don Pedro possesses the ability to perceive the real situation at hand. He does not panic to issues that are out of his control. He will adapt his strategy to the given scenario.

Plans need to be accelerated to combat the continued articles detailing Don Pedro as the sole person responsible for every Colombian and for that matter, the world's problems. Should Don Pedro approach his friends in the Colombian government and sincerely and civilly discuss an outline for his eventual retirement? Continue with the plan to change the battlefront?

Previously, his enemy combatant mediated a retirement deal, and as a result of the talks, the individual temporarily resided on a mountaintop in a beautiful residence with limited guards. All the combatant had to do is last a short time in this de facto confinement complete with party girls and great food until the public forgot what he did. However, he ruined it for people like Don Pedro as the combatant leaves the confines of the residence, embarrassing the government only to start another civil war.

Now, if Don Pedro petitions for a similar scenario, it is unlikely to be considered. Hopefully, he can outlast this problem, and maybe in another few years, he can readdress his retirement package. He reaffirms to himself that the only viable plan is to move the battlefield from Colombia.

Chapter Six

Seamus O'Malley, the superhero in his mind, sits at his desk and reviews old cases to identify potential human Sources to approach for new case development.

He also glances at the newspaper headlines:

"Kosovars Killing Serbians"

"Mex Fed Killing in Nuevo Laredo"

"Taiwan No Longer Part of China Proper"

"Mexican Minister of Interior visiting Italy." No doubt a 'good old Danny Boy Catholic.'

"November elections coming...Uh, oh, that will affect me."

At the same time, O'Malley's supervisor Eddie invades his pod space. Eddie is forty to fifty years old, and a modern-day administrator. Wiping his glasses with his only tie, Eddie speaks, "Senator; 'I want to keep my job' has indicated that he will seal the Texas border from the onslaught of narco-terrorism."

"Narco-terrorism a new buzz word that means?" O'Malley asks.

"That means that you have been selected, including six of your worthy peers to assist the Border Patrol in enforcement along the southern border; specifically, Laredo, Texas."

"When do I go? I must add that I do not care about the border. I am sure much thought went into the selection process. Let me guess not one good old boy or girl is on that list. Let me look at that." Seamus steals the list from the supervisor's hand. "Exactly, what I thought. You guys are a bunch of clowns; not one ass kisser is on the list."

"It is what it is."

"It is what it is," Seamus repeats, shaking his head, "Yea, don't try changing things."

"Look, I don't care about the border and my and your boss don't care about the border. Nobody cares about the border. You still have to go. It's such an exhilarating assignment." Puffing out his chest, Eddie tries to act serious holding the crumpled list. "Try not to screw it up, or they might make it a permanent assignment."

"I'll call you, not my new supervisor when the crap hits the fan down there and it will."

After hearing that, Eddie displays a nervous smile and resembles a moonwalking hermit crab as he leaves O'Malley's pod. Thank God, this Seamus asshole is out of here for a while. Standing tall a 'post-it-note' stuck on his shoe, Eddie briskly walks to his boss' office to inform him that the big managerial mission is complete. Man, another fire has been put out.

O'Malley summarily sets off for the border, himself and six others traveling at sunset in their respective vehicles through the vast expanse of South Texas. Seven agents in their separate cars resembling pathfinders staging to attack the western Russian offensive similar to Hitler's Waffen SS in the later stages of World War II. Of course, in no way matching the intensity. Their mission is to augment the gaps in the US Southern Front.

All to save a Senator's job who is reacting to recent polls indicating that his 'paying' constituents want to eliminate the narcotic and illegal alien/refugee flow into the US. The Senator, no doubt tired of hearing the constant drumbeat from Texas law enforcement and Texas ranchers frustrated with Mexican vehicles, smuggling who knows what, entering from Mexico into South Texas tearing up valuable ranch fences and lands. The same cars generally left abandoned turning Texas ranches into used car lots, landfills and cemeteries.

The seven conscripts are already counting the days until they are relieved of their southern border duties and transferred back to civilization. Like, Serbian police transferred to Kosovo after the breakup of Yugoslavia, only the best and the brightest were sent to serve. Yea, about that.

After arriving in Laredo, O'Malley teams with a youthful and energetic US Border Guard. To O'Malley's surprise, the Border Guard's exuberance begins to reinvigorate him. O'Malley thinks that this might be a decent temporary assignment. If he enjoys the task, he will not tell anyone that he enjoys this job. Out of spite, management will transfer him back to Houston. After all, you cannot be happy at work.

O'Malley makes the best of his days patrolling amongst the dirt roads that parallel north of the Texas/Mexico border. These border patrols bring back memories of his past days while on city police patrol. He was responsible for a 'beat' within a city 'district' all overseen by a particular station house. A designated dispatcher manages communications amongst the districts and beats in each specific station house. Back then, a constant communication gap existed between different station houses. If you are assigned a patrol beat that borders an adjacent separate station house you are seldom if at all advised of ongoing criminal activity such as burglaries, robberies, narcotic dens and accompanying stolen vehicles that occur beyond the fractured communication line.

Occasionally, active events: a stolen car or robbery suspect chases broadcast to the impacted station houses. However, the transmission of everyday crime analysis along the station house frontiers with the affected patrol officers of the adjacent station houses is rare. Small units exist within each station house to analyze the criminal activity and react to these events, but again, the illegal activity rarely shared with the ordinary patrol officer. Now, as O'Malley patrols, the southern US border he has no communication with Mexican law enforcement (foreign station house) at all and that is how Mexico wants it.

Night patrolling their stretch of the Rio Grande, Pete the youthful Border Guard drives a four-wheeled SUV, towing a tire attached to a rope erasing the SUV tire tracks from the loose patchwork of decaying plants and sand. Eyes are everywhere. The criminals identify the origin of the smooth paths and attempt to time their narcotic smuggling between patrols. In this environment, Seamus begins his nightly discussion with Pete, the Border guard. The topic tonight the meaning of life, to pass the time.

"Who is smarter, the human or the pet animal?" Seamus asks.

O'Malley answers his question, "the human. We have a thumb, and that differentiates us from the majority of the animal kingdom. Also, we have the power of reason. We are the masters of the animal kingdom. Dante said we are not to live like animals but to seek knowledge. Animals can't reason or seek knowledge, but the confusing part of Dante's statement is animals adapt. A monkey puts a stick in an ant hole and pulls out ants to eat from the stick. That is smart."

Pete, the Border Guard, replies, "Okay, then who takes care of the pets or the animals in a zoo? No one? I say the animals are smarter as they have convinced the humans to take of them."

"Good one. Yes, humans do. Look at the animal support groups, PETA, SPCA, and some of those environmentalists. They are all well-meaning and sensitive people. Humans are taking care of the animals, and the animals are giving nothing in return. We provide them with the basic needs of life, food, and shelter. I guess they give companionship? You are right. Humans chose to do such a thing. Then, do animals rule over humans? Nobody rules anybody. We are all a product of cycles, events."

Pete rolls his eyes and continues scanning the horizon. The discussions are similar to Jenkins' and Seamus' conversations, but serve to pass the time until it is time to eat. They motor along the vast expanse of the Rio Grande river separating the US from Mexico. Various parts of the river one can walk across, farm, swim, and or ride the rapids. The river allows easy access to both countries, especially during the recent drought.

O'Malley believes Pete's job is not complicated. When Pete arrests subjects and seizes drugs, Pete completes the internal paperwork. Pete's role is 'Cat and Mouse.' See the perpetrators and arrest, simple. He then contacts the DEA, resembling FedEx drivers with guns who in turn pick up all the pieces, transport and charge the subjects. End of Pete's responsibility. Oh, Pete might get subpoenaed to testify but highly unlikely due to the plethora of plea cases. Seamus' job is to make sense of the arrest and evidence and find a way to climb the ladder of the criminal organization. Seamus knows Pete, and his buddies think all of the new arrivals are cowboys.

Seamus and Pete approach a section of the river that can be crossed by foot, southeast of Laredo.

Pete is the first to pick up the signal. Seamus was manipulating the SUV's 'good time' radio dial in a losing effort to locate American music instead of the illegal boosted Mexican music also invading the United States. Tire tracks Pete did not see before are now discernable on the dirt path in front of the Border Patrol vehicle. Lights flash from afar; it is hushed. Pete shuts off the headlights permeating the metal slits covering the vehicle bulbs. Silence paralyzes the area. With the headlights off, darkness sets in and give Seamus the impression of being placed inside a water well. Images of brush and rock begin to reappear. Pete is upset for he usually drives in the bush without vehicle lights wearing night vision glasses. Seamus wants to ask Pete what is taking place, but Seamus understands this is Pete's world, not his. Seamus' world is one of stumbling through files, Informants, tracking cloned phones, cellular calling cards that lead nowhere, all to piece together a means of infiltrating trafficking organizations. Just as there are gateway drugs that lead to harder drugs, narcotic investigations lead to more significant crimes: government corruption, weapon trafficking, money laundering, and wholesale murders. The narcotic traffickers are the weak links providing entry into these greater crimes.

Seamus struggles with his concealed weapon and rusted handcuffs. Pete wearing fatigues readies for war. Pete possesses a compass, power bars in his pockets and water bottles that roll on the SUV's backseat accompanied by a snake bite kit. Seamus holds a pen and a pad of paper. Their two worlds are colliding.

This time both Pete and Seamus observe the momentary flash, just east of their location along the north side of the river, State-side. Pete motions for Seamus to exit the vehicle. Neither slam the vehicle doors only to push the doors closed with a click to reduce noise and extinguish the SUV's interior light. Pete and Seamus low crawl on a dirt path. Seamus' pants fill with dirt at the waistline, and he simultaneously wonders if Pete set the SUV's car alarm. They conceal their motion towards the observed light by moving along the larger rocks and limit contact with any brush. They scale a small mound of dirt. Tiny pebbles roll from rock crevices and sound as loud as marbles landing in a tin cup. The humidity is thick, and the air still.

Seamus yells with astonishment and points in the darkness, "Holy Christ, its Poncho Villa!"

"Shut up," Pete whispers.

"My God, where is General John Black Jack Pershing when you need him?" Seamus is grinning.

Seamus views an incredible sight. Ten to fifteen horses ridden by Mexicans with dark, thick mustaches and goatees, their bodies, thin and tall in the saddle dust blowing in their wake, in the moonlight give the impression of a dream. These smugglers are born to ride. They race from the Mexican banks of the Rio Grande River to the US side of the border. Hooves from the trailing horses' clop on the river rocks splashing the horses' sides. The horses and men lock on to the dark pickup truck parked on the (US) north side of the river. Now, determined to be the source of light that Pete and Seamus had seen. This light was used to signal the Mexican raiding party.

"Son of Bitch," Seamus says, "what the hell is going on?"

Pete, in a hushed manner, radios their position complete with a synopsis of the current events to a matter of fact night shift dispatcher.

The Mexican cowboys rush the stationary pickup throwing saddlebags from the horses backs into the rear of the truck. The two groups remain silent. The groups understand the delivery is the most dangerous time of any deal, the transaction of dope from one group to another. Who's responsible for the smuggled drugs at this time? Is there going to be killing, a Source secreted in one of the groups? Is the other side compromised resulting in the police interceding arresting everyone? Both narcotic groups received their orders from unidentified bosses. Some in this transaction infer who the real boss is. Everyone's senses are peaking.

The horses' hooves click the ground near the pickup. The Cowboys pull the horses' reins. Spit falls from the horses' mouths their eyes glow in the darkness as if possessed by a mythical master. The horses' hair is slick with water and sweat. The animals breathe excitedly from the race to the pickup. Their nostrils flare. No one is at ease, including the horses after being forced to cross the unforgiving terrain at night.

Realizing support will eventually arrive, Pete makes a unilateral decision to act. Pete storms the truck laden with narcotics. Seamus has ideas of his own. Seamus is trained to investigate.

At the same time, the smuggler lookout standing on the bed of the pickup truck spots the top of the Border Patrol vehicle. He breaks the silence and relays the news setting into motion the return of the Keystone Cops, and all hell breaks loose.

Pete and Seamus are too far from the Border Patrol SUV to drive to the smugglers truck. The cowboys circle their horses to face south towards Mexico. The driver of the pickup, now containing the narcotics, flies from the fixed location towards the Border Patrol SUV, as it is the only route out of the area. Pete is in their path.

Seamus rushes the horses. The dope comes from the south, so he follows the cowboys.

Pete runs back to the SUV grabs his rifle aims at the truck slips on a rock and lets off a round agitating the driver who increases his speed and clips the tail end of the SUV. Pete says to himself that just cost me at least eight hours of paperwork. The pickup occupants begin their rodeo ride bouncing in the rear of the truck attempting to close the tailgate. The impact of the two vehicles jettisoned one of the saddlebags from the back of the pickup truck. The saddlebag bounces on the path exposing the cocaine bricks. The pickup truck disappears in the darkness with its bountiful harvest eventually reaching a haven in a nearby ranch's barn circumventing the hard-surfaced roads and Border Patrol air capabilities.

Meanwhile, Seamus continues what he believes to be a run; in reality, control falls in the direction of the horses and cowboys. Candy bars, pens, pencils, explode from his pockets his pistol buried in its holster attached to the interior of his belt. Dirt is rolling from his waistline down his pants — the majority of the horses' sprint to the safety of the midpoint of the Rio Grande. The horses rear legs kick at invisible threats.

Seamus gets to his feet and touches the rear of a trailing horse, startling the already nervous horse and cowboy. The horse rears its hind legs, kicks and dislodges its rider from the saddle just missing Seamus. In their haste, the remaining cowboys ride from the mid-point to land south of the Rio Grande not aware of the missing cowboy. The injured cowboy lays motionless on the ground. The cowboy's horse bolts into the sagebrush never to be seen again. Pete reaches the Border Patrol vehicle and turns on the searchlights, illuminating both sides of the river. The cowboys ride off, leaving Pete, Seamus and the cowboy.

Seamus the consummate smart ass tells the half-conscious cowboy that he is dying and needs to let Jesus into his life.

"You need to tell me whom this dope belongs. You're sure going to die for your sins. You are going to hell. Poisoning people. Killing people and all that other bad stuff." He quips, "You need to relieve yourself of this burden and come straight."

Pete kneels next to the wounded cowboy with the saddlebag containing the cocaine. Seamus looks briefly at the cocaine bricks.

The cowboy tries to assess his wounds, his mind, and heart racing like a scared rabbit. He is not sure if the American tells the truth or not. Pete translates in Spanish in the event the injured cowboy contracts selective hearing or ability to speak English.

"Tell me, or you will go to Hell," Seamus whispers. The cowboy is shocked at Seamus' blasphemous words.

He looks up and mumbles, "Jo, Jo, Jo."

"Jose?" Pete intercedes.

"Si. Si," the cowboy replies.

"Oh, that's great. Do you know how many Jose's there are in this world? Tell me; be more specific."

The cowboy did not understand anything the American said other than "Hell" and "Jesus."

So, Pete translates again and asks, "It's Jose, si, si."

"Si."

The cowboy incoherently whispers in Spanish and fades away. He's in and out consciousness. How would the cowboy's statement look in court? Half unconscious, lying in the desert. Interviewed —Yes, his rights read to him —Yes, a dying declaration is admissible in court.

"Beware," the cowboy says in a thick Mexican accent as if personally upset with the 'gringo' for speaking so nonchalantly with the Lord's name. The cowboy struggles to place both elbows on the ground. He then uses his arms as support, raising his back from the field.

"What?"

Now, looking up at O'Malley, the cowboy leans towards Pete. "He says to beware of El Negro Gato, Negro Gato."

"Beware of the what, what a bunch of Bullshit."

"The Black Cat! The Black Cat!" The cowboy falls back to the ground.

"What the hell is this guy saying, the Black Cat?"

The cowboy passes out his head, leans left. The cowboy's slim frame is barely discernable in the dirt.

"Frightful old chap," Seamus says in a bad English accent. Who is Jose, the Black Cat? Is he a boss? The worker bees are not to know who the owner of the load is, but no one can control rumors.

Chapter Seven

"There was no other way to get the dope across. The Mex Feds have effectively sealed vehicular traffic into the United States. I guess in search of the Colonel's killers or giving the impression they are looking for them. I needed the money to pay off the debts owed to Don Pedro. This delivery was the last of his dope." Sanchez blurts out. "Don Pedro is not a forgiving person."

"Yes, I know. We have been through this before." Jose states. Jose is shorter in height, slim, and darker skinned than Sanchez but more streetwise. Sanchez is a book worm.

"They have nothing. The cops captured one of the cowboys. The rest entered the horse carrier and got away into the night."

"What if the kid talks?" Jose asks. "Did they seize any dope?"

"He won't, and if he does, the worst they will know is your name, Jose. You weren't there, but you coordinated the initial delivery to the ranch."

Comforting, thinks Jose. Although that is not good, how many Jose's are there in this world?

"The lead cowboy indicates one bundle seized."

"So, they did seize dope with the 'crown' markings, a small amount." Jose pauses, "They will not delve deeper into the seizure."

"You're right."

73

Sanchez and Jose sit at the Matamoras office miles from the shipment of narcotics into the United States. The remaining drugs are destined for New York City via Houston, Texas. In Houston, Sanchez's smugglers break down the bundles of cocaine into smaller caches secreted in various tractor trailers. If law enforcement seizes one of the lower loads, the impact on the Sanchez organization is negligible.

Sanchez recounts the Romans, the Germans before World War II and the Americans all constructed roads to conquer and or to expand their respective countries financial reach. Eventually, invading armies make use of the same routes to invade Rome and Germany. The Americans are now experiencing a silent smugglers re-conquest via its infrastructure.

We are not an organized army, but in time, we might be designated terrorists. The United States administratively wrestles in adopting an adequate strategy in neutralizing terrorists. Terrorists are extraordinarily transient and operate without stagnant command and control. Sanchez questions if it is better to be designated a terrorist or not.

So far, Sanchez's most significant threat is internal as a more radical person/group always sprouts from the original group. Sanchez recently read an article detailing Yasser Arafat, the leader of the Palestinian National Authority (PNA), negotiated efforts with representatives of Israel and other world leaders. Because of this dialogue, a more radical contingent within the PNA concludes Arafat is a US conformist or worst a US Informant. Sanchez remains vigilant for any signs of an internal uprising.

When law enforcement identifies Sanchez as a smuggler, he hopes the US categorizes him with a military rank deflecting the American public from who he is, a terrorist. The designated grade provides him with a sense of legitimacy and integrity. He anticipates 'Lieutenant.' He will strive for 'Captain.' Sanchez is not aware that if he is designated a terrorist, then US law enforcement infiltration tools in dismantling his organization become very limited. United States government officials can give no aid or comfort as a means to infiltrate terrorists groups only directed law enforcement techniques to locate the terrorists can be attempted. Successful tools making use of undercover buys and money laundering operations are to be avoided by law enforcement in investigating terrorists interpreted as giving aid to a terrorist group.

Sanchez, in deep introspection, knows the US will never compile a complete and accurate list of its unsolved murders and missing persons associated with the numerous smuggling operations. He knows these unsolved murders and missing persons are the first phases in creating an undercurrent to break the US' 'rule of law.' The 'real professionals' will enact the next stage. He wonders when the professionals will initiate the next phase.

Sanchez is a student of history. He realizes the US is not aware or refuses to accept that the Mexican government is in decline. The Mexican government will cease to exist mimicking the fall of the Roman Empire. As the Roman Empire grew, the Roman central government paid the legions salaries and adequately provided goods and services to conquer new lands and people successfully. The spoils of war fed the Roman coffers much like Mexican oil reserves and mineral wealth keep Mexico afloat, today.

With the advent of corruption in both Rome and Mexico, salaries and services remain stagnant disenfranchising the military and police. To supplement their wages, prominent Roman Generals located and acquired new sources of income. The spoils of war remained under Generals control. The Roman Generals paid the legions salaries and become more important and influential than the central government. In Rome, the Generals eventually replaced the central government as the soldiers pledged their allegiance and loyalty, not to Rome, but to their Generals.

Mexico is now in its death spiral as prominent military members and police are acting much the same as the Roman generals. Troops swear allegiance and loyalty to the Mexican Generals.

The exploitation of mineral and oil wealth and receipt of criminal organizations 'payoffs' are the Mexican Generals spoils of war. Extortion and kidnappings reign in Mexico. Criminal groups are even extorting Mexican farmers avocados and tomatoes found on US tables. The populace continues to flee this corruption to the United States.

The problem, for the US, when it enters into Mexican agreements, there are no guarantees since the actual Mexican decision makers have not shown their faces.

Meanwhile, Seamus and Pete work on a draft related to the cowboy's statement and the seizure of the narcotics secreted in the saddlebag paperwork necessary to justify their respective budgets. One hour of action equals 10 hours of paperwork. While writing the draft, their 'valley' supervisor, Bill, directs Pete to complete his accident package. So very important, this decree will encompass two days of work, three autobody shop quotes and pictures.

Seamus asks supervisor Bill if he needs to locate the pickup driver to ascertain if the smugglers are okay, any bumps or bruises. Do they intend to sue the government? Does the pickup driver possess liability insurance? You know Mr. Bill, the accident forms require all of the above. Bill walks away, acting as if he does not hear O'Malley. Bill stops in his tracks, snaps his fingers turns towards Pete and Seamus and states that they are to remain available tomorrow and the next for interviews related to Pete's discharge of his weapon.

More wasted days. No doubt, Office of Professional Responsibility (OPR), internal affairs agents are parachuting into the region at this very moment for the impending interviews. A shot heard around the world. An American agent shoots his gun near the border. My, oh My. While on the other side of the 'ditch' gunfire is heard nightly. Bullets originating from Mexico randomly fall on the office's parking lot. Time spent on analyzing the markings on the dope not 'gonna' happen nor attempts to interview the cowboy.

They are taking Pete and Seamus 'out of the line' forcing Seamus' cohorts to pick up the slack in the daily seizures. Seamus buddies direct their scorn towards Pete, not Seamus because they heard that when supervisor Bill asks Seamus' side of the story about 'The Shot,' Seamus said he was struggling with "another horse's ass."

Seamus saw Pete stumble when he shot. The bullet probably landed south of the border in a big pot of steaming caldo soup. Bill seethes after hearing Seamus' remark. Seamus will not let up. O'Malley tells Bill all the lines in the accident package need to be filled out. People will die if the forms remain inadequately processed. O'Malley tells Bill he will be responsible for the Administrative Officer's impending heart attack as a result of the incomplete forms. Bill turns to Seamus, wanting to say something but walks away realizing this Seamus guy is here temporary. Nobody is willing to reduce the ridiculous paperwork.

Sanchez and Jose openly operate. Sanchez still seated behind his seldom-used office desk is assessing the overall, reviewing whom to trust.

Jose receives a call from Flaco requesting that Jose "stand by" for an incoming call. Flaco does not provide the future caller's name. Flaco tells Jose to treat the caller in high regard. The conversation concludes.

Within a few minutes, the aforementioned individual contacts Jose from a different cellular telephone. These telephone calls remind Jose to obtain new phones. When acquired, the new telephone numbers are 'texted' in reverse order to existing organizational phones, indicating a change in communication devices.

Jose briefs Sanchez before the second call. Sanchez answers the phone. The caller instructs Sanchez to activate Sanchez's other (third) cellular telephone. They hang up. Sanchez responds to the ring on the third cell phone. The voice tells Sanchez that he will meet him a few blocks away at Rosarios's Cantina. Joaquin, the caller, says he will approach Sanchez. Joaquin terminates the phone call. Sanchez walks from the office into the constant heat.

Sanchez wonders if Joaquin is one of those up and coming extremist terrorist, who wants his repayment for the missing drugs now counter to Don Pedro's decision. There is always one person 'who leaves the reservation.'

Sanchez dodges a few vehicles and continues his walk to the cantina, orders a coffee and waits. Within a few minutes, a white man approaches Sanchez and speaks with a formal Spanish accent, not Mexican Spanish.

The conversation is short and to the point, no pleasantries. Sanchez detects an Eastern European accent. What he asks for is interesting. The timing could not be better. Limited data provided by Joaquin will relieve the stalemate at the northern Mexican border caused by the increasing presence of the Mex Feds. Sanchez possesses what the foreigner demands. Why is this of importance? Sanchez learns from the short conversation that he will not play a significant role. Maybe, Don Pedro reinstated Sanchez in good standing. There is no doubt, Flaco will enjoy every bit of Sanchez's new reality.

Without delay, Sanchez obtains the requested information from his office; the new 'meet location' was given to Sanchez by Joaquin at the bar.

Chapter Eight

Pete and O'Malley's 'valley' boss, Bill, makes it known to a captured audience and those willing to listen of his significant role in obtaining some support and exchange of limited information regarding the small amount of cocaine seized by Pete and Seamus east of Laredo. Everyone, but Bill is aware of the inherent danger in this information exchange. The odds are the Mex Feds merely want to ascertain what is known by US authorities on a specific Mexican narcotic organization. Not for action, but for consumption by their real bosses. Seamus eventually discovers Bill lied about his role in the limited exchange. The Mex Feds initiated the request making the cooperative effort even more suspect. Based on the small amount of cocaine seized, it makes little sense for the Mex Feds to cooperate. Rest assured, Bill will receive kudos for pushing the false narrative at the expense of Seamus and Pete's lives.

The 'cooperating' Mex Feds, indicate the disembarkation point of the smugglers' horse trailer was a dirt road paralleling the river. They found many boot and horse hoof impressions in the soil, no evidence retained. Horse trailer tracks lead to a hard-surfaced road.

The cowboy arrested on the US side is uncooperative and refuses to give further statements. Pete and Seamus were busy charging the almost dead cowboy, processing the dope, completing the accident report and somewhat participating in the weapon discharge interviews. Translated: Neither attempts additional meetings with the cowboy.

Thank God, the US Marshals accepted custody of the cowboy as he recuperates otherwise Seamus, Pete and the happy others from his office would be delegated by Bill to conduct 24-hour guard duty at the hospital until the cowboy recovers from his injuries. No one wants to be involved in an in-custody death inquest. Besides, more seizures are coming their way.

Continuing the Mex Feds brief to Bill, the participating Mex Feds identify the injured cowboy from a US-provided photograph as a farm hand of the Garcia-Gonzalez ranch about sixty miles south of Nuevo Laredo. Possibly a major break. Naturally, the Mex Feds possess some intelligence on this matter.

The Mex Feds arrive at the Garcia-Gonzalez ranch and are unable to match the horse and cowboy descriptions provided by Pete and Seamus. The ranch hands are not talking even with the perceived threat of torture. The Mex Feds are not willing to torture. They are aware information obtained in this manner is 'fruit of the poison tree' evidence. If given, to US authorities who act on the data, arrests will be dismissed, embarrassing Mexico and the United States.

The owners of the Garcia-Gonzalez ranch are very amicable to the Mexican authorities in providing no useful information. Seamus thinks the Mex Feds are just going through the motions. Pete and Seamus' lying US supervisor relates some of the above. Bill forwards the events from memory as he is too lazy to write notes from the Mexican briefs. Supervisor Bill denies Seamus and Pete requests for access to the Mexican managerial or agent counterparts. US management reminds them 'to know their role,' too subtle for bulls in the china closet to comprehend.

Not revealed to Bill or US authorities at the initial brief, the Mex Feds leave the ranch. They lose their bearings amongst the dirt roads. While lost, the Mex Feds discover a burned hulk of metal. Sitting upon the metal, vultures feast on the remains.

"What is it?" asks the Mex Fed driver of the vehicle.

The captain replies, "A burned vehicle, possibly stolen."

"Why steal a car and leave it so far from nowhere?" The driver inquires attempting to impress with his investigative powers, obviously bucking for a promotion. He is a driver. A driver is not interested in working cases.

He has the driver position to seek advancement through his access to rank. A philosophy also practiced by other drivers in larger US Police Departments.

"I don't know, but let's check it out," says the captain.

The car's interior is burned to the metal and contains two charred human bodies — one on the front seat the other in the trunk. There appears to be a belt buckle with a partial engraving laying near the backseat. Weapon remnants remain.

With the recent killing of Mex Fed Colonel Pablo Corrion in Nuevo Laredo, the captain decides to remain at the scene until more units arrive. Can it be related to the Colonel's death or just another crime? They stumbled into something significant, the gravity unknown. The unknown is always a concern.

During this period, Seamus the consummate public relations agent uses his time off to frequent the local bars in Nuevo Laredo. Seamus is on temporary assignment, so effort by local traffickers to identify him will be fruitless. If they do, who cares? Seamus will not participate in undercover operations down here.

Seamus eventually settles on one particular cantina, The Wooden Nickel. It avails a good view of the streets. From this bar, he views aged, weathered women carrying large purses walking on the sidewalks. They wear bright, colorful clothes. The lively colors divert their focus on the darkness surrounding them. The women rock as they walk. As they walk, their legs remain straight, not bending their knees. They move their legs from their hips. Is the rocking motion a learned defensive act in case inaccurately identified as a target for a sniper? No, not these women. He first learned of making small random moves in a conflict zone. A soldier told him, if he intends to stand outside for an extended period, it would be beneficial to his health if he randomly repositions his body. The move could reduce the effectiveness of a potential sniper. What those women's eyes have seen, experienced, and cleaned up, being born into this part of the world. The younger kids wear jeans and shirts and run around the women on the sidewalks. Still happy and joyous, shielded from their harsh reality by the aged women.

At times, Seamus sits on barstools at the Wooden Nickel and watches soccer on the television. He previously viewed a beautiful woman at the bar, and when he returned to the bar, she enters again. While Seamus stands at the wooden bar, she orders a drink and surveys the interior of the bar to locate an ideal seat. Seamus initiates a conversation with her, and after having a few drinks, they discover both are involved in law enforcement.

Seamus knows cops around the world, regardless of origin, share a particular bond. A bond that one joined the force to do good. Through their conversations, Seamus learns that following the killing of Colonel Pablo Corrion, she received orders to travel to Nuevo Laredo. Occasionally, the two will meet at the same watering hole in Nuevo Laredo. Exchange law enforcement tales that become more grandiose as the drinking intensifies. Maria practices her English and Seamus practices his Tex Mex. Seamus is in awe of the Mex Fed. How does she survive this working environment?

Maria appears to be a loyal sharp cop. How many more are like this particular Mex Fed? How will Seamus react if stuck in the Mex Fed's world allying oneself to the Mex Fed in charge, like the Colonel? What if he discovers that his boss is crooked? Poverty or death is inevitable if Seamus does not go along with the corruption. He would have to resign. Luckily, the US does not have such prevalent problems, yet. To Seamus, US corruption investigators appear to have kept up with the incidences, not so in Mexico.

The real problem for the Mexican Government related to the Colonel's killing is the movement of 'new' Mex Feds into the former Colonels' area, threatening established ties between Mexican traffickers and existing law enforcement in the Nuevo Laredo area. The new Mex Feds, now operating in a different geographic area with its own established links to corruption, might work. They could combat crime to create pressure on the existing criminal groups as a means of developing new connections. Additionally, initiating 'shakedowns' on the residents. The new troops might look for new tits. Placing the central Mexican government in an awkward position as it may be necessary to separate the Mex Fed groups for everyone's safety. What will happen if one Mex Fed group entering the area has received money from a criminal organization in conflict with a criminal group aligned with a Mex Fed detachment already in Nuevo Laredo?

Admittedly, Seamus is not a ninja cop. He is capable of defending himself with his hands and feet, training by himself not divulging his abilities to his compatriots. If he tells anyone he 'trains,' he will hear each day, that we train too. Come train with us. I am a blue belt, a pink belt. What? My belt glows in the dark. What belt are you? My 8-year-old boy breaks boards with his hands. O'Malley broke a wooden pencil once when listening to Eddie, his Houston supervisor, lecture him about the 'Big Picture.'

Seamus O'Malley is proficient with a small arm. At present, it is not necessary to carry a long gun (rifle). Of course, the administration places so many restrictions on its availability that in reality the only administratively approved location to secure the weapon, is at the office. There are not many crooks running around in the office.

Seamus is aware of his surroundings when necessary. Staying in a constant state of readiness can exhaust you mentally. His primary concern is the furtherance of the case. Moreover, if it is terrorism, narcotics and large amounts of money he will follow the case despite his boss' wishes to the end it, especially if the case involves the investigation of corrupted foreign government officials. It is these corrupt officials that allow the narcotics and proceeds to flow. Source information usually leads to the highest foreign officials. This Source reporting will force the manager to remain knowledgeable about the long-term case. Seamus has had to deal with supervisors asking why they should stay vigilant in understanding the long-term Source reporting when the smaller investigations are just that easier to oversee and weigh the same in the budget process?

Drinking with Maria, the Mex Fed can be in fun, passing the time, a honeytrap by Mexico or it can turn into a working relationship. Seamus goes along with the meetings to ascertain which scenario unfolds. In the event, a meeting turns into a kidnapping, Seamus advises Pete in advance as to when and where he will meet the Mex Fed — providing Pete, a place to start the investigation. Seamus gave Pete her name, telephone number, and position. More importantly, Seamus tells Maria her name has been given to his partner, adding a little more insurance. These simple meetings separate Seamus from the regimentation of his organization. It is not grandstanding; it is an attempt to obtain information.

As the weeks go by, an informal working relationship develops between Seamus and the Mex Fed. Seamus tells Maria he continues to investigate a crazy cowboy smuggling case and provides the names, Jose and the Black Cat as associated with the seizure. There's nothing to lose. If she is soliciting compiled US information related to corrupt Mexican officials and their narcotic brethren, she can conclude Seamus appears to have some workable leads. Seamus further reveals that the Black Cat case has developed into a 'hobby case.' He works on 'leads' when time permits. He thinks it is a compelling case and memorable in the way the cowboys rode into the United States. He reveals his infatuation with the mystery subject, the Black Cat. Seamus says the hobby case does not monopolize his days. He and his partner Pete are busy responding to narcotic seizures along the border. However, he reinforces to Maria that he will not drop the case.

One day, Maria releases unactionable Colonel Corrion case data. She took a chance in releasing the information. In turn, Seamus shares additional details on the cowboy case. Seamus is not aware of a linkage between the circumstances, but provides small bits of evidence to accelerate the future transfers of data. To break the ice, Seamus asks Maria if she requires assistance with the Colonel Corrion investigation. Before he is transferred to the border, Seamus remembers reading a headline about a high-profile Mex Fed killing. He confirms she saved his cellular telephone number. Is Maria courageous, or is she acting on orders? Seamus states that she will achieve the rank of Colonel out of this investigation. She laughs.

He asks Maria, "Do you think the Mex Fed Colonel was crooked? You said somebody blew up his house. If he was a good guy, wouldn't the bad guys just discreetly dispose of the body?"

The Mex Fed remains quiet and frowns, "What do you think?"

Seamus does not respond. The Colonel is crooked; he just wanted Maria to reinforce his thoughts. Late in the night, Seamus and Maria leave the Wooden Nickel. Outside the bar, Seamus hugs Maria and she squeezes him harder. As she holds him tightly, he's discovering he has feelings for her. He fixates on her beautiful face and body. Maria releases her hug peering at him like she wants to say something. She seems stressed and abruptly says goodbye. With a lowered head, Maria walks away. Seamus waves, but she does not see it.

Seamus walks the short distance to the northern Mexican border, pays 25 cents to an individual inside a wooden booth and enters the United States. Maria moves throughout the old square of Nuevo Laredo eventually walking inside a weathered boutique hotel three stories in height with a small lobby, as observed by a Mexican American couple. The Mexican American couple remains on the exterior of the hotel standing at opposite corners of the hotel scanning the hotel rooms windows.

Not observed by the Mexican American couple, Maria climbs the hotel stairs and knocks on a door. The door opens, and Maria, the Mex Fed enters sitting next to an older Caucasian woman with a reddish face and long gray hair in a bun on top of her head. The older woman sits near the hotel room's exterior window providing a view of the street. Maria sits on the edge of the bed. The hotel room television roars to deter interdiction — Maria talks without breathing. She repeatedly waves her hands in the air. The older woman listens intently. With nothing left to report, Maria exits the room.

For a few more minutes, the older woman sits in the room scanning the streets below. She allows the Mex Fed to depart first unaccompanied. If surveillance exists the older woman eliminates surveillance's ability to photograph the two together as they exit the hotel, the prized photograph referred to as 'the trophy shot.'

The Mexican American male observes Maria walk from the lobby and onto the street. He advises the Mexican American female by cellular telephone, and they decide not to follow her.

The older woman stands, turns off the hotel room lights observed at that moment by the Mexican American woman. She, in turn, contacts the Mexican American man and advises what she saw. The older woman leaves the room and closes the door. The Mexican American woman tells her partner that there is a 60% percent chance the next person walking out of the hotel is their target. The older white woman walks outside the hotel carrying a large straw bag. She's portly in nature a small stomach bulge protruding from her tight white dress adorned with blue flowers. Her face swollen with accompanying red streaks from broken capillaries throughout her cheeks, her gray hair is in a bun. She wears sneakers and resembles a retiree.

The couple follows the older woman for approximately one and a half hours. The older woman is observed entering and exiting various convenience shops that line the crumbling streets — buying some fruit and milk, here and there. She stops to look through the exterior windows of different curios shops. Ultimately, she enters a condominium complex lobby guarded by a young man.

The Mexican American woman speaks English on the cell, "We've located the general residence of the new contact. We will eventually identify the room number confirming our intelligence."

A responding female's voice says, "Good Job. Have a good night." The Mexican American woman responds in kind, and the conversation ends. The couple eventually departs the immediate area.

On a particular day during one of their attitude adjustment meetings, Maria, the Mex Fed reveals to Seamus the discovery of a few bullets near a burnt-out car in proximity to a suspected ranch purportedly used by the cowboy smugglers, Seamus' hobby case. The development and information are compelling. What is she doing? Can the evidence/bullets link to the cowboy case and the Corrion killing? He does not believe in coincidences. Maria is brilliant, probably why she has such access.

"Was there a body at the scene?" Seamus asks through a slight tequila haze.

She pauses and then says, "I think there were two. The police found part of a belt buckle, and as I said before, at least one bullet and I hear now the police found a destroyed weapon. The situation is fluid. I guess?" She waves her hand upwards and frowns.

"I mean this is a long shot, Colonel Pablo Corrion is shot and killed, and nobody knows who did it. Somewhat close to each other and time, right?"

Corrion, being the same Colonel killing, Seamus previously asked Pete to translate from an article within a Mexican border newspaper. The only reason why Seamus was interested in the newspaper article was marketing. A common practice amongst Mexican newspapers is to place brightly colored photographs of the most violent killings on the front page. Being that the Colonel was a Mex Fed, retaliation against the press for excessively reporting on the incident will not happen. Interviews, from the Colonel's neighbors, who if they say anything indicate they awoke in the night from gunfire and an explosion. Photographs depicting the aftermath of the Colonel's residence, so on and so forth continue to fill the local papers. However, truly 'investigating' the killing as to who did it and why will have ramifications for the reporters of the various newspapers.

Seamus is lucky in locating the article about the Colonels' death. Hopefully, Maria is not just forwarding events she has read about in the newspapers to keep him talking.

After Pete read the articles, it does not appear to Seamus that the residents are demanding answers as to who killed the Colonel. In their eyes, he was a bad guy, and he got what he deserved. It is almost if they wanted the entire episode to go away. They fear something. Do they fear the government's reaction?

"Close in time, but we find burned out cars and bodies somewhat frequently in the desert."

"Yes, but what would it hurt to check ...compare the found bullets to those at the residence? Check weapons found at the Colonel's residence. I saw the discarded weapons at the Colonel's house in the newspaper. Use the weapons at that crime scene in determining if the ballistics match to the ones found at the burnt car or check out the buckle. I wonder if our cowboy knows anything about this? The cowboy's ranch and the burnt car are close together." He did not let Maria know he will not interview the cowboy again.

"I'll check the ballistics, but I'm sure somebody is working on it."

"Hell, make a call."

"I will."

"Did they only find a few bullets and leave, or are there more at the scene including casings?" Seamus says suddenly feeling the buzz of professional excitement. He reminds himself that this is a casual conversation, not an inquest.

She continues, "An assassin's car remained at the Mex Feds' house after the Colonel's murder."

"I had that read to me from the news," Seamus says, "were leads developed from that?"

"They were not able to obtain actionable fingerprints from the car, but an overzealous lieutenant did kick in the door of an old lady down in Monterrey, Mexico." They laugh at the same time. She continues, "The license plates were stolen months ago, and the old lady did not report them stolen for she did not drive the vehicle anymore."

"Oh, what the hell. Hey, if you have any problems with your boss, I'll help you out. He will need to clear it with my boss." Seamus says.

"That won't be possible."

"I understand. Hey, say we decide to take a drive south and stumble on the wreckage."

"Like a coincidence."

"Yea, like a coincidence."

What is Seamus getting into, Pete the Border Patrol agent's vitality rubbed off on him, and if Seamus does not watch his step, big trouble could ensue. Man, this is getting interesting. One problem for Seamus is Pete, with all his enthusiasm to work, is not willing to assist Seamus south of the border.

"Maybe, in the future," Maria says.

"Aye, aye," Seamus says, kicking back his last tequila wincing in pain as he sucks on a lemon wedge.

Chapter Nine

The stranger with the Eastern European accent known to Sanchez, aka the Black Cat, as Joaquin holds the requested paperwork provided to him by Sanchez. Joaquin asks that Sanchez remain available a few days before the operation in the event modifications to the plan are necessary.

Sanchez is given additional orders by the stranger Joaquin at the 'meet location' to plan the acquisition of men and weapons. The meet location is a prearranged setting at a future date and time given in person or through code over the telephone, eliminating excessive electronic communication.

Sanchez forwards Joaquin's orders for men and weapons to Jose. Sanchez is not anticipating further demands from Joaquin related to this matter. Other than he will be required to cryptically forward to Jose a meet location, date and time between Joaquin's people and the newly hired assassins. By having Jose handle the 'acquisitions,' Sanchez creates at least one layer between himself and the new subjects. If breached, Sanchez prepares to 'wash' his association with this issue by eliminating Jose. The anticipated event is extreme. What is driving this violent action? Millions and millions of dollars can be the reason. Who gains in this matter? The stranger Joaquin, Don Pedro? Always follow the money a credo followed by many.

Before Jose's dispatch, Sanchez establishes code words for use by Jose and Sanchez in subsequent telephone contacts. 'Guns' will be referred to as 'Corn.' 'Money' is

'Fertilizer.' 'Manpower' is referred to as 'Farm Implements.' 'Vehicles' are 'Grain.' For example, if Jose experiences a problem and seeks advice from Sanchez, the call sounds like this: "Having problems in acquiring the farm implements, as the owner wants to wait on at least a portion of the fertilizer before 'ground is broken' (the impromptu phrase 'ground is broken', means acceptance). So, let's wait on acquiring the corn as well until the fertilizer arrives. Translated: no commitment from the assassins until they see the money. Until they commit, let's wait on the procurement of the weapons. Sanchez's responses might include: "I agree," or 'go to the other dealership,' meaning to another set of assassins.

Sanchez flies to Culiacan, Mexico as instructed by the stranger Joaquin. These are repetitive orders. The stranger knows Sanchez already has a required presence in Culiacan. The stranger knows this. The stranger is manifesting his control over Sanchez.

Arriving at a predetermined Culiacan hotel, Joaquin greets Sanchez in fluent Russian. Attempting to shock Joaquin, Sanchez responds in perfect Russian. Due to a lack of response by the Russian, Sanchez realizes Joaquin's overall knowledge of the operation. Joaquin is not impressed by Sanchez's Russian response.

The stranger re-introduces himself as Yuri, not Joaquin, and says Sanchez's Russian is adequate stunning Sanchez's ego. Sanchez prides himself on his conversational and intellectual prowess and is taken back at Yuri's demeaning remark. Sanchez is now working for Yuri. Yuri provides additional plan generalities and instructions. Sanchez is now to relay to Jose the meet location between Yuri's people and the recently hired assassins. Jose summarily forwards the meet location to the newly acquired killers.

Two days pass, and Jose meets with the Black Cat at a restaurant close to Sanchez's temporary residence, a small Culiacan hotel. Jose indicates all is in its proper order.

Sanchez orders Jose to leave the area by 'grain' (vehicle) and drive all night to the 'base,' Matamoros. Jose acknowledges. They now instinctively communicate in code during these personal meets — the tension mounts.

Sanchez similarly meets Yuri at a small Taqueria and advises him of the same, Yuri nods. Yuri's preoccupied, engaged in another matter. He planned the event. Maybe, the reality is impacting Yuri. Perhaps, Yuri did not receive his paycheck. It is no secret Russia is in financial ruin. Russia recently gave notice of significant reductions in aid to Cuba.

The Russians are simultaneously having problems with the Islamist in Chechnya and the 'Stans.' A reduction in oil and gas production in the Stans can place a more financial strain on Russia, not including the cost of another small war. Mexico has plenty of oil and gas reserves. Maybe, the Russians are trying to extort Mexico. For what? Follow the money. Ah, that is too big of a scenario. How will this impending operation benefit the Russians? Who's to say Yuri is Russian or even working for the Russian government? Damn, it seems implausible that any legitimate country mounts such an operation as this. Somebody is, and they appear to have committed the best minds to the plan. The action has the appearance of resources to complete the goal.

While driving, what deception Jose thinks to himself. Sanchez directs him to find the 'farm implements' in the US, not Mexico thwarting both countries investigations, due to a general lack of shared information between the US and Mexico. If the mission fails, the acquisition of the farm implements can damage the already frayed relations between the two countries. The US is sending assassins into Mexico as if there are not enough in Mexico, already.

Sanchez still engaged with Yuri at the Taqueria crosses his hands and leans towards the seated Yuri, "You know this is going to help me."

"How's that?" Yuri asks.

"The northern border will be clear of the recent influx of Mex Feds, and your 'target' is a historical royal pain in my ass," Sanchez responds.

"We thought we would do this to make your day, such vanity," Yuri shaking his head, "you know, for the betterment of the team. Don Pedro wants to keep his Indians happy." Yuri recognizes he hit too hard with the vanity remark, so he lightens up, "Slick move with the Mex Fed Colonel. Very well done. Don Pedro still has a way to convey direction to his troops silently." Yuri smiles. "He demands movement, not motion. More importantly, Don Pedro does not want his people to become complacent. Because, if just one 'leader' in the group falls, it might allow law enforcement infiltration into Don Pedro's chain of command." Yuri ends the conversation by telling Sanchez to stay sharp. They say their goodbyes and Sanchez leaves the Taqueria. Yuri remains seated at the table.

Sanchez expressed his personal feelings to Yuri, why? Possibly to find answers, or to see if Yuri's personality will soften. Yuri does not take the bait; he is no fool. Yuri deflects to achieve his goal. Sanchez learns from Yuri's deflection traits.

Before the planned event, Sanchez reviews Colonel Corrion's killing. The Colonel demanded an increase in 'payoffs.' The Colonel was taking money from his enemies. The danger, these unidentified traffickers will persuade the Colonel to act against Sanchez. Sanchez has trouble processing the Colonel's death. The killing of the girl bothers him more.

Sanchez rationalizes that the Colonel was the Source in facilitating law enforcement to seize his dope. The first seizure did not reveal the Colonel's involvement. So, the Colonel becomes more confident and shares more information leading to the second seizure. With the caveat, that the second seizure occurs far from the border, minimizing his involvement in the seizure. The further the seizures arise in real distance from the Colonel's 'hands on' the more insulation the Colonel has in deniability.

In a typical route, the dope transfers to a few pre-selected smugglers, 'throwaways' and or mules. The more dope transfers the US investigators allow, the more confident the Colonel becomes. The Colonel either cooperated to get money from the police, is pissed off at Sanchez and or acted on behalf of his new masters.

In the first seizure, law enforcement surveilled Sanchez's dope the moment it transferred from the Colonel's responsibility at the Mexico/US border to Sanchez's person on the US side. Law enforcement surveilled Sanchez's guy complete with his rented family as long as they could without losing the same. US investigators following the suspect vehicle contacted a patrol unit to develop independent probable cause for the stop: tail light out, speeding, or changing lanes unsafely. The patrol officer finds the dope in the car and writes the arrest and seizure report without mentioning the patrol officer received a call from drug agents that the vehicle may have narcotics protecting the Source, the Colonel. The drug agents have now corroborated the Colonel's information.

So, when the Colonel and or his designees notify the drug agents of a second load, the drug agents are willing to invest resources in surveilling the second load to protect the Source again. Law enforcement follows the tractor-trailer in this case, to a New York City residence. US law enforcement waits and hits a vehicle leaving the New York residence/stash house. Once again, directing a patrol officer to establish independent probable cause to stop the car leading to another seizure of the cocaine from this vehicle. The seized dope allows law enforcement to search the New York City residence. Translated: NY law enforcement stops a car (seen leaving the stash house) for a traffic violation. The driver has cocaine. The driver says he got the dope from the residence. From this statement, law enforcement searches the home and discovers more dope. Reducing the need for law enforcement to disclose that the load was surveilled from the southern border, a result of Source information from the South Texas border. It is this protected/layered US law enforcement action that concerns the 'big boys and girl down south.' An Informant or Informants are in the mist. They smell the Sources. They are worried about larger seizures in the future. Don Pedro and now it appears Yuri are convinced that Sanchez obtained facts leading to his lost seizures. Events that led Sanchez directly to the Colonel. Sanchez understands as a result of the impending Culiacan venture; Don Pedro will temporarily freeze his cocaine supplies. Sanchez will be too hot.

Yuri formulated the plan, individually selecting the target. Days pass preparing for the occasion. Yuri, the consummate professional, halts all communication with his Eastern European boss. The results will speak for themselves. Don Pedro will benefit from the plan.

Today is zero hour. Small businesses constructed of concrete with black steel front doors line the streets of the 'targeted' area. Houses intermix with the stores. The combined roofs are a mix of brown curved clay tiles and corrugated steel. Flowers in full bloom, a kaleidoscope of colors adorn walls close to the streets. Bougainvilleas grow along the sidewalks from the smallest parcels of dirt — some sprout from within the sidewalk cracks. Amongst the sweet aroma of melted Oaxaca chocolate, children skip and chase each other through the streets and sidewalks. The city awakens with the sunrise. The citizens are unaware of the impending events.

Sanchez, the Black Cat, had been summoned to Culiacan by his boss, Cardinal Manuel Torres. The

Cardinal is scheduled to speak in front of a large crowd. The main topic of the speech stresses the necessity to eliminate or at least to reduce the narcotics trade, and the address provides details on how to quell the associated Culiacan violence. Cardinal Torres sends a strong message in summoning Sanchez, the Black Cat, the Bishop of Matamoros. Yes, Sanchez is a priest.

Cardinal Torres obtained limited evidence linking Sanchez, the Black Cat to narcotics trafficking. Sanchez has some details of the speech and is concerned that the Cardinal will mention his relationship with narcotics trafficking. The Cardinal intends to showcase the Black Cat. Giving public notice not only to the Black Cat, but to the regional narcotic traffickers, and to whom he determined facilitates this madness, the state Governor. The Governor will be present at the speech.

The Cardinal plays a dangerous game. The Cardinal plans to have Sanchez, the Black Cat accompany him on the stage. This overt display of Sanchez choreographed by the Cardinal could cast Sanchez a mastermind by the traffickers or as an Informant, a Source. Either way, Sanchez does not appreciate the attention. Inflaming the situation, the Cardinal intends to call out the Governor's role in narcotics.

It is morning, and Cardinal Torres meets with small groups of families at the Culiacan, Presidente Hotel's lobby. Small children wearing their best clothes are ecstatic and grab at his clothes rising on their toes in attempts to be heard by the Cardinal. He pats the children on their heads and makes the sign of the cross blessing the older children. The patient Cardinal makes every effort to acknowledge everyone before he enters the hotel's breakfast room. The families depart the lobby — the Black Cat is scheduled to meet the Cardinal at 8:00 a.m. for breakfast at the Presidente Hotel. At 7:30 a.m., the Black Cat is driven by his chauffeur from his hotel to the

Presidente Hotel. While en route, the Black Cat views a blue Volkswagen van full of nuns singing and clapping their hands. They are traveling to the Cardinal's speech, hoping to acquire front row seats. The Black Cat is torn to his core and turns away from the joyous nuns.

Immediately without notice at 7:30 a.m., Yuri's US gang members attack Cardinal Torres in the breakfast area of the Presidente hotel. The Black Cat has yet to arrive at the meeting with the Cardinal. The attackers are not proficient with their weapons. After they shoot a volley towards the Cardinal, they look over their weapons front sights to locate the direction of the shots. They reengage the bullets in affect walk from one side of the large table to the other where the Cardinal sits smashing plates and glasses in a wavy line towards the Cardinal. Waiters and waitresses run from the breakfast room. Some fall to the ground. Eventually, the novice shooters train the weapons onto the Cardinal as he leans towards the floor. Bullets hit the Cardinal's right side and climb to his head just before it disappears under the table. He falls to the ground.

The Cardinal is mortally wounded. Dying, he says, "Save the children."

Plates, glasses, and the table cloth cover him. His limited number of guards reach for their weapons. The gangsters spray a barrage of bullets at the Cardinal's guards. The guards recover from the initial onslaught and return fire. The attackers are now running from the scene, turn towards the guards, and shoot without accuracy. Most of the rounds hit the interior walls of the breakfast room. Some of the attackers' rounds superficially strike two of the Cardinal's guards. The killers leave the breakfast room as fast as they assaulted.

The attackers carrying their weapons run to the hotel lobby. As the attackers exit the hotel, citizens awaiting the Cardinal's departure line the hotel's sidewalk in hopes of seeing the Cardinal up close. The citizens hear the noise emanating from the hotel. The citizens recognize these running gangsters attacked the esteemed Cardinal. The stricken citizens spent days preparing messages for the Cardinal to view. They acquired wooden stakes and affixed posters with notes: We love you. Pray for us. We are praying for you. The adults hold the stakes in their hands. Young children, dressed in colorful clothes, carry flower bouquets and stand in front of the adults waving the posters.

The friendly crowd grieves and then transforms into the incensed. The large groups were expecting such happiness, and instead, they are shocked again with the incessant violence that plagues their area. The attackers see the now maddening crowd and fear for their lives. The citizens throw what is in their possession. Water bottles, posters, stakes all cascade towards the attackers, surprising them as they sprint towards the three getaway cars. A few of the older men in the crowd approach the attackers and grab at the AK 47s weapons. The attackers are so scared of the immense crowd they do not discharge the weapons but reacquire control of the guns and jump into the escape cars.

The driver of one of the getaway vehicles hits one of the older men. The man rolls over the hood and bounces on the ground near the passenger side of the car breaking his right elbow and ankle. The adults push the children still holding the flowers to the rear of the crowd as others swarm the assassins' cars. A wooden stake penetrates one of the assassins' car windows. An assassin reacts and fires through the broken window into the crowd shooting two short indigenous abuelas/grandmothers who crash to the ground in pain. The grandmothers' clean white dresses adorned with handmade embroidered little red cardinals perched on branches are blood soaked. Angelic strangers now on their knees tend to the injured women. The site of wounded women lying abandoned in the street would be unfathomable — the mob retreats from the shooter's car.

Two of the assassins' cars escape to the exit of the hotel parking lot before the encircling crowd closes the gap.

The crowd then reengages with the trail car. Trash litters the street. The citizens gather it and throw it towards the last car. The car advances in its escape when within the crowd, multiple blasts from the Cardinal's guard detail hit the vehicle — exploding the cars' windows shredding the occupants. The car crashes into a streetlamp. The pole flexes downward from the impact. The lens appears to lean into the vehicle obtaining a quick assessment of the shooters. The streetlamp then retracts, but now with a 35-degree permanent bend. The streetlamp bulb flashes on and off as if delivering a Morse Code message. The message received by the 'Old Man of the Building' who begrudgingly assimilates the data and adds it to the daily misery index. Following the issuance of the Morse Code message, the streetlamp goes dark.

The 'Old Man of the Building' has previously received initial reports delivered via electricity regarding this growing terror group when the Black Cat spread his terror from Matamoros to Nuevo Laredo. In Nuevo Laredo, the streetlamps view and reported the assassination of the Mex Fed Colonel providing the 'Old Man' intelligence on the Black Cat's assassins.

The faithful crowd swarms the wrecked car and tries to open the doors to continue the assault, but the engine catches fire. The mob moves from the vehicle as the flames approach fuel leaking from the gas tank. The car explodes burning the already dead occupants. The remaining cars race from the area taking separate routes from Culiacan.

It would have been easier to kill the Cardinal en route to Culiacan, but suspicion could have led to the Black Cat for only a few at the Mexico City Diocese were privy to the Cardinal's itinerary including his protection capabilities. The Black Cat was one of the few with knowledge of the trip outside the Mexico City Diocese. Yuri decided to have the Cardinal's whereabouts known to the Culiacan public. The Cardinal would not be allowed to make the speech.

One flaw in the plan known to the Black Cat is the eventual capture of one assassin by the Mex Feds. If captured, at least one of the US shooters will inform on the rest. Mexican-American shooters cannot fathom Mexican Police interrogations or threats of Mexican imprisonment. Their imaginations cannot imagine cultural juxtapositions.

Following the Cardinal's assassination and the exit of the assassins, the Black Cat arrives in the vicinity of the Presidente hotel. He sees smoke at the main entrance to the parking lot. A vehicle is on fire. The Black Cat's chauffeur barely reaches the sally port of the hotel.

People incoherently walk on the parking lot and sidewalks. Citizens cry. Some stand speechless. The children with beautiful bouquets are dazed not able to comprehend the commotion. In an attempt to reach the Cardinal, some of the adults try to breach the hotel. The Cardinal's bloodied guard detail and accompanying Culiacan police force the people back. The same Culiacan police who do not fire one shot in the attack.

The Black Cat is genuinely shocked. Yuri never briefed him as to the exact details of the assassination. The Black Cat makes it to the Cardinal's body lying on the floor, leans over the body and extracts the Cardinal's bloodstained speech from his shirt. He directs the guards and hotel staff to maintain security at the hotel until the body can be safely moved. He instructs the hotel manager to address the citizens of the death of the Cardinal and asks that the manager politely disperse the crowd by stating that additional updates will follow.

Ultimately, in collusion with local officials, the Black Cat organizes the Cardinal's funeral and burial. Large numbers of Catholics participate in the funeral. Children present at his killing approach the Cardinal's casket and place the same flowers they carried at the hotel onto its exterior.

Following the burial, the Black Cat returns to his post in Matamoros. Jose is also a priest and is under the Black Cat's command. The Black Cat observes signs of Jose's mental deterioration. To get him away for a while, he allows Jose to attend a brief study abroad. Jose used intermediates to layer himself from direct contact with the US assassins, active gang members. To the Black Cat, this provides some comfort.

As the weeks drag on, the image of the female assassin invades the Black Cat's dreams. They are growing bolder more life-like as the nights' pass. He fears the need to sleep.

Eventually, an older Cardinal, Juan Carlos Ramirez-Vazquez fills Cardinal Torres' position. As a result of the Cardinal's assassination, the Mex Feds split their full deployment at the northern border near Nuevo Laredo to assist in the Cardinal assassination in southwestern Mexico. Questions abound from several reporters in the local newspapers. Was the Cardinal killed because of his stand against narcotics? Who did it? Why?

During weeks of inactivity, Yuri does not surface. Flaco calls the Black Cat occasionally advising of one rescheduled shipment after another. Don Pedro is diverting loads to other transshipment points avoiding the Black Cat's Nuevo Laredo access point. That's okay with him. His nerves are frayed. By focusing all of his efforts towards his diocese, the Black Cat buries his dark thoughts.

The Black Cat struggles each time he conducts the daily mass; this is his most dangerous hour. Reading scripture, he has visions of his victims as they congregate at the entrance of the church and race to the pulpit. Occasionally, the congregation observes the Black Cat contort in nonhuman ways to divert the invisible threats. The parishioners wonder if he has a disease, maybe Parkinson's.

The Black Cat makes every effort to be as public as possible. He is hoping to instill in his flock that all is well. Staying busy at work distracts him from the daily accounts of the sensational killings. The Black Cat exercised significant roles in the Colonel and Cardinal's murders. As of yet, the police do not suspect his involvement.

The Cardinal's matter is tenuous. The Black Cat provided the Cardinal's itinerary to Yuri, and he instructed Jose to obtain the weapons and the assassins. The Mex Feds captured some of the US gangsters in northern Mexico. As expected, they turned against each other. The suspects implicated others in the US.

All in all, Jose did an adequate job in insulation. The Black Cat and Jose attended Jesuit schools. The Black Cat even spent a few years studying abroad. Jose conducted charity work in Africa. Following the seminary, they requested assignments to Mexico's northern border.

The church subsidence is minimal, and they board with influential Mexican business people to save money. It seems that in time, they chose to board with one or another narcotic trafficker, significant contributors to the church. Eventually, the Black Cat, with his formal training combined with other unidentified assistance conquers his little part of the criminal world. He is called the Black Cat because of his cunning as well as his affinity to wear all black, the Jesuit wardrobe. His black garb is worn only on diocese property leased from the Mexican government or on special occasions. The Mexican government considers the Catholic faith a threat to its teetering government.

There still is no reason as to why Yuri with the help of Don Pedro killed the Cardinal. Although, the Black Cat concludes the killing is economic in nature.

Chapter Ten

"So, they decided to leave you in Nuevo Laredo?" questions Seamus.

"Si, mi amigo. After we talked, I asked questions about the bullets; they said there were no casings discovered. A bullet found in one of the burnt bodies, maybe the male's calf matches a Colonel's soldier's weapon. Those two burned suspects are involved with the crime, but there is no way to identify them. No foundation exists to initiate a search from available dental records. If nobody wanted to investigate further, the case could be 'administratively closed.' You know, you almost deserve a medal," laughs Maria, the Mex Fed.

"I should shoot myself. Your boss contacted my boss at work," Seamus moans, "and tells him how you loved me and behold; I'm staying for a while."

"I'm sorry, my friend. Should I 'hold up' the official correspondence to your boss?"

"No, let it go through. It will remind me to keep my mouth shut. I appreciate your offer. I'm starting to enjoy the change in the environment. Regardless, my old supervisor was driving me crazy. I'm sure I was driving him just as crazy."

"They won't keep you much longer, the elections are over, and the US Senator will be off your back."

"You're right, well while I'm here why don't we go to the site where they found the burnt-out car? I'm sure there is more to be discovered." Maria does not answer the question; instead, she points to the restroom and walks towards it.

Seamus and Maria realize they have come to another impasse, the point at which one genuinely weighs the ramifications of their actions. Should they enter into an area where they recognize if they left good enough alone, nothing will happen? In every investigators' mind, there is always the want to find the truth, but more importantly, to continue the hunt, regardless of the ramifications.

Seamus O'Malley's unsanctioned actions will violate Mexico's sovereignty. Would he allow Maria to operate in the United States with his concurrence informally? He does not have an answer to that one.

Maria carries the most risk. Maybe Seamus is 'just being played.' The overt Colonel's killing leads the ordinary Mexican citizen to conclude the Mex Fed Colonel is crooked. The Colonel's assassination is no random incident. Is the cowboy case related? The burnt assassin's car is relatively close to the ranch hands who smuggled the dope across the Rio Grande. It would be easy to direct the ranch hands to dispose of the car. However, the car is left. The Cowboys are not contacted to move it or did they move it to its present location. There has to be a relationship.

Why should anybody in law enforcement care? A known crooked cop/soldier murdered, who cares? It is barely misdemeanor murder. Good riddance. Should he say "the hell with this."

There is nothing to lose. What can the supervisors do to him, send him to the border? He's already here. Is there a border? To Seamus and his colleagues, the US/Mexico border is only ceremonial in nature. Seamus read a recent article indicating that a US border city requires its government correspondence written in Spanish. The town suffers from an identity crisis. Corruption tends to fray at countries' borders.

If he wanted to get away from the border right now, Seamus could take advantage of this town's edict. He'll author an administrative subpoena, of course in English. Serve it to the local authorities requesting a subscriber on water and sewage service related to a subject in one of his new seizures. Then, wait for the town's lack of response.

Seamus presents the failure to comply with his new 'valley' supervisor, Bill. Seamus explains that the town official refuses to act as the official request is in English.

Bill dutifully forwards the 'O'Malley' problem up the chain of command. This supervisor questions Bill, and asks what the real story is? Bill returns from his meeting with his supervisor and tries to persuade Seamus that the subscriber information is not integral to his case, and further directs that Seamus is not to pursue the matter for fear of opening pandora's box. If Seamus does not cooperate, they might quietly transfer him back home. Seamus admits that he has become quite agitative, lately. If transferred back to the home office, Seamus needs to go into stealth mode because the 'home office' brass will retaliate.

Seamus breaks from his daydream when Maria walks from a pay phone in the narrow hallway leading to the restrooms.

"When do we go?" the Mex Fed repeats.

"What?"

"Let's go tonight."

"Okay," Seamus answers with sudden intensity.

Seamus with a cooler of beer accompanies Maria who drives south from Nuevo Laredo. He justifies this as a weekend vacation.

Seamus perceives strain on Maria's face. While she drives, her eyes squint, and she moves her face closer to the windshield. To break the stress, O'Malley starts talking.

"Hey, Maria."

"Yes, my friend."

"How many Ex-US Presidents have been forced to live abroad following the conclusion of their terms in office?"

"Uh, I don't know of any."

"There are none, my friend."

"Okay, so am I supposed to guess, stand up or sit down? What's your point?"

"None. Let's see. The Shah of Iran, oh, wait, he was not a President. The Shah of Iran was forced to leave his country. Dictator Marcos and his wife, from the Philippines, were forced to live in a shoe shop in Hawaii.

Uh, Pinochet, no they want him back in Chile from Great Britain." Seamus opens a car of beer and continues. "Wait, he did extradite to Chile. Great Britain is trying to be the world's self-appointed moral compass out of remorse of its colonization legacies."

"Again, what's your point? Isn't the Shah and the Marcos' friends of the US?" Maria smiles at Seamus.

"Good point and Pinochet previously assisted Great Britain. That's why Great Britain tried to help him. Tried to keep him from being sent back to Chile."

"Yes, yes, and the Shah and the Marcos' go to the US."

"I think you are right. The Shah went to the US for medical treatment and then asylum in Egypt when militants seized our embassy." Seamus offers a beer to Maria, but she declines. "Have you ever been told to quit thinking at work?" She gives him a confused look. "Never mind, don't answer that. Let's see, Idi Amin, the galloping cannibal gourmet. Did he leave Uganda and flee to France or Saudi Arabia? Oh, Saudi Arabia, but he died of too much meat, you know. High cholesterol." O'Malley laughs at his joke. "Where do the former Presidents of Mexico retire and for that matter their closest ministers? I don't see Mexico having the capacity to protect these guys."

"I do not know?" Maria interrupts, "I do not know where the former Mexican presidents live? They might still have houses in Mexico."

"What do you think happens to former Mexican Ministers. I am sure they made many enemies. If you cannot protect the ex-presidents, how would the former Mexican government ministers fare? I read in the paper where a Minister of Interior, I think his name was Gomez, before retirement officially traveled to Italy. I think Rome. Why there? Wouldn't he need prior approval from your congress to travel abroad or something like that? Moreover, why was this even in the US papers? About his travel? I forgot why he traveled there."

"Good Lord, a thousand questions, what is with you? To answer all your questions, I do not keep up with Mexican politics as much as you do."

"Who is the Minister of Interior, Gomez? What does he do?"

Maria squeezes the steering wheel, "I don't know."

"Is he Catholic?"

"Possibly, I don't know," Maria says, "again, I'm not political. Nor, am I that curious."

"You know there is always a reason for somebody, institution, or country to act as it does. They don't just do it out of the kindness of their hearts. Sometimes, it is best to get completely away from something if you know things are going to go bad. You know, out of sight, out of mind. Maybe, the Minister of Interior soon to be Former Minister of Interior knows things are going to get worse for him in Mexico when his boss leaves office, and he's creating his exit strategy or retirement. Maybe, in Italy? Are the Minister of Interiors, or Foreign Ministers appointed?"

"Wait a minute, let's go back. Why do you insinuate that the Mexican President is a dictator? You put him in the same category as the other dictators, Idi Amin. Are you crazy? The Mexican people elected him. Mexico is a democracy."

"Is it? You always hear about voting irregularities and corruption. I think the Minister of Interior is looking for a haven to insulate himself from something. You see, he was instrumental in free trade with the US and Canada. I read more 'ministerial' than the Mexican Foreign Minister. Many people owe him favors for this agreement. If he was involved in drugs, and the US knew it, he wouldn't be able to live in the US, so why not Italy? There are plenty of money laundering havens in that area. Do you think he is crooked?"

"How, am I supposed to know that?"

"Maybe, he feels closer to God? Vatican City is close to Rome. Maybe, the Minister was seeking forgiveness, making amends, got kicked out of the church for past wrongdoings trying to get back?" Seamus looks at Maria who is ignoring him. "All right, I see I am boring you. Okay, I will stay quiet for a while. I can see it is a sensitive topic with you."

"You may talk like that, but it is not healthy for me to say such things."

"And you are still a democracy?" She scowls at Seamus.

"Okay, okay, I will change the topic to soccer. How about that?"

"Much better."

Within a few hours, they find the location. The burnt car remains at the scene. Seamus and Maria uncover additional bullet fragments in remnants of the front seat, evidence to be analyzed by Maria. These bullets can be a real find, Maria states. Boot prints most likely from the cops trample the area. The only sign of a crime scene perimeter is the police officers discarded coca cola and water bottles that encircle the scene. The boot prints have covered any possibility in the recovery of spent shells.

Maria says she will analyze the bullet fragments with the aid of a few trusted comrades. The bullets discovered in the front seat metal frame were challenging to find. Why did they not melt, Teflon coated? Maybe, some other kind of metal. A Colonel targeted for assassination by narco-traffickers, it is highly possible ranking officials above and below the Colonel's rank are involved in narcotics. Therefore, the first responders knew it was not necessary to conduct a quality investigation. Observe and report, mission complete.

As Seamus approaches the front passenger seat, he unexpectedly gets a little nervous. A presence exists he feels or does he hear it speaking in an unfamiliar language. Somehow, he understands the words. Something tells him

to look further. A female voice utters, "Closer. Closer.
There, take this. Do not stop in your quest. You will
encounter undefinable difficulties. Do not weaken."
Seamus acts as instructed. Maria does not hear the voice.
Why not? Man, he must have drunk a lot getting here.
Was it the wind? It had to be. The area is haunting, dark
— time to go.

"The gun that killed those people will never be found,"
Seamus remarks.

"I know that, but we have the bullet evidence. I would
go crazy knowing that the evidence is deteriorating or more
like buried by sand in the desert." Maria says.

"All right, let's go. Let's stop at the Broken Nickel on
the way back. I'm already out of beer. Do you think it is
still open?"

Maria looks curiously at the anxious Seamus and
questions, "Broken Nickel, it's called the Wooden Nickel.
I'd say the bar is still open. Nothing closes in that town."

On the return trip, Seamus reviews the mysterious
presence; it does not speak English similar to the fake
nonreality ghost shows. He smirks at the nonsense on
television. The voice spoke in an old language, a language
Seamus assumes is centuries old. How did he recognize
the language and for that matter understand its roots are
poetry? This presence is real, serious, a threat to its
enemies. Why did he say "Broken Nickel?" He passes out
in the car.

Before entering the bar, Seamus purchases some chiclets
and a newspaper from a young boy at the entrance. He
slowly scans the paper and fingers an almost intact bullet
and a spent casing in his pocket. Seamus has a buddy who
will look at them. Without Maria's knowledge, he found
the housing on the ground in front of the car and the bullet
near the rear seat. The voice told him where to look. Who
is she? She is a powerful friend. She has to be.

Chapter Eleven

General Comstock and Yuri make use of encrypted cellular telephones.

"It's a small world, Yuri," Comstock relays on the phone, "your buddy is close to you."

"Who?"

"The American. We've identified him as Seamus O'Malley."

"No, unbelievable."

"Yes."

"How do you know?"

"Our Mexican Intelligence General based in the big city called weeks ago. The general said that he received information that a Mex Fed formed a friendship with a US investigator. So, I told the General to identify the agent. The General called back and said it is Seamus O'Malley. I asked the General to forward investigative details to his contact in comms with the female Mex Fed. The female Mex Fed was directed to forward the same to O'Malley. They are working on the Colonel Corrion killing. There has also been some talk about a seizure related to the Cat. It is a bit of luck on our behalf."

"He stumbles and fumbles into my US money secreted at the Miami warehouse. Money to be sent to our Russian irregulars operating in Chechnya."

"Hey, no one got arrested. If your watchman did not give O'Malley a consent to search the warehouse, O'Malley would have left penniless. I admit I do not understand why O'Malley was even at the location. He was not able to identify others in your organization. More importantly, as best as we understand he does not know, the origin of the monies, who controlled the money at the warehouse, and its destination. No problem."

"No problem on that Miami mess you're right, but Inspector Clouseau is now looking into the Cat, and he could uncover what we are doing. What do you propose?"

"I think that we might want to wait it out."

"How long?"

"We will know his every move. Right now, they spend their time in the desert and at the Wooden Nickel. Like I said before, we have no idea how he infiltrated the Miami organization. The next thing we knew is O'Malley, and his buddies dismantled the cell. We do not know how much evidence O'Malley obtained from the seizure and the cowboy arrested in the US. O'Malley did confide to the Mex Fed that as a result of the seizure, he learned the names Jose and the Black Cat. We, like I said before, via the Mexican General forwarded some tidbits about the Colonel's killing. With the hope that O'Malley will reciprocate in kind, with emphasis on the cowboy's statements or if he has linked the Colonel and Cardinal assassinations to the Cat. More importantly, where is he going with his investigations. It does not appear yet that O'Malley has connected the alias the Black Cat; specifically, to Sanchez. However, something tells me he may have. O'Malley did tell the Mex Fed that he would not drop the Black Cat case. Without the Mex Fed's knowledge, I guarantee O'Malley found something of interest in the desert."

"You say the word."

"I know. No, maybe," Comstock watches and listens to children playing at a park. "I'm leaving red going to yellow thinking about the green light. Uh, let me think. We have a handle on where O'Malley might be going. I am talking out loud. Can we control him?"

"It will be risky, what else?"

"The meeting is going to take place over here. All the parties will be gathering."

"Serious money?"

"Yes, sir. Contact the 'displaced one' (Mexican Minister of Interior) and have him call the recently assigned Mexico City Cardinal (Juan Carlos Ramirez Vazquez). Remember, the Minister was instrumental in setting up the introductions that started this program. We will take advantage of Cardinal Vazquez's' age. Four Catholic priests have been chosen throughout the world to participate in the talks, and Cardinal Vazquez will select the fifth. A written dispatch from our Spanish friend Emilio in Vatican City will request that the Mexico City Diocese approve Sanchez, the Black Cat as the fifth participant in the talks speaking on behalf of Cardinal Vazquez. Cardinal Ramirez Vazquez is not aware of Sanchez's' history. If the Cardinal's aides attempt to persuade Cardinal Vazquez of Sanchez's purported drug connections an additional call from the 'displaced one' will force Cardinal Vazquez to relent to Sanchez's selection. Our friend in the Vatican, Emilio is also oblivious to Sanchez's criminal history and is cooperating solely for the benefit of Vatican City."

"And the Black Cat will never know of our involvement in the selection process, that is correct?"

"Yes, that is correct."

During this same period, the Mexican American couple who followed the portly women aka red face after her meeting with Maria the Med Fed in Nuevo Laredo, decide they will be more proactive with this particular case.

The Mexican American couple is US Intelligence officers with operations in Mexico.

The US Intelligence officers previously received a dispatch indicating that Eastern Europeans were intent on capitalizing on the continued unrest in Mexico. The unidentified Eastern Europeans were to partake in some political or spectacular assassination. The assassination was to occur shortly at an unknown specific location, but possibly on the western coast of Mexico. Intelligence is not always perfect and complete.

Following the murder of the Cardinal in Culiacan, it is incumbent that the US Intelligence officers identify and stop the Eastern European subjects. This spectacular assassination is the event referenced in the dispatch. They devote more time to monitor the portly women; others in their group are exploiting additional resources to understand the workings of the Eastern Europeans. In miles, Nuevo Laredo, Mexico is far from Culiacan, but the distance is irrelevant when one investigates Transnational Crime.

The female US Intelligence officer, an avid runner, is tall and slim. The male officer, somewhat similar in height, participates in P90X fitness. Both are in excellent health and approximately 30 years of age.

They have identified one friendly, DEA Agent Seamus O'Malley, who unknowingly operates on the periphery of the Eastern Europeans. They decide to find out what he is doing. The female contacts Seamus' US Border Patrol partner, Pete at his office and notifies him that they are agents assigned to the US Inspector General Office (IG). They will masquerade as IG agents.

The IG investigates transgressions by US government employees. State and local police have a similar investigative agency referred to as Internal Affairs. Usually, Inspector General office personnel out of courtesy contact a supervisor not involved in the purported investigation and notify the same that they will be in the area. By doing this, IG personnel are free to conduct ambush interviews of agents, who may have worked all night — coercing them into mandatory recorded statements regarding an event that could have happened months ago.

The US Intelligence officers, not accustomed to having procedures lead their investigations, allow common sense to be their barometer, not process. Processes are for dumb asses. Because they are not real IG personnel, no prior contact occurs with Pete's chain of command.

The female officer advises Pete; that he is not to reveal to anyone in the office that the IG contacted him, and she orders him to meet them in a few hours for a typical IG ambush interview. Because of the short notice, the female agent convinces Pete of their identities.

The female officer does not reveal they are purportedly investigating corruption amongst US agents operating on the US southern border, but Pete assumes that will be the issue. They tell Pete that they will approach him at the local coffee shop and summarily display their identities to him. After the telephone conversation with Pete while in their office, they acquire their IG I.Ds.

Seeing his identity, the male officer complains that it is a conspiracy that his first name is always stupid; this time he's Todd. Last time, his name was Chad. He crumbles his lips as if to make a lousy kiss and whines, "Todd" repeating it even slower, "Toooooodd…I am going to need to change into docker pants, a button-down shirt, where are my leather shoes, off with my socks." He continues, "You know what agency wears these kinds of clothes, yes, those 'press conference' people." Shaping his right hand into the figure of a pistol, thumb up index finger pointing at the female. He winks at the woman. She smiles, shaking her head throughout his theatrics. When Todd clips his badge and his gun in a holster on the outside of his belt for all to see, she waves at him to stop.

"Cut that out. Put all that away." She opens her credentials and smiles at Todd. What luck. Provided the name Socorro, she intertwines her fingers and places her hands gently against her right cheek as if posing for a photographer. Socorro means fox in Spanish. "My name is Socorro." She smirks. Todd shakes his head, looks down, and throws up his hands. They walk from the northern Mexico office and drive north towards the US border.

The US intelligence officers, Todd and Socorro, observe Pete seated at the coffee house. He is extremely nervous. As they approach, he stands and rubs his palm. Pete guesses it is them. He wants to get this interview over. They identify themselves and remind Pete not to disclose the contents of the meeting. They provide various employee names familiar to Pete. They ask what he thinks of the individuals, and Pete provides what little he knows. The given names are diversionary to give the impression they are looking at numerous agents to distract Pete's attention on O'Malley. The pair then asks about Seamus O'Malley. The questions are direct. Pete squirms in his chair. He crumbles a paper napkin in his left hand as they continue to drill down on Seamus' whereabouts, his working hours, telephone number, and what does he do when in Mexico.

Pete gives them O'Malley's cell phone number and says, "I knew there was something wrong about that guy. He is out here operating in Mexico without anybody's knowledge, except me. He is putting me in a difficult situation. I am glad I can now talk to someone about this. You guys are great. O'Malley was instructed to communicate with the Mex Fed but not to go operational in Mexico!" His voice cracks. He begins talking like a child, "…he regularly meets with Maria the Mex Fed at the Wooden Nickel in Mexico." Pete almost whimpers. Bubbles of spit are visible on his lips. "I can't believe this is happening during performance evaluations," Pete lowers his head onto to his right palm.

Following Pete's incendiary statements, Socorro's disbelieving gaze directed at Pete moves to Todd with his arms folded. She bites down on the outside of her upper lip, making her nostrils flare. She ends her nonverbal tirade by rolling her eyes up visible only to Todd and says to herself, "What a dick, this Pete is."

Seeing Socorro's reaction, to keep her from backhanding Pete, Todd takes over the questioning. He asks if Pete knew the Mex Fed's full name and if he by chance has her telephone number. They already acquired some of this information, but they are looking for corroboration. Pete fumbles in his man purse containing his pistol and raises a piece of crumbled paper listing Maria's number. Paper stained with gun oil. Socorro grabs the paper. Maria's telephone number is safer with her than with this guy. If confronted by his supervisor about the Mex Fed's number, Pete would probably eat the paper, something he learned from a bad movie.

Pete voluntarily shares that Seamus provided details of a cowboy smuggling case to the Mex Fed. "Seamus is a nut. He was sent to the border by his home office as punishment. Seamus never listens to authority; he always calls managers talking heads."

"Well, are you saying Agent O'Malley is cooperating with the enemy. I mean giving them protected information," asks Todd.

"Oh, I don't think so," responds Pete.

"Because you are required to report without delay illegal actions or procedures violations when observed."

"Yea, well."

Todd points his index finger at Pete. "Yea, well how long has this been happening, you have sat on this information how long why did you not report it until now?"

Pete repositions his body in the chair and mumbles, "O'Malley, I mean Agent O'Malley is following up on a theory that some guy named Jose and the Black Cat associated with the cowboy smuggling case might link to the Colonels' assassination how no one knows maybe because the two incidents happened close to each other and were somewhat spectacular. Not that uncommon around here. I told him not to go to Mexico."

Socorro regains her composure and says in a slow deliberated voice, "But, you did not advise your supervisor promptly." She looks directly at Pete, letting him absorb his failure to report and then asks, "Where is Seamus now?"

"I was preparing to update my supervisor. I was. I think he was going to check out the Colonels' assassins' vehicle found in the desert. Also, he was with that girl! He's out of control what could I do? I did not see him at work this morning. Probably screwing off." Pete, the cop ninja, falls on his procedure manual sword to save himself. Socorro was not that surprised at Pete's statements. She's experienced it before.

However, in a rude remark in front of Pete, Socorro speaks to Todd, "Let's get out of here." Leaving Pete seated in the chair, unaware of what will transpire in the future. She is more than aware she should have thanked Pete and verbally massaged him. Explaining to Pete that this would be the final interview, and everything should be resolved in a few weeks. That way, Pete would not feel compelled to call a 'binky' anyone for support. Her remark was worth risking the investigation. Plus, she feels better after saying it. She says to herself, "Fuck hem. Let him sweat a while."

While walking to their car, she leans towards Todd, "Seamus is working, and he is looked at by his partner as a malcontent, rogue, a maniac."

"From the sounds of it his office too, well, we are going to have to do our best to give him coverage, but it's not like we have that much manpower ourselves."

She would not let it drop. "Seamus is most likely trying to develop his case, and the only way forward is to develop Sources and maximize the data received from the same. My dad used to tell me, 'Hell, I don't care what you do. Just do something even if it's wrong.' At least, he is doing something."

Todd is somewhat put back at Socorro's remarks as she rarely confides in him about her past. He thinks she is enjoying tracking O'Malley's nonconformist ways. "I know. I know. We will step this up. 'Ole red face' or as you call her 'the portly woman's' phone is now providing good stuff about an Eastern European. This new communication could be significant."

Todd recognizes that Socorro hears him, but she enters the vehicle without acknowledgment.

Chapter Twelve

The former Mexican Minister of Interior Gomez prepares to call Monsignor Romero assigned to the Mexico City Diocese whose duties include direct correspondence with Vatican City.

"A call for Monsignor Romero."

"Yes, who is it?"

"The former Mexican Minister of Interior."

"What does he want?"

"You don't ask him what he wants, at least I would not."

"Yes, yes, of course."

"Hola, Father. Como Esta, mi amigo?"

"Bueno, Minister. What, may I do for you?"

"I have a friend, in fact, a Bishop by the name of Federico Sanchez."

"Yes, yes."

"Well, I would like to suggest his selection for the final position in the Moscow negotiations. As I understand it, the negotiations will attempt to settle the ownership of Russian Orthodox possessions."

"Quite right. It just so happens that I received a Vatican dispatch," Monsignor Romero says, "indicating Father Federico Sanchez's consideration for the same assignment. The dispatch authored by Monsignor Emilio, assigned to Vatican City. Father Emilio's coordinating our church's side of the negotiations. In 'Vatican' speak, 'consideration' means Sanchez is strongly recommended. It is a nicety, making our Cardinal aware and summarily allowing our cherished Cardinal's blessing."

"I understand. The Catholic Church has immense hierarchy and certain workings must be followed."

"Very good; you have had a good education. You never cease to amaze me," replies the Monsignor. "You know this Bishop Sanchez; he is very good with the money, fundraisers, bazaars, and donations, this man."

"I was not aware of that."

"Yes, well," Monsignor Romero reads from the dispatch, "an odd thing…it appears the Vatican recommended Bishop Sanchez and our beloved Cardinal because the Greek/Eastern Orthodox Church, the second party in the impending negotiations, balked if Vatican City-based personnel are participants in the impending negotiations. Interesting. Why, I have no idea? Maybe, they believe we are more organized, centralized, you know." The Monsignor reflects and continues to read the paper. Then looks up and says, "The Eastern Orthodox lack organization, no real Pope, no order." While speaking, Monsignor Romero uses a toothpick to pick between his teeth.

"Are the Eastern Orthodox and the Greek Orthodox separate religions or the same? Are the names, Eastern and Greek interchangeable? That is what confuses me," the Minister asks.

"The Eastern Orthodox Church is the second largest Catholic group behind the Roman Catholic Church, and as I understand it technically the Greek Orthodox Church refers to churches in Greece. However today, when referring to the Eastern and Greek Churches you equate it solely to the Eastern Orthodox Church." Monsignor continues to read the Vatican dispatch. "Well, four Roman Catholic church delegates have already been chosen from North America,

South America, Eastern Europe, and Asia. Let's see, the representatives are two senior priests and two Bishops." As the Monsignor speaks, he makes smacking and sucking noises dislodging a piece of meat from his teeth. He looks at it and throws it in the trash. The Minister interrupts.

"Yes, I am familiar with that…. Each geographic region was to select one Roman Catholic priest to participate at the negotiating table against the Eastern Orthodox Church. Bishop Sanchez speaks a variety of languages, one is Russian, a major asset. Keeping the Russians happy is very important in achieving our mutual goals for the Catholic Church."

"Why Bishop Sanchez, Minister?"

"Well, the few relatives he has have been long friends of mine."

"Oh, well he does seem to fit the puzzle," The Monsignor leans back in his thick cushioned leather chair. He gazes at the lush foliage outside his office window and pours a glass of water from a clear vase. "You are a longtime friend of the church and very much respected. Your request will be accepted as soon as I brief Cardinal Vazquez. You know Cardinal Vazquez has a lot on his plate. I will ensure the Cardinal concurs. Following acceptance, I will notify Bishop Federico Sanchez of the appointment, immediately."

"I ask that you do not tell Bishop Sanchez the contents of this call," Minister Gomez's eyes widen. His forehead wrinkles. His mouth recedes. He hopes Romero will concur. "You know, I want Bishop Sanchez to feel his merits resulted in his selection." A short pause in the conversation ensues, Minister Gomez does not want Sanchez nor Romero to finger him if this thing 'goes south.'

"Yes, yes, of course."

Gomez finally exhales, "It was good speaking with you again. Adios, mi amigo. Good Luck, Father."

Good Luck. Why did Gomez say that?

Chapter Thirteen

The Black Cat maintains his moratorium of smuggling and killing people. In his perverse way, he recognizes that if his parishioners uncover his illicit activities, they will forgive him of his treachery as long as his celibacy remains intact. His flock loves him.

The Black Cat pays a majority of his debt to Don Pedro from earnings associated with one last sizeable successful load before the attack on the Cardinal. He thinks maybe the dead Mex Fed Colonel was the leak, the Source.

On a few occasions, the Black Cat met with Yuri in Mexico City. It appears to the Black Cat that Yuri was assessing his ability to continue his stamina, his loyalty. Additionally, the Black Cat forwards to Don Pedro partial proceeds given by Yuri for his assistance in the Cardinal attack. Initially, the Black Cat believes Yuri shortchanged him for his role in the Cardinal's assassination. He comes to his senses as Yuri's tasking related to the Cardinal's assassination is why the Black Cat was assigned to Matamoros to conduct operations such as these when directed agreed to many years ago.

If invited, the Black Cat will address his remaining debt at the annual year-end financial accounts meeting in Cali, Colombia before the Christmas season. The yearly meeting encompasses a review of account receivables and liabilities. The traffickers discuss new routes, future delivery contracts agreed on, and decisions made as to who will die in the upcoming calendar year. Don Pedro has not adopted the fiscal calendar, yet.

The Black Cat learned Don Pedro's organization intends to employ a person from the Dubai of Central America, a Panamanian. This Panamanian is expected to develop and implement more sophisticated shell and shelf accounts necessary in the ever-changing money laundering world.

About that year-end meeting, maybe it's best to stay away from Flaco. For some reason, the Black Cat perceives him to be a threat. The Black Cat boils at the thought of how amused Flaco must be following his new relationship with the Russian, Yuri.

The Black Cat knows someone is manipulating him more so than ever. What the hell is going on? Maybe, his past training is needed? He never realized it would reach these levels. As a result of the assassinations, one thing is sure, the Black Cat is becoming more callous, cold, distant, almost amoral and more confident or vain as Yuri told him.

The Black Cat sits in his dusty office attached to the church and looks out of the open window observing people crossing the brick streets while others navigate the broken concrete sidewalks. Brown dust swirls enter through the window mixing with incense protruding from the church. The odors seem to attack each other; the reality of the street appears to win against his lost faith. The Black Cat holds a worn rosary, and temporarily forgets what prayers to say as his fingers move across the beads. The Black Cat talks to himself. He cannot confide with anyone, not even Jose.

"It's time to grow up."

"You have to play it out."

"And believe it, nothing will stand in my way."

Weeks pass without notice. Occasionally, he still reflects on the killings and that damned girl; he experiences anxiety during these 'down times.' He thinks he is managing it. By dwelling on the past, he deflects his attention to his uncertain future.

Jose returns from his study abroad. Jose immediately buries himself in the diocese duties, participating in the daily services, baptisms, and confessions. Plunges himself into his work, thinking it will absolve him for his violent past. Jose is still justifying his actions as the only means out of destitution. Even though he voluntarily took a vow of austerity. Jose does not know how to spell hypocrisy.

One sleepy hot afternoon Jose enters the office with correspondence from Cardinal Vazquez's Mexico City office. The Black Cat reads the document and learns he has been selected to participate in a negotiation team organized by Vatican City-based Monsignor Antonio Maseru and Monsignor Emilio. As not to upset the Eastern Orthodox Church, Maseru's role is ceremonial. Maseru and Emilio will not participate in the direct talks. Maseru's real purpose is the Vatican City designated point of contact (POC) in the upcoming negotiations with administrative duties including communication and logistics. Monsignor Emilio's duties are liaison in nature.

The Mexico City-based Cardinal Vazquez leads the Catholic Church negotiation team. The Mexico team will collaborate with selected Catholic delegates chosen from North America, South America, Eastern Europe, and Asia. These delegates are directed to arrive separately to the 'talks' as coordinated by Monsignor Maseru. The Black Cat and Cardinal Vazquez are responsible for arranging their mode of transportation to the negotiating table. The correspondence stresses that their means of travel create optics of strength and power.

The singularly Catholic/Eastern Orthodox delegations will enter into talks with Russian government officials representing the Russian Orthodox church. A few Russian Orthodox delegates will also participate. The conversations will occur at Peredelkino City southwest of Moscow, Russia future home to the Russian Orthodox Patriarch, and purportedly will determine the ownership of age-old disputed Catholic/Eastern Orthodox lands in Russia with additional emphasis on Russian Orthodox Ukrainian assets. Russia hints of repatriation of some of the Russian Orthodox properties. With the development of Glasnost, Russia appears to be acting more transparent, making it public. The former USSR is cash strapped.

The free market is crushing what remains of Russian state-owned operations. Russia has entertained the possibility of relinquishing these Russian Orthodox disputed lands claimed by both the Catholic and Eastern Orthodox churches in exchange for hard currency. Payments assumed in a yet to be developed form will be transferred by the disparate negotiation teams for the disputed lands. The participants never mention bribery.

The Black Cat learns he is the chief negotiator for Vatican City and the Eastern Orthodox Church is his adversary in acquiring Russian Orthodox Church possessions.

The disputed Russian Orthodox lands include undeveloped tracts, buildings, and churches located throughout present-day Russia, including its possessions and Ukraine, illegally seized during the advent of the communist regime a century ago. The Catholic Church and the Eastern Orthodox Church believe they have legal standing in the negotiations. The Russian Orthodox holdings are immense.

The correspondence specifies that the talks do not include Russian Orthodox Church holdings outside Russia's influence. The Russian Orthodox Church in effect split into two separate churches with the disputed holdings in Russia and the Ukraine from the Russia Orthodox using the same name outside of Russia's influence.

Russian Orthodox parishioners worship within their churches. Russian Orthodox outreach activities are prohibited. The Russian Orthodox Church historically operates very quietly, under the radar of Russian intelligence. Because of these secret activities, it is difficult to determine the actual number of Russian parishioners. If successful in acquiring the tangible assets and the new Russian parishioners complete with tithings, both the Eastern and Catholic churches can add millions of dollars in new annual revenue.

For some time, Vatican personnel have diligently worked on a Russian acquisition plan. Presently, the Catholic Church is riding on a wave of enthusiasm with its recent successes in saving new souls in India, a Hindu majority as well as in Japan, a predominantly Buddhist/Shinto country. The Vatican is succeeding diplomatically and participating in numerous victory marches because of these new souls and associated tithings. The Vatican does not march reminiscent of the Crusaders but is nonviolently acquiring the spoils of economic war.

The Black Cat assumes another Vatican goal could be an attempt to reduce Eastern Orthodox influence in Eastern Europe. The Vatican's power in Eastern Europe is meager compared to the Eastern Orthodoxy's supremacy. The historical struggle between the Eastern Orthodox Church and Catholicism has waged for centuries. If the Vatican acquires critical geographic Russian Orthodox assets, it could create a physical and financial pincer on the Eastern Orthodox Church reducing the Eastern Orthodoxy's ability to expand.

What chance does the Catholic Church get in persuading the Russians to go 'Vatican' not 'Eastern'? Therein lies the mystery. Who stands to prosper and profit? The Black Cat understands his importance to this new mission. More significant events are at play; it is imperative that he complete the task. The Black Cat deals drugs, two thousand dollars a kilogram when bought in Colombia, thirty-five thousand a kilogram in Europe. Maybe, they want him to move drugs from Colombia to Russia. Alternatively, from Mexico. The profits would be immense.

The Black Cat reviews the past activities, Don Pedro, the leader of the Cali Cartel has taken advantage of the situation at hand. You might say beneficial cycles. When the Mex Feds moved additional personnel to the northern Mexico border because of the Colonel's death, Don Pedro's organization smuggled significant amounts of dope through the Eastern quadrant of Mexico and into the southeastern US. Don Pedro's organization has had a historical relationship with the criminal group controlling the Mexican Tamaulipas State encompassing this valuable entryway, including Nuevo Laredo to the northwest. Matamoros is one city in this state.

The Black Cat, assumes that Don Pedro in collusion with Yuri, assassinated the anti-drug Cardinal Torres in Culiacan. Cardinal Torres would never have approved of his posting to the Vatican/Eastern/Russian talks.

A second result of the assassination of the Cardinal was that the Cardinal killing occurred geographically in what historically is controlled by the Medellin, Colombian Narcotic Cartel. Presently, the behavior of the Mexican government is ambiguous in protecting Colombian traffickers from arrest. In response to the high profile killing of Cardinal Torres, the Mex Feds are pursuing narcotic traffickers in the Culiacan area.

The Culiacan residents continue to protest the Cardinal's murder detrimentally impacting the effectiveness of Don Pedro's smuggling competitors, the Medellin Cartel. Mex Feds have deployed in strength to Western Mexico resulting in a thinning of Mex Fed reserves in Tamaulipas State opening a considerable gap in enforcement in northeastern Mexico.

The Medellin Cartel already viewed by the general populace as a very violent group leaves the Mex Feds without options. They had to act against the Medellin Cartel. The citizens are aware the Medellin Cartel overtly operates in Mexico without restraint. The general populace blames the Medellin Cartel for the Cardinal's assassination. So far, the Medellin Cartel is absorbing the Mex Feds assault, and no doubt is soliciting assistance from its people operating within the Mexican Government.

A third result of the assassination and the ensuing battle in the Culiacan area is that it drains financial resources of the Medellin Cartel and Mexican Government. Yuri devised the plan. The Black Cat now knows he is Russian and his government benefits when the country bordering the US remains unstable and quite frankly broken.

The numerous Colombian articles exposing Don Pedro, articles now confirmed created by the Medellin Cartel, forced Don Pedro to go on the offensive. Don Pedro could not escalate the violence in Colombia as his government supporters might relieve him of his command. So, the Cali, Colombia Cartel brings the war to the Medellin Cartel in Culiacan, Mexico. The Cali Cartel is using the Mex Feds as their proxy army. Very Clever. The Colombian citizenry will never associate the escalating Mexican violence with the Cali Cartel. It is too far away.

In an effort to rid both the Cali and Medellin Cartels from Mexico, the Black Cat wonders if the rising rival Mexican organized groups are providing intelligence to the Mex Feds on both Colombian Cartels. Does Don Pedro understand the danger related to these emerging Mexican criminal groups?

Yuri is subordinate to somebody big in Russia and his actions related to the Vatican issue. The Black Cat thought Yuri was just a hired gun. He wonders if Yuri is still alive after the killing of the Cardinal. He bets that Yuri is still living. Yuri could be the 'chance/hope' that the Vatican believes will persuade the Russian government to sell the lands to the Vatican instead of the Eastern Church. However, Yuri is middle management, a high-ranking soldier. More likely, Yuri's boss must be the ace in the hole for the Catholic Church. Who is that? What does the Russian government get? Money. What does Yuri get? Will Don Pedro profit from the Vatican negotiations?

The Cali Cartel is profiting from the Mex Feds enforcement against the Medellin Cartel which is threatening the Medellin Cartel's western and central Mexican northbound narcotic smuggling routes into the US as is the flow of revenue southbound from the US through Mexico to Colombia. Southwest Mexico, including Culiacan, is aflame with violence. Mexican Government officials, Medellin Cartel personnel and innocent civilian bodies are beginning to fill the now empty streets. Instead of entering this fighting, the proxy war allows the Cali Cartel to expand its operations.

The Mexican citizens in the Culiacan region are demanding action. There are weekly protests in the streets demanding that the central government act. They want justice. They hope the few remaining good people in the government hear their pleas. The Cardinal was not crooked; he was their friend, a savior. The citizens desire an end of their enslavement and or occupation by the Medellin Cartel.

The Culiacan protests are a far cry from the reaction of the Nuevo Laredo residents after the Colonel's killing. The Nuevo Laredo residents knew the Colonel was crooked. Nobody would listen to their concerns. To them, the Colonel's death was a vigilante killing.

The results are unbelievable. The Vatican would not sanction this, but man operates the church, and 'man' is infallible. If someone, possibly Monsignor Maseru believes Yuri's boss can turn the tide in the negotiations, Maseru might 'turn the other cheek' in the acquisition of millions of Russian and Ukrainian souls. It is highly unlikely that Monsignor Maseru has any knowledge of Yuri. Smart, very bright for all, very big. One foul up and the Black Cat is dead.

Chapter Fourteen

It's freezing in Switzerland. Trace amounts of snow drift to the ground, some of which remain on the ground.

The snowcapped mountains stand enormous amidst the cloudless blue sky. One's breath is seen exhaling the crisp air and brittle when inhaled. Pedestrians wrap themselves in thick jackets. The temperature is tolerable as there is no wind.

The now-former Mexico Minister of Interior Gomez sits inside a Geneva café sipping coffee. He ponders his past indiscretions hoping that his and his family's future is not one of isolation. He is fleeing one country or another fearing extradition because of his kleptocracy and the possible existence of a US narcotic arrest warrant. One 'targeted' nation must accept his plea for citizenship because of his introductions and persuasion of the Black Cat's selection to the upcoming Vatican/Eastern/Russian negotiations.

It is imperative that Gomez's future country allows him access to his 'war chest.' He is soliciting Vatican City naturalization. There are approximately two hundred Vatican citizens, it is a small country, but the citizenship will allow him access to his money and eliminate extradition to the United States. With the help of friends, he and his family could then transit into Italy and throughout the European Union. Maybe, being close to the church will do him good. His family remains in Mexico protected by his bodyguards, but their security will not last. He made many powerful enemies, and it is just a matter of time until they strike at his family in Mexico.

Gomez introduced Yuri and Yuri's boss, General Comstock, to the Cali Cartel leader Don Pedro when directed by a Colombia official. The Colombian official did not want to make direct communication to Don Pedro related to this matter.

Gomez recently heard that General Comstock frequents Don Pedro's bar in Cali. The old man loves the ladies. Who doesn't?

Gomez, while the Mexican Minister of Interior, had cleared the way for Don Pedro's organization to smuggle large sums of narcotics secreted in the cargo area of commercial aircraft from Colombia to the Benito Juarez Mexico City, Mexico Airport. He and he alone knew that Yuri's boss, Comstock, could assist the Catholic Church in the upcoming negotiations. Gomez is optimistic General Comstock will advise Vatican City personnel of Gomez's essential work in the matter of the future talks.

Monsignor Emilio, in close association with Monsignor Maseru, recently provided correspondence to the Catholic Pope detailing Gomez's vital assistance in the talks. The communication requests the Pope's consideration that Gomez and his family acquire much-coveted Vatican City citizenship status because of Gomez's work. With the Pope's concurrence to proceed, the correspondence reveals that the citizenship process is exhaustive. Gomez and his family will have to meet numerous qualifications for acceptance. Meaning there are no guarantees for citizenship.

The Pope is only aware of Gomez's unique and valuable position in the talks. However, the Pope is following the ongoing negotiations and its potential benefit to the church. Monsignors Emilio and Maseru are not crooked. Saving souls is their mission and the talks will further advance this goal.

When the former Minister of Interior Gomez, a Catholic, suspects the existence of a US indictment combined with Comstock's concurrence, Minister Gomez contacted church personnel with a proposition that benefitted the Catholic Church in the impending Vatican/Eastern/Russian talks. They listened. Gomez revealed that Bishop Sanchez/The Black Cat and General Comstock are their aces in the hole. From that moment on, Spanish Monsignor Emilio treated Gomez with respect.

By introducing Yuri's boss, General Comstock to Don Pedro, Gomez settled an old debt owed to Don Pedro. Minister Gomez first met General Comstock while on official business to Russia as the Mexican Minister of Interior. The Interior Minister trumped the Mexican Foreign Minister on this trip, as even back then Gomez was seeking a potential home following his fleecing of Mexican government coffers. The Russian trip involved the negotiated purchase by the Mexico government of AK-47s and accompanying ammunition. Gomez never followed up these negotiations.

Today, seated at the Geneva coffee table, Gomez observes the men approach. He will not be fortunate enough to see an assassin's approach. Yuri wearing fashionable European tight jeans and a long sleeve shirt, enjoying the beautiful weather, leads the frail Russian General Vladimir Comstock. Gomez dressed in layers, the outermost a bloated black jacket buttoned to his neck, sits inside the heated café.

Yuri enters the restaurant first followed by General Comstock. A small bell attached to the door announces their presence. Comstock is the head of the Troika panel, representing Russia's 'Church Problems' on behalf of the Russian Orthodox Church.

"Good morning," Gomez stands from the table.

"Good Morning, Sir," Comstock replies, not mentioning Gomez's name. The two shake hands.

Yuri intervenes and tells Comstock that he will remain inside the café but would return with a coffee for the General and another cup for Gomez. General Comstock and Gomez walk from the restaurant's interior and sit at a small table on the sidewalk. The little bell signifies their exit. No other patrons are seated outside. Comstock out of routine prefers to discuss business outside in an attempt to reduce any 'overhears' from curious bystanders or intelligence assets. Yuri knows all the plan's details. The former Minister does not know this.

"Everything appears to be in order," Gomez states.

"Good, good work," the General states, rubbing his gloves together. "This weather is invigorating." He deeply inhales the frigid weather, and idle talk follows.

Gomez understands Comstock will side with the Vatican in the anticipated talks, but he learns Comstock is prepared to give the Eastern Orthodox Church a small portion. Comstock's people are presently coordinating a means to receive an economic windfall/contribution for his services. As part of the anticipated acquisitions, the Russian government will require future scheduled payments from the Vatican and the Eastern Orthodox.

In addition to this windfall, Gomez knows Comstock's reasons to side with the Vatican. The then Colonel Comstock fought in Afghanistan and in the first Chechnya war enduring enough of what he calls the 'Islamic' problem. The Eastern Orthodox Churches exist in areas under assault by the Muslims. Comstock believes the Muslims are slowly co-opting the Eastern Orthodox. In Comstock's mind, the 'Eastern Orthodox' are losing the battle against the 'Islamists.'

Also, the Eastern Orthodox financial resources pale to the Vatican's immense financial strength. The Vatican's financial resources can buffer the ever-expanding growth of the Arab/Muslim religion. The principal deciding factors for Comstock to side with the Vatican are that he lost a son in the Afghanistan war and a niece in Russia from an Islamic orchestrated train bombing. Comstock is a loyal Russian and will do anything to keep the Islamist ideology from spreading further in Russia.

Gomez knows that you can't hinder or for that matter stop the Islamic ideology because the Islamists are simply having more babies than other religions. When Gomez attended university, he learned that T. E. Lawrence,

Lawrence of Arabia, even concluded you couldn't make enough bullets or something like that. Gomez believes it is a failed strategy, but it is not his business.

Yuri returns with the coffees and retreats to the interior of the café. He is situated much like a sniper from his recessed vantage point. Yuri scans the area. Comstock and Gomez express their gratitude to each other as the plan appears to be coming to fruition.

"If this goes through as planned, it will be a wonderful occasion for all of us," bellows Comstock, his cheeks a bright red.

"Indeed."

"If successful, my people will wire money, because of your services, into your bank account," Comstock motions his shaking hand to the UBC bank across the street where Gomez opened a disguised account.

"Thank you, sir and my family thanks, you as well."

The cordial meeting concludes. Gomez walks from the table, first. If surveillance is present, a surveillance team, usually without enough human resources, will have to decide whom to follow.

Yuri sits next to Comstock telling him the lack of observed surveillance in the area. Comstock finishes his coffee and pushes the coffee glass next to Gomez's. Yuri discreetly wipes the fingerprints off each drink. They slowly walk from the area.

Chapter Fifteen

"Who is the Black Cat?" Seamus asks the Med Fed, Maria, his leg on the table at their defacto office, a bar.

Maria replies, "So many people use that alias."

She's forgotten how much information to divulge to Seamus. The pressure is immense on her; she never played this type of game before. If you can call it a game. She assumes Seamus read the articles about the Cardinal's assassination. One article mentioned that Sanchez/The Black Cat was present in Culiacan as part of his official Catholic duties.

A smaller Culiacan publisher posted photographs of the Black Cat at the Presidente hotel following the assassination. The Black Cat, dressed in black for the formal function, is seen coordinating the funeral with local church officials. The local press refers to Sanchez as the Black Cat. She's sure Seamus is continuing to consume all open source material regarding the Black Cat/Sanchez.

"As I have told you before everyone uses that alias. They even refer to the Bishop of Matamoras, Sanchez, as the Black Cat. He was in Culiacan. There could be links. Are you thinking what I am thinking?"

"Well, of course," Seamus says, "we know firsthand a person named the Black Cat deals dope. Those smuggling cowboys almost trampled Pete and me. The young cowboy captured at the scene mentions the names Jose and the Black Cat. We can presume the two subjects, Jose and the Black Cat, are associated with at least the Rio Grande invasion then you have those burnt bodies associated with the killing of the Mex Fed Colonel. Timely discovery and close to the Cowboys' ranch. A bullet found so far is linked to a killer of the Mex Fed Colonel. You just told me that there might be a possible link between the Cat and the Cardinal killing. That is what you just said, right?"

"Yes, well, I said there was a Sanchez in Culiacan who is referred to as the Black Cat," her face turns red. Was she supposed to say that? Too late; it is out.

"So, there is a probability that the Black Cat is Bishop Sanchez, but as you say the alias, Black Cat is common in Mexico. We found additional bullets in the burnt car that did not deteriorate. They await analysis."

"Correct," the Mex Fed says. She is recovering from the leak. It was a mistake by her superiors to provide her all the investigative details.

"The bullets initially found in the car by your people have to be different from the ones we seized in or near the bodies of the assassins. The first bullets link to the Colonel's crime scene. My theory is that somebody newly arrived and not present at the Mex Feds residence at the time of the assassination killed the two assassins at the deserted site and then burnt the car destroying most of the evidence. Except for the special bullets you found. One body was close to the front passenger seat another near the trunk. Where was the driver? Could he/she have left the driver's seat and then shot from the front and into the vehicle? Highly unlikely."

"Yes, but that gun is long gone you said that."

"You're right. If you briefed this investigation with its developing linkages to a boss in our country, you might get some support. In yours, I don't know. That brief could be quite dangerous to your wellbeing," says Seamus.

"The captain who found the burnt car and what remained of the bodies is from my home town," Maria says. "in the State of Michoacán. He has the results of an analysis of the bullets. You remember his team identified the bullet in the body of one of the assassins as matching the Colonel's soldier's gun. So, what you are saying is that the bullets we found in the front seat frames and floorboard of the burnt car are separate from the bullets found by the Mex Fed Captain's team? Could the bullets we found in the assassins burnt car be from the Black Cat's gun?"

"Yeah, that's where I am going. Sanchez, the Black Cat, killed the links to him. I don't think the Black Cat was the driver of the car that would mean he participated in the Colonel's death. We only know one other name, Jose. Maybe, Jose was killed and left in the trunk. Alternatively, he was the third person, the driver. He left the scene. You mentioned that the identification of the bodies was impossible." Seamus senses Maria is under pressure; in deep thought, she's biting her lower lip. It's as if she

135

anticipates the next question and looks directly at Seamus. Seamus asks, "Where does the Black Cat live?"

She pauses and states, "at the church in Matamoras."

"Let's go find religion, a one-day outing to Matamoras. I've got nothing to do this weekend. Here we go again, just for shits and grins." Seamus laughs; she does not.

"Sure, just for shits and grins," Maria rolls her eyes and for the first time, involuntarily shows a look of despair to Seamus. She hoped Seamus would drop the case, but her orders are to stay close to him and report.

It would be impossible to obtain copies of the ballistics report or other evidence obtained from the Mexican captain, so why even bother. Seamus thinks. The one distinct bullet, he discovered in the frame of the front seat of the assassins burnt car and a casing were sent to an old friend. A homicide detective who can analyze this bullet. For what it was worth. No questions asked.

The homicide detective told Seamus that the casing analysis can lead to the ammunition factory, but it would require official correspondence. Seamus requests the detective to concentrate on the bullet. Maria is not aware Seamus forwarded the evidence to the States. Seamus is trying to continue the flow of information. For his safety and hers and the development of his hobby case, he believes it is better to keep her in the dark about the evidence.

Following Seamus and Maria's conversation, Maria's Sergeant contacts her and in a shaky voice reminds her to keep him apprised of all of Seamus' activities. He specifically asks if she maintained a 'good eye' on Seamus while at the burnt car. Did agent O'Malley by chance sneak away with any evidence? She's slow to answer, "no evidence taken."

Maria was very cavalier stating that a Matamoros priest, namely Sanchez, affiliates with the alias 'The Black Cat.' Seamus could have spent years tracking down the correct nickname. Mexican law enforcement has not acted on the Black Cat lead. He read, well Pete read, an article in a small Mexican paper indicating that Sanchez, the Black Cat is rumored to have trafficked narcotics. The newspaper also printed a photograph of Bishop Sanchez. Why would she lead him to Matamoros?

Is this Sanchez/the Black Cat protected? Was Maria sending him on a fishing expedition to tire him of the investigation chasing rumors? Did Maria make a mental mistake? She could have been directed to stay as close to the truth as possible. Knowing a highly respective priest would not be pursued. Did she hope that he would not react favorably to the long shot lead? Matamoros is not close to Nuevo Laredo. Why not send him to a dead end, another Black Cat that would be the end of it.

Seamus knows a Black Cat is a drug dealer associated with the cowboy case and then there is the small paper associating Bishop Sanchez, the Black Cat with drugs on the northern border. Is that paper still in business? Is the reporter alive? Who else could coordinate such a high profile killing as the Cardinal? Sanchez, the Black Cat, was there. Pete indicated that the Cardinal was to speak about the need to end narcotic trafficking. Is Maria his 'minder'; a babysitter?

During this period, US intelligence officers Todd and Socorro receive data that the 'old lady' forwarded, to a yet unidentified subject, news of impending travel by the Mex Fed, Maria and Seamus O'Malley to Matamoros, Mexico.

Todd and Socorro based in a target rich geographic area, find themselves stumbling over quality cases. Investigators, including Todd and Socorro, demand challenges in their investigations and additionally, the subjects must be of interest. This Seamus/Sanchez/Black Cat case was beginning to satisfy both requirements. Therefore, it climbed on the priority case list. Plus, they identified in effect an active, credible informant necessary in any investigation, Agent Seamus O'Malley. They are not directing him, but they agree if his organization is not going to support him, they may as well stay close to him and make timely decisions to assist when appropriate.

Socorro volunteered for the present assignment. It was one of five geographic locations available on her 'wish list.' She speaks fluent Spanish and Russian. She possesses an innate ability to filter through the extensive reporting related to their Mexican sector. She cuts to the most accurate and actionable information to maximize her time. Time is a premium in Mexico.

Todd is an adrenalin junky and volunteered for various hot spots throughout the world. Before his graduation and notification of his geographic assignment, his mentor met with him. The mentor displayed pictures of beautiful deserts, sandy beaches, bodies hanging from bridges, tortured lifeless victims discarded like trash in the middle of the streets, beheadings, and remnants of human parts that floated in acid before the oil containers were kicked over by local law enforcement.

The mentor explained to Todd that remnants of the present government from which the photographs originated are fighting a low-grade insurgency. Kidnappings and murders between rival criminal organizations are a daily if not an hourly occurrence. Each criminal group establishes permanent and impromptu roadblocks, nightly. Villagers have 'taken up arms' against the criminal groups and created barricades of their own, encircling their hamlets. The government can no longer protect its citizenry.

Todd interrupted the mentor in mid-sentence, "You know I already volunteered for numerous assignments in the Middle East. I am proficient in Arabic. Why are you showing me these pictures and describing what I am going to experience? I have been briefed in the areas already."

The mentor replied, "Well, I thought you might want your initial assignment close to your parents. I understand they need continued medical care."

"Close to my parents? They don't live over there."

"I am talking about Mexico!"

"What?"

"Yes, go to Mexico; we are getting slammed there."

The next thing you know, Todd is working in the most violent place in the world. Todd can throw a rock from his new assignment and hit US soil.

Chapter Sixteen

An unidentified voice contacts the Black Cat on the phone.

"They will be coming this weekend," the voice declares.

"How many?" the Black Cat asks.

"Two."

"I'll give them a good show, or Jose will."

"Hopefully, we will intercede before he reaches you. We want him to make it to the city. It's far from his office. It will look better. You know, this guy is quite resourceful. I do not want to shock you, but I would not be surprised if he stole evidence from the burnt car without our people seeing. I know your link to the car. I will only ask you one time. Did you use the special ammo?"

"Oh, no. Standard only." He lies so convincingly it surprises him.

"Very good."

Simultaneously, General Comstock receives a cryptic message indicating that the American, Seamus O'Malley, and Maria, the Mex Fed will travel to Matamoras. They are going to surveil the Black Cat. Comstock thinks to himself, the 'War on Drugs.' The war is rarely fought with tanks and missiles, but the narcotics traffickers' tactics are similar to those he combatted in Afghanistan. The Americans have yet to realize the threat that narcotics are to US security.

The cost involved in investigating illegal narcotics, including enforcement payrolls, insurance, and equipment is well into billions of dollars a year. The costs associated when addicts prey on innocent citizens to get monies for their habits: burglaries, thefts, robberies, and sometimes homicides are immense.

Hospitals pass the expenses, for care given to injured suspects and their victims, to uninvolved third parties. Residential and auto insurance bills include the damages caused by the addicts: department stores in rising price tags because of persistent theft, and by the US government via increase taxes all increase. The impact of narcotics is similar to what the Americans referred to as their policy, 'the slow bleed' at the advent of the Russian/Afghanistan war.

Meaning, the US provided just enough aid to the Mujahedeen to keep them in the fight draining the resources of both combatants. The Americans with other Middle Eastern countries then fully supported the Mujahedeen's war in Afghanistan thinking they could control the Mujahedeen only to discover again and again, that as always, a more radical group always emerges from the original terrorist group. A more radical group that cannot be reined in by the creators. Narcotics is America's 'slow bleed' oozing from a pinata.

The Colombians realize the threat as they had Presidential candidates murdered by the traffickers. Central America is teetering into chaos because of corruption alliances between government officials and narcotics traffickers. In Mexico, the government official is challenging to differentiate from the traffickers. These populations cannot ignore such brazen transgressions. General Comstock is sure people with higher clearances than him are responsible for keeping Mexico in a state of chaos. It borders with the US. We just did it once.

Media reports of Mexican killings and violence are so commonplace that Americans ignore the stories. Wealthy Mexicans flee the violence, murders, kidnaps, and extortion to Southern California and Houston, Texas. The rich delegate their business operations to employees who cannot afford to leave. The rich are seen driving Land Rovers, Mercedes-Benzes, and Ferraris. The poorest sneak into the US. Only those who are directly affected by narcotics will take notice.

Comstock's intelligence buddies discussed that they should smuggle narcotics directly into the United States to obtain money for the government and second to psychologically control the population of the United States. Who is to say that his government is not fully supporting this very ideal? He has access to intelligence activities on a 'need to know basis.' Comstock has not been 'read in' on such a mission.

The British subjugated the Chinese with narcotics. It is more palatable to the world's conscience to kill ones' foes with warplanes and tanks than to murder with drugs. Geneva would not like the drug idea; Comstock smirks. Just like they do not approve of the use of poison gas. Chemical weapons kill many people when deployed. How many people are killed daily because of drugs or chemicals? Narcotics dispersed through spectacular explosions causing hundreds of deaths with accompanying hysterical media reports does not happen. Instead, narcotic deaths are constant, an unanswered drum beat and commonplace.

Following travel notification to the Black Cat by one of his subordinates, General Comstock contacts Yuri advising him of the travel to Matamoros by the 'idiot' (Seamus O'Malley's new code name) and 'the cute one' (Maria the Mex Fed's new code name). Code names created from

141

their individual traits. The simple code names make it easier for Yuri and Comstock to identify who either one is referring too. It's risky to assign these simple code names because if an outside agency investigates their activities, they can quickly identify the referenced individuals.

Comstock juggles numerous cases and Sources. By assigning such simple code names, Comstock knows this operation will have a short life span. The probability the 'idiot' and 'the cute one' will survive much longer is low. So, Comstock takes the risk.

"Shall we leak the 'idiots' travel plans to our US friends? Let them handle it. Get the US authorities worked up over the 'idiot' for going rogue? Get him transferred as far away from Texas as possible?"

"No, let it go. What is O'Malley going to find, a priest?" Comstock says. "He does not have any contraband. It is not worth exposing a well-placed US Source over O'Malley."

"Those Medellin people in Mexico are taking a beating as a result of the Cardinal killing."

"Yeah, the Mex Feds have to show something. Our friend (Don Pedro) is hurting his competitor. I might say you conducted a very effective plan." Comstock continues, "We needed to help our friend against the Medellin Cartel. Changing the 'front' was a great idea. Those Colombian articles are dangerous. Oh, make sure you keep paying those Culiacan community organizers. Buy the protestors more pots and pans to bang. They need to continue the protest. Whip up the masses. Keep the pressure on the government. The Mexican government is hemorrhaging money."

"I will continue to make payments to the community activists."

"Very good."

"General, let me add this; the Mexican government is hemorrhaging money, but I wonder if we have accelerated the growth of the Mexican Cartels. The Mexican Cartels took advantage of the publicity of the Cardinal's killing and the blame thrown at the Medellin Cartel. I understand Mexican Cartel operatives are sowing discontent with the presence of both Colombian Cartels."

"You believe the Mexican criminal groups will replace the Colombians in Mexico?"

"It is my belief they are slowly and deliberately feeding the Mex Feds intelligence on Colombians in Mexico; specifically, the Medellin operatives."

"To take overall control of the Mexican smuggling routes?"

"Exactly, they are treading lightly…assessing the Mex Feds reaction to the Medellin Cartel threat."

"Beautiful, the Mexican Cartels are also using the Mex Feds as their proxy army."

"It may not be that beautiful. You will not be able to harness the actions of the Mexican criminal groups. Don Pedro's Cali Cartel presence in Mexico will be the next to go."

"Yuri, you are correct. Let's hope Don Pedro has enough resources to remain in Mexico."

"That's all we can do."

"Yuri, why don't you go to Matamoros. The Mex Fed is not a problem; the American is."

"Arrange a bar fight in a local tavern or have the American rolled by a prostitute and her accomplices, no one would suspect," Yuri adds.

"You are reading my mind. Make the necessary plans, the light is green, and I'll consult with Don Pedro."

Without the usual goodbyes, the line disconnects. Comstock contacts Flaco, Don Pedro's spokesman, via a cellular telephone and asks to speak with Don Pedro. Flaco provides the phone to Don Pedro.

"Si, Senor," Don Pedro answers.

Comstock provides a cryptic message:

"BC goes to D.F. (Mexico District Federal) (Capitol).

Idiot (Seamus) Norte (US) ahora (now) un problemo (problem) will correct.

Prepare the white cars (cocaine).

Contact BC with details of cars that is your baby.

As previously explained security, my baby, as soon as it departs." The call terminates.

Don Pedro is a powerful man, but Comstock runs the show. The Colombians respect the Russians. The Colombians control the product, but the Russians have a superior organization formally trained in intelligence operations.

While drinking his vodka, General Comstock thinks about how Don Pedro has become such a good ally. Former Minister of Interior Gomez possesses considerable US knowledge an attribute to exploit in the future. Gomez was instrumental in the introduction between Don Pedro and him. Should Gomez remain in the wings of this 'op'? Gomez's termination would be a future cost saver. Who would object? Gomez is a public figure. We don't need publicity if this thing falls apart.

The problem, if our allies discover that we make it a practice to kill those that have helped us, people will not be willing to give us valuable information or act on our behalf. Gomez is a shell of a man and professes to have found God. God did not exist in my country for decades. Gomez is emotionally weak. Gomez's future is now in Comstock's hands.

Former Mexico Minister of Interior Gomez lays in his bed, his eyes staring at the hotel's ceiling. He struggles to sleep. Gomez is oblivious that someone is considering his fate. How many people go about their daily activities with the possibility that they will be 'gone tomorrow.'

Chapter Seventeen

Sanchez/The Black Cat responds to his orders and travels to Mexico City, Mexico leaving Jose as the 'acting' Bishop of Matamoras. Before departure, the Black Cat tells Jose he will attempt to return to Matamoros by the end of the week to personally assess the American and Mex Fed agent problems. Following the appointment to negotiate with the Russians, the Black Cat tells Jose that Don Pedro is likely linked with the Russian issue and gives limited details. The Matamoros' populace is in awe of the Black Cat's temporary appointment to Mexico City.

Outwardly, Jose is stoic, but he is emotionally unstable. He is too close to the Black Cat, Don Pedro, and Yuri. Jose gets no relief from the reoccurring girl's image. Disappearing and reappearing as he raced from the Colonel's killing. Her face haunts him day and night. Following the Black Cat's departure, he's rational enough to realize something terrible will come his way.

Jose views photographs hung on the office wall. Most of the pictures depict Jose's and the Black Cat's early years at the seminary dressed in their black cleric clothes. The color makes sense. Black like the night, the color of death. How appropriate. Will he experience an epiphany, so his colors can change? Does he want that? Maybe, he's grown up and now understand things in a new reality.

If anything goes wrong in Mexico City, Jose will be expendable. The Black Cat is ignoring the dangers surrounding him. Jose walks the office's perimeter walls rereading framed glowing letters of appreciation and love given to them from their flock. Similar framed letters of praise from priests stamped with the insignia of Jesus are on the office desks.

In stark contrast to the letters of appreciation, is a hole in the lower part of the stucco wall caused by the weapon that killed the girl assassin. Some books are stacked to conceal a portion of the depression, but for some reason, Jose cares less if the hole and the casing are discovered.

There is a break, a chasm developing between himself and the Black Cat. He is not sure he will remain loyal to the Black Cat.

A priest enters the office, thankfully disturbing Jose's thoughts. Jose turns to speak to the young man. The priest speaks to the need for an impending trip to a pueblo on the outskirts of Matamoras. A family member requests that the priest administer the last rites to a young man. The young man cannot travel. Jose authorizes the priest to go as if he would say no. When, and who will read his last rites. At this rate, it will be soon.

Chapter Eighteen

The Black Cat walks to meet the now fragile and senile Cardinal Vazquez at his temporary quarters at the Shrine to Our Lady of Guadalupe. The Cardinal's residence is undergoing extensive renovations. So, the Cardinal decides to reside at the Shrine to converse with the Mexican delegation members.

The Shrine encompasses many acres. Hundreds of thousands of pilgrims travel to pray at its large circular shaped church devoted to an appearance of the Virgin Mary. Daily, priests try to say mass amongst the noisy crowd. Walls comprised of exposed volcanic looking rock mixed with mortar flow throughout the premises. A parking garage and large metal gates lead the pilgrims to the Shrine with its beautiful terraced gardens surrounding immaculate buildings. Viewing the Shrine from afar is difficult. Mexico City is flat; built upon a swamp surrounded by mountains. Because of this depression, thick pollution remains in the City. The Shrine, with its beautiful gardens, reveals itself to the astonished pilgrims as they walk through the gates. It is then that the pilgrims see the terraces.

The premises are immaculately maintained by poor residents who receive job security for life as a perk of their coveted employment. Upon their retirement, the aging gardeners and house staff generally pass their duties to young and eager family members.

Modern electric and motorized gardening tools are available in the city, but the gardeners use handmade straw brooms and rakes. Manuel saws and leaf clippers are used to prune the trees and gardens. The gardeners place water sprinklers in various green spaces throughout the acreage. Some hold hoses spraying water upon the purple, red and yellow flowers that are always in need of its life-saving liquid. The use of manual tools and water hoses instead of power tools and permanently installed underground sprinklers, allow the Diocese to employ more people in a small but needed effort to assist the poor. The rift between the lower class and upper class is widening.

Because of the mild annual climate, the flowers bloom throughout the year. Large trees throughout the premises provide shade for the pilgrims. Air bubbles continuously explode in water fountains sounding of small brooks. Vines take hold of the walls reducing the feel of a compound.

The acreage beams of life as dark-skinned gardeners wearing straw hats and green uniforms go about their daily outdoors chores; the majority a little overweight, the rest quite skinny. Short women housekeepers wearing blue and white uniforms clean the church, windows, rooms, and sweep the building entrances. They encounter each other while pushing their full cloth baskets on wheels containing cleaning implements, toiletries, towels, and sheets. They use these brief meetings to spread innocent rumors and jokes. They also can't wait to meet other housekeepers to be the first to tell the others what they just heard, read or watched on television about their favorite soap stars.

To continue without disruption its nominal citizenry life support, the Mexico City Diocese tries to remain neutral in politics. Recently the church was placed in a precarious position as one of its priests actively demonstrated in support of the indigenous Mexican Indians residing in the State of Chiapas, Mexico. The State of Chiapas is located in southern Mexico and borders Guatemala. The Indians demand equal rights and more government financial investment in their area. The church decides to support the Indians cause quietly. It is in the peaceful confines of the beautiful gardens, terraced walkways, fountains, birds nesting in the trees, the busy 'full of life workers' and the care provided by the Catholic Church that enters the Devil himself.

"Buenos Dios," The Black Cat says. Cardinal Vazquez seated behind his desk, squints his eyes from the morning sun that floods the small room with its lush potted tropical plants. The Cardinal motions for Bishop Sanchez to be seated.

"We have heard nothing but the good news of your appointment to be the lead arbitrator involving 'our' church lands. I hope you will make yourself at home." The Cardinal is small framed and fragile looking. The Cardinal wears black starched shirt and pants overly large for his frame. His gold ring on his finger dwarfs his shriveled hand.

The Black Cat nods and sits waiting for the Cardinal to continue the conversation.

The Cardinal becomes unexpectedly agitated but does not reveal it to the Black Cat. His blood pressure spikes and feels the development of a massive migraine. He puts a handkerchief on his mouth and detects a small amount of blood. "Please excuse me, I have urgent matters to attend. I'll see you tomorrow at the noon service and after we will talk." The Cardinal rises from his chair and calls for his aide to walk the Black Cat from the small office. His staff will attend to his needs. The Cardinal motions the Black Cat to the entrance of the small office.

"Yes, my Eminence." The Black Cat is not surprised in the change of the Cardinal's demeanor.

Following the Black Cat's departure, the Cardinal struggles to reach his chair, putting one hand on the armrest. He drops on the thick leather cushion, his back pressed against the leather. He raises his shaking right hand to his forehead. He tries to massage the pain above his right eye. He wonders if he should seek medical attention but the feeling subsides.

The Black Cat converses with a few of the Cardinal's staff and handles some administrative details. The Black Cat borrows a motor pool vehicle and abruptly drives from the Shrine. The Black Cat meets with Don Pedro's man, a sinister, light-skinned thin framed short Colombian. Interesting. This man is not Mexican. Do the Medellin Cartel and their associated/allied Mexican National traffickers know what is happening here? A Cali Cartel based Colombian National is operating in central Mexico. Don Pedro trusts this man as he must be highly skilled in the trade. The Medellin Cartel and their Mexican allies are actively looking for revenge. Don Pedro has to be anticipating a counter strike.

"How are you?" the Colombian male identified as Jorge inquires. The Black Cat only nods.

Unbeknownst to the Black Cat and Jorge is an olive-skinned man, unshaven standing in the shadow of a small business wall. He conceals himself amongst the pedestrians on the street. The man focuses on the meeting. Either, the Black Cat or Jorge failed in their counter surveillance routine, or the olive-skinned man's presence is just a coincidence.

When Jorge meets the Black Cat there are none of the usual jokes about him being a priest and saving souls? Jorge's mannerisms were quite severe. Jorge understood the dangers. Jorge hands the Black Cat a cellphone and a piece of paper with a telephone number.

"Call this man associated with the cell number. He will arrange your delivery."

"Delivery to where, who, when?" Sanchez waves his hands in one direction and the other.

"You probably know where but not how."

"You are correct."

"I am glad that I know nothing else," Sanchez mumbles.

"Buen Suerte (Good Luck), Bishop Sanchez we will talk more in the future," Jorge says as he walks into the flow of numerous pedestrians disappearing into the crowded, noisy environment. The Black Cat walks to his vehicle and drives from the area. Looking at his vehicle mirrors, he attempts to locate counter surveillance. Not observing any, the Black Cat returns to the Shrine.

Chapter Nineteen

While traveling to Matamoros, Seamus O'Malley is genuinely concerned, more like scared. He risks the loss of his job if anything goes wrong. What does he have, case wise: a dying cowboy, a little dope, the murder of a Mex Fed Corrion, the killing of Cardinal Torres with no actionable linkages? Maria revealed they could be linked. 'What the hell, over', you're supposed to work narcotics.

Seamus is thinking about his home supervisor, Eddie, signing monthly car reports and time sheets. Maybe, Eddie is reading a synopsis of 'supported' narcotic investigations making use of wire intercepts. Eddie is probably upset as Source reviews are due. As a result of the regular Source reviews, numerous Sources are 'deactivated' during this period, reducing the number of mandated Source package updates and supervisor Source interviews. The lack of human resources nearly crippled the CIA in the late 1970's. The cycle is about to repeat itself in law enforcement.

O'Malley and Maria close on Matamoras. A strong wind blows from Matamoros east to west; sand strikes the windshield. White clouds turn gray. They observe yellow heat lightning cross the clouds. They smell the rain, but it is doubtful the clouds will release its bounty on the parched earth.

Why is he going to Matamoros, who cares? Is it worth it? Well, maybe he still wants to do something useful. Seamus' bureaucracy rarely backs serious investigations making use of 'real Informants, Sources.' In an effort to understand the Black Cat investigation, he needs to develop Sources. The potential Sources are generally close to the target. If the situation is right, Seamus may locate a Source. For years, the administration convinced itself that these 'real cases using real Sources' that lead to the highest violators must be ignored or shutdown. These cases frighten the risk adverse supervisors. So, the administration invented the go to shutdown phrase to be delivered the agents with intentions on working large Source driven cases, 'there's just too much liability and drama.'

A majority of agents have relented to this managerial roadblock. Deciding not to pursue the case because of management's big lie, 'fabricated liability and drama' reinforced to the agents over and over. The supervisors reinforce that only 'rogue' and 'lone disgruntled federal employees' continue to work these Source driven cases. Wire intercepts are the future, not Sources.

The problem with these supervisorial labels is twofold. A 'rogue' agent is a misnomer when it should be defined as a real 'working agent' without managerial support. Secondly, the supervisorial label of 'lone disgruntled federal employee' is synonymous to that of the 'lone wolf' terrorist designation. Management does not acknowledge that agents such as these exist in the plural just as the government does not want to acknowledge that terrorists and their organizations are anything other than singular in their action and scope. There are always more than one lone wolf terrorist just as there are legions of 'rogue' and 'lone disgruntled federal employees.' Another issue is that the number of quality Source cases discontinued by agents as a result of fabricated liability and drama is not tracked.

Seamus is familiar with the fifty percent supervisor rule. He gets a good supervisor and a few years later a bad one. Recently, he has outlasted three bad supervisors in a row. Unprecedented, and because of this, he is exceptionally jaded. The last three have been 'political' supervisors, the worst kind, they actually support and believe in fabricated liability and drama.

Politics enters amongst the first line supervisor ranks. There has been an increase in the promotion of 'political' supervisors as hysterical fears of liability have morphed to accepted willful omission. These 'political' first line supervisors are chosen amongst the ranks to remain at the same office or traded to other offices out of favors to those he/she will work for, but more importantly, chosen with the knowledge that their new immediate supervisor can easily manipulate the newly promoted 'political' supervisors.

The newly promoted 'political' supervisors sell their souls for promotions and now 'Drink the Kool-Aid' content in relaying nonsensible job expectations to their subordinates to remain average. Excellent performance appraisals are given by the 'politicals' to agents who have 'little cases and therefore little problems.' An excelling agent should remain at this level.

An agent cannot have 'no cases, no problems' unless he/she is the supervisor's snitch or drinking buddy.

An agent must not ascend with the assistance of quality human Sources to the level of 'big cases, big problems.' If an agent reaches this level, then he/she is reminded of the fabricated liabilities and drama associated with working such cases as these. If an agent ignores the 'political's' attempt to terminate the case, then the political uses other means to inhibit the investigation.

A supervisor does not order an agent to refrain from working 'big cases' reporting on crimes, such as official corruption and its facilitation of powerful narcotic contractors. Instead, managers place roadblocks in the agents' way. The political supervisors do not want 'big cases' as they take some time to develop. The Federal drug budget primarily awards 'targets of opportunities', smaller cases, the same as cases reaching the highest levels of criminal activity.

Meaning the administration looks more favorably on grabbing the lowest hanging fruit from the tree comprising the most stupid suspects. To the federal budget, the arrest of a non-designated major violator is equivalent to a 'street slinger.' For an agent to succeed in working quality Source cases, the agent needs to treat the political supervisor as a speedbump.

Meaning, the agents need to practice established management techniques like forgetting the contents of the meetings, purposely misinterpreting the meeting, or never recalling there was a meeting. At the same time, the agents continue to direct the Sources, corroborate the Sources information and have a detail plan on how to proceed. Most importantly, the agents need to cover all the possible investigative outcomes before the supervisor thinks he/she needs to provide input. Political input is hazardous.

Maria and Seamus O'Malley continue east on Mexican Federal Highway 2 towards Matamoros, the same highway used by Jose and the twin assassins.

"We are approaching a roadblock," Maria says.

Seamus sits up in the seat, "Is it a legitimate roadblock?"

"It should be it is daylight," Maria reaches into her front pocket and retrieves a piece of paper.

"What do we do if it is a 'bad guy' roadblock? Will you run it?"

She does not answer.

They observe bright orange traffic cones placed in a manner to close one lane incrementally. Two Mexican Federal pickup trucks are stationary facing the roadblock on the road shoulders near a third truck parked on the closed road partially blocking the one open lane. Mex Feds sit in the two vehicles parked on the shoulders, protecting them from the growing movement of sand.

Maria slows the car behind a line of approximately ten vehicles. Two Federales standing by the third truck direct the drivers to stop, and they approach the cars from opposite sides. As Maria gets closer to the designated stop area, she observes a fourth vehicle facing east. This truck is a chase truck if a driver decides to run. The remaining pickup trucks are occupied and most likely serve as security for the two Federal officers.

"They wear uniforms and the trucks look genuine," says Maria. "I will take over the conversation, just nod and smile."

"Got it."

"We are on vacation. We are going to South Padre Island, Texas, for a few days."

"What hotel? That's where they will get us if they are real."

"I'll handle it."

Maria's car is now first in line.

The Federal officer raises his hand and motions her to stop.

"Let's see your identification," the Federal officer standing next to Maria orders. Sand blows into the car. Maria reaches into her purse and hands her driver identification to the officer the other officer looks through the passenger window at Seamus.

"Where are you going?" the same officer asks.

"First to Matamoros and then onto to South Padre."

"How long do you intend to stay in North Padre?" The officer purposely changed Maria's destination to observe her reaction.

"A few days," responds Maria, nonchalantly.

The officer observes nothing unusual in the way Maria answered.

Seamus becomes nervous as Maria unconsciously or consciously affirmed the officer's change in their destination from South Padre to North Padre. He suspects that this officer and Maria are working together to justify Seamus's arrest.

The questioning officer probes further, "Where's your luggage?" The officer is turning up the heat now looking for involuntary facial twitches and excessive sweating from the occupants. Again, the officer observes nothing suspicious.

Maria is about to say something. She rubs her thumb against a piece of paper in her right hand. If the officer says 'pop the trunk' there will be problems.

Seamus knows they are doomed; there is no luggage. If the officer looks in the trunk, Seamus goes to jail. Alternatively, Maria and this guy get into a verbal altercation, or this is part of Maria's plan. These officers arrest him and then dispose of his body.

The officer moves from Maria before she answers. The questioning officer looks into the backseat and flicks his finger against Maria's identification. The other officer walks to the rear of Maria's vehicle. Seamus mistakenly cranes his head to the rear of the car alerting the officer near the trunk. The questioning officer next to Maria observes the growing traffic and wipes the sand from his mouth. While working a checkpoint, the questioning officer realizes he only has a few minutes with each car's occupants to assess the situation.

The officer returns to Maria's window and hands her identification to her, "Have a good day."

"You too, thanks."

The officer motions her to leave and orders the car behind her to move up. Maria puts the identification and the paper into her purse. Seamus wonders what is on the paper; it has to be an internal form of insurance. Maria wanted to get through the checkpoint without using it. Roadblocks can be dangerous and discretionary.

"That was close," Seamus says.

"Close to what?" Maria says, sarcastically.

She must be exhausted; Seamus returns to his thoughts about investigations. The roadblocks for case development by the political are multifaceted. A political generally accepts a promotion to the supervisorial role because they no longer want to work, one barrier. Of those working agents, now supervisors, that are under the illusion that their new group will work on numerous valuable/quality cases they will learn that mindset is not appropriate, roadblock two. Other barriers are that the political supervisor does not want to take the time to understand the quality Source case, lacks curiosity in his/her job, or was advised by his/her supervisor that the quality Source case should be shut down.

How does a political shut down a quality case? The political does not want a fight on his hand. So, the political reaches out to weaker agents motoring along with 'no cases, no problems.' These agents are tasked by the supervisor or through their own initiative eavesdrop in an effort to understand the working agents' case. The incompetent agents acquire 'case' overhears from the working agents' conversations and phone calls. When the agents are satisfied with their incomplete information, they forward their case analysis to the political. Precisely, the inadequate and flawed information the political supervisor craves. The erroneous information justifies the supervisor to withhold payments to the agents' Sources, thus reducing the effectiveness of the case and causing the case to die on the vine.

Monies for Informants/Sources generally originates from the home office budget. By withholding Source payments, the political supervisor eliminates the embarrassing need to request Source money through briefs to his/her supervisor on a case he/she never cared about or took the time to understand. Sources used in the 'quick hit' low hanging fruit cases will receive office money instead. The political supervisors are expected to use Headquarters money designated for wiretaps.

Wiretaps initially make use of Sources then it is determined the Source has plateaued, and eavesdropping ensues. A problem, a bulk of Source monies exist in Headquarters for a few questionable Headquarters agents, too lengthy to think about, Seamus is developing a headache.

During the case development process, another problem hits the rogue agents; the 'parallel case' impacts the 'shelf life' of a quality Source case. The 'parallel case' can occur from the inferior briefs by the political 'pets' to the political supervisor, but also in other forms. When the 'parallel case' develops, the working agents are forced to expend half their time to defend the case, correcting the damage from the managerial designated 'dumb ass agents' vacationing on the no cases no problems life style.

Seamus awakes from his thoughts as he observes a low flying aircraft descend south over the horizon. Where is it going? Who's onboard? The passengers are well above all this traffic, bumpy roads and excessive heat. How relaxing is that?

"You would like to be on that plane?" Maria asks Seamus.

"You are reading my mind."

"Me too, sometimes this work is sad, dark and not very rewarding. Sometimes, I would like to get away."

"You are wiser than you think," Seamus smiles at Maria, and she returns her focus on the road. Back to his thoughts.

In the case acceptance decision-making process, the supervisor understands that the arrest of subjects as a result of a two-day investigation has the same budgetary weight as non-designated high-level subjects. So, the supervisor attempts a balance of the short term, medium, and long-term cases. However, when you balance, you cannot devote the time necessary to conduct long term Source cases.

You can acquire the approval of a long-term case with an accompanying high-level designation the caveat being a wire intercept is expected, consequently shutting out Informant driven cases. Eventually, wiretaps will not be a useful tool as technology will make it impossible to intercept conversations.

If, an agency can crack the technology, would it be wise to have it disclosed in court? 'All the eggs' have been placed into wire intercepts leaving quality Informants/Sources dormant and abandoned. There has never been a healthy balance of intercepts to Informant/Source driven cases. The reason, Informants/Sources are believed inherently troublesome. An intercept is nice and neat, and the direction of the Sources is not needed. An Informant could double cross you. It could, but that is the nature of the business. An agent must look for the signals and advert the event before it happens. In the future, multiple agencies will be without 'real Sources.'

Because of fabricated liability and drama engrained into the 'political' supervisors' psyche, they seek prosecutor case acceptance. The agent now enters a nonphysical 'fatal funnel.' There are a limited number of prosecutors, who in turn communicate and coordinate with a multitude of local, state and federal officers/agents all vying for case acceptance and maintenance. The political supervisor is aware that prosecutorial acceptance of long-term cases is challenging to obtain. The lack of prosecutorial support is another 'out' for the political supervisor. Lack of prosecution acceptance threatens Source monies.

Prosecutor acceptance transfers the fabricated liability and drama from the political to the new 'binky,' the prosecutor. Case acceptance does not ensure seizures or arrest, but it none the less gets that requirement off the supervisors 'to do list.' Translated: a 'to do list' is also referred to as 'putting out fires.' Management through make-believe crisis.

Hiring more paralegals would ease the excessive burden on the prosecutors. Paralegals are not necessarily attorneys but work supervised by attorneys. The paralegals could act as subject matter experts on various cases allowing the working agents time to infiltrate the criminal organization's command and control. Direct agent brief's and current reports given to the paralegal will allow a better flow of information. The paralegals could then schedule interoffice briefings between them and the prosecutors. They can assist in the preparation of court documents. Court documents then reviewed and finalized by the prosecutors. Paralegals will eliminate the need for prosecutors to filter agents calls. Surprises will cease. People go into shock and shut down when overloaded with data.

The paralegals and prosecutors speak the same language. In the past, the 'same language' issue occurred between O'Malley and a prosecutor. One particular word became the focus of the debate. O'Malley said Webster's Dictionary defines the 'word' as this or that; the prosecutor replied that Webster's definitions mean nothing as there is a separate legal dictionary trumping the English language. Seamus is cognizant the expansion of paralegals will require years of review. The hiring of additional prosecutors and paralegals will require Congressional approval adding to the length of time for acceptance of this issue.

The agents' case briefs to the prosecutors can be by telephone or consist of lengthy PowerPoints. If a prosecutor declines the case, an agent can contest the decision of non-acceptance and receive a written 'refusal' and or written 'declination' provided by a state or federal prosecutor, respectively. The prosecutor details the reasons he/she is not willing to accept the case. An agent can contest a declination, but the prosecutor's boss reviews the declination.

At present, the prosecutors are outgunned and outmanned. Many factors lead to case denials. Seamus thinks 'denials' of long-term infiltration cases could lead to an increase of cookie cutter cases driven by 'go-byes' (redundant past cases) relying on simple sting operations. Meaning in the case of terrorism, time spent on infiltrating a group ends when a subject acts on law enforcement provided 'bunk' material, faulty weapons, inert gunpowder leading to its immediate arrest. The premature arrest leaves the investigators without the overall of the criminal organization.

Although an agent or police officer can receive written refusals/declinations, most agents and officers 'wave their hands in the air' and go on their way. Verbal prosecutor refusals, denials/declinations are not logged. As stated before, cases shut down by the 'politicals' are not tracked at all. So, what is the real number of quality Source cases never receiving support?

If a significant target and its organization continue its activities because of a lack of supervisorial and or prosecutorial support, the organization may come to light after the criminal group takes over a part of a country or kills someone of importance. Rarely, are the case agents questioned as to what happened to the case.

Back to the 'parallel case,' Seamus was thinking of when interrupted by the aircraft, is its impact on Upper Management and HQS who interject unsolicited/unwarranted demands on the case. The parallel case thrives when HQS continuously receives flawed briefs or communiqués from the lowest supervisors filtered through a chain of command consisting of various humans all interpreting the facts differently. Erroneous data trickles upwards creating a parallel case that has nothing to do with the real situation.

Why? Numerous managers in the chain of command are not always available for the case briefings, so no one person in the chain of command is an expert of the facts except the 'first line' working agents.

When upper management decides to make a non-solicited decision on the parallel case based on the so-called facts, the choice in most cases is to shut down the investigation, because of erroneous briefs or inaccurately concluded fabricated liability and drama.

The decision by HQS to resort to such a drastic decision occurs as the data received is similar to a middle school lesson. In this school lesson, the teacher whispers a phrase to a child sitting on the first row of his/her class and instructs the same child to forward that exact message to the next child who in turn whispers the message to the next, repeating until received by the last child sitting in the back row of the class. No different than briefs forwarded up the chain of command.

For example, the teacher tells the first student, "The Rocky Mountains are in the western US, and the Appalachian Mountains are in the eastern US." When the last student receives the message, the student proudly stands and states with all sincerity that, "Rocks are thrown on the eastern side of the class." The student is designated a rogue and an idiot, and their best friends are labeled the same. Of note: You have a real problem if the first brief by a supervisor or in this case, the teacher's statement is inaccurate — the cards stack against the shrinking quality Source investigations.

Seamus could go on for days about the problems associated with cases, 'big cases big problems' but then he would have to field, well, what about this? What about that? It is not like you make it sound — you are mistaken. You don't know the Big Picture. Yours is a simplistic explanation of the topic. It is not worth thinking about this anymore. Who is going to fix it, anybody, Bueller, Bueller?

Seamus awakes from his thoughts, a slow roll of his head, and massages his neck with his right hand. He scans the surroundings.

"There is BC's place," Maria points to the office.

Seamus slowly turns his head in the same direction. He squints his eyes and hopes he will not see the office and that the Black Cat is gone. Seamus goes back to his thoughts; sure, supervisors are necessary for controlling that 10% of nutty agents and officers, but the resulting draconian oppressive rules related to Source/Informant use detrimentally affect those still willing to work.

Because of the immediate Source environment, Seamus is determined to seek out Sources operating on the periphery of the criminal organizations who possess independent financial means, reducing the need to beg management for Source monies. Defendant Sources working off or reducing their sentences are damaged goods. Anything they provide will be short-lived, ancillary, and not substantially related to the criminal organization they were involved unless they are uniquely placed.

Maria drives the vehicle by the Black Cat's office, observing no one inside the office. She moves the car in a big circle through the stifling traffic and brings it to its original position. Seamus observes a lone cop directing traffic; some drivers follow his hand commands. Others do not even acknowledge his presence. Corruption is a huge problem in Mexico.

Years ago, Seamus summed up Mexican corruption through his 'ticket theory' which originated from one conversation he had with a person living amongst it. One day a Mexican Police officer directed the person to stop its vehicle. The officer told the person that their vehicle license plate ended in an even number, which means that on this date, only cars with odd numbers could travel to the interior of Mexico D.F. The government's attempt to reduce traffic and pollution.

The officer explains that if the person is willing to give him 20 dollars, the officer will not write a ticket. The officer indicates that the ticketed offense costs 40 dollars in fines and court fees. The person pays the officer 20 dollars, and both go their separate ways. The person revealed that the police officer was friendly, for saving the person 20 dollars. Nowhere, in the conversation, did the person mention corruption. Bribery is endemic throughout the system.

However, corruption is not always black and white if you are poor. A person with limited means cannot afford the ineffective, without credibility hated government requirements; they have to go to the 'fixers.' The fixers fill the gray area. They have no other recourse. Is it right, who knows?

Seamus' bosses in Houston are aware of the information exchange with the Mex Feds. However, they are not mindful of Seamus' Mexico operations. Seamus random in his thoughts, wonders if Mexico would tell the US that the traditional smuggling routes into the US have been highjacked and regularly used to transport bomb components or terrorists? Alternatively, would the Mexican government remain silent until the tragic events occurred in the United States? Would they hope, cross its fingers that most of the smuggled evidence or persons are obliterated. Would anybody be held accountable in Mexico?

Like the United Nations peacekeeper who watches in dismay as Rwandans are hacked to death right in front of he/she because orders are given not to intercede, the field agent is 'handcuffed' in much the same way. At present, this inability to effectively act on foreign soil is perceived by the traffickers as a covert activity when, in fact, there is limited activity. When the traffickers reach the conclusion of inaction by US authorities, you may as well get the hell out of the way. Illicit drug prices have remained constant. Increased effectiveness should result in increased rates. Seamus does not realize the Black Cat, and his new terror group concluded for some time that there is no covert police activity.

So, what about the lone wolf terrorist? What if intelligence does not exist identifying large groups of terrorists associated with the lone wolf? That is a dangerous thought. Hum.

Yuri standing at a nearby store near the Black Cat's office smokes a filter less cigarette, and observes the small compact containing Seamus O'Malley and the Mex Fed Maria circling the church and the priests' office. Yuri smirks, what an idiot that O'Malley is.

"Now, what do we do?" Seamus asks while eating the remaining of a gordita managing to spill half of it on his new jeans. Portions of the gordita fall between his legs onto the car's seat cushion.

"Look for dope. Ha. I do not think the Black Cat is there. It looks unoccupied and deserted. If we go in, we should enter the church. Blend in. We will only have one shot at this. It will look bad to walk up to the office door and find it is locked. How would you explain your second approach? You will lose your ability to conduct an ambush interview. Let's wait until we confirm someone is there. Let's go get a drink." Maria is speaking at 78 revolutions per minute. "I know a great bar; it is close to here. Wait it out for a bit and come back."

"He won't have the dope, yes." Barely listening to her. "Let's go inside and seek an audience. We came this far." Seamus responds feeling like he needs to win one battle after losing one with his lunch.

"Oh no, I can't, there's nobody there," She slows the car.

"Well, I can. The Black Cat and or this Jose guy don't know who I am. I look like a typical tourist. I think my clothes will confirm that." Seamus steps from the rolling car. Maria unsuccessfully reaches with her right hand to stop him. Seamus walks towards the office. She's in shambles. Yuri drops his cigarette from his mouth, burning his shirt as it falls to the ground.

Seamus enters the office.

"Yes, may I help you?" Jose asks, walking from the hall to the central office area.

"Yes. Do you speak English?" Seamus does not wait for a response. "I would like to know what your mass schedule is? I am visiting the city for a few days." Seamus is amateurish in his one-sided conversation. He memorized what he is going to say and blurts it all at once to the individual.

Jose introduces himself to Seamus in English and says, "They are daily at six a.m.., twelve p.m. and five thirty p.m. and on weekends…."

So, this is Jose. O'Malley asks if English masses are available. Jose says there is an English mass on Wednesdays at three p.m. O'Malley thanks him for the schedules. O'Malley asks to use the restroom as his stomach is turning somersaults from the lunch.

"Of course," Jose replies.

Jose leads O'Malley by the Black Cat's desk. The Black Cat's not present. The Black Cat is detained by his Eminence in Mexico City and will not return to Matamoros until Saturday evening. Maybe. It is noon on Saturday.

The Black Cat relayed the possibility of a visit. Lacking photographs of the two, Jose suspects the American is O'Malley. He is supposed to be accompanied by a female. It's odd the way the stranger arrives with no family in tow. Single men asking for the mass schedule in Matamoros is a rarity. Vacationers are not here for religion. What is he supposed to do, kill him in the office? The Black Cat told Jose that Yuri would handle the entire O'Malley matter. Letting O'Malley in the office is handling the issue? For Christ sake, he is standing in their office, a bold move by the American. Typical though. Americans always assume they are invincible. Chewing their gum and bouncing as they walk thinking they are impervious to death, so confident.

Jose bets this O'Malley never encountered twelve years of age African males wearing women's dresses and wigs carrying AK47s and machetes during the ever-going African revolts. Jose has.

As Jose leads O'Malley through the office, O'Malley observes the impact in a wall caused by what has to be a bullet. What appears to be a bullet fragment is in the wall. There is still a bullet casing underneath the desk. What a stroke of luck!

"What was I supposed to do?" the Mex Fed Maria speaks through the open passenger window.

"You stupid M.F.." Yuri speaks intently, "Don't stop, circle the car around the block. Convince him that this was too dangerous. Maybe surveil the place and then go have a few drinks at the cantina. Your captain's people are waiting there!"

"Yes sir, yes, I can still do that!"

"You will still do that," Yuri orders, "no telling what could happen in there."

"Thank you," O'Malley says as Jose shows him the restroom. Jose is frantic while O'Malley remains in the bathroom. Jose is rubbing his hands together; pacing the floor. This American seems to know everything. O'Malley wonders if Jose knows who he is. O'Malley needs to create a diversion. Forget about his stomach pains.

"Fire! Fire!" O'Malley yells running from the restroom. O'Malley is laughing at the absurdly of his action and dances about the office, "Fire! Fire!" pointing to the restroom. O'Malley draped toilet paper from the roll to the agape restroom window and used a scented lit candle on the bathroom sink to light the paper. The fire climbs the cement walls.

Jose runs into the restroom, back into the hall and then to the bathroom sink for water to extinguish the fire. O'Malley passes him in the hallway. He cannot be the American; he's an idiot. He has got to be a crazy guy. My paranoia is killing me! Where is he?

O'Malley goes directly to the Black Cat's desk. It is the Black Cat's desk as framed pictures are on its surface. Pictures of Jose and others, but the common denominator is the tall skinny male dressed in black, Sanchez, the Black Cat. He digs the slug out of the wall and retrieves the bullet casing. What are the chances that the bullet from the wall matches the one found in the seat frame examined by his homicide buddy? The specialized bullet lifted by O'Malley at the burnt-out assassins' car. Shit! He commits arson in Mexico. In a few seconds, the flames will extinguish. Fuck them.

A brief flame snaps from the restroom window to the street. Yuri stands transfixed on the window. If he did not need the cute one, she would be dead, now. Pressure builds in Yuri's head. A pain develops over his right eye. Are his eyes bleeding?

"You were sent to me to monitor O'Malley's activities, and look, now!" Yuri points to the Black Cat's office.

"Do you want your money back?" She thinks Yuri has overstepped his bounds as this is her country.

Yuri is incensed at the remark. His eyes bore into her exhibiting pure rage and hatred. Both recognized they reached the crossroads in their relationship.

"I'll get him out of there!"

"No need, he is running out of the front door. Get O'Malley and get him to the bar."

"Yes, comrade Lenin, yes, comrade Stalin," Maria sarcastically replies. No wonder Russian General Secretary Andropov, a KGB guy, lasted just a year and a few months on top —acute kidney failure. She'd drink every day too. These Russians are ruthless. She knew not to mess with Yuri, but he pissed her off. She hopes there is a way to make amends.

O'Malley in full trot runs across the street. His tall legs are galloping like a donkey, not a thoroughbred. He looks for Maria.

Maria positions the car closer to O'Malley and stops. O'Malley enters the vehicle and sits on the front passenger seat.

"Jesus, let's get out of here!"

"I got it. I got a bullet and a casing from Sanchez's, the Black Cat's office."

"What?" Maria's face turns white and simultaneously feels a pain in her left chest. It can't be true. "What, what did you say?" She cannot believe it.

Yuri watches the car speed away. His face flushed and lights another cigarette. At least, it heads in the direction of the cantina.

Seamus repeats, "The bullet had to be fired by someone in the office. It had to be the Black Cat. It was right near his desk. Maybe, he killed someone in there. Who knows? The odds are completely against there being a match, but what the hell."

"Oh, Dios (God)." Immediately by her tone, O'Malley realizes he is set up. Anybody else would be ecstatic; she isn't. Maria is in deep thought. She acquires a nervous tick to her lower lip.

He burned down or almost burned down a Mexican church on a weekend stroll with a turncoat Mex Fed. How can he write this letter to his supervisor? Forget that, move on. Without a suspecting voice, O'Malley says, "I have to hit the restroom again, my stomach is killing me."

"What is wrong with you? You need to learn to let things go."

"I was scared to death in there. We came to see these people."

She regains her composure. Her orders are to proceed to Rosarios Cantina. Go there as instructed by Yuri or bury yourself. Her captain's men await at the bar. They will take care of O'Malley once and for all. His death will resemble a drunk rolled by a prostitute.

The car screams down narrow dusty streets with limited signage from the tourist area and enters the barrio. The weakened shock absorbers cause the vehicle to bounce and squeak uncontrollably. O'Malley asks where they are going, but she ignores him. O'Malley inquires again. She ignores his questions. She should have just said, oh this is the way to the bar, and that would have placated O'Malley, but she does not. Sweat pours from O'Malley's head. His fate appears to be sealed, from Diocese dancer to dead US agent.

Watching the uptick in the Mex Fed's vehicle speed combined with O'Malley's demonstrative hand motions towards the Mex Fed Maria, US Intelligence officer Socorro without speaking rockets with abandon over the potholes and discarded trash creating a tornado effect of rising debris in the rear of the car also occupied by US Intelligence officer Todd. Socorro and Todd strain their eyes to maintain a line of sight on O'Malley; there is no need in remaining covert.

They received data of the impending trip by the Mex
Fed Maria and Seamus to Matamoros. While en route, they
received incomplete information that 'elimination' or
'conclusion of a problem' was to coincide with the
Matamoros trip. The recent data leads them to believe that
Seamus' life is at stake. They cannot trust local assets in
such a delicate matter, so Socorro and Todd decide to
conduct unilateral surveillance in Matamoros. They are
now providing their first aid to Seamus. They conclude
that Seamus needs a diversion.

With a clearing of traffic on the narrow street, Socorro
maneuvers the vehicle into the intersection three cars
behind the Mex Feds vehicle. Todd holds a Heckler and
Koch MP5 weapon within the passenger window out of the
pedestrians' view. Todd is cognizant not to shoot the Mex
Fed, nor does he want to harm Seamus.

Based on the angle of their vehicle to the Mex Feds
vehicle, Todd's forced to shoot the back-right window in a
trajectory that will not come close to Seamus. The first
shot bounces off the Mex Feds rear window sending it
careening into a wall. The second shot pierces the back
window sending the bullet through the back-seat passenger
window and into the same wall. After the second shot,
Socorro swerves the vehicle left while in the intersection
disguising it from the Mex Fed's view and for that matter
any other unobserved counter surveillance. Socorro
immediately positions the car in a parallel path to the Mex
Feds vehicle on an adjacent street.

At the sound of the breaking rear glass, O'Malley jumps
from the vehicle and falls onto the unforgiving rocky road
rolling into a curbside metal juice cart. The juice glass
bottles hit each other, spilling the tropical red cherry juices
onto his shoulders. His head hits the ground. He touches
his head a small amount of blood is present, and a bruise
already swells. The cherry juice makes his wound appear
more omnifarious. The Mex Fed does not hesitate in

stopping the vehicle in the street and commences to fire as if it is her dying act wildly.

Bullets ricochet amongst the adobe, concrete and brick walls that line the streets. O'Malley continues to run; a running target is harder to hit. Cops practice shooting at stationary paper targets; he hopes the Mex Fed did the same. She probably only possesses a few bullets.

The bullets are skipping off walls and cars — seconds behind him. Innocent pedestrians duck for cover and some layout on the ground, spilling groceries and goods throughout the sidewalks and streets. Vehicles occupants in the impact area are only able to sprawl out on the floors of their cars as only a few lead drivers sped from the scene. There is no method to her volley, except that this Mex Fed was not going down until she expends all of her ammo. The Mex Fed pursues O'Malley on foot, slowing to a stop when she loads her magazines and charges her weapon.

O'Malley's heart pounds because of the bullets zipping by him, but also the possibility of being wounded, captured, tortured, and then killed. His boss will do nothing to save his ass. Why is he doing this? Maybe, he is at a time in his life when he seeks adventure or a sense of doing something significant.

As the Mex Fed reloads her weapon, the street fills with additional civilians, as this is a daylight shooting. It must be 'amateur hour,' the pedestrians think.

With her head down, loading her gun, O'Malley escapes through a door along the street and exits onto the opposite road.

Now, as the Mex Fed fired shots at O'Malley, Todd readies his weapon to kill the Mex Fed. Socorro drives the vehicle through the intersection in front of the abandoned Mex Feds car. Todd sees O'Malley run into the first door.

Socorro turns the car just in time to see O'Malley exit a building on the opposite side and then on to the sidewalk. With a bullet and casing in his pocket, he's on his own.

Race to the border, before communication alerts the Mexican Border Guards. Simple. He rubs his head again. The bump is pronounced. O'Malley walks fast on the sidewalk observed by both Todd and Socorro. Todd places a jacket over his weapon and sets it beside his right leg next to the door.

Socorro positions the car so that Todd is on the same side as O'Malley.

"Get in the back seat," Todd says through the open car window.

O'Malley somewhat confused wonders if heard English.

"Get in the car." The car's keeping pace with O'Malley's steps. Todd repeats in a way a buddy would ask a close friend. A friend who was involved in a bar fight and summarily thrown out of the bar and now in need of a ride home.

"We saw what happened. You have no chance of getting out of here.
 Make a decision. If we are bad people, we will not let you sit in the back seat, unrestrained."

Socorro scans all three of the vehicle's mirrors for threats.

O'Malley enters the vehicle. Socorro slowly drives from the street entering a complex maze of alleys and rocky roads leading to the US border city adjacent to Matamoros: Brownsville, Texas. O'Malley does not ask the identities of these people, and they do not ask who he is.

As they near the border, Socorro says, "This is as far as we can go. Walk to the other side. Be careful."

With all that had happened, O'Malley's looking directly at Socorro's legs. Those are running legs, shapely. Man, she's beautiful. She catches him staring. She looks at the road in front of them and makes a small smile. Oh, he is crazy but exciting. It is a mystery what people ponder in a crisis, Socorro wonders what his house is like, no apartment. No, he probably lives in a camper. Full of empty beer bottles and dirty clothes. He's a workaholic, back to work.

There are no silly parting remarks by the two individuals to forget them. Alternatively, this assistance never happened. They do not say they are tourists and just driving by. Seamus is not about to question their presence as he knows they would give a nebulous response. Secondly, if the truth be told, he does not want to know. Also, thirdly, if he asks the two who they are, they will probably think he is an idiot. Are these two individuals responsible for breaking the Med Feds rear window? Most likely. Are they monitoring his activities? Who are they?

If ever by chance asked by his management to identify the two, he would answer what two people? In reality, he is at a loss in describing the male, but he's capable of expressing every part of the beautiful woman. Seamus will make it his mission in life to find this lady again.

Seamus exits the vehicle and follows their recommendations. Socorro drives the car in a westerly direction from the border out of sight of Seamus.

"Let's get back as soon as possible this was a confirmed attempted hit on an American. On top of that, a US Special Agent."

"Ol' red face, the fat woman's wire will be down after this fuck up," Todd adds.

Socorro then calls their supervisor Rebecca on the encrypted phone and provides a short a brief.

"They've elevated this shit. We can't just stand by. Like, we already talked if this is confirmed and it now is, I'll make the arrangements right now to have the "three" make haste in our direction. It's on."

Socorro unsuccessfully tries to get a word in. Rebecca continues, "We can't let old red face get away, with y'alls work we know her pattern of life. Get back as soon as possible. You and I know "his" people will not want to act because they think he is "rogue." More importantly, they will not even believe him. He has unjustifiably lost credibility in their eyes."

"Got it," responds Socorro. The line is disconnected. "Man, Rebecca is seething."

"Good, it's about time we go proactive."

Within minutes, Seamus makes it to the Texas border. He briskly walks to a car rental agency returns to his Laredo apartment, gathers his belongings, and immediately seeks refuge in a hotel.

Seamus placed numerous ice packs on his head on the long drive to Laredo. His neck is killing him. It's over. Will, they kill him in the US? Kidnap him? Shit, he's in trouble. Once he settles down, he knows the Mex Feds will not make this an issue. Tomorrow or Monday he will go to work, process the bullet and casing. His actions are a borderline sovereignty issue.

Seamus will list the Mex Fed Maria's name in a report detailing the initial finding of the bullet and casing in the Nuevo Laredo area related to the burnt car. He will need to get that evidence back from the homicide guy. Seamus will list her name on a second report detailing the discovery of the bullet and casing in Matamoras. If the Mex Fed is reported dead, his story will be validated, and he will finally be allowed to go home. Although the Mexican government could blame him for her death, his gut tells him the Mexican government will not respond that way.

Seamus O'Malley contacts his homicide buddy who states that he needs the suspect weapon to match the bullets. The homicide detective has to fire the gun in a water drum or something like that and then compare the finds. Seamus tells the detective there is no weapon. The detective says again he can examine the casings and determine the factory of origin, but it will require official correspondence from O'Malley's office. Seamus tells him thanks and asks that the detective mail the evidence to his

Houston office. Seamus believes that he will be sent home. His evidence chain of custody is in tatters.

Immediately, the shit hits the fan, and the Laredo supervisor, Bill transfers O'Malley back to the home office. Sovereignty, sovereignty, O'Malley can finally spell the word. He awaits days off, threats, and silent treatments. O'Malley lives up to his label 'a rogue agent.'

The evidence listed in the reports will take months to process. Management then stalls O'Malley's request for analysis and puts the case further on the back burner. Mexico authorities report the purported suicide of the Mex Fed Maria. She went missing following the Matamoros incident. Coincidently, Mexico's willingness to exchange information with the US in the Laredo area terminates.

O'Malley at his Houston residence cannot sleep. Something is bothering him. The feeling is similar to the deja vu he experienced at his house while talking to his neighbor, Jenkins. Is he alone?

Seamus searches the house and senses evil, feels it. He moves to the dark hallway and observes a face with dark red eyes; its mocking laugh pierces his eardrums. Seamus covers his ears. A chill speeds towards him, so he races to his bedroom, grabbing his weapon and returns to the hall. Seamus thinks it is threatening him. Can it be him? He aims his gun at it. It disappears, and the laugh slowly recedes.

The laughter and feeling are different from the helpful vision in the desert; it is menacing. The doctor said he had a concussion. This vision is dangerous. He turns on the lights and walks the length of the hall, nothing. He is now entirely confused. He was drunk during the first vision at the burnt car and now with a concussion sees and hears this. Although it is exhausting, it is time to increase his situational readiness.

Chapter Twenty

Days pass without home office administrative backlash giving Seamus a momentary sense of job security. He's moved within his Houston home office to 'the land of broken toys.' Arriving at his new group, he recognizes agents in various forms of trouble from travel voucher discrepancies, to sexual harassment claims from the translators in the 'vaulted' wire room, to agent Murphy who recently told his boss to go fuck himself. Seamus sits next to agent Murphy. Seamus weighs into his rickety, broken chair, causing him to lean to the right. He gathers paperwork spread throughout his desktop and feeds all of it into the shredder, not bothering to ask anyone if the papers belonged to them. Finds the closest coffee pot to rob and returns to his desk. As he sits, Murphy points at the supervisor's plant, 'agent do- nothing' living on the mantra, 'no cases no problems.' Seamus nods in the affirmative. Seamus has to wait until someone else screws up, and the blow torch will move to them.

Seamus spends his days reading various newspapers. Weapon experts tour Iraq; British and the Real IRA warring. He reviews a list of the number of the Real IRA bombings, attempted bombings, and murders. The numbers are staggering. How difficult is it to stop determination, the Real IRA thinks the original IRA is weak, so the Real IRA continues the struggle. Interesting?

There's an update on the USS Cole incident. Vatican City seeks disputed lands in Russia. Chief Vatican negotiator identified as Bishop Sanchez. "What? I never knew that! All I had to do is read the newspaper. The Black Cat is a negotiator?" Typical, Open Sources: newspapers, books, and magazines tend to provide timely valuable Intel. Confidential information is just that 'confidential not disseminated' and the corollary of no use to anyone.

Seamus now knows Sanchez, the Black Cat, is a narcotics trafficker who played a role in the Colonel and the Cardinal's killing. Seamus followed evidence leading him to Matamoros. Why else would they try to kill him? That's how the Mexicans get rid of the good cops. Especially, cops/agents interfering with their business. It's just in their nature.

What can he do? Seamus' hands are tied. He can't say, "Mexico," without being questioned by his new supervisor. For an agent to travel abroad, the agent needs prior country approval from that country's personnel that the agent plans to visit. Seamus now requires authorization to go from the Houston office to the outer highway loop.

Seamus asks Murphy, his new office buddy the supervisors' whereabouts. Murphy reveals they are attending the weekly afternoon management conference. Ok, at this time his last three 'political' supervisors have approached the eighth hole.

Seamus visualizes the 'politicals' standing in a row on the green. O'Malley, his new pod mate, Murphy and a few others especially, wild man Moody, are the topic. The mention of their names causes them to cup their hands. The first covers his ears, the second covers his mouth, and the third covers her mouth, Larry, Curly and Ms. Moe. After the brief conversation, one supervisor after the other fold their arms across their chest and state in sequence, "Rogue, malcontent, disgruntled government employee, and what an idiot." All three then say, "Yup, Yup, and Yup," frown and bob their heads in affirmation. The remaining of the management meeting identifies who can get them promoted or transferred to a better Field Office. "Four!"

Disturbing his thoughts, an 'office do-nothing' walks by his and Murphy's hallway pods. Hallway pods they both believe will eventually be moved to the stairway.

177

"Oh. I see a bruised head. Did you get rolled by a whore down there? He, He." The nerd squeaks like a house mouse.

"You might say I rolled down there."

"What are you two working on?"

"Nothing you can comprehend. It has nothing to do with planning birthday parties or women baby showers."

"Damn, shot across the bow," Murphy laughs. "Awesome."

The do-nothing shakes his head and walks away.

"Probably running upstairs to see his 'daddy.' Fucking manifest safety hazard."

"Man, you are angry."

"Fuck hem."

In the meantime, unidentified friends acquire an old Hawker Siddeley corporate aircraft (A/C) for use by Cardinal Vazquez's large staff for travel to the upcoming negotiations. For security reasons, the same friends allow the aircraft to base at a Fixed Based Operator (FBO) at Benito Juarez International Airport in Mexico City, unheard of as only commercial planes have access to this busy airport. The few private A/C making use of the Benito Juarez airport have been granted authorization from the highest Mexican authorities.

Correspondence from the Russian government distributed to the participants in the impending discussions advises that the talks will take place soon, and the delegates are encouraged to fly into Moscow's main airport. The Hawker Siddeley aircraft is capable of making the trip to Moscow, Russia with a fuel stop at Teterboro, New Jersey Airport and a subsequent safety/fuel stop at Heathrow Airport, Great Britain. Maintenance and excessive fuel consumption can change the route. The fuel stops allow the aircraft occupants, including the pilots time to use the FBO facilities, obtaining beverages and food.

Law enforcement is not expected to search the aircraft as its flight will be designated by someone, who, is not known, as a quasi or diplomatic flight on behalf of Mexico or Vatican City, but it is not entirely clear to the Black Cat if that is true. After all, what country will officially sign off on this bold smuggling plan? The aircraft manifest identifies the occupants of the aircraft. The Black Cat will instruct each occupant when asked by the authorities that they are on an official mission on behalf of the Mexican and Vatican City governments. Additionally, the priests, including Bishop Sanchez and Cardinal Vazquez are to wear church vestments when landing at each destination.

In Mexico City, a small non-descript cargo truck transports several boxes to the entrance of the FBO's controlled access gate. The FBO has a small passenger terminal, an aircraft repair station and a fuel truck. While parked on the exterior of the controlled entrance gate, the truck driver calls the FBO receptionist. She tells the receptionist of a delivery destined for the Cardinals' aircraft, all perfectly legal. The driver receives clearance from the receptionist who remotely opens the gate. The truck driver moves the truck to the opposite side of the gate and stops. The gate closes, allowing only one vehicle to enter the tarmac at a time. The truck driver drives its contents onto the tarmac and parks next to the Cardinal's aircraft. The Black Cat personally loads the boxes to the back of the plane behind a rear curtain and closes the broken storage door. Some of their luggage will have to go between the seats.

At the bottom of each box are kilograms of cocaine covered by a combination of baby formula cans, children clothes, baby wipes, expensive Tequila bottles, and pharmaceuticals. "What a deal! Too easy," the Black Cat thinks.

Diplomats have been known to use diplomatic pouches to smuggle something at one time or another, but not to this magnitude. The boxes contain a total of three hundred kilograms of cocaine. The Black Cat marks the boxes as diplomatic. The Black Cat knows the first delivery is a test load. If, the first smuggling venture is successful, more significant amounts will follow.

Before departure, Yuri directs the Black Cat to mark the boxes 'Property of Vatican City,' and Vatican City insignia tape affixed on the same. The tape and markings should reduce over anxious custom officers' inquiries. The Black Cat obtains the Vatican tape from Monsignor Romero based in Mexico City, the designated conduit to Vatican City. Initially, the Monsignor said that you don't just give "this stuff away." The Black Cat mentions the contents of the boxes are a small conciliatory gesture to "our friends" in Moscow.

Romero is not aware of the cocaine's presence. Romero asks why do you need the tape? The Black Cat explains that at least five of the boxes contain the finest Mexican tequila valued at $130.00 per bottle. The Black Cat offers to show the bottles to the Monsignor, knowing he will not wish to view the bottles. The Monsignor is very good with finances. He adds the customs duties if declared. The Monsignor delays, the Black Cat repeats that our friends in Moscow requested the tape. It's just tequila. The Monsignor relents and coordinates an overnight tape delivery from Vatican City to Mexico City. The Monsignor does not want the blame if the Catholic Church is unsuccessful in its bid for the disputed lands because the Russians tequila is tampered with or seized. It's just tape.

If by chance a narcotic canine is present at the delegation's arrival in a particular country and the canine 'hits' on a specific box, the Black Cat is prepared to open it. He will display the pharmaceuticals as the reason for the 'positive hit.' He will use all of his persuasive powers and is determined to remain calm throughout the route. It is a huge responsibility.

No problem, the flight departs Mexico, fuels at its designated points and subsequently arrives in Moscow, the site of the Vatican/Eastern/Russian talks. It is almost anticlimactic at how easy it was to transport cocaine to Russia.

Don Pedro and Yuri's organizations exercised extreme tradecraft. Everyone with a role in the transaction is given just enough information and duties to complete the individual task — the taskings given to the subjects as close to the time of the deed. In the event an Informant is in the mix, each person's role compartmentalized not allowing anyone to put the pieces together.

Arriving in Moscow, Yuri and his associates drive two vehicles through the FBO gate and park next to the Cardinals' aircraft. The boxes are loaded into the cars and transported from the FBO. Let's say, a cost of $11,000.00 a kilogram of cocaine in Mexico with a minimum price of 38,000.00 a kilogram of cocaine in Russia, when the shipment transits through the back door (east) of Europe. A gross profit of $8,100,000.00, pretty good for a test load. The Black Cat is incredulous.

The Colombian Jorge had to predict everything that was going to happen. Jorge has to be in charge of Don Pedro's air operations. The scheme is too easy; law enforcement did not conduct searches on the corporate plane. Maybe, law enforcement viewed the aircraft itinerary before it arrived in New Jersey. Law enforcement must have designated the flight as a non-priority as no narcotic canines were at the fuel stops.

Since 911, the Black Cat knows the bulk of the worlds law enforcement canines have moved to commercial airport terminals, bus terminals, ship terminals, the subways, courthouses, and for use in law enforcement traffic stops. At each fuel stop, the occupants of the aircraft provided their passports to the pilots who in turn gave them to the respective border officials for viewing. The officials

181

reviewed each passport, unable to find derogatory information and returned them to the passengers.

According to Jorge, while traveling within the US, passengers making use of private aircraft enjoy the luxury of no personal or baggage police searches. Metal detectors are not present at the FBO's. Also, there are minimal searches upon making entry into various countries. How much dope, weapons, unscrupulous people, and terrorists for that matter fly in corporate planes within the US without interdiction?

Based on the Black Cat's observations, law enforcement does not deem corporate aircraft a threat. The use of larger planes than their Hawker Siddeley would eliminate the need to stop at various countries. A nonstop flight from one corrupt country to another would be a goldmine in revenue, but more importantly, a secure means to transport the principals, those in command and control or real terrorists spreading their ideology. The use of corporate aircraft is the way to go.

While in Moscow, the negotiations between the Russian General Comstock, the Vatican represented by Cardinal Vazquez and Bishop Sanchez/The Black Cat and the Eastern Orthodox Church represented by Bishop Papadakos continue for three days. The Black Cat treats the other Catholic delegates as a nuisance. He slyly insults and shames the two Bishops for their lack of geographic and historical knowledge of the lost Catholic lands. As a result, the Bishops remain silent during the talks.

The initial discussions reveal that the negotiations will continue for at least six to eight months. It is apparent to the Black Cat that Yuri and Don Pedro have covertly succeeded in taking advantage of the open talks. They will reap massive profits. By agreeing to supply the cocaine, Don Pedro's Cali Cartel might be paying back the Russians for their participation in the Cardinal's assassination. Because of the assassination, the Culiacan based Medellin

Cartel is fighting for its life. Don Pedro's profits will soar with the acquisition of these new Medellin Cartel routes.

The aircraft plan detailed that the proceeds from the sale of the cocaine would return on the same delegation's corporate aircraft. Yuri's team members advised the purchasers a tight window for repatriation existed. So, the purchasers set aside a large amount of the debt anticipating a lag in some of the account's receivables from Eastern Europe. When Yuri's organization controlled the aircraft contents, the former Minister of Mexico Gomez received his first wire transfer to the Geneva bank.

The second delivery of cocaine will probably consist of five hundred kilograms of cocaine. The corporate aircraft will approach its manufactured weight capacity. Traffickers seldom abide by safety recommendations. The Black Cat may have to reduce the number of the Mexican negotiation team or direct some to travel commercially. The pilots, as with all pilots, already complained about the idea of adding more weight. The pilots do not even consider to look into the luggage or boxes. They are experienced Mexican based contract pilots who have turned off their curiosity meter years ago.

In a subsequent meeting with the Colombian, Jorge in Mexico City, the Black Cat suggested to Jorge, Don Pedro's air operations manager, that five hundred kilograms might require that weights are placed in the aircraft nose to offset the additional burden placed in the rear of the plane. The Black Cat is not an aircraft expert, but he is intelligent enough to discuss the issues. Jorge explains that the aircraft nose is fiberglass and any modifications there might interfere with the installed aircraft avionics located in the plane's nose. Jorge asks the Black Cat to obtain solutions from the pilots.

Regardless, the Black Cat is to stress the increased weights are not negotiable. The extra weight will affect fuel consumption and have some effect on the plane's maneuverability. If the pilots feel compelled to fly at the highest altitude in the thinnest air to reduce fuel consumption bouncing off the atmosphere, then so be it. Assure that the aircraft oxygen tanks are full. The occupants might have to suck oxygen at those heights.

With its weight constraints, the use of the aircraft is still the best mode of smuggling. In general, corporate aircraft can fly over countries in various states of confusion. Fly over law enforcement, terrorists, and smuggler roadblocks eliminating interdiction.

Just think about it, Jorge would say to the Black Cat when you drive your car, you can be stopped by law enforcement at any time. There are thousands of private planes. They can't search each one when it lands. You don't get pulled over in the sky. Because of the Montreal Convention, aircraft can fly over countries without being forced to land or stopped and searched. States cannot shoot down civilian aircraft. Well, there is one South American country that will light you up if you do not land when ordered. However, this plane is not traveling there. If law enforcement believes the aircraft is smuggling weapons, people, money, dope, you name it, they cannot shoot you down, so take advantage of it while it lasts.

Yuri's boys in Russia acquired almost all the one-hundred-dollar bills in Russia and placed them in newly acquired suitcases. Using the higher valued currency reduced weight and space for the return trip to Mexico City. The Black Cat places the luggage in the aircraft's storage area.

Upon his return to Mexico City, the Black Cat generally remains in his room at the Shrine of Our Lady of Guadalupe except for the meeting mentioned above with Jorge. It was at that meeting that Jorge briefed the Black Cat on additional aircraft capabilities, and both discussed a general smuggling timeline.

As Acting Bishop in Matamoras, Mexico, Jose continues his mundane duties. Jose occasionally travels to the Mexico City Shrine and meets with his boss the Black Cat updating him on local church business. The main reason for his travels is to get away from the haunting memories of Nuevo Laredo. In Mexico City, the Black Cat provides Jose limited details of his and Yuri's new relationship. These generalities are tactfully eliciting Jose's experienced input. To Jose, the Black Cat was initially concerned about his new appointment, but for some reason, the Black Cat is becoming comfortable and confident.

With the assistance of local Matamoros traffickers and contrary to Don Pedro's orders, Jose orchestrates the smuggling of the Black Cat's smaller independent loads. The Black Cat permits him to do this. The Black Cat realizes it is necessary to keep Jose content while he is away. Also, they need to fill their depleted resources.

By allowing Jose to work on the smaller Matamoros loads, the Black Cat hopes to divert Jose's unhealthy fixation on the recent assassinations. Jose confided to the Black Cat his visions of the female twin disappearing and reappearing after the Colonel's murder. Jose's disclosure is not taken lightly as he too is severely impacted after killing the twin. The Black Cat does not tell Jose of his nocturnal visions, nor the images he sees racing towards him during mass.

Jose coordinates small amounts of cocaine, five kilograms at a time, by tractor-trailer through the US/Mexican border. Mexican law enforcement interdiction at Mexico's northeastern border effectively ceased to exist — a result of the ongoing war between the Medellin Cartel and the Mexican government in the Culiacan area. So far, Jose's loads penetrate the US border at an 86% success rate.

The secreted loads of cocaine are then transported northbound on highways 281 and 77 crossing the US

Border Patrol checkpoints at Falfurrias and Sarita, Texas respectively. The two inspection stations are southwest of Corpus Christi. If these checkpoints are a hive of police activity, then Jose will instruct another group to take receipt of the cocaine from the driver before the Sarita or Falfurrias checkpoints. This group by truck or foot walks around the Sarita and Falfurrias checkpoints and delivers the cocaine back to the tractor-trailer driver.

Presently, Jose drives as a 'lookout' in advance of a tractor-trailer with a secreted load. His duty to determine the existence of marked or unmarked law enforcement vehicles on the highway and to advise their presence to the tractor-trailer driver. Jose has to decide if law enforcement is conducting 'speed traps' or interdiction.

On this particular route, Jose plans to travel to Houston, Texas where he will direct the tractor-trailer driver to 'offload' its cocaine to Jose's designees. Following the Houston delivery, Jose will travel to Dallas, Texas. In Dallas, he will reside at the Hyatt downtown hotel, relax and party with some personal use. He's becoming lazy and confident; the recent cataclysmic events cause him to abuse drugs at an excessive rate.

Jose varies his northbound travels in concert with the tractor-trailer. At times, he leads and then follows the truck. His disparities are intended to throw off unseen law enforcement aircraft surveillance who may become interested in their movements. Jose, leading the tractor-trailer, exits the freeway while the tractor-trailer continues north. Jose drives to gas pumps operated by a nearby convenience store. He enters the store gives the attendant thirty dollars to be credited to the gas pump. He does not want to leave a 'paper trail' as the route has been successful. Jose returns to the vehicle and sets the pump handle to fill the tank. Back to the convenience store to go to the restroom, then returns to his car. Jose is not going to relieve himself in empty water bottles as the trucker was doing throughout the trip. The tractor-trailer driver is discarding the bottles of urine from the truck's window creating his yellow brick road. After filling the vehicle's gas tank, Jose accelerates eventually reaching the highway. It will take many minutes to catch the tractor-trailer truck traveling at the posted speed.

As Jose approaches within a mile of the tractor-trailer, he witnesses the activation of emergency lights from a Texas Department of Public Safety (DPS) trooper's vehicle directing the truck driver to slow on the shoulder of the highway. He sees the rear of the trailer swerve left a result of the driver frantically turning his head to look in the driver side mirror in disbelief.

An additional trooper driving a low-profile vehicle with a jet-black paint scheme, bolts like an alligator from high weeds amongst the highway's feeder road. As Jose passes the trooper's car, he sees mud fly from his vehicle's rear tires. It skids in a controlled manner on the grass until reaching the hard surface causing the tires to squeal. Even with the road noise, Jose hears the tires squeal as well as the trooper engine's roar locking onto his vehicle.

There is no doubt; this gator is going to catch his prey. Jose realizes he and the trucker traveled into an interdiction team (Wolf Pack). The team possibly observed them mimic each other's actions on the highway. Alternatively, Jose and the trucker's activities are radioed from 'down south' to the first available troopers, or there is an Informant, a Source in his mist.

The worst part, Jose possesses a ¼ kilogram of almost pure cocaine in his car for use at the anticipated party. The gator is within striking distance. Jose will 'be popped.' He panics with the knowledge of his associations in the killing of the Colonel and the Cardinal. Paranoia directs his actions. Is this a directed traffic stop a result of the murders? Was the DPS alerted to his past indiscretions, and that is the real reason for the stop? He shakes, sweats, and sees black spots.

The inevitable arrest for possession of cocaine is nothing compared to what the Black Cat will do to him, ordered by Don Pedro. Jose nervously consents to a search of the vehicle. Seeing the 1/4 kilogram of dope in the trooper's hand, he says, "I'll tell you everything, but I'll only talk to Senor O'Malley." O'Malley is the only one capable of doing this right. He knows what is going on. Jose has a front row seat to the circus developing at the tractor-trailer stop. The trooper cuffs and stuffs the tractor-trailer driver into the trooper's backseat. Jose looks up but knows no support will come from that direction.

Chapter Twenty-One

"O'Malley!" yells O'Malley's new supervisor, John.

"What?" O'Malley yells back thinking, "What a dick this guy is. Doesn't he know I'm scanning open source material." O'Malley's in time out, benched. Will the administrative storm pass? Is John going to make him participate in the yearly evidence inventory, applicant background investigations, or duty agent for life?

Lately, Seamus O'Malley distastefully emulates office survival skills learned from the 'no cases, no problem' agents. Always look busy. Head down while at the desk. Periodically, splashing water on his forehead to resemble sweat. Walk the halls with miscellaneous paper in your hands, shaking your head back and forth, acting as though you are under considerable pressure. Nodding at people as you hurriedly pass. Your destination always the restroom.

"DPS at Corpus Christie, Texas called, and they have a crook named Jose."

"And." Not bothering to get out of his chair. Seamus will yell back at this dick. After all, John, the supervisor should get out his chair, first. The supervisor will lose much-coveted video game points if he leaves his office.

Seamus succumbs stands and walks to John's office. His 'pod mate' Murphy reading the 'discipline boards' decision of his suspension, raises his head and snickers, "You have been summoned to the principal's office." Management 101, if you treat your people like kids, they act like kids.

"Jose. Uhm…," the supervisor did not take notes of the phone conversation with DPS. "Uh, he's from Matamoros." John, not looking at Seamus, hits a computer key and takes out two alien ships. "Yea, um...was popped for a small amount of coke and will only talk to you." John looks up briefly, "How did he get your name?"

"What?" Seamus ignores the supervisor's question. The supervisor laser gun needs power.

John concentrates on the game, "Drive down there with your new buddy who needs anger management school- listen, take notes, do not ask too many questions, come back, and report. Do not go any further than that, understood?"

"Yes, Sir." This guy is clueless as to what transpired. Seamus leaves the office hearing the computer blare, "You are dead."

"Dammit!"

The trip down is euphoric; it has to be the same Jose who introduced himself at the Matamoras church. This lead could put the nail in the Black Cat's coffin. If you hang in there long enough leads like this come your way.

Seamus explains to Murphy, Jose's significance and his role within the Black Cat's organization.

Murphy asks, "What additional information did the supervisor provide about Jose's arrest?"

"Nothing, John did not take notes during the DPS call."

Murphy raises his arms in the air and adds, "John never takes notes allowing him deniability on everything. Why do you think he is down here with us? His people realize he is worthless. That says a lot."

Seamus and his new partner drive south on highway 59 then on to 77 towards Corpus Christi. The 'good time' radio blares.

Murphy was dying in the office. He is glad to be away from the nursery.

Chapter Twenty-Two

The transportation of the dope to Russia and the return of the proceeds was all too easy. Profits distributed in Russia to Comstock and his government partners. The proceeds are US currency because Russian rubles are not easily transferable. Don Pedro's profit returns on the delegation corporate plane. The subject who delivered the cocaine to the aircraft in Mexico City was replaced by another who retrieved the suitcases laden with the currency. The Cardinal is oblivious to the smuggling venture.

Don Pedro's money transfers to shell and shelf accounts located in Colombia, Panama, and Liechtenstein only to be wired into separate shell and shelf accounts created in the United States. Shell accounts can be formed by anyone, for anyone with limited due diligence into identifying the real identities of those involved. Shelf accounts are the same as shell accounts only that they have a supposedly historical existence. Proceeds of the cocaine sales, via the shell/shelf accounts, are invested into US and European brokerage accounts, property, vehicles, businesses, and aircraft.

A recent but limited safe transfer of illicit funds is the transfer of subject monies into US-based law firms. The funds held in abeyance for anticipated defense purposes. For whom? As with shell and shelf accounts, law firm personnel are not required to conduct due diligence in the identification of the real owners of the funds. Law firms are not bound to the same rules as financial institutions, namely banks which are required to 'know your customer.' The clients of the law firms transfer funds in and out of the designated accounts at the direction of 'somebody.' Investigating the origin of the client funds is difficult as one encounters attorney-client privilege. There are so many ways to hide ill-gotten proceeds, but the constant among the most successful traffickers is to make use of the most efficient financial system in the world, America.

The Russians are satisfied with the smuggling operation, and that's all that mattered. They are the real professionals in crime as their government's existence intertwines with crime and corruption — 'Thieves in law' Soviet criminals are well known in and outside of the Soviet penal system. A knee star tattoo means they hate government authority; a star tattoo on their chest or higher, means 'Beware.'

There is a historical liaison between the long-established criminal groups who operate regardless of who is in power whether Lenin, Stalin, or Krushev. The criminal groups work in unison with various Soviet regimes. It is a simple explanation of the Soviet system, but how dissimilar is it from Mexico. Upon abdication, deals are stuck for the safety of the Russian leader and his family. Not much different from Mexico. Did the present Soviet government originate from crime? Was the Soviet in charge a criminal when he accepted the position or did he become a criminal when in office?

Russian General Comstock exploits capabilities of weaker countries in facilitating the movement of narcotics from source countries like Colombia, Peru, and Bolivia, the final destination is generally Europe. He develops and maintains numerous smuggling routes. The various routes reap US currency for the Russian government. Russians are not wealthy enough to buy coke; vodka serves as a cheaper, more available substitute.

Drugs delivered to Russia are 'backdoored' into Europe via 'restless' states like Bosnia and Serbia. General

Comstock will eventually abandon his frontal assault of narcotics into Spain from Mexico and Colombia because the Spanish authorities have infiltrated the 'cell' resulting in recent seizures and arrests.

The Black Cat sits in his Shrine apartment smoking a fine Cuban cigar. The smoke leaves his open window and rolls over the rock and mortar wall topped with multi-colored glass fragments. The glass fragments cemented in the top of the wall act as a deterrent to trespassers. From his studies, he learned that man could destroy anything created by man. To prove his case, the simple use of cardboard or a small rug thrown over the glass fragments enables easy access to the trespassers.

How long can this last? Eventually, Don Pedro and Yuri will open the valve loading the plane beyond its capacity. It will take a real miracle to keep the aircraft aloft. The Black Cat will reduce the weight of the cover loads and allow fewer passengers.

The Cardinal views the goods as a nice gesture. The Cardinal's staff recently expressed to the Black Cat their concerns about the Cardinal's failing mental and physical health. The Black Cat will continue to exploit this weakness. Looking at the cigar smoke, he knows it will only take one Source and maybe two to expose the entire operation — the cigar smoke hides in the darkness, much like a Source.

Chapter Twenty-Three

Todd and Socorro, the US intelligence officers, conclude briefs on various cases to their boss, Rebecca. They move to an update regarding Russian involvement in their theatre, Mexico. A quick 'overall' before they act. Neither agent monopolizes this brief as they have enough on their plates. Plus, at this time in their careers, they are only interested in working cases, not managing.

Todd and Socorro identify a previously referenced Eastern European as a Russian National named Yuri. Yuri was intercepted on the Nuevo Laredo's portly woman, 'Ol' red face' telephone. 'Ol' red face' is also Russian. Her name is Netanya. As a result of the Matamoros 'cluster,' Netanya most likely 'dropped' the phone as calls have diminished. Netanya is really of no use to anybody, but us. She does not appear to be a decision maker, only a 'pass through.'

A subsequent analysis determines Yuri as a former Spetnaz soldier now operating as a Russian contractor. There is some mention that Yuri was present in Chechnya. It's believed that Yuri's boss is a regular Russian Army General with a last name of Comstock. HQS completed a bio of him. However, we do not have definitive evidence of Comstock's involvement in Yuri's and Netanya's activities.

As we put the investigative pieces together, there is a high probability the Russians were involved in Cardinal Torres' killing. Preliminary data leads one to believe that Yuri directs Bishop Sanchez aka The Black Cat.

The Mexican government reels once again because of the Cardinal's assassination in Culiacan. The 'hit' is another example of continued Russian involvement in the destabilization of Mexico. Secondly, indications lead us to believe the acquisition of hard currency is a byproduct of the Russian 'hit.' To what extent is not yet clear.

Continuing their brief to Rebecca, a new cable originating from their Kiev, Ukraine Country Office (KCO) distributed to Washington HQS then passed to the HQS Aircraft Investigative Group (AIG), Bogota CO (BCO) and the Mexico City Country Office (MCCO) seems to confirm linkage between Yuri, Comstock, and Sanchez/The Black Cat. Contents of the cable indicate that Sanchez makes use of an aircraft for travel from Mexico City to Moscow, Russia. Sanchez is a member of a Catholic delegation who wishes to acquire Russian Orthodox lands possibly accessible as a result of Glasnost. Catholic Church delegates compete for these disputed lands with Eastern Orthodox Church delegates. Both delegations are very much interested in acquiring the same properties as well as the new Russian parishioners and associated donations.

Socorro ends the cable brief stating, "The KCO Source reporting suspects the use of the delegation's aircraft in yet determined illegal activity."

During the brief, Todd and Socorro specifically leave out their meeting with Seamus' Border Patrol partner Pete as they crossed the line both figuratively and literally. With this recent information, they now have a bonafide investigation without a US nexus. They plan to request resources for the Russian case formally, but with the limited budget, they realize resources might not be that readily available. It is worth a request.

"Man," Rebecca says while taking off her glasses and rubbing her eyes. Rebecca somehow remains a 'worker' while employed as a supervisor. She has a colorful history of telling everyone diplomatically to "Get the fuck out of the way, real workers, real officers coming through!"

Rebecca continues, "Do you think we will be able to obtain the aircraft tail number? You know, we could do a lot with that number." She pauses and quietly states, "Source reporting possible suspect aircraft activities." She looks at Socorro. "I know you already thought about the tail number, I'm just running the details through my mind. Because we are going to sever a link."

Socorro states, "We hoped to get the tail number from our Sources. Right now, Sources are flooding Toluca, Mexico, next to the main private corporate aircraft airport northwest of Mexico City, but are unable to locate the aircraft."

"If we do locate the aircraft and the subjects, what are your initial thoughts related to action?" Todd asks.

Rebecca leans in her chair and asks the officers for time to reflect on the case. Usually, this statement means a slow death for an investigation, but not when it comes from Rebecca.

"First, let's take care of this issue."

Rebecca instructs, "Todd, I mean Chuck. I can't even remember your real names anymore bring the cargo van around. Socorro, dammit, Angelica come with me in my car. You know, I am just going to keep calling you Todd and Socorro. Y'all are briefed and know the plan. Socorro call Fred. Linda and Joe and have them stage. Let's go."

They enter their respective vehicles and drive towards Netanya's residence. She's due to surface in about an hour. Todd in the van leads.

"Ok, good there is one of the new guys who drove all night from the US to enter at a separate Point of Entry (POE) from our other two colleagues you will see soon. Jesus, that guy is huge."

"Damn, you're right. Where does our agency get these guys?"

"All right he is in Todd's van. Okay, Fred is driving his car out of the lot now. That car will be through the Laredo POE in minutes. As you are aware, Fred will walk back in. Just in case somebody reacts."

"Okay, Todd stay in sight."

"Will do."

"How y'all doing? Did you have a good trip?" The front of Rebecca's car rises, and the shocks moan when the two large men sit in the backseat. Rebecca and Socorro look at each other in astonishment. Socorro starts laughing, seeing Rebecca looking curiously into the rear mirror at the boys. Their large bodies almost touch. Looking at the rear mirror, Rebecca can barely see the road behind them.

"We are doing great — long night. I entered through the El Paso POE, and he entered through the McAllen POE. A little closer."

"Roger that, this is Socorro." They shake hands.

Socorro points and states, "You can see Linda and Joe just got your cars. They will drive your vehicles back into the United States."

Rebecca adds, "We will notify your people on the US side when to retrieve your vehicles."

"Thanks," says one of the men in the backseat.

"I apologize for the all-night thing I do not trust the backdrop on our credit cards. I felt this is more covert not letting you guys use a hotel, last night. Here's a picture of Netanya." Rebecca gives the picture to the boys, and one of them hands it back to Socorro.

"No problem on the logistics. We will get our sleep soon."

"Socorro will pick up anything she drops. Your concern is the grab only."

"Got it."

"Good timing. Todd's positioned well. Here she comes." Rebecca points to the lady. "The old lady walking with her back to you. You good?"

"We got it." They exit the car. The shocks sigh in relief. The two men briskly walk after the old lady. Todd drives the van next to her. The van sliding door opens, and the two large men throw the old lady into the interior. Duct tape strips line the van's interior. The man located in the cargo area grabs the lady and places duct tape over her eyes. One of the boy's lands on top of her and tapes her arms behind her back. The remaining boy slams the van door shut. While Todd slowly drives to the airport, the three men finish taping her legs and mouth. The men stuff the woman into an empty chest placed in the rear of the van. Socorro retrieves a straw bag left on the sidewalk and reenters Rebecca's car. They follow Todd to the airport.

Todd drives to the private side of the airport, enters an FBO's tarmac and then drives to a waiting jet. A solitary guard waves at the van. Two of the men carry the chest inside the plane. With the jet engines warming up, the third follows and closes the aircraft hatch. Todd drives the empty van from the tarmac as observed by Rebecca and Socorro and all leave the area. The pilots initially filed a flight plan to Mobile, Alabama. The jet taxis and takes off. Approaching Mobile, the pilot electronically changes the aircraft tail number and flies directly to Guantanamo, Cuba.

"Netanya will be eating white rice and black beans for some time. She will prove useful in a swap later on."

Socorro looks in the old lady's bag, "At least, we have her phone, and it looks like some documents to exploit."

"We had no other choice. We needed to do something. They tried to kill an agent, for Christ sake."

"Oh, I agree," says Socorro.

"Before I forget, what happened to DEA agent Seamus O'Malley?"

"I hear he is on a tight leash in Houston," responds Socorro.

"Um hum," Rebecca murmured.

Yuri and General Comstock enter into a conversation.

"Yuri."

"Yes, General Comstock."

"We will not unload at the same place. We need a destination change for the 'bricks' (cocaine). It's become necessary to reduce risk. The Russian Secret Police associated with this decided it is politically unwise to have the Cardinal's aircraft fly directly into Moscow. If uncovered in route, the high-profile cargo will stain the new administration." Comstock continues, "There has to be another reason the Secret Police want us to change the disembarkation point. Is there a leak in our operation?" Comstock does not expect a response related to a potential leak. Yuri predicted there would be a leak. Yuri with his head down could be vindicated on his concerns about Source infiltration.

"Yes, yes, we can change the location," Yuri, second in command to General Comstock remarks.

"We must again exploit unrest. As we always have, exploit particular regions and associated government weaknesses to achieve our goal."

"I understand," Yuri states.

"We are making some money, but as you know, we must pay others above us to continue this operation. They reap the reward, but as usual, they'll have plausible deniability if this falls apart. They'll justify it as a means to obtain US currency for the government. Man, the plan is solid, good until revealed. You said it, Yuri. It is not on paper."

"There's unrest in the Middle East, always has been. I know you don't care to work with the Arabs with the double-dealing and your misfortunes with respect, Comrade." Yuri nods at General Comstock.

"Yes, yes, but right now delivery of our other loads into Europe are suffering. The German border stiffened a few years back after the discovery of some of our uranium. You know how efficient the 'robots' are. Those Waffen bastards could seize the next 'brick' shipment and trace it to Moscow. We have to get around the eastern German border."

"To get the dope to Europe, let's first make use of the Palestinian controlled Gaza airport."

Lowering his head and folding his hands, Comstock quietly states, "I don't know."

"It's perfect."

"It's too new and not yet fully developed. Very touchy, it's a hotbed."

"Perfect... instability. Isn't that to our advantage? You said so yourself. You're right about a hotbed, but what about the talks?"

No answer from Comstock.

"Sir, move the next meeting to Israel as a means to obtain a neutral setting for the talks. We request that the Cardinal's aircraft land in the Gaza Strip, not at Tel Aviv-Ben Gurion Israel airport. The world will view this landing as a small step of legitimacy to the Palestinian State. Additionally, an olive branch extended by the Russians to the Catholics, Eastern Orthodox, and the Palestinians. The movement of the talks and its subsequent acceptance by each delegation would be interpreted as compulsory to remain in good graces with us. Maybe, a small step towards peace in the area." Yuri looks at General Comstock listening intently.

Yuri continues, "It will allow Palestinian's first foray into the diplomatic world. As you know, Gaza controlled by the Palestinians borders the Mediterranean Sea with Israel army and navy interference at the borders. We fly into Gaza and reduce some of the Israeli interdiction efforts. We unload the 'bricks' from the Cardinal's plane with the help of our Palestinian friends then smuggle from Gaza by vessel west on the Mediterranean Sea. We smuggle through Kosovo, Bosnia or Serbia to Italy then onto France."

Yuri drinks from a bottle of water and concludes his long dissertation, "Um, the Kosovo government has increased its searches for weapons. They will quickly find our dope. Instead, I say we go from Gaza into Marseilles, France by water and distribute from Paris, as usual."

Comstock pauses and then says, "that's plausible, Yuri it's ambitious, so dangerous. I might say well thought out. Don't take this as an insult, but I did not realize you are so well versed in geopolitics." He nods his salutations to Yuri. "We will need, of course... to make the necessary preparations. The first route was successful. So, let's increase the load to 500."

"Of course, General. We will have to develop an alternate route as a backup. Right now, the aircraft could refuel in Shannon, Ireland or Italy to Gaza and then the 'commodities' route by vessel into the Mediterranean, and on to France. It would be simpler if we had people in place at these transit stops."

The General states, "the Gaza airport must stay open. It's in a volatile area. I believe it is called Yasser Arafat International Airport. Hopefully, Don Pedro agrees to 500 kgs. I bet he already told his people to load 500."

"Yes, hopefully," Yuri pauses and thinks.

"We need a good man, one who asks no questions, and for that matter, one who does not even think about the questions but who is focused solely on completing the mission."

Immediately, the General smirks and reminisces. Years back, Americans and Russians were kidnapped in Lebanon just north of Israel. The Americans tried to negotiate with terrorists for their release. At least one American died. The Russians, well, they sent in Boris' group. His group located the kidnappers' associates and mailed their balls stuffed in a box to the kidnappers. The Russian captives were immediately released. Boris will be the contact in Gaza. He's capable of getting the dope from the plane to the boat off the coast of Gaza. Boris' contacts in Gaza have a good chance at subverting Israeli marine patrols. They've done it before, but in reverse weapons originating from vessels into Gaza.

"Make the preparations, use Boris for the Gaza operation. Right now, he is in Lebanon." Comstock orders.

"Yes, General."

"I'll call Don Pedro and make the necessary preparations. He doesn't need to know the new route, yet. He only needs to know when to load the Cardinal's plane in Mexico City. It looks like the Black Cat is going to Palestine, the Israeli occupied country. Yuri, ensure Boris has enough for payoffs. If we have to, we will buy everybody at Gaza airport."

"Yes, Boris can also make payment in 'product.' The Palestinian National Authority (PNA) headed by Arafat and its 'strong arm' Fatah is still unaware that Gaza is about to be hijacked by greater heretics with the accompanying hysteria, Hamas. For now, Fatah will lead, but I think Hamas will run the show. Who knows, after these future deals, they will probably kill each other. Fatah will agree to trade their heroin for coke and triple their profit. They will continue to strap their children with explosives and blow up the Israeli soldiers. However, now, the suicide bombers will be high on coke before detonation." Yuri adds.

Ha, the General thinks.

"Comrade Comstock, how do we get the Cardinal to land in the Gaza Strip instead of the Ben Gurion airport? Ben Gurion is modern and of course safer? The Cardinal could conclude that the delegation can easily convoy from the Ben Gurion airport to Gaza to meet with the Palestinian leadership. The Israelis will find the narcotics at Ben Gurion."

"Let me handle that, Yuri, do not allow the loading of the dope on the Mexican aircraft until I get the Mexican delegation to commit to a landing in Gaza. I want the other delegation to follow. If the Eastern Orthodox do not have corporate aircraft at their disposal, well, let them land in Israel. The talks will occur in Israel, but it is necessary for the Mexican delegation aircraft to land in Gaza, first. I want to see media photos depicting Palestinian youths waving flags and cheering at the arrival of the plane. Just another sideshow, you might say. It will be a lot for the Israelis to digest, but we will promise to speak favorably of Israel's peace efforts."

General Comstock leans in his chair and releases a plume of cigarette smoke. "I am determined to make use of the Gaza airport. You know Yuri, Catholics love Jesus, and he is an Arab prophet. If I have to, I'll remind Israel that they sent Jesus to his death." He slams his fist on the table. "The Israeli Defense Forces (IDF) effectively encircle the Gazans and patrol Gaza City securing the remaining Israelis. The IDF patrols act like visitors at a zoo. The Gazans strike back like caged animals, and the IDF reciprocates. The deadly cycle continues as each party blames the other for firing the first strike." Yuri does not respond.

Comstock reflects and realizes. What choice does the IDF have when the Gazans strike? It's an impossible situation for both. Both are right in their actions, except those Palestinians who make use of human shields. Why do the crazies store their rockets in the basements of hospitals, in schools and maintain command and control in innocent civilians' residences? We all know why, to protect the same. Comstock thinks it is abhorrent to make use of human shields. However, somebody in his government, as well as other Middle Eastern patrons, continues to agitate the situation. What a cluster.

Comstock extinguishes his cigarette and lights another then continues, "The airport is a big problem for the IDF because its very existence gives the idea, like you said, that anyone can easily smuggle weapons into the heart of Gaza circumventing border searches. So far, the IDF searched numerous aircraft without results. So, I am sure there is a decline in IDF aircraft searches. The typical Palestinians are not making use of the airport. The IDF discovered that important people like movie stars and diplomats are the only ones making use of the airport. The rich think it is cool to fly into Gaza." Yuri shakes his head, swallows a shot of vodka and continues to listen to General Comstock. "The IDF is cognizant of the ill will each evasive search causes amongst the super-rich. To reduce the IDF's desire to search the plane, I will request our Foreign Ministry stress to their Israeli counterparts the need for Israel to exercise proper protocols related to the occupants and aid stored on board. We will make public the aid stuffed into the boxes to be distributed to the Gazans. I am taking a big chance, Yuri. If the IDF find the dope, I am doomed, branded 'rogue' and disavowed." Yuri nods his head affirmatively; Comstock almost inhales his entire second cigarette. He commits to Gaza.

"Contact Boris."

"Yes, sir."

General Comstock contacts the former Minister of Interior Gomez residing in Italy and request that he call Spanish Monsignor Romero assigned to the Mexico City Diocese. Gomez complies. Gomez makes it known to Monsignor Romero that he has back door access to the negotiations. From this access, Gomez advises there will be a change in the negotiation's venue. The talks will occur in Israel, but the Mexican delegation must land in Gaza.

The use of Gaza by the Mexican commission will demonstrate support for the Palestinian cause, a cause that the Catholic Church supports. More importantly, a cause supported by Russia. Who knows while in Gaza, the Catholic Church might persuade the Palestinian Authority to accept Vatican funds for the renovation of the Bethlehem church? Comstock's people contact the Eastern Orthodox representatives and demand the same.

Chapter Twenty-Four

Not expecting such a small interview room, Seamus O'Malley stumbles in the entrance (the famed fatal funnel again) and comes to an abrupt stop. He balances on his left leg to avoid hitting the interview table. His grip releases a pencil and a notepad both sliding across the interview table. Because of Seamus' sudden stop, Murphy aka 'full of hate' plows into Seamus' back almost causing Seamus to fall on the seated Jose.

Jose, with his mouth open, concludes he's doomed. He drops his head into his hands. He can put this guy O'Malley unto the Black Cat's operation. Specifically, the Black Cat's relationship to the Nuevo Laredo seizure or maybe even some crooked Russians. What the hell, his future depends on this guy. How the hell does America survive?

Seamus now standing erect on terra firma initiates the interview and asks Jose to pray out loud. Seamus folds his hands. Seamus is a bigger asshole than Jose remembers. (Normally, Seamus treats all potential human Sources or current Sources with their due respect. However, Jose broke all traditional bounds. Many Sources operate within a corrupt foreign system with its pre-determined maligned code of ethics. Systems whose existence breathe on governmental corruption. If a Source makes mention of its complicity with murder, rape, and child abuse, the interview is over. Agents do not give Sources immunity. The key to human Source development is trust. Trust must develop and eventually exist between the agents and the Sources. If it does not, then a significant case cannot proceed as the informational foundation is cracked.)

With his recent transfer to the land of misfits and broken toys, Seamus behaves within the confines of his immediate environment. He resembles a child. Following this transfer, Seamus is on the verge of giving up on the entire program. He recovers from this temporary insanity and laughs to himself, realizing his bosses are not aware of what will develop from this simple interview. How desperate he and Jose are. Strangely, they are linked.

However, Seamus cannot resist sprinkling the room with his designated holy water shaken from his plastic water bottle. He could not help himself on that one. Murphy is a quick learner, and equally a cynic tells Jose that Seamus is exorcizing from Jose the evil spirits of our lady of dope.

Jose rolls his eyes.

"So," O'Malley says, "you work with the Black Cat."

To end the theatrics, Jose asks, "What will I get out of this, if I give you seizures and or the Black Cat?"

"Well," O'Malley replies, "Jesus will enter your heart." Seamus is still unusually cruel and sarcastic. In his mind, Jose, a purported priest, broke through the mythical 'line of acceptance' related to decency. Seamus' statement is a quick verbal shot of disdain. It needed to be said early in the interview process to suggest O'Malley and Murphy will remain distant until Jose proves himself.

O'Malley is following the interview checklist: good cop bad cop, emotionally bounce the subject about and then finish with an agreement to work in the future. Murphy and Seamus conduct interviews while other agencies conduct interrogations; there is a big difference.

"Shit. Is this guy for real? Are you making this personal?" Jose points at O'Malley and looks for Murphy's support making his first mistake in his attempt to separate Seamus from Murphy. Murphy does not fall for the trick. Jose is knocked off balance and tries to correct so as not to alienate himself from Seamus. He does not need another enemy. The agents could get pissed off and delve deeper into his past. He adjusts his mistake, "Ok, look, O'Malley give me something, some reduction in my sentencing for this info." Jose's stomach grumbles.

"Well, you know we will have to consult with a prosecutor. Give us some generalities of what you are prepared to provide, and we will get back with you." O'Malley points his index finger at Jose impersonating a grinning pearly white tooth, fake baked tan, game show host celebratory advising Jose he won a prize. Following this round of theatrics, O'Malley shakes his head to see if

Jose will connect with him. Connect in their disdain of authority. O'Malley guesses Jose does respect authority.

"You got an attorney?" Murphy asks, smacking and popping his gum with the rhythm of an accomplished musician.

"What for?"

"So, the attorney can take all your money. The attorney will delay your case until the attorney is satisfied, your money is drained and then tell you to plead the case. That's why, welcome to America."

"That's it," Jose clinches his fist, "The Black Cat, the one you're looking for — he's moved to Mexico City."

"We know that." Seamus recognizes he acted foolishly. It is not reasonable to disrespect caged animals. Once caught, the US judicial system is strong enough to break them if they have enough sense to realize it. Jose possesses that good sense and is not stupid.

"Well, he's smuggling dope."

"Yes. I am listening. I know, but how do we get the BC?" Seamus replies, calmly.

Jose now knows Seamus is listening. Hell, he deserved what Seamus threw at him, he's been screwing up for some time, well before he met Seamus. Seamus sits on a steel chair next to Jose.

"It's easy." The jokes are over, and Jose is now what they say 'off the fence.' He believes Seamus is trustworthy. More importantly, he will act on the data. Because of O'Malley's theatrics, Jose initially questioned his decision to ask for O'Malley at the traffic stop. However, even a bad guy, can sense when the good guys are experiencing bad days.

"He's working for the government," declares Jose.

Seamus maintains a curious gaze and slowly shakes his head up and down, processing the statement.

Murphy smiling stands from his chair and ceremoniously bangs his fist against the interview room's cinder block wall and says, "this is great." Murphy thrives on this kind of information.

"Our government?... Whose government?" Seamus grins.

"That's what you have to deliver to your prosecutors." Jose rolls the word prosecutor out to at least 30 syllables in complete disgust not directed at Seamus and the amused Murphy, but for authority do-nothings. Jose's face turns red. The cards are now on the table. The games end soon.

"What is the 'handler's' full name?" Murphy asks.

"No more information, I want the deal first," Jose sneers. The negotiations turn in his favor.

Murphy points to the camera in the interview room. Is it operating? Who cares it might as well be. No need to be in the Internal Affairs digest. No need to designate Jose a poster child for civil rights abuse by US officials against helpless Mexican National subjects. Yelling and screaming at suspects as you see in the movies and crime dramas never work. When you work at the highest levels of crime, your actions need to be well thought out and plans reviewed and discussed with the Sources for authenticity. Operations need to be realistic and viable, so no one gets killed. Agents and Sources have to communicate continually. Because of this, the relationship cannot be in a state of hostility.

Seamus wonders if the troopers contacted the Mexican Consulate office, as required after the arrest of a Mexican National. He shrugs his shoulders. Who cares, he's not the arresting officer. Let the Mexican consulate official wearing his pointy shoes, and European jacket drive down to this country outpost and complain to the tobacco-chewing troopers. "Huh, what the hell are you talking about? Fuck notification," the troopers would say.

After hearing the trooper's response, the skinny consulate official would scurry back to his office and relay the 'big' issue to his boss. His boss would look at him and ask if the 'arrested' could receive capital punishment? The skinny guy says no, discussion over.

Mexican Nationals arrested in Texas have become such a problem that the Mexican Consulate cannot provide minimal representation. The consulate office now accepts faxes notifying of their arrest. In reality, this US notification serves as an early warning system alerting the criminal base of potential harm from the arrest.

Oh yeah, Seamus is sure somebody read Jose his Miranda rights. Might be a problem in the future. Maybe, but Seamus and Murphy's interest lies in Source development and the 'overall,' not a simple possession case. Jose is a defendant Source, one strike, but Seamus and Murphy are aware his information could be valuable and actionable as it reaches the highest levels.

Seamus and Murphy will become comfortable working with Jose, not fighting with Jose. Understanding a subject's environment to extract valuable Source information will develop as Seamus and Murphy listen and discuss the issues with the Source. Seamus and Murphy will not instruct the Informant it has to be done this way or that way unless they have encountered the same scenario in the past. Seamus and Murphy will listen to the Source on the proper way to go forward. It's not as though Seamus and Murphy were criminals when growing up. Seamus knows it is necessary to listen and learn from the Sources, a lost trait.

Seamus and Murphy leave the interview room abandoning the seated Jose, advising him they will reach out to 'authority.' Jose amused Seamus in the way he slowly said the word, prosecutor. O'Malley leaves a message with a federal duty prosecutor to ascertain if the prosecutor wants to take the case federally. Seamus and Murphy reenter Jose's holding cell. Jose will have to wait for a prosecutor's response. Seamus expresses their interest in Jose's information and will move on actionable leads if given the go ahead. Seamus is aware he reduces his leverage by this statement but does so to extend an olive branch. Following the remark, Jose is satisfied that he made the proper choice in asking the trooper to contact O'Malley.

Following the olive branch, Seamus asks Jose to give personal information related to Sanchez/The Black Cat. Jose does not have a problem with this inquiry. Is the Black Cat a smart ass? What are his deficiencies? Seamus' last question to Jose, in one word, what is the Black Cat's weakest trait? Jose replies, "Overconfidence," and adds, "Vanity." That's two words; they all laugh. Jose, O'Malley, and Murphy understand that future official interviews will result in some actionable information, but not the 'real deal.' They know why. This investigation will be a slow roll, but it will eventually pan out.

Before Seamus and Murphy leave the interview room, Jose reveals that it is not common for the public to enter the rarely used Matamoros office. Visitors always come through the church. He states that the stacked books were placed in front of the bullet hole, by whom, not identified. Obviously, the books did not serve their purpose. He says the Black Cat is aware of the theft of the bullet and casing. Seamus and Murphy remain silent and shrug their shoulders, wondering why Jose is telling them this? Did Jose reveal something important?

Then Jose randomly details what he saw, on his northerly trip before being arrested, rows of 'corn and farm implements.' He found the sights relaxing. Seamus and Murphy curiously look at each other. Murphy comments in the presence of Jose, "are you into nature?" Jose only shrugs his shoulders. Seamus and Murphy leave the interview room. Jose realizes that O'Malley and the other guy, whatever his name is, were not listening to his phone conversations. During the Cardinal's assassination, corn was code for guns and farm implements referred to manpower/assassins. Jose hopes the agents do not discover those dark days.

Hours pass into days without a reply from a prosecutor. Years ago, Seamus gave up in repeatedly contacting the prosecutor for updates, so he waits. In the meantime, Seamus continues his routine of reading various daily newspapers and plows through numerous non-fictional books. Eventually, the federal prosecutor contacts Seamus. The prosecutor says he spoke with Jose's defense attorney and it appears the defense attorney wanted this incident to conclude quickly.

The prosecutor advises Seamus, Jose is a first offender with a listed occupation as a priest. Following a thorough 'official proffer session' (interview), the prosecutor sets Jose's plea to three years of incarceration with final concurrences of the defense attorney and the judge. Seamus gets the impression the prosecutor does not believe anything of note will surface in the anticipated proffer session.

As a result of the prosecutor's recommendation, O'Malley and Murphy travel to the Corpus Christi court annex to conduct Jose's interview with his defense attorney. The prosecutor could not attend. Jose, a tactician, specifies that the Black Cat is run/controlled by the Montreal Police. Seamus and Murphy conclude the cop is not crooked. Most likely labeled a 'rogue,' a real worker, as Canada has strict rules for Cooperators/Sources.

At least someone is willing to work in Canada. Eventually, police officers and agents beaten down by internal controls (directed towards the most stupid agents/officers) will have no choice but to sit at his/her desk or remain idling in his/her "shop" (patrol car) because of management administrative liability phobias.

Back to his thoughts. "What's his name?"

"I don't know, but here's the telephone number," Jose provides a piece of paper to Murphy and says, "The Black

Cat carelessly wrote in small letters 'dplaertnom' next to the number. I had to look at it for some time until I figured out what it meant. We write our phone numbers backward after looking at the letters it spelled Montreal PD. It shocked me, so I copied it when I found it in the Black Cat's Matamoros desk. You know, I held it for insurance reasons."

Jose indicates that the Black Cat was dispatched to Mexico City 'maybe' to deliver dope that is all he knew. Stay close to the truth he thinks as Seamus has not revealed his knowledge related to their activities. Jose needs Seamus' help. The Black Cat will be okay with this leak because half of Mexico already suspects Sanchez the Black Cat of dealing drugs. O'Malley asks if the Black Cat is smuggling dope within Mexico, Mexico City, and or into Texas. Jose says nothing.

The Black Cat will disavow Jose. As a result of Jose's arrest, if known to Don Pedro and the Cali Cartel, the Black Cat will tell Don Pedro that Jose was smuggling without his authorization. Jose, without close family members, is still worried. Don Pedro's men will locate his distant relatives and kill them if he cooperates. Jose's cooperation will result in his death while incarcerated. So, his formal collaboration is sketchy and limited.

The Black Cat will view Jose's information favorably because Jose's information of Sanchez's cooperation with the Montreal Police puts the Black Cat in a good light with law enforcement. Jose, Seamus, and Murphy understand that Jose vies for more time. Jose's Montreal PD telephone number keeps O'Malley and Murphy in the hunt.

If Jose links the Black Cat/Sanchez to the Cardinal's killing, Don Pedro's Cali Cartel will kill him. Because of Jose's association with the Black Cat's plan unleashing the Mex Feds against the Medellin Cartel in western Mexico, Medellin henchmen will also target him. Plus, he will implicate himself in the murder. Jose is smart enough to realize that formal interviews are public records for all to review. His defense attorney, hired by the Black Cat, will immediately forward the information to the Black Cat. Jose has to stall. Because of the official interview details, O'Malley will get the 'I told you so' from the prosecutor. He can live with that for now.

Chapter Twenty-Five

Seamus sits on his Houston desk and calls the Montreal PD telephone number provided by Jose, no answer. Murphy was summoned upstairs for some BS. The voice mail associates the number called with a Peter MacDougal. O'Malley bypasses his Canadian office representative to locate the officer. Official correspondence from O'Malley requesting why and what would take too long. If this officer does not want to work with Seamus and Murphy or is crooked, Seamus will save a lot of time and effort. It is no longer a secret that O'Malley is interested in the Black Cat. If the Montreal police officer alerts the Black Cat of Seamus' inquiry, it will not affect O'Malley's investigation. O'Malley waits a few more minutes and calls the number again.
"Hello?"
"Who is this?"
"You called me," the Montreal police officer is pissed right out of the box. The police officer hates it when someone calls him and asks him whom they are speaking to. Shit; they called the number. The caller should know who, they are calling. The caller is probably selling crap or an Internal Affairs dufus.
Not a good start, his mistake. "I am looking for Peter MacDougal."
"Yes, this is Detective Peter MacDougal with the Montreal Police. Who is this?" MacDougal sours upon

hearing the American's voice and thinks that he'll speak French to this guy and he will go away.

"I'm DEA agent Seamus O'Malley, and I would like to ask a question regarding the historical activities of Juan Federico Sanchez, aka the Black Cat."

"Who?" He's going French, MacDougal regrets returning to his office to retrieve his jacket. He knows better to answer the phone this late. It's always something terrible or BS drama. Someone is having anxiety and wants to get it off of their desk and send it onto somebody else so that they can get a good night's sleep. The late-night calls are as bad as the Friday afternoon calls. The Friday call initiator wants to have a peaceful weekend.

"Well, I know what I said is a shock, and I do not expect you to provide any information from this first inquiry. I can shoot you a government email, that will include my office number and cell verifying my employment."

" Oui, Oui. Well, send me an email with your contact numbers, and I will decide if I know what you're talking about." Without another word, the connection terminates. A couple of days pass before Detective MacDougal contacts O'Malley.

"You must keep this to yourself, but Sanchez or some call him the Black Cat worked with me in the past when I discovered that he was involved in smuggling aliens by vessel from Mexico into Canada. A few of these aliens were popped for possession in Canada and dropped his name with no real actionable evidence. Mind you, this was a few years ago, and Sanchez was living in Mexico – Texas area. I think? He worked for someone, never identified, but Sanchez, the Black Cat, used to say that if he were smuggling aliens, it would only be the act of a priest concerned for the plight of the poor…. you know humanitarian reasons."

O'Malley listens and writes notes of the conversation as fast as he can. O'Malley does not prematurely interrupt the

Detective. If he hinders the stream of consciousness, he knows the Detective will stop talking and become introspective. He knows just as quickly as MacDougal provides the information, that he can turn the conversation into an inquisition.

"You still there?" Detective MacDougal asks.

"Still here, good stuff," replies O'Malley.

MacDougal continues, "But as I said some of these poor people possessed small amounts of dope attached to their bodies. Occasionally, Sanchez provided information on the whereabouts of a few of the aliens, but he was playing both sides of the fence. He was making some money from this new route, so he was forced into this relationship with me. I had little to develop the case, but enough to make Sanchez think I knew more of the internal machinations of his organization. I believe Sanchez easily absorbed the loss of the narcotics. The alien smuggling is a sideshow compared to the future narcotic smuggling proceeds. I think Sanchez is probing in our area to ascertain its potential."

"Yes, yes, go on."

"Well, to preserve his reputation as a priest, Sanchez cooperates reciting generalities of the smuggling route. Sanchez always stresses he is not involved. He's not involved. Yea, right. He purportedly makes inquiries as to who knows what about the routes and forwards the replies to me. None of the arrested will testify against Sanchez. The last time he provided information to me was I believe a result of an arrest of a Coyote and a few aliens outside of Quebec City, Canada. None of these subjects had narcotics. This lead was his way of staying in good favor of the person above Sanchez….um…down there, as well as a way to keep us happy up here."

Detective MacDougal continues, "I am sure the aliens that have made it here traveled further south down the St. Laurence River…right by Mount Royal, Montreal. Sanchez probably told the aliens to reflect as they boated past L'Oratoire-Saint-Joseph du Mont-Royal (St Joseph's Oratory). You've ever heard of that place? The L'Oratoire?" MacDougal coughs and clears his throat. MacDougal does not wait for O'Malley's answer and continues his brief. "It was and may still be a good route as they are most likely transiting south near the US/Canada Point of Entry on your Highway 87 into New York State. I am sure their destination is the Greater New York City area." MacDougal finally takes a breath and hopes by providing so much information, so fast, that the curious DEA agent will say, 'Okay that's enough.'

"Man, that is much information. Well, by any chance can you contact Sanchez?"

It did not work, "Yea… ah…no…a yea, why?"

"Well, I don't know, but it could be helpful. Oh. Did you guys part in a bad way or are you okay with Sanchez?"

"Okay, I guess. I requested that Sanchez travel here to testify against a few of the aliens and that Coyote guy. He refused. What was I going to do? The case was done on the side if you know what I mean. Plus." MacDougal coughs. Sounds of him swallowing can be heard on the phone. O'Malley thinks he probably took a shot of whiskey most likely hidden in his desk drawer (not judging) "Well, as you know, I was taking a big chance...was I directing him? If so, he could be designated an agent provocateur under our laws. Oh, man," MacDougal moans, "and, if decided that while he was here that he was a provocateur, Sanchez could have been incarcerated, complicit, you know, for the same crime. We are working with our hands tied behind our backs up here." MacDougal coughs again. This guy should get that cough looked after. When it snows almost every day up there, no small wonder half the population is under medical attention.

Seamus understands the challenges the Detective faces and will protect the Detective's information. Seamus visualizes the alien smuggling route as outlined by

Detective MacDougal. The aliens are traveling at night by boat in a southerly direction from the Gulf of St. Lawrence and eventually reaching to their right, the Montmorency waterfalls and gorge north of Quebec City, Quebec. The site, mid-1759, of a British armed forces naval assault lead by General Wolfe against the French armed forces headed by the effective General Montcalm resulted in a British retreat.

The Montmorency waterfall conflict also called the Battle of Beauport, led to the Battle of Quebec. The Battle of Quebec, the final decisive battle between the British and the French armies for control of Canada, resulted in the death of the brilliant French General Marquis Louis Joseph Montcalm on the Plains of Abraham, adjacent to the present Citadel of Quebec City. The same battle claimed the life of the legendary British General James Wolfe.

Seamus reminisces of the greatness of General Montcalm who succeeded in battles despite inadequate French-Canadian government support. The French-Canadian government officials were too busy fleecing Canada, via the fur trade. The French-Canadian administrators were only concerned about their aggrandizement, kleptocracy. Similar to present day Mexican government officials or in his small world, the 'politicals' minus the kleptocracy but adding willful ignorance in targeting real threats. Oh, that is bad, did he think that?

With limited government support, General Montcalm's forces were still able to destroy the British at various engagements. General Montcalm's most decisive battle was in New York State, Fort Carillon or known to the British as Fort Ticonderoga on the western shore of Lake Champlain. At Fort Carillon, General Montcalm destroyed the famed British Black Watch from redoubts hastily prepared at the steps of Fort Carillon/Ticonderoga. Wave after wave of Black Watch soldiers, storm Montcalm's earthen western perimeter only to be repeatedly beaten back. Adding to the British problems was the death of British General Lord Augustus Howe in the same battle.

General Montcalm remained loyal to France even while he and his troops froze and starved, some to their death, during those winter campaigns. Seamus identifies with Montcalm left out in the cold; operations left to die on the vine. Through all of the conflict along St. Laurence River, Seamus finds it fascinating that the Montmorency Falls has remained intact and undisturbed.

Detective MacDougal said the aliens and associated narcotics made use of the St. Lawrence River south to US Highway 87. Sanchez, the Black Cat, was making use of the same invasion and retreating routes of the British and French armies. The Black Cat's plague entered the Gulf of the St. Lawrence River and then south to the Richelieu River at Sorel, Canada. Its sparkling river in summer is difficult to view because of the sun's reflections. The Richelieu River empties into Lake Champlain, New York. The plague then journeyed south overland to Lake George and eventually to the Hudson River which ends at New York City.

US Highway 87 parallels the routes of the US, French and British armies from Canada, to Lake George and to Albany, New York. Back then, the commanders understood that by controlling this route one can conquer the Eastern United States.

However, Seamus remembers a peculiar event during the British and American war, north of Albany during the battle of Saratoga, the American General Benedict Arnold fought with bravery in defeating the British. Seamus wonders what eventually caused Benedict Arnold to turn from his country and serve the British. Was it Arnold's vanity? Was the Black Cat a student of history? Strangely, Seamus thinks the Black Cat participated in these past wars?

Following the death of the French General Montcalm at Quebec, Canada, the French administrators lost control of French-administered Canada. French forces were forced to flee Canada, and British troops took control of Canada for centuries.

As history is known to do, it repeated itself once again, with emphasis on government administrations inability to grasp the situation plus self-serving motives, and no better example was how the message of the loss of France's possession of Canada was justified. One French-Canadian civil servant, Pierre Vaudreuil, who had inhibited French General Montcalm's efforts relayed to King Louis XV the loss of French Canada to the British. This self-serving public servant tells the French King it was not a big deal. Hell, Seamus thinks, France lost an entire country. However, Seamus believes there was another reason for France's defeat in Canada but back to his conversation.

"Understood, well, well. I recently received some forensics, although negative, regarding a couple of bullets and shell casings I found that killed assassins related to the killing of a Mex Fed down in Mexico. The bullets are very high tech."

"Goodness!" Detective MacDougal responds, wondering to himself how far will he be drawn into this impending cluster. Maybe, he should get amnesia.

"I think our man has graduated and moved up the food chain since your last dance."

"What are you going to do with the forensics?"

"As I said, they met with negative results. My office has downgraded the investigation. I still think it is worth investigating Sanchez, the Black Cat."

The Detective is momentarily caught up in the hunt and says, "yes, of course."

"Well, I'll call you if I ever come up with any additional material. Good day, eh."

"Yes, good day." Holy Shit! I hope O'Malley does not find anything else. Get a hold of yourself. What the hell, if he can get some free time, he'll review the files and see if they contain anything that could help out this crazy O'Malley. At least, O'Malley is doing something.

After the call, the visuals of Quebec Province remain. Montcalm, Wolfe, the Oratory. So much history to absorb. The more you learn, the more you realize how little you know. On many occasions, O'Malley visited Quebec Province including Montreal, Quebec City, Montmorency Falls, Fort Carillion, and St. Joseph's Oratory. The L'Oratoire as MacDougal calls it. The Catholic faithful throughout the world have for years undertaken pilgrimages to this site to the impressive building constructed in terrace fashion from the parking lot steps climbing to Mount Royal's summit. The Oratory's green dome can be seen for miles as one approached northeast on the main highway from New York and can be viewed in all of its glory from western Montreal.

By visiting the Oratory, hundreds of souls claim cures of various diseases and ailments. Wooden and metal crutches of the healed hang from the roof adjacent to the lower church. The faithful crawl on their knees on the Oratory's exterior stone steps from the parking lot to the smaller church below the main Basilica, at least two stories in height. Praying, seeking penitence and or in search of healing. The populace believes that one day Brother Andre, a long-term parish priest, will be designated a Saint.

The Black Cat/Sanchez has chosen to spread his evil in this environment. The Black Cat's actions in this theatre pale to the historical events that predated him. However, the Black Cat is smart enough to capitalize on the historic routes. Alternatively, did the Black Cat have firsthand knowledge related to the known invasion route? Why does this thought keep invading O'Malley's mind?

The Black Cat's overconfidence and vanity revealed by the priest, Jose, are the Black Cat's debilitating traits. The Black Cat's confidence to 'play' anybody blinds him to reality. One sure thing is that if one believes that one is fully in control, then one will eventually be shaken to one's core when discovering that this is not the case. The Black Cat's overconfidence provides him the fuel to continue, increasingly ignoring danger signs and or signals that he should seriously consider. If these same signs had been evident in the past then they would not have been overlooked but instead would have resulted in suspension or even termination of impending smuggling ventures. Because of his vanity, the Black Cat does away with real-time situational awareness. At the right time and place, O'Malley plans to shock the vain Black Cat by taking full advantage of any situation that presents itself.

Vanity is such a debilitating trait, one who exercises vanity is not even aware of its ramifications. Nothing sums up vanity more than the non-loyal French-Canadian civil servant Pierre Vaudreuil, a servant of France's King Louis XV during the fall of Canada, the same one who delivered the news to King Louis XV of the fall of Canada. Vaudreuil's vanity resulted in personal hatred of General Montcalm and without hesitation Vaudreuil gave away Canada no other reason.

Seamus knows Christians equate vanity as a trait of self-appointed apostles of God; more specifically, the mark of the Devil. Was Vaudreuil an apostle of the Devil? Or, the Devil? There was another French-Canadian administrator who acted like Vaudreuil, he too ignored General Montcalm's pleas for assistance. What was his last name, Seamus thinks it started with the letter B? Was this second administrator, the Black Cat, operating in Canada centuries ago breathing in the cold crisp air while confidently striding throughout the region?

Because of the loss of Canada, Vaudreuil received a short sentence in France while the second administrator received a much longer sentence. Both were eventually released from French detention to continue to spread their poison. Very interesting. Where did the Black Cat go after his release from French incarceration? To Mexico? Is the Black Cat replacing the past commanders with groups smuggling drugs making use of the known invasion route to control the Eastern United States?

O'Malley reflects on a straightforward example of danger signs within his small part of the world. Danger signs that if ignored will lead to disastrous outcomes. For example, an overconfident and vain undercover (UC) agent may believe that he/she has completely 'hoodwinked' either the purchaser or seller of the narcotics overriding his/her partner in allowing the suspects to change the previously agreed upon meet location.

If one were successfully playing the role, this 'location' change should never occur as there will always be another deal. Additionally, by not agreeing to the change, the UC gains respect from the suspects. By not conforming to the location change, the UC sends a message to the suspects. The undercover is wise, and is not desperate. Again, there will always, always be another deal.

Changing the meet and time is a well-known mechanism for suspects to identify established surveillance and or more importantly forces the undercover into an environment without a safe exit strategy. The lack of an exit strategy is the suspects' method of prepping the 'rip' and or murder of the undercover. With the intentions of stealing the UC's money for the acquisition of the suspects' narcotics, and/or purported drugs for sale to the suspects by the undercover.

Of course, there are measures to reduce the threat of a 'rip,' but again, the change should never occur. There are other reasons rationalized by the UC to agree to such change, but in general, they hinge on the UC's overconfidence. One cannot correctly investigate if one is not absorbing the overall environment.

Suspect rational thought is almost nonexistent as one investigates these 'gutter rats' who listen to ghetto and country nursery rhymes. Some rational thought enters into the narcotic equation when one rises from the primordial ooze of street slingers to kilogram vehicle deliveries, to bulk kilogram smuggling via tractor-trailer, railcar, vessel, and aircraft. Seamus believes that the Black Cat's vanity causes him to ignore the threats.

There are times in this narcotic world that even if all of the danger signs are known and discussed, a tragic event will still occur. That is because one is always dealing with losers. Losers without remorse, without scruples, willing to poison the defenseless. Also, they are blasted out of their minds from the same product that they are slinging.

Following the telephone call with agent Seamus O'Malley, Detective MacDougal decides to review his Black Cat 'hobby' case. Yes, another shot of Crown Royal whiskey is needed. He reads: providing small jail bonds, a Honduran National mother and her Honduran daughter leave Canadian custody. MacDougal's team, with RCMP support, arrested them, the charge, illegal entry into Canada. They did not have narcotics. When MacDougal interviewed them, they were severely traumatized from their long trip from Tegucigalpa, Honduras to Montreal, Canada via Veracruz, Mexico.

The Honduran women told the following to MacDougal, and he was able to piecemeal the rest through other Sources: their Honduran family was threatened by a Honduran gang weekly, if not daily, to pay for protection. He shakes his head and realizes 'protection from the same scumbags threatening them.' When the money runs out, the daughter's father tells the gang leader that he is penniless. Later in the evening, the gang members return to the house and drag the father onto the street. They stab him to death for failure to pay. As they depart, they tell the mother and daughter that they better have the money in the future or be prepared to be gang girlfriends. How stupid are these animals? They kill the only source of income not only for the family but to them as well.

The mother does not borrow money from her immediate family as they are making the same extortion payments. The mother and daughter sell all of their possessions and begin their trek to America. They travel by foot, bus and even hitch a ride on the roof of a train boxcar in Mexico. The train called 'The Beast.'

Detective MacDougal recognizes Mexico encourages the refugees to 'pass-through' and continue to the United States. He wonders if someone or representatives of a particular country request that Mexico allow the refugees to enter the southern Mexican border at Guatemala and then into the United States. Mexico cannot economically support the transients. If a real wall existed on the US southern border, the effect would resemble a clogged kitchen sink.

Refugees occupying Mexican tent cities will drain the already depleted resources of the Mexican government. Future earnings from the 'tent' refugees wired to their relatives 'down south' will dwindle breaking the economies of numerous Central American countries and leaving the inhabitants in the home countries no recourse but to attempt US entry, themselves. He digresses. He should have invested in a company that made tents. Somebody did.

Stopped in Mexico, the 'tent' refugees will revolt from the undesirable conditions at the northern border. The Mexican government will physically react the same as did the US to the Cubans refugees during the Mariel boatlift. The difference, Fidel Castro's government, supported the expulsion of Cubans, some criminals. Tattoos placed on the hands between the index finger and the thumb by Cuban authorities identified them as robbers, murderers, and thieves. The Honduran mother and daughter are not to be categorized the same. Nor, does he believe the Honduras government is complicit in forcing their citizens to leave the country.

During the mother and daughter's journey to America, they learn that the Coyotes become more aggressive and more violent as they approach the Northern Mexico border. So, they decide not to travel that far north. They make it to the eastern port city of Veracruz, Mexico. A stranger introduces them to a 'Coyote.' The Coyote declares his organization can smuggle them as far as Canada, but they are on their own in entering the United States.

The mother and daughter provide almost all of their monies to the Coyote and stowaway on a freighter. The water route appears to be much safer. If they make it to America, they plan to wire earned monies to their Honduran relatives. These wires keep the economies of Honduras, El Salvador, and Guatemala afloat.

While on the freighter, the bad guys order them upon reaching Canada to smuggle narcotics from the ship to a medium-sized boat and then to a yet to be declared land location. The medium sized boat will take them into Canada. Both refuse to transport drugs. In exchange, they offer to cook and clean throughout the voyage. Because of the refusal, the corrupted crew repeatedly rape them throughout the journey. The crewmembers will dispose of their bodies later.

When the mother and daughter reach the disembarkation point at the Gulf of St. Lawrence, Canada the corrupt crew order the women to the deck of the stationary freighter, a small moon provides limited light on the freighter's deck. A storm develops, and lightning flashes in the distance. The crew does not suspend rope netting on the freighter's side to the water. The women instinctively understand they will throw them into the dark ocean, like dead fish. The corrupted crew just had to keep the women a little longer; instead of disposing them into the Atlantic Ocean.

From the vessel's deck, the women observe the medium sized boat with its searchlight alight as it slowly approaches the stationary freighter. That is their ticket to the shore. Holding hands both jump into the ocean. They expect the impact to kill them or at least to break their legs, striking the ocean's surface the daughter becomes unconscious. The mother's left leg aches and her clothes become entangled. The mother sees her daughter's pale face floating in the moonlight. She swims to her daughter. She panics as her leg stings and the weight of her clothes drag her below the now forming swells. She's not an accomplished swimmer. She asks herself; does she have the resolve to save her daughter? She exhausts herself in the swells.

The mother grabs her still floating daughter and swims to the barely visible approaching boat. Were these crew members friendly? It did not matter. The mother has no other option. Hide from the newly arrived, and they are guaranteed to drown. They have come so far. Her body becomes fatigued in the cold water. Her legs are heavy, and she's losing feeling in her hands and feet. She is drowning, and her daughter will succumb to the same fate. She feels guilty. Guilty for what happened to her daughter on the freighter. Why live? Give up. Let the ocean absolve you of your sins.

Even though they jumped from the deck, they are still very close to the freighter. Flashes throughout the freighter's deck signal crew member gunfire streaking towards the women. Swells absorb the bullets. The swells rock the ship not allowing the derelicts to zero in on the women. It is imperative that they kill these two victims of their savagery.

Seeing the flashes from the freighter, the Canadian captain of the arriving boat determines the shots are heading at him. The Canadian captain does not observe the women when they jumped from the ship. The captain is wise enough to realize that regardless of the number of deals done in the past between criminals, you always need to be on alert for a 'rip' or in this case an assassination. Did an organizational member get 'short-changed' and the crew members are seeking revenge directed at him? Did the crew members think he is an Informant?

The Canadian captain is a Quebec Separatist; specifically, a member of the Quebec Liberation Front. He believes the French-speaking Quebec Province should secede from the rest of Canada. Detective MacDougal thinks, the captain is a product of MacDougal's 'toothpaste theory.' The captain's parents were ardent supporters of General De Gaulle and then President of France, De Gaulle. His parents and President De Gaulle believed in Quebec separation from Canada. The parent's beliefs influenced the captain to think the same. No different if the parents used Crest toothpaste and the captain used the same in his youth. The captain will continue to use Crest toothpaste. If his parents are Catholic, the captain would be Catholic. If the captain's parents practiced Islam, the captain would practice Islam. It is that simple to Detective MacDougal. However, this Separatist captain is particularly dangerous; he is a skilled bomber. MacDougal suspects the captain in at least one bombing on the outskirts of Quebec City.

The shots continue to fly from the freighter. The captain couldn't care less about why they are trying to kill him. He struggles to turn his boat from the massive ship as increasing swells force his boat closer to the freighter. A bullet strikes the bow of his small boat. Fuck them, he yells. His boat heaves on top of a swell, and the bow drops on the backside of the same swell. Its stern points up above the swell exposing the boat's twin propellers to the air. The propellers throw the remaining water off, and they squeal for water lubrication. His boat slides the length of the swell as the propellers grab the water.

The captain's modified boat's motors possess an impressive 600 horsepower, and extra fuel tanks litter its deck. He makes use of 'red pumps.' Pumps that transfer fuel to the boat's fuel supply enabling him to stay on the water for extended periods. The boat's propellers tear into the water and climb the next wave. The Canadian captain reaches for the switch to turn off his searchlight. A strong tide turns the boat sideways. The captain struggles with the horsepower and steering. It's raining heavily, and water pours off his body. He slips. Hitting the hard deck. He pushes his arms against the floor, regaining a standing balance.

A massive volley, of small lights stream from the freighter's deck. Lightning strikes the freighter's antennae. He reaches again for the searchlight button and at that moment sees a white image floating on a wave. The Canadian captain focuses on his starboard side and determines that the image is two women being thrown about on the ocean's surface. He succeeds in turning off the searchlight, momentarily disappearing from the shooter's view. He's expecting two women. These women are his passengers.

Are they dead? Should he leave them? He can go, and nothing will come his way or will it? If they are alive, how will he get them on board? Standing and controlling the boat is almost impossible. A swell slams the women against the starboard side. No more thinking. A wave then pushes the women away. They are floating together; he can still see them. They are alive. The shots increase in intensity from the freighter and haphazardly spray in every direction.

A wave pushes the women towards the idling boat. He ties a rope to his steering wheel in the direction facing the shore. He touches one of them, but she is motionless.

Immediately, the older woman clutches the side of his boat and times a wave propelling her onto the deck. The captain grasps the non-responsive woman while the older woman lifts herself from the floor and grimaces from the pain in her leg. Her 'see through' clothes stick to her body. The captain concludes the women do not have the cocaine.

The older woman's hair is pressed against her head and covers her left eye. She seizes her unresponsive daughter's arm, and they tug her into the boat. The boat uncontrollably circles towards the freighter. Also, the waves are forcing him towards the ship. The captain unties the rope from the steering wheel. Well, if that is where the ocean directs us, then that will be the way we go. He tells the older woman to lay down next to the other lady and hold on. He accelerates the boat motor as they fall on another wave. He steers towards the freighter. He slams the throttles forward and the engines pop sending fire from the exhaust. He catches a swell flowing to the port side of the ship and pushes the motors to their limit. He crosses dangerously in front of the stationary freighter and yells at the crew again, to go fuck themselves. Let them eat my engine flames. Away from the pull of the waves, his boat disappears into the darkness. He will make it a priority of locating the freighter when it docks on the St. Lawrence River.

They travel south for an extended period on the St. Lawrence River passing Quebec City, ultimately docking the boat on the northern shores of Montreal. The captain directs the now conscious daughter and mother to the nearest clinic. While undergoing medical care for their injuries, a nurse contacts the local authorities. The police question and detain them for illegal entry. When asked by MacDougal's team, if they have heard of Sanchez and/or The Black Cat as it is determined this is a route used by him, the women cannot confirm. When asked again, they state that only the 'Devil' would treat them as they had been on the freighter.

When the women make bond, they visit the L'Oratoire. MacDougal's people instructed them to seek social services found at the church. Before requesting social services, they seek penance. Confess nonexistent sins to the priests at the vestibules inside the church. They individually tell the priests they are sorry for breaking the law when they illegally entered the country. They describe their harrowing story and repeat that only the 'Devil' could have done this to them. They did not know the leader of the criminals. They tried to help the police. They continue their one-sided conversation with the priests. The police kept telling us that the leader of the criminals is most likely a person called El Negro Gato, Gato Negro, the Black Cat. We cannot say yes; it is the Black Cat. We do not know. The women uncontrollably cry after their stories stating that they cannot lie. In an unprecedented move, the priests leave their respected vestibules, cancel penitence, and lead the women to social services.

Another entity noticed unknown to all, including MacDougal and the priests, these Black Cat and Devil statements given by the women in the church.

Reflecting on the women's stories, MacDougal realizes that theirs is not an isolated event similar stories occur on almost every continent. These women are not terrorists but terrorized. Countries fear refugees. Fear is caused by the unknown never having contact with these new refugees, and their culture.

Is there a good reason to worry about refugees who illegally enter a country, yes because there is always that 1% who are evil. Where does that 1% percent number originate, he wonders? Legal entry reduces that threat through a background investigative process. However, 1% already exists in police departments, nursing, manufacturing, attorneys at law, in all fields. The simple refute by keeping them out of one's country is you eliminate the additional 1 percent, and that argument is hard to defeat.

If there were a reasonable means to track illegal entry refugees within the new nation until their cases are reviewed in court, then this fear will subside. You cannot ignore the drain on the economy caused by the refugees. So, if there is no existing tracking mechanism for illegal entries, then make the refugees previous/home environment safe, complete with life support. If successful, the refugees will remain stationary in their own country. Walls can slow illegal entries, but they don't halt the corrupting factors leading to their exodus — both substantial propositions.

How many bails, probationary, parolee jumpers, and wanted outlaws are there running amuck in our country right now? Who knows? We are so lucky up here. The US filters most of the immigrants, and for that matter, contraband before the problem reaches us. We screen again at our southern border. However, this Black Cat character is planning to eliminate US interdiction efforts. What if the Black Cat decides to fly directly over the US and straight into Canada? Also, continues to use vessels to smuggle contraband and aliens pass the US directly into Canada? What a big mess.

Chapter Twenty-Six

It would be easier to put a bullet through the Black Cat's head and end this situation, Moshe ponders. Moshe, a former Mossad intelligence agent, is employed by the devastated Medellin, Colombian Cartel based in Mexico. Moshe is assigned to locate the Black Cat and ascertain who in the Cali, Colombian Cartel controls the Black Cat and take them out. By now, everyone knows the Black Cat orchestrated Cardinal Torres' killing.

Moshe receives information from a Mexican intelligence agent that a Cali operative recently arrived and presently resides at a small hotel in central Mexico City. The Mexican intelligence agent did not know the significance of the Cali individual. Moshe decides to follow the Cali operative from the hotel.

Moshe hit pay dirt when he observes the Black Cat meeting with the same Cali Colombian Cartel operative later identified as Jorge, in Mexico City. Following the first meeting, Moshe follows the Colombian Jorge through numerous barrios of Mexico City and loses him. To Moshe, the Cali operative is more important than the Black Cat. Lucky for Moshe, the Cali Cartel operative Jorge meets a second time with the Black Cat. Moshe follows Jorge to a hut terraced on the outskirts of the metropolis. He determines it is Jorge's very low-keyed Mexico City base.

Somebody is going to pay for the Medellin Cartel's problems in Culiacan. Moshe sits next to a sidewalk taqueria cart able to observe the Colombian walk to and from the hut. The Colombian Jorge repeatedly leaves the shelter to obtain proper cellular communication. Jorge is burning up the phone. Maintaining a low profile, Jorge operates without an observed protection detail.

Moshe's boss, in charge of the Medellin Cartel in Mexico, lost wholesale narcotic caches, that for years were protected by the very same Mex Feds forced to seize the same. The arrival of additional Mex Feds exacerbates the problem. He realizes the distinct Mex Fed groups may 'go at it' with each other if they have received monies from competing criminal groups.

It is Moshe's opinion as an outsider that the Med Feds are corrupt regionally, specifically, within Mexican States boundaries ruled by individual governors. Mexican

231

Governors rule their fiefdoms with limited intervention from the central government and allow corruption in their theatre. The Central government has its hands in other things. Whether it is the Medellin or Cali Cartels with operations in the governors' states, they need to pay to play.

Moshe voluntarily left the Service over allegations of theft. He is a good investigator and uncovered an internal bribery scheme and reported his findings to his boss. Moshe then became a target. He is well schooled and even wrote a lengthy dissertation on how dictators rise to power. Moshe is bitter from the event, and because intelligence is his only skill, Moshe decides to seek employment in Latin America. Now, he works for the Medellin Cartel.

Moshe thinks that the Colombian Cartels are not the only criminals operating in the various Mexican States. Mexican organized criminal groups began accepting the Colombians cocaine for payment to smuggle the dope within Mexico into the US. These Mexican groups then established a separate customer base. To the Colombians, Mexico is becoming too unstable for even the Colombian Cartels. So, the Cartels outsourced the transit of the drugs through Mexico to the Mexicans. With their new spoils of war and associated confidence, the small Mexican organized groups expand into kidnappings for profit, murder for hire, and extortion. Extortion of business owners, including farmers.

The Mexican criminal groups benefited from the Colombian Cartels outsourcing. Now, the Colombians need to reign in their creations. They still employ Mexicans. Now, they need to remind the Mexicans that they are still in control. History is repeating itself. The crazies always take over the established.

While working in Colombia, Moshe realized that Colombia's regional corruption mimics Mexico's corruption. The longer the Cartels exist regionally, the more power they amass. The Cartels in Colombia and

Mexico are never satisfied with their standings, so they expand. Their tentacles eventually reach the central government. With the assistance of existing criminal groups in other countries, the Cartels establish international bases.

Looking at Jorge using the phone Moshe knows the Medellin Cartel boss based in Mexico, Eduardo, wants 'blood' to spill. Medellin's retaliation will be extreme. Eduardo reports to his boss residing in Medellin, Colombia, and acts without administrative malaise. Eduardo commits to doing something, anything. A common trait instilled in people who are successful in their trade.

Moshe will torture this new Informant using the 'water test.' This technique has existed for years. There are other methods of torture, but he wants Jorge to live as long as possible to extract as much information as possible. This poor Colombian will reveal something before nightfall.

Chapter Twenty-Seven

"We're opportunists, Yuri, you know. The US calls it conspiracies. We merely take advantage of ever-changing events; events that we have little control over. With this coke, we can poison France and Germany and acquire US hard currency at the same time. When you add up the numerous smuggling routes, the amount of money is just enormous! The US expends resources in narcotic interdiction very similar to their Vietnam War. The FARC in Colombia is doing its small part as well. Our FARC Communist forces started with some seed money, and are now self-funding from the drug proceeds. Who knows maybe one day they will threaten Colombia's democracy?"

Yuri and General Comstock are in Nicosia, Cyprus, eating lunch. Decades ago, Turkey invaded the country, and as a result, the country is split between Greece and Turkey, but the Cypriot government is supposed to administer the entire island.   An associate refers Cyprus to General Comstock to make use of its liberal banking institutions. The island has become a money laundering haven and will eventually be a flashpoint with leaked preliminary reports of large gas deposits that will be claimed by Israel, Cyprus, Greece, and Turkey.

"Hopefully, I will receive a promotion to 'Soviet Direct Activities' because of my successful supervision of numerous smuggling routes. I hope to get more proactive in activities directed towards the United States. The oligarchs (boys) are doing a great job acquiring hard currency by flooding Europe and Asia with minerals, oil, and gas. So true to their form, the boys raise the rates of oil and gas every winter. If a country steps out of line like Ukraine, the boys manufacture a fake terrorist attack on the natural gas line, of course during winter, and freeze the Ukrainian citizens. They are bringing in much money. If you add our weapon proliferation in the Middle East, Asia and Africa combined with the mineral, gas, and oil sales, then you are talking billions in wealth!"

Yuri lights a cigarette inhales, exhales and follows with a shot of pomegranate raki while listening to the General. Raki is a smooth sweet drink made of grape seeds and skins leftover from making wine. Yuri pours another shot for himself and refills the General's glass.

The General continues, "Oh, we may get caught skimming some money, but don't you forget, Yuri, I'm a Communist, and that is one ideal I will always have."

A cellular call from Boris to Yuri interrupts General Comstock. Boris provides a cryptic brief indicating that the initial Gaza preparations are complete. Following the conversation, Yuri forwards the information to General Comstock.

Following the call, Boris prepares to leave his Beirut, Lebanon hotel. He packs his clothing bags and gathers the necessary documents to travel to the Gaza Strip. He will

drive to Syria transiting Jordan into the Occupied
Territories, Israel and finally into the Gaza Strip. His
concern is the numerous Israeli checkpoints; this will not
be easy. Luck has to be on his side.

Beirut was once referred to as the Mediterranean's
French Riviera before Syria's occupation. Syrian troops
entered the Bekaa Valley in western Lebanon following a
US troop withdrawal. Boris, a western movie buff, knows
'there are drugs in those hills,' and Syria wanted them. The
US withdrawal is precipitated by a suicide bombing
causing the deaths of hundreds of US Marines. Boris'
surreptitious route to the Gaza Strip is necessary as the
northern Israeli border with southern Lebanon is
permanently sealed. Gaza is south of Israel, and presently
under the Israel Defense Forces (IDF) occupation.

Boris drives southwest and with plenty of time on his
hands reminisces on the past. The US was believed to be
the most powerful country in the world. Well, they learned
in Vietnam. How did they expect to win a civil war,
Buddhist against the minority Catholic ruling party based in
Saigon, Southern Vietnam? The US supported the corrupt
Saigon regime. The US believed it could control the
corruption but it was so prevalent that the Saigon ruler
accepted a bribe allowing an organized crime member to
act as the mayor of Saigon. The foundation to succeed was
fractured because of this corruption. It was around 1974
when the US left Vietnam.

In 1979, the US puppet Shah of Iran was deposed. Boris
knows the US felt compelled to support the Mujahedeen in
Afghanistan to stop recent communist advances. In
Afghanistan, the US initially adopted a 'slow bleed'
campaign whereby enough aid was given to the 'Muj' to
keep Russia and the 'Muj' battling for years. Then, the US
provided rockets to the 'Muj' and effectively destroyed our
land and air assets. Ultimately, we left Afghanistan;
eventually, the US will have to battle their creation the

'Muj' in the future, mark my words. Well, we will restore our bruised prestige with the destruction of Chechnya.

How long will this war between the US and Russia last? Britain, Spain, and France fought for centuries. Who benefited? The US, of course. Who will benefit from our endless skirmishes? China, of course. He lights another cigarette and blows the smoke outside his slightly opened driver's side window.

Boris continues his drive south through Lebanon then into western Syria, his country's ally. His relatives live in Syria; he's not seen them for a while. His sister married a Syrian and they have a beautiful family. She's quite content as many Russians live in Syria. They meet regularly at parties. He makes a mental note when this Gaza issue concludes to visit them.

Without incident, he reaches the main Israeli highway, paralleling the Mediterranean Sea. It seemed a little too easy. Maybe, luck is on his side. He's masquerading as a Russian Jew. The only danger so far has been when a tourist bus almost ran him off the road. Israel is clean, orderly, and the farms are lush within sections of the desert. He once tried to ski the slopes in northern Israel, but something ruined his plans. The remaining Roman aqueducts are in decent shape. Probably, because of the dry air. He admits history abounds in the area.

Israel is the homeland of the Jews, the US' politically correct puppet country. Those Germans killed millions of Jews, it was terrible, and it served no purpose at all. That paled to mother Russia when Stalin killed millions of his people. Because of Stalin's paranoia, he ordered the slaughter of innocent Russians. Stalin was insane. It is abhorrent. The Nazis were inhuman, but Boris is smart enough to realize so was Stalin. Back then, he and his family were insulated from the Stalin purges because they lived in Siberia. His family already lived in a gulag.

Because of the Russian genetic trait paranoia, when Russia perceives a threat whether real or not, Russia will use all of its power against known or unknown enemies. The cold war is not over. Tactics only change. He guesses his country decided to make money from these drugs. Some degenerate General probably presented it as a means to poison our enemies, to degrade their effectiveness and economies.

Boris doesn't like it. He's not thrilled that young kids will get addicted to this stuff. His sister has little kids. Why are they open game, now? He's a good operator, but this drug deal is not palatable. What is he going to do? Well, orders are orders. Wow, he sounds like a Nazi or a Stalin henchman. At least his country will never have a drug problem. We can't afford them. Uhm, well, maybe.

Before entering Israel, Boris fills the gas tank. In Israel, he intends to fill up when the gas reaches ¼ of a tank. He does not want to run out of fuel and desires to limit his exposure in the country. Boris enters the last IDF checkpoint into Gaza with the assistance of his comrade a Palestinian friend, Muhammad. At this checkpoint, the soldiers curiously peered at Boris and Muhammad. Upon seeing them, one soldier walked to another and may have pointed at them. Boris and Muhammad remained calm. Without further questions, Boris and Muhammad were allowed to enter the Gaza Strip. Boris' cover was he was to provide construction maintenance to the new Gaza airstrip. He is aware; the airfield is giving the Israeli government permanent heartburn.

Muhammad entered Boris' vehicle at a gas station in eastern Jerusalem. Boris trained Muhammad in Source recruitment, development, and management. Boris and Muhammad worked together on a few missions in Southern Lebanon. Muhammad and his teams became quite proficient in the uncovering of Israeli assets (Sources) operating in Southern Lebanon. It is a nasty business.

When Muhammad's team discovers a purported Israeli asset, the Source seldom survives. Muhammad's way of protecting his teams' involvement. Muhammad is a hero to his Southern Lebanese comrades as he successfully 'flipped' a confirmed Israeli Source. Muhammad was confident that the new Source would not tell his Israeli's boss of the contact. Muhammad sent the Source back to Israel. To this day, Muhammad receives information from this Source. Somehow, Israeli Intelligence has yet to discover Muhammad's actions.

Boris and Muhammad enter the Gaza Strip and coordinate receipt of the dope at the Gaza airport. They remain in a Gaza safe house until contacted by Yuri. The stage is set.

A short Russian government dispatch details to local Moscow media that the next meeting in the talks for distribution of Russian Orthodox church lands will take place in Western Jerusalem, Israel. Russia believes the location provides a neutral site to both the Catholic and Eastern Orthodox churches. The meeting occurs in a few weeks.

Representatives of the Russian government send the same dispatch to Eastern Orthodox Church representatives in Constantinople, present-day Istanbul, Turkey and Catholic representatives in Vatican City. The movement of the negotiations from Russia to Israel, via Gaza, is debated within the Vatican. Following a recent visit by the Pope to Israel, Gaza as a destination for the Mexican delegation corporate aircraft is considered a step in the right direction. After all, the Catholic Church has been at odds with Israel's occupation of the Holy Land. Making use of the Gaza airport will signal a sense of legitimacy to Palestinian autonomy.

The different administrations then forward correspondence with concurrences to the actual delegates. The delegations have no choice but to rubber-stamp the change because the Russians are the negotiators and decision makers in the Russian Orthodox land dispute.

Within a few days, Cardinal Vazquez reads the Vatican correspondence and concurs. He is advised to use the newly built Gaza airstrip.

General Comstock advises Don Pedro, the leader of the Cali Cartel of the change. The flight will originate from Mexico City making use of the same Mexico City FBO with a route, via Teterboro, New Jersey, Shannon, Ireland and right now possibly Italy and onto the Gaza Strip airport, Palestine. The narcotics will be safe in Gaza. Comstock orders 500 kgs. of cocaine.

Before the call, Yuri advises Comstock that the Nuevo Laredo, Mexico based asset Netanya does not respond to telephone calls. They enter into a discussion related to various scenarios on her silence and how to proceed. Presently, it is too risky to send a person to her domicile. She might have died of a heart attack. She was in ill health. Maybe, she's still in stealth mode as she was instructed to shut down after the Matamoros clusterfuck involving Agent O'Malley. Could she have been murdered, during a burglary or a robbery? She is operating in Mexico.

Alternatively, the worst happened. Someone is tracking Yuri's activities, and as a result, Netanya was killed or captured. Comstock orders Yuri to have his people scan Nuevo Laredo press clippings and news reports to ascertain if the police recover her body. Yuri says calls to the Nuevo Laredo morgue met with negative results. Following more trips to Gaza, they will dispatch people to her Nuevo Laredo condo. They will have to remain vigilant. Comstock does not advise Don Pedro of this new development.

Don Pedro wonders why Gaza. Where is Gaza? Uhm. That's over near Israel. He thinks. What a cauldron. What happened to the sure thing, Russia? Russia is foolproof. Well, the same Mexican registered aircraft will still be used to smuggle the cocaine. The listed owner, he has been assured is a Mexican financial company. Two individuals own this commercial company. They registered the plane in the company's name or was it a fake name resembling a legitimate company. He thinks the owners are close friends of the Mexican Finance Ministry. The Mexican financial company leases the aircraft, when not in use by their personnel, to affluent and well-connected businessmen and women.

Don Pedro remembers Flaco recounting a conversation with Jorge, Cali's chief air operations man. Jorge tried to obtain a plane with US registry, the tail number starting with a letter 'N.' Jorge is more comfortable with US registrations as countries believe all the paperwork and pilots are legit, less interdiction. Jorge confirmed that the pilot in command and co-pilot involved with the first delivery would fly the second load. The same crew and aircraft provide some consistency.

Don Pedro still instructs Flaco to personally ensure the 500 kilograms coke have no markings identifying the origin; namely his organization, the Cali Cartel. Don Pedro, a professional marketer, has standing orders forwarded to his supervisors to press the symbol of a king's crown into each kilogram of cocaine and a 100% decal affixed to the wrappings. The markings assure customers that the origin is Cali and the quality of each brick guaranteed. Each taped cocaine brick is to be vacuum sealed with plastic. However, again, for the Gaza delivery no markings.

Flaco also assures each taped cocaine brick is not numbered. Meaning, in the Gaza delivery, Flaco will tell the workers not to write on each brick: 1 of 500, 2 of 500, 3 of 500, and so on. If something goes wrong, the less law enforcement knew, the better. Don Pedro does not want the investigators to know his organization is the source as identified by the king's crown and the 100% decal. Nor, does he want the investigators to know the total amount of smuggled bricks. There is only one customer, Comstock's people.

In a standard established Cali delivery, multiple brokers provide their share of the entire load. Each with a different number of packages. When delivered to the secondary Cali distributors, the numbering system reduces mistakes in the ensuing fast distributions to the next customers. A typical load might have bricks marked 1 of 50, 1 of 25, 10 of 350 so on and so forth. Brokers with the same number of bricks on the first load would inscribe on the outer wrappings an alias or another symbol. The word 'President' written on bricks with the same number of bricks would go to a 'President' customer. The same amount to be delivered to a different customer uses another symbol, an eagle, or a USA decal. A simple children's sticker of an image of a teddy bear or gold star can also differentiate the same broker amounts for delivery to their customers.

When the entire initial load hits the secondary distributor in Houston or El Paso in a matter of hours, distribution begins to each of the designated tertiary customers. The secondary distributor gives the established tertiary customers the date, timing, and general vicinity. The exact delivery location eventually provided to the tertiary customers who then arrive at the temporary warehouse or designated area within their timeframe in their vehicles. Alternatively, the secondary Cali secondary distributor plan with the established tertiary customers to make use of 'straw purchased' loaded cars for delivery to the tertiary customers. The Cali secondary distributor leaves the 'load' vehicle keys on a tire, and the customers drive the loaded vehicles from the area, a parking lot or street corner. The tertiary customers can return the same car loaded with money to another pre-designated location for pickup by the Cali secondary distributors. These deliveries are modified. In shipments of 800 to 1000 kilograms per 'straw' vehicle, the tertiary customers abandon the cars after the transactions. Again, there are other variations.

The real reason Don Pedro instructs Flaco to eliminate markings is a seizure of just a few Cali bricks with Don Pedro's king's crown in Gaza, Israel, or anywhere in that theatre could identify Don Pedro's organization as the source. Don Pedro's identification could reduce his shelf life. Don Pedro weighs the value of his marketing compared to being designated a high-value target (HVT) by US and European intelligence agencies. With the possibility of discovery/seizure of his bricks in that theatre, the same intelligence agencies would conclude that Don Pedro is complicit in providing narcotics to terrorists.

Terrorists often sell drugs to fund their activities. Don Pedro is not entirely clear on what it means to be designated an HVT. Through his own experiences, he knew a few HVTs, and these same HVTs have a higher tendency in getting killed than captured by the same intelligence agencies. Too much for him to handle, Don Pedro does not need those hunters in his jungle. He is already fighting with the Medellin Cartel, some Colombian Forces and US drug agents. He does not need these additional lethal enemies.

Don Pedro must stay in a position to feed the beast. Much as Spain gave them their physical attributes, they also gave Colombia its feudal bureaucratic corruption. Politics and crime start locally. The politicians ascend from the cities to state institutions and on to the federal level. Don Pedro climbs the criminal ladder paying some of these same politicians. Presently, Don Pedro is regionally dominant hence the Cali Cartel. His enemy, the Medellin Cartel, is another regional power. In his mind, the only difference between him and the politicians is the politicians are designated core government employees with inherent credibility and rights. He is a contractor without job security.

When Pablo Escobar was the leader of the Medellin Cartel, he asked for his retirement package, and the central government granted it. Negotiations eventually broke down between the two and Escobar left his cushy confines. With the assistance of his co-opted regional politicians and his inroads into the central government, Escobar transcends his organization to national power. War breaks out, and the US, France, and Colombian forces strike back. Why does war break out, he asks? What causes the Colombian central government to hit again at Escobar? Does the central government act on behalf of the citizenry or on behalf of themselves?

How does Don Pedro identify the 'line of acceptance?' At what level is he accepted? Unable to define the line of acceptance, Don Pedro decides to use his new-found wealth to continue to subvert the central government. He is strengthening his international bases. Right now, Don Pedro intends to control the central government. He learns from Escobar's and Carlos Lehder's mistakes; he will attempt to remain at the 'level of acceptance.'

The US government is pouring millions into the fight buying vehicles, increasing salaries for upper management, security for secret judges, surveillance missions, eavesdropping equipment, and training. Don Pedro admits the jungle training has hurt his organization. The elaborate investigations have not.

If this extra money went to increase the salaries for the cops on the street, he could get damaged further. These newly highly paid cops may not bend to the corruption; they could ignore the bribes, secure their families; they are Colombia's first line of defense. A dedicated group of cops could efficiently 'run' low-level Sources with provided Source monies and work their way up the chain forcing Don Pedro in attempts to stop it at a level above them.

There are large numbers of these cops; he cannot control all of them. They are the real threat that could cost him time and millions of dollars. This first line cops can restore the rule of law. To counter the new strategies and influx of funds, Don Pedro pinpoints his payments: to specific prosecutors, surveillance imagery and intelligence specialist, linguist and a few well-positioned generals and politicians.

For now, Don Pedro feeds the beast. For now, he accepts 'trickle' economics. Not 'trickle-down economics,' where the government supports the people, but 'trickle up economics,' where he aids the corrupted officials.

After spending a day in the Mexican barrio near Jorge, Cali's air operations man, Moshe, the former Mossad agent coordinates on behalf of the Medellin Cartel, Jorge's demise. Moshe hopes to conclude this business today. However, Moshe is ordered to perform a mission in Tijuana, Mexico. The narcotic competition between the Colombian Cartels in northwestern Mexico is escalating. The Cali Cartel is succeeding in acquiring a coveted 'plaza' or route into the United States. Moshe is needed to plan an assassination in Tijuana, but not to participate in the actual 'hit.' The target is the newly installed Cali plaza boss.

Following a brief of the Medellin Cartel's Tijuana plaza boss death and Cali's takeover of the plaza, Moshe believes the assassination was conducted by the local Mexican organized crime group. He wonders if Medellin personnel in the area should stand down and see if the local group strikes again, this time killing the newly installed Cali boss. Moshe is exhausted and decides to finalize the Tijuana mission plan returning to his recently acquired team who had by now commandeered a hut within sight of the Colombian.

Moshe and his men watch as Jorge the Colombian walks from his hut onto a dirt footpath leading to a dirt road. As soon as he walks on the dirt road, Moshe's team members dutifully push Jorge inside their van. To this day, Moshe fears vans. Jorge flails at the assassins unsuccessfully maintaining a grasp on the assassins' limbs. Their limbs resemble vines. Vines attached to a narrow bottomless hole he now descends. The hole Jorge knows leads to Hell.

Once captured in this fashion, the Colombian or anyone else involved in this line of work concludes it is over. Jorge does not hold out in providing some data in an attempt to save his family. He is not sure if this organization has kidnapped them. Jorge tells Moshe and his team most everything the Cali Cartel is up too and what he knows of the Black Cat's plans. Excluding the location of the Black Cat's aircraft. Following Jorge's disclosure, Moshe's men drive him to a Mexico City residence where they kill Jorge.

The killers do not hide Jorge's body. They cut him into pieces and discard the remains at the steps of massive wooden doors. The wooden doors serve as the entrance to Palacio Nacional, the Mexican Presidential palace located on the perimeter of Zocalo Square, Mexico City. The large Mexican flag in Zocalo Square remains limp along the flagpole.

The disposal of Jorge's body means war by the Medellin Cartel against the Cali Cartel, their Mexican associates and the Government of Mexico. It's a stinging rebut; Mexican Officials have been bribed for years to remain neutral in their designated theatre. Now, Mexican Government officials in the Medellin minds, are enforcing the law on behalf of the Cali Cartel. The Cali Cartel have successfully co-opted the Mex Feds to do their bidding. The Medellin Cartel declares outright war! They are back!

As Jorge's body parts are strewn unceremoniously at the doorstep of the President's building, the evil act does not go without notice from the adjacent Mexico City's centuries-old Basilica/Cathedral (Metropolitan Cathedral of the Most Blessed Virgin Mary into Heavens) a building that appears to be barely breathing because of the city's altitude and pollution. Its massive brown walls are turning black. The disadvantaged citizenry sits on its sidewalks, benches and its pews. The building is doing its best to keep from sinking further into the former swamp, Mexico City. Its walls resembling massive forearms with clenched fists are slowly losing the battle in keeping the building erect. The fists are slowly shifting back and forth in an attempt not only to stay afloat from the drained swamp but also to try to elevate the building walls from the strain imposed on it by the constant requests of much-needed aid from its parishioners. Its two weakened towers strain to extend its bent legs from the weight of misery, pushing it into the ground.

Its thick wooden doors are drying as an older man's skin. The grotesque disposal of the human observed by the 'Old Man of the Basilica' his formal name but referred by his friends as the 'Old Man of the Building.' This 'Old Man' of the Basilica is the same entity who received the Morse code message from the Culiacan lamppost advising of the assassination of the Cardinal and the killers, and previously the recipient of dispatches from the lampposts identifying the new Matamoros Black Cat terror group responsible for murdering the Mex Fed Colonel in Nuevo Laredo.

An image forms on the entrance of the building. The image forms into 'Old Man's' face. The 'Old Man' cranes its head to get a better view of the vicious act. The old man says to itself: the leaders have abandoned the disenfranchised, sick, and weak. The good people need immediate assistance. Moreover, in the popular vernacular of his friends up north, it says to itself, "It is time to take names and kick ass."

During this period, thousands of miles away a woman and man walk on a cold, damp brick street. They just left their favorite bar. The man politely escorts the woman within a block of her apartment. They embrace and separate. The man walks across the street towards his studio out of view of the female. The woman continues toward her apartment. Initial reports indicate that a man walks within a few feet of the woman and fires three shots from what appeared to be a low caliber pistol. The woman dies at the scene.

Todd, the US intelligence officer, continues reading from the correspondence providing quick summaries, "There is more in the cable. They are awaiting an autopsy. There are limited leads. It appears following the shots; the shooter enters a dark sedan. Kiev, Ukrainian government officials are still interviewing the female's neighbors. So, and so forth...."

Todd moves his free hand back and forth, looks at Socorro and Rebecca and continues, "It's believed the killing is reminiscent of the Russian Secret Police. Also, if you see the references on the cable, it was her, the deceased, who provided the information indicating the use of an aircraft by the Black Cat/Sanchez. The Black Cat is a negotiator regarding the Russian Orthodox lands including those in Ukraine that are purportedly for sale. The Source, if you remember indicates suspect activities related to the same plane."

Socorro then intercedes, "One of our Sources has a sub Source who believes it found the location of the Black Cat's plane. It is at the main Mexico City Juarez named commercial airport within a small FBO for large as well as private aircraft. To have access to the hangar, you need Mexican government authorization."

Rebecca interrupts, "So, someone in the Mexican government is involved in the upcoming negotiations. No doubt another official or officials have figured out that it would be another money pit to tap. I wonder when the plane flies? Is it under diplomatic cover or is it just privately flying around the world with the other twenty to thirty thousand corporate planes?"

Rebecca leans back in her chair, moves her arms above her head, and then places her hands on her head, taking a deep breath. "If it has a US registry number, we have problems. US registrations lead to PO Boxes. It's easier for me to register a plane in the US than my car in a State. Is there a Mexican official on the delegation's corporate aircraft?" She looks at Todd and Socorro. "This is certainly escalating."

Todd and Socorro glance at each other but do not interrupt. Rebecca continues, "There is a high probability that the Kiev Ukrainian Source's killing is related to this fucking Black Cat deal. Some of the Russian Orthodox holdings are in Ukraine. The Source must have been close to the negotiations. Was the Kiev Source killed in response to our action against Netanya, the portly one sent to Guantanamo?" Rebecca places her hands on the desk. "Regardless, HQS plans to send paramilitaries our way." She points her hand at Todd and Socorro. "Interview the Source related to the Sub Source today. I will plan for y'all to interview the Mexican government official Informant with 'one mission at hand': find out if Yuri and/or General Comstock are still in the area. I think we have enough on Yuri. We need more on Comstock. We have to get on him, too. If you find Yuri, we will have one target for HQS."

Socorro raises her eyebrows, curiously looks at Rebecca, and says quietly, "So, we have moved from collecting data to targets?"

Rebecca does not answer.

Socorro advises, "We will interview the airport Source, first. After we interview the Mexican official at the safe house, we will be close to the commercial Benito Juarez airport. It makes for a long day that will lead into the night."

To break the uneasy mood caused by Socorro's target question, Todd immediately follows Socorro's remarks, "If we see something of significance we will stay in the area. We will keep you updated. We have acquired a private FBO list at the commercial airport, and there are not many." Todd pauses, "I was under the impression that smaller private aircraft are not permitted to land at the commercial international airport in Mexico City. They are to use Toluca."

Rebecca does not respond to Todd's remark, "I hope they starve that fat bitch in Guantanamo." Again, Todd and Socorro remain quiet. "She won't provide any information to us. Uhm. Let me know what happens."

"Will do."

The strain on Rebecca's face is noticeable. A result of cutting the Netanya link that might have led to Yuri and possibly Comstock. Rebecca reviews the past action and reaffirms to herself that bagging the bag was the only the option.

Before the anticipated departure of the Black Cat from Mexico City, a Cali Cartel 'Lieutenant,' not referred to as the stone-cold psychopath he is, is ordered by Don Pedro to meet with the Black Cat. The Lieutenant gives a quick brief of Jorge's death. The Black Cat questions the Lieutenant further about Jorge's death, but he does not have any answers. The Lieutenant is not concerned that Jorge might have revealed damaging information before his death that could prove deadly to them all. This Lieutenant is overconfident in his abilities.

The Lieutenant orders the Black Cat to prepare to take receipt of the narcotics in hours. Nothing like cutting it short. They are scheduled to leave tomorrow. Because Jorge did not contact him, the Black Cat is under the impression of postponement of the next load. Compartmentalization continues.

The Lieutenant's men will deliver the narcotics inside the same private Mexico City Fixed Based Operator (FBO) hangar, and the Black Cat will load them on the plane. The

Lieutenant reveals the customary payoffs have been made to the airport authorities to 'turn their heads,' 'take a long coffee break, or 'just feign sickness and leave for the day.'

Following this meeting, the Black Cat rushes to the FBO. While driving, he makes a note to contact his people in the National Liberation Army (ELN) another Marxist Leninist group operating in Colombia, similar to the FARC. At one time, Catholic priests acted in leadership roles in the group. Don Pedro is acting irrationally, and the Black Cat needs protection, an insurance policy or at least more information on Don Pedro's organization.

The Black Cat is Jesuit educated but chose to work at a Parish. In the past, he met priests sympathetic with Colombia's downtrodden the ELN is established to assist them. However, like a majority of groups, they are being hijacked by more radical personnel, and the ELN is now moving in a violent direction.

The Cali men deliver the packages inside the hangar next to the aircraft. The Black Cat puts the boxes in the plane. Numerous Cali associates remain near the corporate jet.

Once again, this time Moshe's team observe the Cali Lieutenant meeting with the Black Cat. Jorge provided Moshe's men the location of the Black Cat's temporary lair and followed the Black Cat from the Shrine residence to the Lieutenant. Losing Jorge after the Black Cat's first meeting with Jorge was beneficial to the Medellin Cartel. Because of the delay, the Cali Cartel is at a loss on how the Medellin Cartel located Jorge. Moshe plans to follow the Black Cat until a majority of Cali Cartel's operatives are identified and killed.

The Cali Lieutenant notifies Don Pedro of the successful delivery of the narcotics to the aircraft. Moshe's team follows the Cali Lieutenant accompanied by his guards subsequently observing them eating outside of a Zona Rosa restaurant near the Golden Angel monument. A roundabout encircles the Golden Angel monument close to the US Embassy on Reforma Street.

Moshe is content with Jorge's information, and because of that, they are not kidnapping the Lieutenant and his guards. Plus, one of Moshe's men recognized the Cali Lieutenant linking him directly to Don Pedro, himself. Moshe now possesses corroboration of Cali Cartel interference. The Black Cat and Don Pedro instigated the Medellin Cartel's recent 'troubles' with the Mex Feds. Moshe reaffirms his plan to delay action against the Black Cat. The proxy war has proved so devastating to the Medellin Cartel, that Moshe's boss, Eduardo contemplates a temporary moratorium of smuggling in Western Mexico.

Moshe relays this newly discovered information to his boss, Eduardo. Within a few minutes, Eduardo calls Moshe with his decision.

Moshe in his vehicle follows his assassins in their car. The traffic moves ever slow, bumper to bumper as always. The temperature and pollution rise and the sun is cracking the skin on Moshe's left arm as it rests on the driver's door. The vehicles in tandem slowly maneuver next to the parallel parked cars alongside the sidewalk of the Zona Rosa restaurant.

The assassins' sedan passenger side, heavily tinted windows, facing the Lieutenant and his guards are rolled down. The driver's side windows are also slightly rolled down to reduce the impending percussion of bullets. In a matter of seconds, the murderers let out a volley of shots decimating the patrons seated at the sidewalk tables. Bodies drop hard onto the dirty sidewalk. Plates, glasses, and tables are in shatters. Following the melee, Moshe and his killers slowly drive from the scene. The traffic does not permit otherwise. The vehicles move in separate routes eventually to be replaced by other cars disappearing into the massive city.

Moshe wonders, how far will the killings go? Will Don Pedro go down next or the Black Cat?

Flaco, Don Pedro's spokesman and his right-hand man, immediately notifies Don Pedro of the Lieutenant's death. Flaco, present in Mexico City, assumes all Mexico City operations. It's evident to Flaco and Don Pedro that the Medellin Cartel spent thousands of dollars acquiring intelligence throughout the city. The loss of Jorge and now the Lieutenant might impact the pending load to Gaza as well as future shipments. Don Pedro leaves Cali to a ranch fifty miles southeast.

Flaco, with the assistance of established Mexican based affiliated operational assassins, retraced Jorge's death. Flaco burns through thousands of dollars to obtain the data he needs. He learns Jorge's death and the Lieutenant are hallmarks of one known notable killer group. Flaco identifies Moshe as the killer. Flaco is now going hunting, concluding again that the root of these problems is the Black Cat.

Moshe briefs Eduardo of the Colombian Lieutenant's demise. Eduardo asks about the whereabouts of the Black Cat. Oh, shit, Moshe thinks.

"Sir, my team was spread thin when we observed the meeting between the Black Cat and the Lieutenant."

"And you?"

"I concentrated my men on the Lieutenant. As stated before, he was identified by one of my team members as a direct link to Don Pedro."

Because of his sweaty palms, Moshe loses the grip on his phone, and it falls to the floorboard. He snatches the phone from the floor. His heart pounds. He anticipates what Eduardo will ask. "When my men located the Lieutenant at the restaurant, we held in the area until instructed." There is an uncomfortable pause.

"Yes, yes."

"And then I dispatched a man to the Black Cat's Shrine residence."

"You'll never get another chance. He has to know at least one of the contacts is dead. He might get a call that another contact has fallen. He's in the wind."

"I know he is there," Moshe's experience tells him the Black Cat's personality will not let him leave the area.

Eduardo indirectly orders Moshe to kill the Black Cat.

"I will get him."

Eduardo terminates the call without warning. Moshe is handling this matter; Eduardo is overseeing the overall proxy war. Moshe's head pounds, his ears turn red, and sweat pours from all of his pores. He sits motionless in the vehicle, his phone lays on his left palm as he stares into the massive congestion. He will act; he has to do something.

Moshe instructs his men to surround the Cardinal's residence. After loading the aircraft, the Black Cat returns to the Shrine before Moshe's men established an effective perimeter. The Black Cat will remain at his apartment and accompany Cardinal Vazquez the following morning to the airport.

Flaco assures Don Pedro the existence of twenty-four-hour surveillance of the aircraft. Flaco tells Don Pedro that our guy here hired many loyal men. Additional reserves covertly arrived in the vicinity of the Black Cat's temporary quarters. Flaco concludes the conversation that his men have established a 'good eye' on the exit the Black Cat is to use on the following morning. Flaco is steaming. He is now providing security for this asshole.

While the Black Cat packs his suitcase, Montreal City Detective MacDougal calls the Shrine's operator.

"Yes, sir."

"Yes, this is Pierre an alias known to the Black Cat for MacDougal, and I would like to speak to Bishop Federico Sanchez."

"And the nature of your call?"

"I'm an old friend. He will be glad to hear from me."

The telephone operator notifies Sanchez of the contents and identity of the caller before forwarding MacDougal's call to him. A moment of silence occurs. The Black Cat assimilates the reason for MacDougal's call. The operator asks if everything is all right.

"Yes, yes, I'll take it. Wait a minute. Hold on."

Jesus, what's next? The Black Cat reviews the recent meeting with the Lieutenant; the Lieutenant was not concerned if Jorge leaked valuable information. Someone is on my heels, and now out of the blue, Mounties or Detective MacDougal or whatever his title is, calls me. What the hell does the Detective know? The dope has to go through it's on the plane. The plan will continue. What the hell does this guy want? More importantly, again, what the hell does this guy know?

How did Don Pedro's people conceal the smell or residue of the cocaine? Was cocaine residue left on the exterior of the vacuum-packed kilograms? The dogs will 'hit' on that. Are the packages going to smell in the aircraft? The boxes will be on the plane the entire night. Hopefully, detergent strips are comingled with the contents to deter the smell. Who knows if that helps, but it should make him feel better? His paranoia is out of control.

Detective MacDougal remains on the line; a recording in Spanish mentions Jesus. He understands some of the messages. At least, it isn't a Black Cat recording, reciting verses. He shakes his head; this is crazy shit. MacDougal places the call on behalf of O'Malley, to probe the Black Cat's whereabouts, nothing more. O'Malley believes the Black Cat is a dope dealer, killed a Mex Fed and was probably involved in the killing of the Cardinal. O'Malley can prove nothing. Just think about it. A priest, well respected, flimsy evidence, a priest assigned by the Pope to meet with Russians regarding lands owned by the Russian

Orthodox Church. Who would get involved in a mess like this? MacDougal will.

MacDougal justifies the call to the Black Cat as a means to obtain updated intelligence related to alien smuggling operations in his area of responsibility (AOR). He, too, believes the Black Cat is a drug dealer.

MacDougal listens to church music. It's not that bad; it's soothing. He hums along, and he reaches for his bottle in the desk drawer and wonders if the Montreal Canadians are expected to do well this year? He is starving, and not one Timmy Horton's donut remains in the box. A bunch of savages surrounds him.

The Black Cat slithers down his leather chair and fights to remain conscious. His eyes roll up into his eyelids. Does MacDougal know he is flying to New Jersey? Does MacDougal know the dope is on the plane? It just got loaded. Does he have eyes on the ground? Okay, get yourself together. He's in this business to succeed. Okay, he will reveal facts as close to the truth as possible. Should he talk to him at all? How did he get my number? I'm public. All MacDougal has to do is inquire at my Matamoros diocese. My staff could have given him my telephone number. That is why Jose was invaluable; he would have filtered the call. The Black Cat stands and rubs his hands together. Runs his hands over his head and takes a deep breath. Shit, okay, stay close to the truth. He picks up the receiver from the coffee table.

"Okay, operator send it through."

"Yes, sir."

"Yes, my old friend. How have you been?"

"Good, good; it's been a long time."

"It has. I hope you are still doing the Lord's work up there."

"And you as well 'down there,' Bishop Sanchez." What a wise ass in saying, 'down there.'

"I am and most recently, as I'm sure you are aware, I'm personally negotiating with the Russians for the repatriation of Catholic possessions in Russia. It is a great honor."

"Yes, I have heard, and yes indeed, it is a great honor. That is why I am calling."

"It is?" The Black Cat almost pisses in his pants.

"I was wondering, well, I was wondering…I hate doing this…."

The Black Cat involuntarily twitches and squeezes the phone. He interrupts the Detective in mid-sentence in an attempt to make MacDougal terminate what he might be contemplating.

"I'm coming to New Jersey tomorrow," the Black Cat interrupts.

"You are?" MacDougal is somewhat perplexed.

"My duties require that I go to the meetings and we have to refuel in New Jersey, as you probably already know. If you are in the area, we can meet and have a quick coffee at the FBO. Of course, it is far from Canada."

The Black Cat has mastered plane talk. After all, he is quite coachable. Deflect and knock off balance is a trait he learned from Yuri. No need to mention the Gaza landing. The landing was made public, but MacDougal probably is not scanning every newspaper in the world. Divulging his itinerary is a bold move. If MacDougal is contemplating an interdiction in concert with his US buddies, it might cast doubt that his new sophisticated transportation is being used to smuggle narcotics.

"Well, let me see. It is short notice." MacDougal takes a quick shot of Crown Royal. He heard from a friend that one day there would be a maple Crown Royal, that will be dangerous. The drink warms his body and mind. "I will need authorization to get off work. You know, the girlfriend always wanted to go to see a play in New York."

Get off work? Is he not working? Maybe, he just said that and he plans to target the aircraft. None of the aliens arrested by MacDougal in Canada knew of the aircraft. The vessel captains, whose ships the aliens disembarked to enter the smaller boats, might have heard of the operation. They are all Cali associates. Rumors are dangerous, and so is his paranoia. The Black Cat is determined to control his fear.

MacDougal says, "If we make it down there, I can give you my girlfriend's bible and crucifix so you can ask the Cardinal to bless them. The Cardinal that is traveling with you." MacDougal mentions the Cardinal to indicate that he has some knowledge of the Black Cat's activities.

"His Eminence might be able to sign the bible and bless it as well as the crucifix at the refueling stop. We can work it out."

"Thanks. I was checking in to see if you had additional information on those people up here. You know what I mean."

"Uhm, no, I know what you mean. I have not inquired. I've been quite busy. When I have some downtime, I'll reach out to some people. If I learn anything, I will get back to you." This MacDougal is good probing everywhere, not exposing his real intentions. He did not ask for the aircraft tail number? He has to know it.

"Sounds good. Let me know. It is always good to hear from a friend. I'll try to call you tomorrow. You still have the same cell number or another?"

"I have the same cell. Call me early for I'll leave early."

"I will. Buena Suerte (Good luck)." Good luck? What did he mean by that? Does he know? An interesting move.

Events are moving fast. Moshe's men converge on the Shrine as observed by Flaco's stationary surveillance. Flaco is eighty percent sure that these new arrivals work for Moshe. Who else is after the Black Cat? That is why he leaves a twenty percent chance out there. This Vatican deal is now, the only priority in all of Mexico City.

At the concentric surveillance, Flaco sits in his car. He wonders if there is a way to orchestrate a move that enables Moshe's men to kill the Black Cat and then he kills Moshe. The thought lasts a second. Don Pedro has a lot riding on this deal. More importantly, the Russians invested in the Black Cat with the Cardinal's killing and the Black Cat's subsequent promotion to the negotiating table. To the Russians, the Black Cat must stay alive for at least six to eight months.

"Keep the men alert, Juan," Flaco relays on the portable radio.

"Yes, sir," Juan replies.

Juan was awake the entire night, personally approaching each of his men without detection from Moshe's men and reminding them of the importance of this mission and relaying locations of known or suspected Moshe's associates and their expected capabilities. Finally, advising each to remain cryptic in their radio conversations.

Flaco maintains cellular contact with the group guarding the dope on the aircraft.

"Everything secured?"

"Yes, sir," the voice replies.

"Report anything out of the ordinary, understood?"

"Yes, sir."

Flaco does not advise the Black Cat of the presence of Moshe's men, and the Black Cat does not relate the MacDougal conversation to Flaco. The Black Cat will be a suspected Informant. If this goes bad and he forwards the contents of the MacDougal conversation, Flaco will kill him. Unbeknownst to the Black Cat, Flaco held out a twenty percent chance someone else could be after the Black Cat in Mexico. Flaco is right. He just selected the wrong geographic region; the twenty percent threat is from Canada.

Following MacDougal's conversation with the Black Cat, MacDougal contacts O'Malley.

"I spoke with Sanchez, the Black Cat."

"Good, what did he have to say?"

"He's traveling tomorrow on Vatican business and will land in New Jersey to refuel."

"Interesting. I bet it is a private plane, that's why the Black Cat said they will need to refuel in Jersey. You don't say that if you are traveling on a commercial plane. I wonder if there are narcotics on that plane? Man, using an aircraft. Did you get the tail number?"

"Shit, I was shocked when I heard it. I plain forgot. I did not think about it." MacDougal hits his hand against his forehead. "Tail numbers are just like license plates, man I screwed up, sorry. About the dope, who knows. He's untouchable." MacDougal says, half convinced.

"He volunteered the plane information?"

"Yes, he's either very confident, or he's not moving dope. I tried to get a new number for him, but he did not provide one. He says he is still using the old cell."

"He's a dope dealer. Is he moving it now?" Seamus O'Malley reviews MacDougal's information. "Thanks, on the number try. Don't worry about the tail number; I'll figure it out."

"It's fifty-fifty on the dope thing, but the odds are ninety percent against and ten percent for dope. I know that does not make sense when you put into play a possible semi-diplomatic status. Do they have diplomatic status or just flying around like everyone else? Uh. Take into account the heavyweight occupants. If they smuggle on the aircraft, it will be bold. There are big people behind this. You know if they are doing it, they are saying fuck you, fuck all of you; bring it on!" MacDougal is fired up about the case. "Who will search the plane, if there is no dope they will be screwed."

"Yea, maybe. My question is, would they jeopardize the talks to smuggle dope? The talks are big money — however, it's perfect who will suspect smuggling on the

259

aircraft. Well, let me think about it. Hey, thanks for the call. If you need help down here one day, give me a call. Remember, we have real Texas B B Q, not that Alberta beef and we have Lone Star beer."

"Oh, yea I heard, but we have hockey! Oh, the Black Cat says he would meet with me in New Jersey."

"But what would you find? A priest. A Cardinal. What's in the plane is what's important. Man, what a mess."

"Well, think about it and give me a call. I'm in. If there is a way to help."

"Hey, thanks a lot."

"Seriously, stay in touch."

"I will."

Following the conversation, MacDougal full of energy and a few shots, goes for a workout. When it comes to losing weight, he is on a mouse wheel. After his workout, MacDougal walks pass the Notre Dame church in Old Town. He sees joggers amongst the abandoned locks and turns at a beautiful boutique hotel and enters an Old Town Montreal bar and watches hockey. While watching the game, MacDougal reviews the aircraft case. He remembers the news mentioned that there are only a few military jets that patrol all of Canada. O'Malley told him there are thousands of private corporate aircraft. He shakes his head and tries to enjoy his Canadian beer.

In this part of the world, Mexico City, Heaven, and Hell will visit with all of its might. Without remorse, two rival groups are about 'to go at it.' Flaco bets, Moshe's men will not kill the Black Cat when they observe him with another Catholic Cardinal. They cannot withstand that much heat. Moshe will stalk the Black Car waiting for an opportune moment, and that will be it for the Black Cat.

Flaco is operating at a disadvantage because he was not able to determine how much information Jorge provided. Flaco's men at the FBO have not identified counter surveillance. Moshe's men remain at the Shrine. Why Flaco asks? They do not know about the aircraft and the FBO, that's why. Jorge did not divulge the whereabouts of the plane. When the Black Cat's plane departs the airport, Flaco's team will strike first.

"'J,' we will 'shop' (attack) near the 'freezer' (airport) following 'check out' (take-off). That means we cannot lose any 'vegetables' (Medellin Cartel) when they roll from the 'freezer.' Be prepared 'to clean up the spill on aisle 1' (protect) if the 'vegetables' (Medellin) 'shop' (attack) the 'asshole' (the Black Cat) before 'check out' (take-off)."

"Got it. Yes, sir."

Why, Gaza? The Palestinians are throwing rocks at the Israeli soldiers, and the Israeli's retaliate with rubber bullets. The violence is escalating, but Boris is ready as soon as the plane lands at the Gaza airport his men will offload the boxes and secure them. This will be dangerous.

The Israeli and the Palestinians situation worsens. That Ariel Sharon, Boris thinks, whose payroll is he on? Whoever it is, they did not pay him enough. Did he want more money and more power? Maybe both, so he says to himself. I want to be the President of Israel. Approximately a year and a half ago, Sharon takes it upon himself to walk into the third largest Middle East ant hill, the Dome of the Rock in Jerusalem. The third holiest shrine to the Muslims behind Medina and Mecca, respectively.

Sharon did not walk into the area unaccompanied or with a few plainclothes guards, but with numerous guards. To the Palestinians, Sharon's theatrics are an invasion. Again, why? He said it was to reinforce Israel's control. Sharon, a war hero, is the cause of these recent skirmishes. This conflict will boil over. In this part of the world, one drinks tea with your family one day, and the war comes right to your front door, the next. What choice do you have in becoming a war hero?

"This time it is more serious," Boris tells Muhammad. They sit at a table outside a Gaza Strip café. In this pre-war climate, they decide to remain in Gaza throughout the recent troubles. If they leave Gaza, the Israeli Defense Forces (IDF) might not permit them to reenter Gaza.

"Yes, it is," Muhammad replies.

"I know it's more serious than usual, I feel it," Boris swats at a fruit fly.

"The Israelis went too far this time. Sharon pushed through the 'line of acceptance,' invading our holy site. Our Jericho soldiers are ready. It is a Second Intifada." Mohammad frowns and shrugs his shoulders.

"I'm sure they are ready. You're right; this is another Intifada. You know why it is worst?"

Muhammad does not answer.

"The Palestinians attacked some tourists."

"Yes, they have."

"My friend, tourism is the lifeblood for your occupied country. They are biting the hands that feed you."

"Yea, well. Emotions are hard to put down. Fatah and Hamas are competing for publicity; their suicide bombers are striking everywhere. Other groups are getting in the action as well. Maybe, Hamas is taking advantage of the situation. Hamas has the luxury of not being forced to work with other political leaders."

"Hey, has Arafat lost his grip on these extremists?"

"Extremist. I can't believe you said that. Man. It's too early to tell, but when the number of martyrs' mounts, tensions rise. They shoot at us, and we respond with suicide bombings, gunfire, and knives. However, our Qassam rockets will be released soon."

"I hope this does not blow tomorrow."

"'Inshallah.' There are more tanks on the eastern border of Gaza southern Israel and down towards the tunnels with Egypt near Rafah than there were yesterday. I've noticed an increase in IDF patrols."

"Not good," Boris sips his strong coffee. "Muhammad, I am growing tired of these conflicts. They never end. I traveled from Lebanon. Conflict. Then to Syria, constant antagonism between the Alawites, Shiites, and the Sunnis. To Jordan, with their large PLO population displaced when forced to flee Israel. Then, the PLO tries to take over Jordan. That was put down. Sinai, Egypt, Iraq, Kuwait, the entire Levant, and the Middle East has always been at war. The Balfour Agreement after WWI was supposed to settle these problems by making artificial boundaries. Nothing was solved. People are constantly being forced to flee their homes for one reason or another."

"Yes, they are, and then the families settle down at one location and are forced to flee again, Sunnis, Shia, Alawites, Jews, and the Yazidis. You're right; it never ends."

"You need peacemakers. That may sound strange coming from me, but even I can see the constant problems. Families, now refugees on the march from this conflict to that conflict. From this country to that country. Marching on. Marching on." Boris raises clenched hands from the surface of the coffee table. He repeatedly moves his arms up and down, mimicking a marching soldier. He smiles and shakes his head at Muhammad. "Everybody in this entire area is on the move, shuffling here shuffling there, marching. Dragging all their possessions with them; families transformed into refugees. Clouds of desert dust rise from the refugees' footsteps as they flee dust clouds identifying the origin of the latest atrocities. These dust clouds transform into sandstorms. You know, Muhammad. I think the sandstorms are not a weather phenomenon but caused by the refugees." Boris pauses and glances at Muhammad. Boris says this in jest. Muhammad listens. "Maybe, the refugees will never have a permanent home. I mean look at Moses and his people, they wandered in the desert for years. I am making a joke." He puts his left hand on Muhammad's shoulder. "But nothing has changed since then."

"It's changed."

"No, it has not," Boris snaps back. "Muhammad, do you want to occupy Israel because it is a secure, productive country? Are you jealous? I drove through it with its modern infrastructure. Its lands are clean, no litter. Is that why you have it in for them? Or, are you fighting to get your ancestral lands?" Boris pauses again. "Don't answer that. I am tired, forget what I have been saying. It's just that coordinating this narcotic deal here seems so fruitless when compared to the refugees' plight. Who helps these people?" Boris swallows the remaining coffee from his cup. He is working on this deal so some fat Generals will get access to a dacha. A Dacha?

"Boris, it is not as simple as you make it sound. Try growing up in this area. You can't keep turning the other cheek to the injustices I have seen and heard of."

"I know what you are saying. It's just that this is a mess. Now, I am joking." Boris raises his open hands to his chest and continues, "But, is it so fucked up around here because of the intense heat, the sun beating down on everyone? Now, please don't hit me. Is it the historical inbreeding?" Boris laughs with clenched fists and puts them in front of his face to deflect a blow from Muhammad.

Muhammad only smiles as these nonsensical conversations always occur when there is downtime. "You are fucked up."

"You married your sister, right?" Boris laughs out loud. He tries to get a rise out of the always stoic Muhammad.

"She's not my sister. What's wrong with you? Shit. She is a 2nd cousin twice removed or something like that." Mohammad tries to make a joke. He almost laughs.

Finally, getting him to loosen up, Boris drops the inbreeding subject but continues on the refugee issue. "Muhammad, deserts and sand blanket this violent area. It as if the sand hides dark secrets." Boris points east. "I believe the refugees, throughout the centuries, have trampled what remained of life to dirt? I mean it Muhammad, and I'm serious. Something has to change. It is sad."

"I know my friend. I see the people around me. What can I do? It is complicated."

"You're right."

Boris reaches into his shirt pocket and gives his cigarette box to Muhammad. Muhammad places his index finger in the opening and retrieves one cigarette. Boris lights it. Muhammad then leans his head over the back of his white plastic chair. Inhales deeply and exhales a plume of smoke that slowly rises above them. The smoke gently flows to the outdoor market. Without speaking, they turn their attention to the civilians shopping at the market.

The market is an explosion of noise and bright colors. Vegetables and fruit lay in various wood and plastic cartons. Owners of the goods swipe at fruit flies making use of stalls passed down through the generations. Occasionally, the proprietors squeeze the fruit and vegetables, assessing their freshness. If needed, they rotate them within the carton. If overly ripe, they place them in separate containers for sale or trade to the fruit juice vendors. Wooden barrels contain pistachios. The vendors with their metal scoops sift and eat the pistachios. A healthy supply of bulk rice and chickpeas exist. Small fish are laid on the ground and then plied with ice. Lightly colored textiles mix amongst the food stalls.

Patrons frequent specific vendors. They selected these vendors following past disputes with others. They have long memories. The shoppers gently squeeze the fruit determining its freshness, give it to the proprietor, and repeat moving onto the vegetables. To pass the time, some vendors place friendly bets amongst themselves as to how many times a particular shopper will squeeze the items and/or ask the repetitive question, "When did you get this item?"

Various spices yellow, red and green in color fill the wooden barrels. When asked, the proprietor scoops the spice and pours it in a bag, weighs and gives the price to the shopper.

Young children surround the juice carts. They are jumping up and down and pointing at their favorite juice. The vendors race to fill the orders. Children seeing the same carts beg for their moms' attention. As if the moms are not aware of the location of each fruit cart. Other children drag their moms by the sleeve to the fruit wagons. Worn soccer balls bounce throughout the maze followed by shouts of young children.

The smell of freshly brewed tea fills the air. Tea waiters walk the market holding metal trays complete with four glasses and a hot tea receptacle. Ready to pour the sweet tea into the glass for a thirsty customer.

Boris breaks the serene silence. "Seriously, I have told you this before, I know, I am a small part of the refugee problem. However, the other side is just as guilty. I am still getting headaches and those reoccurring nightmares. I keep seeing that child I told you, about. The traumatized child can no longer speak and only cries following the destruction of her family home. They are forced to flee their home. They only carry necessities as their car is damaged. They keep walking in my dream, the father, mother, son, and daughter. There is no color in my dreams, just black and white. Her beautiful, clean shoes, her dad spent a personal fortune to buy, get dirtier as she walks. The girl's well-groomed hair becomes matted as she walks. Her dress begins to fray. Over and over, she looks to her mom as if to ask why are you doing this to me? Her mom, with tears in her eyes, does not answer."

"The skinny girl grows weaker and weaker. She leans as she walks and drags one foot and then the other. To bolster her strength, her family relieves her of the small possessions she is carrying, everything except her favorite stuffed bear. The little girl maintains a firm grip on her bear and cannot keep pace with her family. The impetuous dust is everywhere."

"The family slows and waits for her. I tell them in my dream, "Pick her up!" "Carry her!" They do not hear me. They are all so weak and have no more drinking water. They wait for her, but she continues to separate from her family. She tugs on her bear as if it was her mommy. I say to her, hurry up or you will be left behind."

"She stumbles, and she falls into a cloud of dust. She clutches her bear in her right hand and places it against her chest. Her beautiful face covered with wet sand. Then, she is no longer in my dream. Where is she? I try running after her. My legs barely move. They are heavy. I grit my teeth and pull on my legs with my hands to move them. I then try to push them down, but they do not move. I rock my arms back and forth to create some momentum, but my body does not move. My legs then barely move. I awake in a sweat. I am disturbed by this dream. How do you think they feel?"

Boris puts his right hand over his lowered forehead and rubs it as if trying to massage away another headache. He couldn't care less if Muhammad thinks he is growing weak every time he tells Muhammad of his dreams. After repeating the story this time, Boris hopes to get a transfer. Alternatively, he desires that someone will just put him out of this misery.

For a short time, Muhammad does not respond. He then replies, "You are just burned out."

"No, I'm afraid it is more than that, my friend."

To change the sordid topic, Muhammad moves to another, "I hope it goes as planned."

"I guess I do too," Boris raises his finger to quiet Mohammad, "let me get this done." Boris contacts Yuri by cellular telephone.

"Tensions mounting. Am monitoring."

"Is it still open?"

"Affirmative."

"Best guess."

"A couple of days. A week perhaps a few weeks. It is simmering over here. Can you abort?"

"Too late, the woman gave birth, already."

"Understood."

Boris and Muhammad hear the sound of a Qassam rocket lifting off from Gaza City towards Israel. Muhammad points to the sky. He had just predicted it would happen, a surprise before the talks.

"What was that?" Yuri asks.

"You heard that?"

"Yes."

"You know what that was," Boris raises his arm in despair, "we will watch the reaction from here. It should hold out until it gets here. It is getting dicey."

"Good Lord, what's next in this deal?"

Yuri and Boris' cellular connection is disabled. Boris is familiar with the sporadic Middle East and Levant cellular service. He observes a few fortunate shoppers possessing phones as if choreographed remove the phones from their ears and curiously look at the face of their cellular telephones. The few push the send buttons several times and place the useless phones into their pockets or purses. Not good, Boris thinks. He does not tell Muhammad what he sees. It has started; the Israelis are testing their control of Gaza's communication system.

Boom! The sound echoes through Gaza City's small multi-dwellings. It is not that close. The ground shakes from the IDF's response to the Point of Origin (POO) of the

Hamas rocket that passed overhead while Boris and Yuri were talking.

The Black Cat and the Cardinal uneventfully travel from the Shrine of Our Lady of Guadalupe in Mexico City, Mexico and towards the Fixed Based Operator (FBO) at the busy Mexico City international airport utterly oblivious of the many animal eyes piercing their bodies. One of Moshe's men says, " Boss, our guy is with a significant person." Another surveillance team member states, "He's just like the bird that went down on the west coast."

Moshe responds, "Let's stay with them as long as we can. If the Black Cat departs from the bird, then we will act."

The dark limousine containing the Black Cat and the Cardinal is driven to the FBO entrance and summarily towards an aircraft on the tarmac.

Moshe yells on the radio, "Hold on! Stand down! It can't be done here." Immediately, Moshe's men within their convoy turn from the road next to the FBO's exterior metal fence and return from the direction they arrived. Moshe continues, "He's flying out; he will be back." Many voices on the radio confirm Moshe's orders.

Simultaneously, Moshe detects parallel movement. Shit, why did he not see it before? He let his defenses down — damn tunnel vision. His boss, Eduardo, rattled him. Moshe will survive not doing the hit as another Cardinal accompanies the Black Cat. Eduardo will understand. Moshe must deal with this problem, first. The Black Cat has to return to Mexico City. We've identified the FBO and will eventually locate the exact aircraft and complete tail number.

"Be on alert, boys," Moshe commands on the radio, "I see 'counter.'"

Moshe's team members form into a tight vehicle convoy and leave the vicinity of the airport. Moshe updates his men of observed counter surveillance. This counter surveillance is likely protecting the Black Cat.

Todd and Socorro interviewed the Source in comms with the sub Source who indicates 'it' is trying to surveil the government FBO. However, a majority of the planes are locked in the hangar making it impossible to obtain a tail number. The same sub Source indicates it is working on who in the Mexican government is involved in the deal.

They finish the Mexican official's interview and conduct the usual 'heat runs.' Driving in random patterns to identify possible counter surveillance. Satisfied there is no counter-surveillance, they move in a southerly direction towards the few private aircraft hangars with specific emphasis on the government FBO at Mexico City's international airport.

The plane containing the dope occupied by the Black Cat and the Cardinal's delegation takes off from the runway without incident. The plane arcs in a northerly direction, it's activities not observed by Todd and Socorro.

As the Medellin Cartel convoy leaves the airport, Moshe orders his men to strike first. At a stop light, two of Flaco's Cali Cartel men following Moshe's men, are shot through their windshields. The Medellin Cartel convoy stops and the Cali Cartel position its vehicles almost encircling the Medellin Cartel in complete disregard of traffic lights, pedestrians and innocent civilians within their cars. Nobody will escape.

Bullets from the subjects AK-47's (Automatic Kolesnikov 1947) spread throughout the air. Plumes of gun smoke equal that of a North/South American Civil War battle. Neither side retreats. The combatants fire volley after volley. Their vehicles are stationary three to four feet from each other. Ten vehicles contain Cartel subjects. Moshe's men occupy five, and Flaco's men use five; approximately 34 men in the impending massacre.

Todd and Socorro turn and unexpectedly drive to the rear of a few of Flaco's Cali vehicles and become pinned in a semicircle crossfire amongst the stationary civilians' vehicles. Moshe's team bullets plaster their bulletproof windshield. Todd and Socorro temporarily lie on the floorboard. While on the floorboard, Socorro reaches for her camera and slowly raises it to record the battle. They do not know the subjects, but the recording could be of use to someone in the future. Todd reacquires the steering wheel. They are safe in the vehicle. If they engage, which is highly unlikely, who would they shoot? They would have to open the doors, exposing themselves as the electric windows do not work. They never work. The windows are too heavy for the little motors. Additionally, there are no gun ports on the car.

The battle intensifies. Grenades will follow, but the vehicle's plating will not withstand them. Todd and Socorro are operating covertly; their overall mission is to gather intelligence not to engage in battle. They need to escape.

The noise is deafening. Moshe's and Flaco's teams' cars, are peppered with bullets, tires deflate, and steam blows from the radiators. The assassins yell orders, shout obscenities and methodically replace clips, one after another. Blood flows and the causalities mount on both sides. Brain fragments string throughout the interior and exterior of the vehicles. Detached limbs lay next to the fallen assassins; Medellin vs. Cali. It's that simple. The bullets are so numerous that a misstep in any direction cuts a person in half. Moshe and Flaco's earned statuses are meaningless in the melee.

City blocks are affected by the bullets. The incessant lead barrages decimate outdoor clothing, music and periodical businesses exploding newspapers into confetti. Vendors run for cover from the metal hailstorm; most of the innocent citizens reach safety. The concrete walls are pop marked, and wall fragments spray into the air like irregular snowflakes. Judged by the number of assassins left alive, both sides are losing, the flow of bullets diminishes in spurts. Mexican law enforcement and ambulances sirens reverberate throughout the streets. Seven dead. The wounded are gathered and placed in their vehicles. The metal tornado increases as the subjects reload. They reposition their cars for better cover from the exploding grenades creating booms and counter booms, leaving many vehicles aflame.

Moshe is shot in the left arm and jumps into the back of a car. He rips his shirt and applies a temporary cloth tourniquet. With his right hand, he puts his rifle between his legs and loads a magazine into his empty gun and with the same hand uses the edge of the seat to charge his weapon. Flaco's unscathed so far. The Black Cat's aircraft flies over the battlefield. If the Black Cat looks out the aircraft window, the Black Cat can see ground flashes of automatic fire.

Todd slams into the now vacated remnant of a vehicle to his rear. Bullets skip off their SUV. Boom! A grenade explodes ten yards from their car, hitting the left front tire. Todd rams the left fender of his vehicle into another vacated vehicle to his left. He pushes the car partially onto the sidewalk. Socorro continues recording. Todd slams his rear bumper again into the car behind them, creating an exploitable gap. He accelerates from the battlefield. The battle reaches its apex.

The lights slowly extinguish and reappear, and then all electricity leaves the L'Oratoire in Montreal, Canada gently stranding pilgrims on the numerous escalators and elevators. The same L'Oratoire mentioned by Montreal Detective MacDougal in his conversation with Agent Seamus O'Malley and the same pilgrimage site visited by the two Honduran women smuggled into Canada by the Quebec Separatist to Montreal. A tri-lingual priest conducting mass asks the citizens to remain seated and calm. The priest is perplexed as the electrical generators have not engaged. Except, for exterior light entering the stained-glass windows accentuating the images of Mary, Joseph, and Jesus, there is complete darkness.

Simultaneously, two giant fists strike the Zocalo grounds sending energy deep underground hundreds of miles south of Mexico City. A few farmers in the sparsely populated area, hear a developing groan deep within the earth spooking farm animals. Barns and houses sway as the energy builds. The farmland slowly rocks then rolls.

The rumble and associated energy felt in Southern Mexico races underground at 7,000 miles an hour. The power resembles a bullwhip. The handle of the whip originated in Southern Mexico and as the rumble closes on Mexico City, the whip arcs at its highest point midway from the handle and then levels out ¾ the length of the whip. The energy in the bullwhip concentrates at the tassels culminating at the very street of the Cali/Medellin Cartel shootout.

Above the weapons fire, the assassins hear the encroaching rumble of an earthquake. They temporarily stop shooting, scan, only to be rocked with such intensity that they and their vehicles fly into the air. The cars crush a majority of the assassins. Blood soaks the street gutters. The evacuated businesses, walls made of concrete with iron garage doors, heave and twist cascading on the surviving killers. No sooner than the earthquake arrived, it dissipates. It limits its force to this one particular street.

As luck would have it, the most treacherous survive. Moshe and Flaco escape, but there is hope; eight to ten of the dead include off duty Mex Feds and Police Officers lying in or near both Medellin Cartel and Cali Cartel vehicles. The Mexican government will have a hard time explaining the obvious; both Colombian Cartels had hired Mexican law enforcement.

The 'Old Man' at the Mexico City Zocalo Basilica/Cathedral is seen taking a deep breath and slowly exhales. By producing the earthquake, he's temporarily drained of his energy. The 'Old Man' gives thanks to his much younger colleague by centuries, the L'Oratoire in Montreal, Canada, in providing the needed extra energy/electricity enabling the 'Old Man' to produce the earthquake.

L'Oratorie responds that her country's population is much smaller than that of Mexico's and 1/10th in population size to that of the United States. It further indicates that its land mass is too large to guard against those with evil intentions. When two Honduran females disclosed in my church that the Devil's tentacles are distributing poison and abusing refugees up here, a response was necessary to stop The Black Cat's actions.

The lights in the L'Oratoire slowly return, and the slightly scared masses regain their composure. Worship resumes without the worshippers knowing what transpired thousands of miles south of their location.

"Reporting in, Todd wrecked the car," Socorro says with a devilish smile as if she is tattling on her brother. They may act like brother and sister, but Rebecca calls them 'Headache 1 and 2.' Socorro, a victim in a Mexican gun battle, still possesses a sense of humor. The vehicle's engine whistles, the left tire is fraying, and Todd is playing hell to keep it on the road.

"Yea, he hit some old lady's car right outside the meet."

"Good lord," Rebecca says.

"No, that is not what happened. I can't tell you everything on the phone, but we need a place to park the vehicle discreetly. Will explain later."

"Basically, where are you and, are you all right?"

Socorro relays her general location and says they are okay. However, they cannot drive much further due to the vehicle's appearance and the engine's shelf life. Something of significance has occurred, and a possible political long-term reaction is at stake. They are near the airport.

Rebecca assumes they stumbled into something and got stung. Rebecca instructs them to park the vehicle inside a 'friendly's' car repair garage near their location. Can they make it? Socorro replies in the affirmative. Rebecca calls the 'friendly' and has the person close the shop before their arrival. She instructs Todd and Socorro to remain with the car until assistance arrives. Socorro terminates the conversation stating that they are en route and will advise once the vehicle situation concludes.

Agent O'Malley cannot rest. The Black Cat's plane will land at the Teterboro, New Jersey airport with a Vatican, Mexican and or US tail number possibly starting with the symbol "XA and or N." He does not know if the Vatican has aircraft registrations and if they do, what they are.

"911 dispatch. …Yea, this is Teterboro."

"There is dope on a plane landing at the airport."

"Yes, there are lots of planes."

The thought of calling 911 crosses O'Malley's mind.

Chapter Twenty-Eight

Agent O'Malley contacts a New Jersey law enforcement buddy and explains the possibility Sanchez aka the Black Cat's plane contains narcotics and is due to arrive in his area, today. O'Malley provides his buddy the background on the case, including a reference that the subject aircraft manifest may list the flight as diplomatic. This statement nearly kills O'Malley's request.

It is a lot for the Task Force Officer (TFO) to digest, but none the less the TFO drives to Teterboro airport. While at the airport, O'Malley's buddy requests airport personnel to provide aircraft manifests due to arrive from Mexico and to query the subject names before arrival into the United States. He identifies the aircraft tail number and arrival time.

The Black Cat observes the police without canines approach the plane in New Jersey. Oh, shit. The Frenchman Detective turned him in. Detective MacDougal knows he was due to arrive in New Jersey, today. He knew it. They are going to search the aircraft. A tired, disheveled police officer slowly ascends the plane's stairs and enters the delegation's plane.

"Good evening, your Eminence," the New Jersey TFO says and half salutes.

"Good evening, Officer. What seems to be the problem?" The Cardinal asks.

"We are just going to conduct a brief entry inspection," the TFO is unable to locate a canine to assist in the search. So, he will try some verbal judo.

"Yes, of course, standard operating procedure."

The TFO explains his intentions to the pilot and the co-pilot; it will be a short non-evasive search. He directs the occupants to leave the aircraft. Take a break, get some food. The pilots previously shut down the aircraft engines, now exit the cockpit, followed by the Black Cat who's fumbling with papers. While deplaning, the Black Cat asks his Eminence permission to remain with the plane to assist with the search of the aircraft. He can speed up the process. The Cardinal agrees and walks with the others to the FBO lobby.

The TFO scans the passengers' passports, and additional officers review the passports to reduce the time spent on the ground. The TFO is at a disadvantage as he does not have the training to search an aircraft, nor a canine to assist. If there is a manual on aircraft searches, where is it? He is also cognizant that the passengers can start some shit if he tosses cushions and trays.

Without introductions, the Black Cat demonstrates what is standard on the plane. The Black Cat points to the cockpit and the rear of the AC. O'Malley gave the TFO the

Black Cat's description and the passport confirms this is Sanchez, the Black Cat.

To stop the Black Cat from running the show, the TFO starts his judo and ask the whereabouts of Jose?

The TFO asks again, not allowing the Black Cat to respond, "Where is Jose?" The TFO purposely invades the Black Cat's personal space. The TFO is within inches of him and getting a little hot with this guy. The TFO is not acting. "I do not see him on the manifest. Where is he?"

"Who?"

"You know who? Your buddy arrested in South Texas." The TFO points his finger at the Black Cat and speaks quieter. "He got caught smuggling dope. He worked for you. Are you smuggling dope?" The TFO avoids revealing Canadian information forwarded by O'Malley. O'Malley provides Montreal Police Detective's MacDougal's data as a general overall and asked that it remain secret.

"Yes, I know him, I am sorry, officer. I was not sure whom you were talking about, I know him. Yes, Jose was arrested. He acquired a narcotic problem. I tried in vain to get him to quit, but I was not successful."

O'Malley also briefed the TFO that Jose had not provided damming information against the Black Cat. So, the TFO is not in a position to drive the faint further. The Black Cat suspects O'Malley's meddling.

"Again, I apologize officer for not putting that name together. I am aware that Jose's arrest puts me in a bad light, but, as you see, we are part of an official delegation. A delegation en route to Israel to discuss the acquisition of Catholic church lands located in Russia. May I?" The Black Cat raises his arm towards the rear of the aircraft.

"Hold on." The TFO knows he lost the momentum. "Go ahead." What a dick.

The Black Cat walks to the rear of the plane and pulls open the broken wooden baggage door leading to the

277

curtain. He moves luggage exposing the boxes marked with Vatican insignia wrap. Upon seeing the Vatican tape and 'Property of the Vatican City' inscribed on the boxes, the TFO regroups. Without asking permission from the TFO, the Black Cat opens one that contains medicine, diapers and baby formula and even picks up a few of the items careful not to expose the cocaine packages beneath. Man, the TFO was not expecting this, Vatican tape.

"Looks clean, Father Sanchez."

"Do you want me to open others?"

"Not needed. Close it up."

"Good, you can never be too safe. There is a hatch outside do you want to look in it. I am not sure what it is for." Someone thoroughly briefed this officer.

"Not necessary. You're right on the safety. We will tell the pilots they can leave." The TFO studies the Black Cat's reactions during the conversation, but the Black Cat maintains a calm composure. Fucking egomaniac.

"Thanks, a lot," the Black Cat says and closes the rear curtain. Was it the Medellin Cartel who alerted the authorities, the Canadian Detective, or possibly that O'Malley goof? If it is O'Malley, he's not to be taken lightly or ignored in the future.

Following the TFO's search of the aircraft, the NJ TFO calls O'Malley advising the search met with negative results but provides the aircraft tail number, XA3097B. If it was a US registration, O'Malley could research the registered owner. Finding the actual owner-operator will be a challenge. O'Malley can still obtain its flight patterns unless the pilots decide to disguise their movements. It is not possible to investigate Mexican aircraft registrations for numerous reasons.

The TFO indicates that the manifest did not designate the flight as diplomatic, but a delegation member is a Mexican Official. Plus, the boxes appear to belong to the Vatican or something like that. Because of the negative results, they realize a second search on the same aircraft will be highly unlikely. The passengers' identities reviewed, and their stories match what is publicly known. They stand on solid ground on a Customs search. The Black Cat says the aircraft is going to Israel.

Then, the TFO starts messing with O'Malley. Ok, let's say this aircraft travels from that hell pit you call home and then here. Just a domestic corporate flight. What is our probable cause (PC) to stop? Was it speeding? Did it make an illegal left turn when it hit a cloud? Was it following too closely to another plane? Can a pilot fly anything just like I can drive any car? Are there aircraft taxis?

O'Malley tells the TFO to ask his supervisor. They both laugh. O'Malley thanks the TFO and states that if he needs assistance in Houston to give him a call. The TFO says he is going to interview some Sources to see if they know of secreted narcotics on oil tankers bound for the Houston Ship Channel. He'll time it during the cold month of August. The TFO's quick response and queries are why O'Malley decided to contact him. The TFO realizes the immensity of the job.

The hostilities abate and the Mexican delegation's aircraft lands at the Yasser Arafat International Airport Gaza to much fanfare. Banners wave from nearby buildings. People line the streets. Balloons are released in the sky as the passengers deplane. The children, given hard candies smile and wave. Viewing the appreciative crowds, it is incredulous to Cardinal Vazquez how a small percentage of terrorists would use these beautiful children and their parents as human shields against the IDF. Upon landing, he learns that yesterday the IDF destroyed a suicide bomber's Gaza City residence. The IDF surrounded the house and ordered the occupants to leave. The IDF then bulldozed the home.

The IDF has demolished other homes because of small arms fire originating from the same. In some cases, the occupants are terrorists and/or aid the terrorists. In others, the combatant commandeered the residence. It is common knowledge that the Palestinian National Authority (PNA) and or Fatah store explosive materials and small arms in hospital basements, schools, and mosques risking everyone's lives. There are no simple solutions.

On the tarmac, photographers record the Mexican delegates shaking the PNA representatives' hands. The PNA reciprocate by hugging and kissing the delegates cheeks. A children's band, not a military band, plays loudly. Short speeches from the participants occur on a temporary stage placed on the tarmac.

The Mexican delegation then travels by vehicle convoy from the airport through Gaza City, a densely populated area. The Gazans are genuinely excited about viewing the procession and even happier they have been trusted by the world to participate in the critical negotiations. Pride in their country and leaders swell as the citizens view their country's security detachment protecting the delegation, not the IDF.

The Black Cat previously asked Flaco to plan with his counterparts to distribute all the legitimate goods from the boxes in Gaza; Flaco told him this was already in the works. The Black Cat understands that demonstrating public aid legitimizes the delegation's flights making it difficult for future law enforcement interdiction against the aircraft. Scanning the area, it did not take an economist to understand that someone, countries or corporations should reinvest in manufacturing, farming, or skill building. However, he knows previous attempts were discontinued or destroyed following another skirmish between the two warring parties. The Israeli's even built Gaza Strip police stations. In his mind, it is hopeless.

PNA convoy security is exceptionally tight. The convoy is converging on the Great Mosque of Gaza, architecturally a former Crusader fort. From afar, Cardinal Vazquez sees the building needs repair. Its sandstone and plaster are crumbling. In his mind, it looks as though it was somehow recently beaten into submission by the Islamic extremists. A strange thought, but he realizes he has not been thinking clearly, lately.

Before the convoy reaches the Great Mosque, a renegade cleric was proselytizing inside the mosque reinforcing a fatwa approving the killing of all Israelis, including military and noncombatants. The Cardinal observes the same cleric walk from the mosque entrance, unaware of his significance. The emotionless cleric looks directly at the convoy as it passes him and his guards. The mosque walls, facing the convoy bend as if just recently punched in the stomach.

"Yes, I will," the Cardinal whispers.

The Black Cat seated next to the Cardinal glances at him bewilderedly.

"Brother, I am in trouble here, this man, so-called cleric, you see has hijacked our religion of love and respect and is trying to change it into a religion of hate, a religion of death."

"I understand."

"Cardinal, are you all right?"

The Cardinal ignores Sanchez, the Black Cat.

"Brother. Please reach out to my colleagues. They do not hear my pleas. If the message comes from you, maybe they will believe. The danger here will move to them if not corrected. It could be there now. You must contact my colleagues in Qatar and Saudi Arabia; please tell them of my plight."

"Sir, are you all right?" the Black Cat repeats. Again, the Cardinal ignores the Black Cat.

The Cardinal responds to the voice emanating from the mosque, "The past few weeks have exhausted me. I am tired I've grown so tired, sick. My energy is gone."

The voice from the mosque says, "Yes, you are. You are tired. You can rest after the meeting. Fight this evil and help us." The Cardinal looks around the Black Cat towards the Great Mosque.

"Brother, you are with the Devil himself. I warn you. I want you to warn my people that evil is winning. I, too, am weakening. You have to remain strong. Look around at your surroundings. Don't forget me!" The voice fades as the convoy passes.

The Cardinal asks, "Who's the Devil? What do you mean? Where is this Devil? I will not rest. I will not forget."

The Black Cat glances at the Cardinal. Turns his head to the side and looks directly at the Great Mosque. The Black Cat's focus bores into the Great Mosque.

"Brother he's close to you. He's next…." the voice from the mosque is no longer intelligible.

"What do you mean? Where? Say, it again."

"You said you would not rest," the Black Cat interrupts.

"Oh, yes. I need some rest. I feel weak — all this travel. I am dehydrated. Can you hand me a water bottle?"

"Yes, sir, here you go."

"Thanks." While in the convoy, the Cardinal tries to recall the past. What was that voice telling me? I must remember. I will remember.

The Black Cat's livid. His enemies are everywhere. He experiences firsthand an attempted religious alliance against him, but he ended it. He's growing stronger. The Black Cat decides to strike at his known enemies wherever they are. It's time to send a stronger message to one.

Lying on the hard ground on top of a brown wool blanket, the first insurgent awakes. Within an isolated olive tree farm, next to him hidden under a separate blanket is the second insurgent. Where is he, the first insurgent wonders? It is late at night. He, the first insurgent now remembers they launched a rocket from northern Gaza towards southern Israel and ran like hell to get away from the customary Israeli's artillery retaliatory strike on the Point of Origin (POO). He looks into the dark sky and sees a green light and then a red light. The lights circle north of their location. The lights move towards the same olive tree farm. All, he can think of was why did he do it? He did not know his actions would have such serious ramifications. He jumps from his blanket, leaving his rifle behind and runs from the lights. The first insurgent hears the Israeli helicopter, the origin of the green and red lights, as its engine cavitates and now locks onto him and his comrade. The first insurgent screams at the helicopter that he did not mean it!

The second insurgent rises from his slumber with a rifle in hand. He sees the same lights and fires at them. He runs. Bullets, resembling sporadic large raindrops in the summer heat, a prelude to a massive thunderstorm, hit the damp dirt behind him, to his right side, then to his left. Hot lead strikes his left foot sending it careening into the air with a large tendon still attached. The second insurgent running tries to maintain his balance and stumbles on the dirt when he puts weight on his left leg. With his back to the source of the bullets, he drops the rifle and raises his hands to surrender. However, the second insurgent is cut down by a hail of bullets.

Seamus O'Malley, the first insurgent, running from the same helicopter observes the demise of the other insurgent. Seamus looks behind then towards the dark sky to see a square 3ft x 3ft box made up of what appears to be 50 to 60-yard darts. Is this a game? As the yard darts close, he sees that they are in fact, bullets. The bullets without souls shake with incredible intensity and move at high velocity; this is not a game. Can they be called back? If he quits?

The bullets accelerate. Visible behind the rounds in the dark sky develop menacing clouds, lightning outlines the Devil's face. Its mouth is agape, exposing its jagged black teeth. The unblinking red eyes cut through him; its head slowly rocks back and forth. The skull-like face accelerates from the fierce clouds and passes through the metal storm towards Seamus. Seamus cannot move his legs. Lightning accents the Devil. It's the Black Cat. Seamus awakes from the nightmare. What was that? What does it mean? Is it a message to back off from the Black Cat? Fuck that guy. It is not going to happen. Seamus will never stop.

As the convoy approaches the IDF southern checkpoint into Israel, IDF personnel and PNA guards treat each other with mutual respect. After all, no one wants this event disrupted in their area of responsibility (AOR). They wish to display their professionalism publicly. During this transition and travel to Jerusalem, Israel, the Black Cat views no signs of armed conflict. What happens if this skirmish moves to war? If it does, will they have access to their aircraft? If not, he hopes the plane is not damaged. Just in case, he instructs a delegate to reserve seating on a commercial aircraft, the destination Mexico City.

With the arrival of the delegates in Israel, the negotiations commence. During the talks, the participants are led to believe the Russians are leaning towards a seventy percent Catholic and a thirty percent Eastern Orthodox split of the Russian Orthodox possessions, but this split is nebulous. The Russians indicate the division does not include all of the disputed lands. The delegates are in no position to quarrel with this new Russian development. The meeting drags on, and the representatives realize the negotiations will continue for several months.

During the Yasser Arafat tarmac greetings and speeches amongst the Mexican Delegation and the PNA representatives, purported airport personnel, unload the boxes from the aircraft to empty cargo vans intermixed with the delegation's convoy to take advantage of the publicity of the moment. Not to arouse the Palestinians, Israeli leaders elect not to meet the Mexican delegation's plane at the airport.

However, the IDF is present at the airport. When IDF soldiers observe the boxes being removed from the delegation's plane, a few IDF sergeants restrain a younger soldier from approaching the aircraft and the boxes. Unidentified Fatah personnel transport the boxes to a large Gaza City dilapidated warehouse. The legitimate contents of the boxes are separated and stacked on tables for display then broadcasted on local TV. Cellular service and broadcasts are operational during the visit. Local doctors and nurses categorize the pharmaceuticals. Large amounts of freshly cooked bread in plastic wrap, oranges, bananas, hard candy, and children's' clothes accompany the delegates aid — the PNA plan to give everything away. The PNA decides to make this a glorious moment.

Hoping to receive the items, small groups of people form lines at the warehouse. From a distance, the IDF monitor the crowds. Before the public display, the Fatah secret 500 kilograms of the cocaine in an adjacent warehouse; a small portion will transit through tunnels in southern Gaza to the Sinai Peninsula for distribution. Only 200 kilograms of cocaine will transit to France. The Fatah members place the 200 kilograms of cocaine in numerous wicker and plastic cartons and cover with small amounts of legitimate goods, bread, and fruit. The smuggling occurs without the residents' knowledge.

Boris' team of women mix with the crowds entering the public warehouse. The women have a small green ribbon on their left wrist. Viewing the green ribbons, Fatah members, not yet identified by the IDF, stationed amongst one end of the tables give the baskets and cartons containing the cocaine covered by bread and other goods to

Boris' team. The team members then follow in line, placing additional fruit and aid into the containers and calmly depart the warehouse amongst the general populace.

The women take different routes from the warehouse. The sun begins to set. Some stop at cafes and others enter small businesses and residences. The women covertly transfer the containers with the cocaine to Fatah operatives. It is now dark. Fatah members, including both men and women, carry backpacks, towels, coolers, inflatable children rafts, all concealing the cocaine, previously vacuumed sealed in plastic by Don Pedro's Cali Cartel, converge on Gaza's western beach. The IDF rarely search beachgoers going to the beach. On occasion, they search citizens leaving the beach. The importation of weapons from the Sea is still a problem.

Boris' team of scuba divers join the citizens enjoying the night surf during the temporary cessations of hostilities. Two hundred kilograms of cocaine is too much weight for the scuba divers, but they will follow orders. Black and gray tents remain on the beach. Various female Fatah operatives conceal the diving components in their hijabs, others inside large towels to the surf. Reaching the water, the beach towels, without the diving gear, are given back to the family members.

The Fatah operatives enter the small waves assemble the diving components and give them to Boris and his scuba divers. While in the surf, additional Fatah members discreetly assemble the sealed cocaine packages in multiple nylon mesh sacks. Now, neck deep in the sea, the scuba divers conduct quick equipment checks and are given the nylon sacks. Boris orders the scuba divers into the night surf. The divers form into a V formation with Boris in the lead. The divers swim underwater towards the awaiting fishing boat.

Mohammad is not a participant in the scuba operation but was instrumental in obtaining rebreathers. Instead of oxygen tanks, the divers rebreathe their exhales with the use of these rebreathers. Oxygen tanks are too prominent, bulky, and provide limited air capabilities. The rebreathers do not produce air bubbles. Some bubbles release on ascents, but the fishing vessel will disguise them.

Mohammad's team stole the rebreathers from Egyptian scuba shops located amongst the Red Sea resorts. The rebreathers were then smuggled in tunnels from the Sinai Peninsula into southern Gaza. The IDF is proficient in detecting anomalies in the ocean. The rebreathers will at least give Boris' team a legitimate chance.

Boris leads the team swimming at approximately 30 feet under water. In the event, an Israeli Marine patrol strikes, maintaining 30 feet eliminates decompression protocols. The Russian military trained scuba divers reach the fishing vessel and heave the nylon sacks to the waiting fishing crew then return to the Gaza Strip beach.

The Fatah beach operatives retrieve the scuba equipment, in the same way it was delivered, and walk into beach tents burying the diving equipment in the sand for recovery later. If found the entire coast would be lit up by the Israeli Defense Forces jeopardizing the fishing vessel. The fishing boat remains in the immediate area casting its nets not to arouse IDF suspicions. Boris is aware they were fortunate. As was previously agreed upon during this same period, the swap of kilograms of cocaine for heroin occurs at the secret Gaza warehouse.

A few of the crew members place the nylon sacks containing the cocaine into the hull co-mingling the sacks with the real catch covering both with a fresh layer of ice. The fishing vessel's destination was Bosnia, but while the delegation's aircraft traveled to Gaza, General Comstock changed it to Marseille, France. Comstock solicited remaining sympathizers of the Corsican mafia, Unione Corse. The Unione Corse maintains a small presence in Marseille. The crew fishes throughout the long trip and are careful to place the fish and ice in a manner providing easy access to it in France.

The vessel captain is a Corsican National approximately 45 years of age who recently inherited the boat upon his father's retirement. His father sailed the Mediterranean Sea for decades. When the boy became a teenager, he accompanied his father.

At times, the Mediterranean Sea is placid but at other times quite violent. The young captain experienced everything you can imagine on this Sea. Besides fishing, he is a narcotic smuggler with links to the Unione Corse. He saves the narcotic proceeds for vessel repairs and a newer replacement. He is without guilt in smuggling drugs to Europe. He believes those living in the comfort of industrialized countries are without cause to abuse drugs. These abusers are weak, lazy, and never experienced real hardships.

The vessel travels west on the Mediterranean Sea, southwest of Cyprus.

"Boats to the bow!" A fishing crew member yells and points in the direction of the boats.

"I see them looks like maybe 15 to 20, it is a big flotilla, canaries in the mine. Fleeing one conflict or another. I bet they are Iraqis."

"I'll say they are African."

"I'll get close to them," the captain advises, "not too close, as the refugees might jump on board. Would you get some plastic bags and fill them with ice and fish? Maurice, get some water bottles together, you know the drill." The captain always maintains a water bottle surplus for reoccurring events such as this.

"Will do."

The captain slows the vessel and scans the refugees overloaded inflatable and makeshift wooden boats. The sea ebbs into the small boats, and the occupants splash it back to its origin. They are Iraqis fleeing the war — no doubt unwanted in Turkey and Syria heading for Greece, a long journey. The Gulf States and Iran have remained silent in accepting the Iraqi refugees.

Tired hands ascend from the boats. Pleas for help spoken in broken English reverberate over the fishing vessel's motor. The captain's crew throw the plastic bags of fresh fish and ice to the refugees. Fresh uncooked fish is better than no food at all. Water bottles follow. The captain and his crew do their small part for these poor souls. The captain leaves the area before law enforcement finds his vessel amongst the refugees.

The fishing vessel continues on its western route. The captain circumvents a large Greek ferry containing tractor trailers, personal vehicles and many tourists that regularly depart Santorini Island bound for Crete, Greece. He is well aware that you do not get in the way of the numerous Greek ferries.

During long stints at the helm of the fishing trawler, the captain wonders if the 'space soldiers' observing armies and wars from satellites, do the soldiers track refugee movements, the great migrations? Migrations, like you see animals do in Africa in the documentaries.

The captain believes the refugees' paths seen from space would resemble ocean currents. The captain views the ocean foam forming on the small waves. Is the foam acting like detergent washing away memories of drowned refugees? He stares at the dark, unforgiving sea. The captain is now at the helm as the trawler steams between Lampedusa island, Italy and Malta. Tunisia, Africa is east of Lampedusa. It's a geographical choke point full of law enforcement interdiction efforts.

"Man, I see them. More canaries."

"These will be Africans."

"You're right."

"Make it quick."

The captain realizes the Africans are fleeing who knows what war, conflict, government corruption, or poverty. The Captain's crew quickly distribute the goods, and the vessel steams from the area. This interaction feeds the Captain's need for action, adrenalin. The captain assists the refugees but understands he has greater financial responsibilities, the cocaine. In this area, he does not want to be boarded by law enforcement and accused of smuggling refugees.

The vessel reaches Marseille, France. With the assistance of the Corsican organized crime group, scuba divers retrieve the narcotics in reverse order from the manner delivered off the coast of Gaza. When they reach the shore, they give the packages to criminals who transport the same by bicycle, car, and bus to a small decrepit warehouse, for eventual distribution and sale.

General Comstock's organization will wire the narcotic proceeds via Cyprus to Don Pedro's Cali Cartel. It is too dangerous to smuggle the proceeds to the Mexican delegation aircraft in Gaza. It is becoming difficult to move money around the Levant as Gaza is heating up. The change is also made to thwart law enforcement.

After the West Jerusalem talks, the Mexican delegation departs Gaza in their corporate plane for Mexico City, Mexico. The Black Cat does not believe they should land again in Gaza. Per local news reports, the conflict worsens. The IDF guards are hardening resulting in a heated discussion between the southern IDF checkpoint soldiers and Fatah security elements when the delegation reentered Gaza. The Black Cat will give the Cali Lieutenant his thoughts.

Chapter Twenty-Nine

In Mexico City, the Black Cat is surprised to meet Flaco, not the Cali Cartel, Lieutenant. Flaco is Don Pedro's, right-hand man. Flaco gives details of the Cali

Lieutenant's death and the ensuing Mexico City airport firefight. Flaco reveals the Cali Lieutenant is cut in half by bullets from Moshe's Medellin killer group.

Following the Black Cat's departure from the Mexican Airport, Flaco indicates many Medellin and Cali Cartel people died next to the airport. Flaco then reveals that during the airport battle, an earthquake hit the area. It was an extraordinary, eerie event. The Black Cat does not know how to reply, so he remains silent. Eventually, the Black Cat interrupts the uncomfortable silence and details the search of the delegation's aircraft at the New Jersey airport. Flaco does not dismiss the Black Cat's report; he only moves his head in affirmation. Flaco is preoccupied with something else. The mounting bodies indicate mounting danger.

There is a problem: what is the origin of the incriminating actionable information? Who knows of the delivery? The Black Cat and Flaco exchange ideas, they discuss the pilot and co-pilot. No, they discount them. The pilots have worn blinders for years. What about the Mexican negotiation aides? No, they are focused solely on the talks. Could it be Jose, the priest? No, Jose does not have a complete picture of the Mexico City operation. The Medellin Cartel is actively retaliating in response to the Cardinal assassination. Did Jorge spew his guts? Were they able to obtain the aircraft tail number? If they did, are they that sophisticated to in effect dispatch US police to search the aircraft? To Flaco, Moshe's team was not aware of the Black Cat's aircraft.

There is that curious Texas agent. He's capable of coordinating the aircraft search. No, Flaco advises, we hear the agent was transferred back to Houston after the Matamoros incident. However, they agree not to take this Seamus O'Malley lightly. The Black Cat has already come to that conclusion. The Black Cat does not mention his relationship with the Montreal Detective, nor does he tell

Flaco that he told the Detective that he would land in New Jersey.

"Somebody is tracking you," Flaco counsels, "you're instrumental in the deliveries. It would be best if you kept a low profile. Stay within the Shrine's grounds."

"I'll be a prisoner."

"Or dead," Flaco snaps back, "catch up on your prayers." Flaco is back to the old Flaco.

Flaco leaves before the Black Cat briefs him of his concerns about continuing operations in Gaza.

Flaco reports to Don Pedro at his ranch located outside Cali, Colombia. "No one following the Black Cat when we met. Nothing at all resembling surveillance on me, or the Black Cat." With a towel, Flaco rubs the sweat off his bald head. A woman servant delivers him a drink. He continues the brief, "The Medellin Cartel are probably regrouping. They'll strike again, but where, no one knows."

"The Black Cat was told to remain in the priests' compound?" asks Don Pedro.

"Yes, he will comply."

"Good, Medellin could reestablish surveillance again at the Shrine or in the vicinity of the FBO. You hit them hard at the airport, as did our boys in western Mexico and here in Colombia. Medellin's meddling in Mexico City is a real problem. The Russians do not need to know their reach." Don Pedro rubs his stub of a finger and swallows a large amount of his Cuba Libre. He looks towards the green pasture and grazing cows. "If the Russians read about the massacre near the airport, put one and one together, or they ask the extent of Medellin reprisals I will have to say the Medellin threat is contained and the loads will continue."

"The loads will continue?"

"Yes. Load it to 525."

"525 kgs.?"

"Yes."

"Understood. Don Pedro, I'm getting reports that Mexican regional crime groups are interfering in our Mexico operations."

"We will need to work out financial and logistical arrangements soon with the strongest Mexican group. I know you are busy, but have someone make inquiries. It will be a dangerous assignment."

"I'll get on it."

Flaco leaves the confines of Don Pedro's ranch and flies via commercial aircraft from Colombia to Mexico City to coordinate the next planeload. While seated in the plane, he visualizes peasants deep within the dense Colombian canopy stomping cocoa leaves into a mash. The mash smuggled from southern Colombia to labs on the outskirts of Cali for processing into cocaine. Trucks, rail cars, and aircraft transport the refined narcotics to Central America and then into Mexico. Isolated paved roads, dirt roads and recently bulldozed ranch land serve as runways for small aircraft smuggling the cocaine.

Northern Guatemala cottage industries evolve selling used aircraft parts salvaged from crashes, and discarded aircraft following failed and successful deliveries. Used small aircraft costs are equivalent to buying a new car. The cocaine purposely smuggled from Guatemala into Southern Mexico, specifically, the State of Chiapas, the location of a recent rebellion by the Chiapas Indians who have been steamrolled by the narcotic traffickers but also by the Mexican government. It is here the Catholic Church has agreed to assist the Indians. Additional cocaine is secreted in freighters departing various Colombian ports, Buenaventura, Barranquilla, and Cartagena bound for Vera Cruz, Mexico. The flow never stops.

The cocaine destined for the Black Cat's plane already exists in Mexico City residences. The cocaine brokers, eight in all, have significant stakes in the next load. Don Pedro controls a majority of the dope, 300 kilograms.

Upon successful delivery to the Russians AOR, the Russians will buy the entire 525 kgs. The Russians will forward the proceeds to Don Pedro's designees, who, in turn, will disperse the remaining funds to the other brokers. If the 525 kilograms do not reach the Russians, Don Pedro is responsible for compensating the brokers for their 225 kilograms of cocaine.

Flaco believes the Black Cat and his aircraft will last for a few more deliveries. Don Pedro's investment in the Black Cat is money well spent. Don Pedro amounts a fortune as the Medellin Cartel is on its heels. Don Pedro is filling the Medellin Cartel vacuum with Cali operatives in Western Mexico. His organization takes temporary control of numerous Medellin Cartel routes into the United States. However, Flaco realizes Medellin will regroup and counter strike.

Flaco suspects the numerous Mexican criminal groups now threaten both Cali and Medellin in Mexico. Because of this threat, Flaco's man will meet with the representatives of the strongest regional Mexican criminal group ceding control of future deliveries into Mexico. However, this Mexico route is just one in Don Pedro's world. Don Pedro's Cali Cartel is moving tons of cocaine, worldwide.

The killing of the Cardinal was ideal. The murder provides the catalyst in unleashing the Medellin Cartel their Mexican associates and the Mex Feds/Federales machismo all at once. Following the Cardinal's assassination, the Mexican Federales were forced into a volatile situation. The Mex Feds under temporary orders from the central government are instructed to make a show of it. The Mex Feds attempt mediation with the Medellin Cartel.

The Mex Feds demand superficial, sacrificed loads and arrests. As history dictates, one of the Medellin operatives and or a ranking Mex Fed get crosswise over a particular seizure and or detention, and all hell breaks out with no return to the warped stability. A synergistic violent tornado effect develops. Oh, man, Flaco thinks as he stares through the aircraft window, when the newly arrived 'outside forces' Federales enter the fray they will be pissed off. Now, everyone is a legitimate target. He hears their tortured screams and sees the carnage. Bodies lay in the street, hang from bridges, are crumbled on vehicle front seats. He's experienced it before; it is haunting. He falls asleep on the plane.

While at his ranch, Don Pedro contacts Yuri, General Comstock's facilitator through a satellite phone confirming the '525' and their readiness. From the conversation, Don Pedro gleans that Yuri and Comstock are unaware of the airport massacre and the search of the aircraft in Teterboro, New Jersey.

The Mexican media has not been successful in making sense of the shootout followed by an earthquake at the Mexico City airport. The media presses the government for a motive and to identify the dead. The press indicates that the Mexican government is deliberately delaying the results of their investigation.

So far, Don Pedro withstands the Medellin onslaught. He doubles his guards on all operations. He does not remain idle. He is expending large sums of money for protection and at the same time expands his operations. His personnel regularly change phones, faxes, emails, and terminates lower level, suspect employees. He does not order the killing of suspected upper management employees. Instead, he allows them to franchise with separate smuggling operations. In the event questionable employees alert the Medellin Cartel or law enforcement of Don Pedro's activities, the franchises provide another layer of insulation. The franchise restricts the participant from gaining valuable knowledge of Don Pedro's organization. The franchise participants merely have to pay monthly to the Don Pedro organization to operate within Don Pedro's

AOR. If they do not pay, they do not play; instead, Don Pedro's people destroy them.

Chapter Thirty

Socorro, the US intelligence officer, reads from a long HQS cable already scanned by her boss, Rebecca. HQS is now fully committed to the Yuri/Comstock case. Reading the teletype, she thinks it contains too much data. Their investigation is now an HQS priority. Per the communique, an HQS cryptologist identifies the codes 'idiot' as associated with Seamus O'Malley and 'the cute one' associated with the now deceased Mexican Federal Police Officer, Maria. The cryptologist cracks the code with common sense by reviewing surveillance photographs and reviewing Todd and Socorro's reports. Additionally, he read the translated Mexico, Ukraine, and France wire intercepts.

The teletype contents reveal a tone that someone in HQS 'actually' understands Rebecca and her team's investigation. The cable is definitive from this moment on there will be no more freelancing.

Although not mentioned, HQS reviewed a previous cable authored by Todd, Titled Source Information (Pete) related to Mex Fed Maria and a possible connection with Eastern European meddling in Mexico. HQS is aware that Pete's interview was conducted in the States without proper coordination. Socorro reflects on the no more 'freelancing.' The 'walls' inhibiting information exchange between agencies were supposed to be coming down? Fuck 'hem.' It would be nice if we had some help over here. Anyone? Anyone? Back to the cable.

The HQS cable reveals agent Seamus O'Malley, aka idiot, obtained photographs depicting the Black Cat and Yuri, taken together. HQS also acquired Agents O'Malley's investigative reports. The pictures originated from whom

HQS believes is a priest who previously worked for the Black Cat while stationed in Matamoros, Mexico. The priest, identified as Jose, is arrested in Texas for possession of a small amount of cocaine. A trucker is detained with the priest, Jose, at the same time for possession of cocaine. However, investigators were not able to combine the cases.

Without the priest defense attorney's knowledge, it is evident that Jose directed his distant family members to deliver the photographs to O'Malley. The pictures, the only known images of Yuri, were lifted from within a Matamoros, Mexico church. Jose indicated Yuri is a Russian. Jose also told his family members it is his opinion the photograph backgrounds are from the Polanco section of Mexico City. A captured partial address discovered in one photograph background and a restaurant entrance from another are the most favorable leads in identifying the whereabouts of Yuri. A priority HQS analysis ensued on the photographs' backgrounds.

Socorro questions Rebecca, "Why did Jose go to such lengths in having his family obtain the photographs and then forward to O'Malley?"

"Jose probably confirmed to O'Malley that Sanchez, The Black Cat, hired his defense attorney in regards to the Texas possession charge. By providing the defense attorney to Jose, the Black Cat restricts Jose in providing damaging evidence against Sanchez. Jose gave insignificant data related to the independent narcotic subjects involved with his possession case. Jose understands he cannot provide relevant information related to Sanchez, while the Black Cat's defense attorney remains involved in the case. Jose's distant relatives could be kidnapped or killed if Jose gives derogatory evidence against Sanchez. Jose may not even know the extent of the Black Cat's activities, but he provides the photographs. He is hoping that O'Malley will speak favorably to the prosecutor and the judge in his anticipated plea agreement.

Somehow, O'Malley disguises the origin of the information, so it does not lead back to Jose. I had the same question as you because I wanted to corroborate the photographs as well. What are the percentages that Jose's information and photographs are genuine right now? I say 85%?"

"Do you think the Black Cat is a Russian sleeper agent controlled by Yuri? He was picked to travel to Russia. Does the Black Cat speak Russian?" Socorro asks.

"Those are good questions. How many more 'sleepers' are out there? In Mexico, Venezuela in the US." No one answers the questions.

As Socorro reads the cable, Rebecca says that our US paramilitaries, our strong-arm people, have incrementally arrived in the Mexico City area. She goes on to describe the Polanco, Mexico City area. The Polanco area is comprised of wealthy citizens, tourists and is close to a large botanical park complete with lakes and the site of a castle on the crest of a hill within the park. Our Marines took control of it with many losses. I think the castle is called Castillo de Chapultepec. Across the street from the park is a beautiful anthropology museum, she visited it last weekend. Bumper to bumper traffic remains throughout the area almost day and night.

Expensive restaurants intermix with small boutique car dealerships displaying Ferraris and Mercedes Benz's throughout Polanco's clean streets. Four and five-star hotels exist along one of the main streets in Polanco. Trees and shrubs line Polanco's streets, and you can walk unimpeded from the Polanco neighborhood through gardens reaching the anthropology museum and the park.

The streets names comprise famous authors of the world, Dante, Milton, and Goethe other streets list scientists, Kepler, Euclid, and Kelvin. Various nationalities enjoy the hotels, and others reside in the area. There is big money in the area. Oh, and some wealthy criminals are living there as well.

At the tip of two of the authored named streets is a busy standalone Starbucks coffee shop serving as the de facto linchpin of the 'paras' surveillance. The 'paras' possess condensed photographs of the Black Cat and Yuri. The 'paras' established permanent posts within rented apartments maximizing their views of various streets and sidewalks. These same apartments provide sleeping quarters and a place to eat. The 'paras' surveillance includes sitting in parked vehicles, and others walk the sidewalks. Their deployment provides a decent perimeter of the area. However, it is a vast area, and more importantly, nobody has seen Yuri, yet.

Rebecca states she is in 'comms' with the para supervisor and Socorro will act as her backup if she is not available. After all, Todd is still one fingering his portion of the Matamoros incident report. Rebecca has repeated that joke so many times, but they always laugh every time she says it.

At the bottom of the HQS cable is a reference from their Tel Aviv, Israel Office (TAO) informing the officers of recent Gaza events. HQS knows that Sanchez aka the Black Cat and his associates made use of the Gaza Strip airport, formally referred to as Yasser Arafat International Airport. Usage of the airport by anyone is of particular interest to the TAO regarding potential weapons, people and contraband smuggling by Hamas and or Fatah. The airport is a direct threat to Israel. There are already unconfirmed reports of Hamas smuggled guns entering into the airport to usurp PNA/Fatah control of Gaza and for that matter to strike at Israel.

In the same cable, a paragraph references a subject identified as Mohammad Bin Zarif. Zarif is a PNA sympathizer but turning towards Hezbollah based in Southern Lebanon. Bin Zarif is a believed associate of an unidentified Russian National (R/N) residing in Lebanon. Bin Zarif recently departed Jordan and met with an unknown white male (W/M) in Israel. The pair traveled to Gaza just before the Mexican delegation's arrival. The TAO requested identification from their Israeli counterparts to confirm if Zarif entered Gaza with the R/N W/M.

Further information indicates this R/N, W/M has ties to Hezbollah. The W/M and Zarif intend to repeat the travel to Gaza as needed, no further information (NFI). Again, the TAO asked for identification of the W/M; they believe him to be the same referenced R/N. It is not clear if the trip by the W/M and Zarif is related to the Black Cat's activities but forwarded for situational awareness.

"Associated with a Russian, Mohammad Zarif goes to Gaza with a W/M around the same time as the Black Cat's arrival. Interesting. The cable indicates that portions of the TAO cable were shared with Israeli Intelligence. The travel by the two subjects is related," says Rebecca.

"It's a good possibility. The W/M is Russian. The Israelis are busy. That explains their delay in identification and notification or the Israeli's screwed up."

"The TAO provides the Black Cat's plane tail number," Rebecca shows it to Socorro and says, "we will have to conduct a historical check as the plane has returned from Gaza."

"We'll get that done. It is probably in Mexico City. I'll have the Source and Sub Source with knowledge of the government FBO initiate surveillance, it's a start," responds Socorro.

"With good intel and some luck maybe, we can ascertain if the delegation's plane is doing something illegal."

"And interdict before it leaves."

"But we have to follow the cars or trucks that visit, service or supply the delegation's plane, and identify what they are doing."

"This will take some time as we are back to an aircraft that is locked in a hangar."

Rebecca impatiently instructs, "Figure out a way to get information out of the FBO or place a person inside the FBO."

"OK, I'll try."

Socorro says she forwarded the airport battle videotape to HQS for analysis. Maybe, it can be of use to someone primarily, if we identify the dead and any wounded. She tells Rebecca the excessive firepower and its proximity to the airport may not be a coincidence. "I think the battle is related to the Black Cat. Right, near the airport."

"Yes. The coincidences are piling up."

"I am thinking out loud. I might just be hoping it is related. The Black Cat attracts a bunch of negative attention. The tape will give us some leads."

"No doubt," Rebecca responds.

"We still don't know where the Black Cat lays his head."

"That bothers me, yea the city is huge. We need help."

Socorro with a smile, says, "Within a flash, we are completely caught up in that mess. You know, Todd really can't drive. You'd think he just learned how to drive. Don't they have cars in Texas or only horses?" Socorro points in one direction and then another and mouths, "F that guy F that girl. Todd shouts at everybody who comes within inches of the vehicle and, in Mexico City, it is all the time. It is pretty funny. He's going to stroke out." With all sincerity, Socorro looks at Rebecca and says, "What's left of the vehicle is all his fault. The entire thing is his fault. Oh, just between us girls. I will never allow him to drive in Mexico again." They laugh.

Socorro continues, "Right now, he's in the back room writing the airport incident report, cussing and yelling. The computer keeps crashing on him. Halfway through his first draft, the computer erased all his work. He keeps yelling; this is bullshit. What a bunch of crap." Socorro covers her

301

mouth with her left hand, trying to disguise her uncontrollable giggling. "He hates paperwork." She's overcome with laughter and tries to smother it, so Todd does not hear.

"He will probably never ask to drive again after this report," Rebecca snaps her fingers, "oh, important. Make sure he makes it clear in the airport report that you all are not the intended suspect targets, that you are victims, or you and he will be transferred out of here for your safety. It won't happen, because that is the truth. Y'all have invested a lot in this Black Cat op. It would be a travesty only to be reassigned, to Bangladesh or wherever."

"Got it. I will pop my head into the computer room and tell him that and then I'll let him know I'm going to work out. He'll explode."

"You got that right."

"Oh, your Mexican official we spoke to before the airport shooting had nothing. I will write that useless report tonight. He acted shocked that we would even ask if Russians are actively operating in Mexico. I did not develop him, and I know you inherited him, but in my opinion, he is holding back on the Russian threat. He became a smart ass and said that if you are looking for Russians then call your US Drug Czar. He said Czar is a Russian word. Look there. Todd almost belted him; he knows. Maybe, we should put him on the no call list for a while. Let him think about what he did not tell us, and then let's see if he comes our way."

"Good idea. By the way, how is Todd's dad doing?"

"Much better, he told me this morning that his dad finished his chemotherapy treatment in Houston."

"Good news. I hear there are good hospitals there. I have to go to my office to catch up. More importantly, to listen to Todd bitch about you going to work out." Rebecca looks towards the floor and then at Socorro. "You know, Socorro, this investigation is getting dark. I feel as if we are missing the real threat. I can't put my hand on it." She pauses as if she made a mistake in revealing her thoughts.

"What do you mean?"

"I don't know. I'm tired. Forget I said it. Go mess with Todd; we need more fun around here." Rebecca shakes her head as Socorro strides to the one finger, typing Todd.

During the Socorro and Rebecca conversation, events occur in the delivery of 525 kgs of cocaine to the Black Cat's aircraft bound for Gaza. The church negotiations commence in Jerusalem the following day. Per Flaco's orders, the Black Cat dutifully remains caged for an extended period at the Shrine until the next delivery.

While at the Shrine during this period, there are whispers from priests that the Black Cat's personality is becoming threatening. The Black Cat's stopped talking to the domestic staff. When seen during the day, the employees avoid him. A priest observes the obvious avoidance and questions a female staff member. She waves her trembling hand at him and refuses to answer. She almost runs over his foot with her cart to get away from responding.

Others on the premises see the Black Cat walking the sidewalks late into the night talking to himself. There is even an unexplained nighttime commotion reported at the church that involves the Black Cat. Employees' reports indicate flashes and thunderous sounds emanating from the Shrine church followed by unintelligible quiet rebukes. One employee equated the observed incident as if a child was yelling at its mother, and the mother quietly responds. When questioned further by the priests, the employees shake their heads and refuse to elaborate. No one dares to approach and ask the Black Cat.

Flaco assumes personal responsibility in loading the narcotics onto the plane. He verifies that the bricks are without markings and confirms the lack of counter-surveillance. The following morning, the Black Cat and the delegation, drive from the Shrine to the airport and enter the aircraft with an unidentified surprise passenger. More weight.

The aircraft takes its place in line for takeoff. Its pilots given authority to take off, the plane accelerates. Upon its rapid vertical ascent, the plane creaks and moans. It's engines roar. The bulk of the boxes piled in the rear hold on the pilot in command (PIC) side, not evenly distributed cause the plane to heave to one side similar in appearance as the space shuttle on takeoff. The traffickers do not have access to a real loadmaster.

Both pilots struggle to level the aircraft. The pilots increase engine power aware of the risk of stalling the engines. The noise is deafening. Before takeoff when the PIC was conducting the pre-flight checklist, the PIC is told that there was approximately this much weight and yes you can make it. Maybe, you should plan emergency fuel stops. Fly higher in thinner air to save fuel. If needed, deploy the oxygen. Just get it done.

In their vertical ascent, the cockpit door pops open. The Black Cat watches the pilots as they struggle with the controls. The plane ultimately levels off. The PIC periodically looks back at the nonchalantly seated Black Cat as if saying, "Are you kidding me?" The Black Cat smirks off his glances. The pilot assumes the worst and now believes the rumors are true.

Socorro's Source surveillance arrives at the Mexican government FBO as the Black Cat's delegation's plane arrives at its New Jersey fuel stop. The passengers clear US Customs and the insanity of takeoff repeats itself. During each landing and takeoff, metal stress fractures mount on the vintage aircraft. The pilots doubt the plane will last for the remaining negotiations. The traffickers could not care less about stress fractures, maintenance, and loading issues.

O'Malley does not receive an update from the Montreal Detective MacDougal. O'Malley periodically monitors a commercial database that displays the movement of the aircraft. What else can he do? He knows the pilots will not disguise their flight. The route is a proven legitimate trip. He has kept track of the war between the Medellin Cartel and the Mex Feds. He knows the Cali Cartel and the Black Cat are running free.

Don Pedro is elated. Without issues, the plane departs Charles De Gaulle airport in France. He reminds himself again of the lack of infrastructure to safely 'offload' the narcotics at Charles de Gaulle Airport. Plush with new income streams, Don Pedro plans to develop this route.

The lowliest street urchin who slings dope and awakes at the crack of noon is never on time for the days trafficking — leaving his customers in a lurch. The urchin treats everyone with disrespect and cares less about schedules or responsibilities. Because of the urchin characteristics, addicts remain in their cars or on foot near a street corner or outside a convenience store anxiously waiting for the arrival of their fix.

As one climbs the narcotic ladder of success, deliveries and meetings become somewhat more punctual as schedules have to be met. Economic scales begin to creep into the equation. Loads secreted on unsuspecting commercial transports, vessels and tractor trailers, need to be delivered on their respective tables. Timeliness and trust become instrumental as the narcotic amounts and proceeds increase. At the higher levels of smuggling, some responsibility enters into the equation. Profits grow integral in greasing the wheels of corrupted government officials, ensuring maintenance and operations.

As if genetic among narcotic traffickers, the Mexican delegation's aircraft is behind schedule. The PIC and the co-pilot are flying the plane at an extremely high altitude. They engage the deicing rubber slates on the front of each wing. The engines operate at peak power. Although they completed one successful landing and departure at Yasser Arafat International Airport, the delegation's arrival is in jeopardy. As much as the Israeli's administration acquiesced in the use of the Yasser Arafat Airport, one issue they did not concede is approval of a nighttime landing. The Israelis are well versed that sophisticated smugglers and terrorists make use of the night. The night provides natural cover for illicit activities.

With the plane resembling a comet streaking across the sky, the co-pilot leaves the cockpit and approaches the Black Cat seated to the rear of the aircraft. The Cardinal is asleep. The co-pilot drops to one knee in the aisle next to the Black Cat. She explains that unexpected headwinds over the Atlantic Ocean have made their timely arrival in Gaza doubtful. As an alternative, she recommends the use of Ben Gurion. She details the measures taken to make up the lost time. The Black Cat looks at the co-pilot and whispers that he does not care what was done by the pilots, we will land in Gaza and concludes the conversation, involuntarily exposing his teeth and flaring nostrils, and states that if he could open the exit doors in flight, she would be the first to go. Of course, to reduce the load.

The co-pilot, caught off guard, stands and tries to control her involuntarily shaking hands. She fears for her life. She concludes that the Black Cat is pure evil. She struggles to walk in the aisle towards the cockpit. Her butt bounces off a seat when the aircraft hits turbulence. She almost falls. She enters the cockpit hitting her head against the door frame. Drops on her chair and exhales. The PIC asks what transpired. She tells him we are landing at Gaza no matter what. Did you explain? Does he know the entire story? She nods her head, yes, and points with her finger towards their only destination, Gaza.

Car bomb! Fourteen Israelis killed, eighty-two wounded within a tourist restaurant in Tel Aviv, Israel, from a bomb left under a breakfast table. A respected Israeli parliamentarian gets shot and killed. A Palestinian terrorist is suspected.

A West Bank shooting of a Palestinian, one Israeli killed, three Palestinians killed, in the aftermath.

Israeli tanks enter eastern Gaza and into northern Gaza from southern Israel in search of terrorists. Columns of tanks roll on hard surfaces led by static Israeli artillery bombardments. Israeli artillery originating deep within Israel proper, directed by covertly deployed commandos in Gaza, to surveil known and suspected terrorist locations. Israeli jets scream over Gaza firing rockets at pre-selected verified sites: Hamas temporary rocket launch sites, PNA command and control, suicide vest manufacturing facilities and arms caches. Jet contrails crisscross the blue sky.

Secondary explosions, a result of Israeli jet strikes, confirm the intelligence of secreted PNA explosive and weapons caches located throughout Gaza. Hamas rockets lift off from northern Gaza indiscriminately striking Israeli towns and farmland close to the border. Vapor trails from Israeli military aircraft and Hamas rockets interlock creating the facsimile of a spiderweb trapping both sides in mortal combat. The web will remain until fractured once again by outside forces — the war rages.

The night is coming and with it, evil. A large flash and dark plume are seen just within northern Gaza. The accompanying noise reverberates through a previously destroyed olive tree farm. A large Improvised Explosive Device (IED) is denotated by insurgents as an Israeli Merkava tank crosses a small bridge. The tank lifts from the now destroyed bridge and crashes on the side of an abandoned irrigation ditch. The IDF previously flattened the olive farm and its trees as the grove was used as cover to launch Hamas rockets towards Israel. It appears the insurgents have planned many surprises for the invading IDF. The violence escalates.

A short transmission invades the Mexican delegation's aircraft radio, shouting as if under attack. An Israeli air traffic controller advises the pilots of a complete Gaza Strip and West Bank blockade. Nothing enters or leaves Gaza, including aircraft. Gaza Airstrip closed.

"But we are on a mission for the Pope; we are to land at Gaza," advises the PIC.

"Denied. You are to divert to Tel Aviv-Ben Gurion airport," the air traffic controller barks.

The co-pilot transfers the communication to the plane's intercom allowing the passengers to monitor the conditions. Scared to death of the Black Cat she hopes the public transmission will absolve her and the PIC of the anticipated disaster. The co-pilot explains to the air traffic controller again that they have official business in Gaza with the Russians.

"We understand, and our people are contacting them as we speak. I repeat Gaza airport closed."

The co-pilot gets a nod from the now awake Cardinal seated a few seats behind her.

"Then, we will comply."

The Gaza events are more significant than this deal. The Black Cat will adapt the plan.

Boris tells Yuri of the closure of the Arafat airport and adds there is a high probability that the Cardinal's aircraft will divert to Tel Aviv. Boris is monitoring the same commercial plane tracking application as O'Malley. Yuri forwards Boris' message to General Comstock.

General Comstock immediately communicates with his contact at the Russian Foreign Ministry and advises of the situation. As a result of the conversation, a Junior Russian Deputy Foreign Minister contacts his Israeli counterpart. The Russian Minister sympathizes in regards to the present Israeli/Gaza 'troubles' and then addresses the real issue. Describing the aircraft situation, the Russian Junior Minister reminds the Israeli counterpart that the passengers and the aircraft are to be treated almost on par with a State visit. When the Israeli Minister hesitates at the request, the Russian Minister threatens that the recent immigration of Russians Jews to Israel will expire. It is known to both, that some of the emigres are incredibly poor and others are incredibly wealthy. The Israeli Minister agrees.

The Black Cat sinks into his chair. What the hell? How are we going to get this stuff off? From the most secure airport in the world. It won't happen. The Black Cat will assure the dope remains on the aircraft.

The Black Cat explains to the Cardinal that moving the goods to a war zone is impossible. Distributing the legitimate products within Israel in wartime will tax Israel's complement of delegation guards. The boxes will remain in the aircraft. The Cardinal agrees.

Will the Israeli's search the plane? The Black Cat is calm throughout the delicate situation. Landing in Tel Aviv, the Israelis keep their distance from the aircraft. The Israeli women Customs officials still question the occupants leaving the plane searching for inconsistencies, they meet with negative results. The smuggling operation is essential but pales to the war. The Black Cat knows Tel Aviv is a primary target of the Hamas rockets. Do the insurgents have the scientific capability to reach Tel Aviv? What if a missile hits the plane? Plumes of white powder burning orange, and then a bright red away from a known fuel supply, not defensible.

The church negotiations sputter in Jerusalem. Israeli defense alarms continue to wail throughout the day alerting of incoming Gaza rockets. As the night wears on, the signals increase. Israel, West Bank, and Gaza residents are sleep deprived.

The negotiations shorten. The security of the delegates is no longer an Israeli priority. Anticipating Hezbollah rocket barrages originating from Southern Lebanon, Israel moves additional forces to Northern Israel.

Focus on the negotiations is secondary to the pain occurring in this theatre. Movement-related to the distribution of the Russian lands is nonexistent. The Black Cat surmises the Russians are not committed to distributing the properties, it's just a ruse. The Russians already receive monies from the Russian Orthodox Church.

The talks do lead to further discussions that the small present Palestinian delegation might accept funds in the rehabilitation of Bethlehem's, Church of the Nativity located in the West Bank. The Vatican is ecstatic with the 'historical' renovation issue. Many issues are separating the various religions in Israel. One persistent example is no one religious claimant of the Church of the Holy Sepulchre in Jerusalem, the site of Jesus' resurrection, controls the keys to open and close the church. Instead, various groups possess the keys. The war continues.

The Hamas rockets do not reach the Mexican delegation's plane. All delegates make haste to depart the area. Before departure within the FBO, an Israeli guard enters into a discussion about the recent Fatah/Hamas conflict with the Cardinal. The guard states that the IDF destroyed the Gaza electricity plant, and there are rumors that the freshwater and sewage facility are severely damaged. The Cardinal asks what about the citizens of Gaza? The guard indicates that these actions are psychological operations. The lack of electricity and water services will put pressure on the PNA administration to end this conflict.

Following the conversation, the Cardinal asks himself if Israel and the various insurgents are guilty of war crimes, crimes against humanity? That discussion will go on for decades, and there will never be an answer. Unless somebody loses, the victor could seek these convictions. So, what value is there to stop? This issue is so inflammatory; what outsider can answer such a thing?

His bosses lean towards Israeli crimes, but the Cardinal does not. The Cardinal sometimes suspects that those declaring 'crimes' such as these directed at a particular country do so to divert attention from their own countries present and past sins. Previously, one young priest explained this 'declaring' phenomenon to the Cardinal through his 'fart theory,' when mentioned the Cardinal nearly told the priest to stop talking, but politely listened. Namely, the first child to accuse others of farting is the real culprit. The Cardinal reflects, maybe this priest, who recently completed his master's degree in international relations is not that juvenile, the theory greatly simplifies the issue. The Cardinal asks himself, do others think like this young priest simplifying complex issues into simple theories?

Also, has the Israeli and Gaza conflict continued so long it too is commonplace much like the violence in Mexico. The Cardinal reflects on his country's actions against its people. Hundreds of thousands of people killed and or missing as a result of violent organized crime groups with operations in narcotics trafficking, extortion, and kidnappings. Right now, instead of uncovering killing fields, the bodies are strewn throughout the country overloading the administration's ability to investigate, resulting in a 10 percent conviction rate. It is an overt war no different than the Israeli and Gazan War. The Cardinal knows what is going on.

There are so many Mexican killings that cold storage is at a premium. When the world gets wise to this overt tactic of overwhelming the administration's investigative capacities, the criminal groups will bury the bodies, the result killing fields.

You can delve into a simple definition of war crimes: the government murders its citizens before or during a war. Is there a declared Mexican war? No, but it might as well be. What about crimes against humanity, whereby the government enslaves and murders its citizens without the use of courts, without the rule of law? Previously, a Mexican Official introduced himself on the Mexican delegation's aircraft. Who is he? Why is the Mexican Official on board? Is he knowledgeable in operating and or perpetuating this madness?

Have the Mexican government officials become so skilled in disguising the contracted killings, extortion and kidnapping of its enemies facilitated by the overt operating criminal groups that the world has never thought to inquire about Mexican war crimes, crimes against humanity? Deflect and place the blame on the piles of bodies on the Mexican 'contractors.'

For that matter, is Iran guilty of war crimes or have they become so skilled like the Mexicans in deflection by contracting their war crimes through known associated Hamas and Hezbollah groups? Hezbollah militarily and politically controls Southern Lebanon. Hamas now strengthens its grip on Gaza. Iran uses these 'contractors' to do their bidding. He sees it firsthand. What about the Iranian Revolutionary Guard? How many political prisoners are there in Iran? For some reason, the Cardinal is now 'opening his eyes.'

These are difficult questions; the US supports the dictator Saddam Hussein in the war against Iran, providing imagery and goods. The Tehran and Baghdad regimes fire rockets at each other's city populations. The Saddam regime gases the Iranian soldiers. The Gulf States are content in having Saddam act as their proxy in the war against Iran. However, the war grounds to a stalemate and the Gulf States order Saddam to pay back war loans. Saddam feels betrayed and attacks Kuwait and even moves transports into Saudi Arabia. Saddam pushes pass an another undefined 'line of acceptance,' toppled from leadership and is then found guilty of war crimes; one war crime is the gassing of Kurds in Northern Iraq. The gassing of innocent Kurds is unforgivably terrible.

The use of poison gas within Iraq's borders is not accepted, but outside its boundaries it is? It's all about timing. Backing a dictator is not easy when the dictator commits additional war crimes that allow his henchmen to run amuck and does not inhibit one of his derelict sons from killing and raping with impunity. However, when it is time to go, whether a dictator, Mexican or Colombian contractors, it is time to go.

The pilots plan the return trip, a departure from Tel Aviv, a fuel stop in Europe, through the States, and the final destination, Mexico. On the return trip from Tel Aviv, his Eminence, the Cardinal decides to visit the Galveston Houston Diocese, in Texas. Because of recent observations of the Palestinian and the Israelis, combined with his knowledge of the Central American and Mexican exodus to the United States, the Cardinal wishes to speak with the Texas Catholic Bishop regarding refugee issues between Mexico and the State of Texas. The refugees' plight and the economic strain on the State of Texas is not a favorite topic among the Texas legislature.

The Cardinal hopes to convince the Texas Bishop to create a concerted and continuous plan in solving the decades' old refugee problem. In the past, attempts to solve the refugee problem have failed, but after observing the Gaza conflict, the Cardinal decides it was worth another try starting in Texas.

Leaving Israel, the Black Cat relaxes. The dope is safe. No one searches the plane as its electronically forwarded itinerary listed the aircraft's destination as Mexico. It is not common to have dope secreted in a private corporate flight leaving Europe bound for Mexico. Yes, smugglers flood the US east coast with Afghanistan heroin via Europe and coke from Latin America through other modes of transportation, but US investigators are generally hesitant to search private planes. The Black Cat will continue to exploit this 'air' weakness. There does not appear to be a procedure to search private aircraft. The Black Cat witnesses just that, if there is, it is not available to the cops. The New Jersey officer was 'making it up' at the plane.

The richest and smartest make use of private planes bypassing a majority of law enforcement and terrorist interdiction efforts. So, when the aircraft is not smuggling contraband, those in command and control (C&C) make use of the same plane — diminishing law enforcement efforts further when the C&C use false passports. At least, that is what Jorge, Don Pedro's Cali Cartel air operative told him before his death. Jorge would know. It was Jorge's business to know, and from the Black Cat's recent experiences, Jorge was right. He forgot to ask Jorge what checks exist to determine pilot names and occupants as the private aircraft travel within the United States? The investigators will view this flight as a return trip from the Holy Land; the police will only identify the occupants as priests.

Additionally, the Mexican delegation aircraft was searched in the New Jersey area, without results. The police will not attempt a second search. The trip will be uneventful. Flaco's associates in Israel indicated that Flaco would take receipt of the dope at the same FBO in Mexico City.

The principals, with an invested interest in the 525 kilograms route, are upset but satisfied that the dope is secure. More importantly, the brokers are relieved the plane is not 'heated up' and the operation not discovered. The church talks will need to be moved to another area until the Israeli/Palestinian conflict settles down. It will calm when someone decides it has passed the 'level of acceptance.'

Chapter Thirty-One

The Cardinal's aircraft, including the negotiation team, clear Customs in New Jersey and land at Hobby Airport in south Houston, Texas. Hobby Airport is the smaller of two major airports located in the city. The Bishop of the Galveston Houston Diocese and his entourage meet the Vatican delegation team on the McKinney Fixed Based Operation (FBO) tarmac. Passengers waiting for their companions to arrive at the FBO are seated in the FBO's lobby. Some view the action through the large FBO windows. Pilots conducting preflight checklists in their respective aircraft also observe the greetings on the tarmac.

The Cardinal's party enter two large suburban vehicles, previously driven from Telephone Road through the FBO's private security gate. The suburbans with the passengers drive from the tarmac; a third vehicle contains the Bishop's entourage composed of numerous priests. This third vehicle follows the two suburbans. The Mexican delegation attends a luncheon at the downtown Diocese. Following the lunch, the Cardinal and the Bishop will discuss refugee issues.

A dark-skinned male, the 'surprised' Mexican Official guest who enters the aircraft in Mexico City, carrying only an attaché case, is the last to leave the delegation plane. The passenger walks into the FBO. A slender male wearing a tight suit meets the passenger. The thin man waves his right hand towards the FBO exit and an awaiting Bentley. Without speaking, the passenger enters the back seat of the Bentley, and the slender male drives the vehicle from the area.

John Moody, a bud of O'Malley, presently exiled to airport duty, no surprise, was drinking coffee, watching the news on the FBO's television, observed the activities surrounding the delegation's plane. The reporter on the news channel reporting live from Jerusalem reveals that intense fighting is happening between Israel and Gaza.

315

News footage shows insurgent rockets streaking across the sky some landing on southern Israeli farms. Videos of Israeli jets are seen heading south from Israel to the Gaza Strip. Additional footage shows the Gaza Strip airport bulldozed by elements of the Israeli Defense Forces.

Business is slow for Moody at the McKinney FBO. He figures he will snoop around and run a few of the car plates. What the hell? Not knowing any of the parties, he remembers O'Malley, a fellow compatriot in trouble, is investigating a priest/pastor/minister, a holy man or whatever they call them, places a call to O'Malley to bust his chops.

Everybody in the office heard the recent O'Malley stories. His pursuit of 'big time' priests responsible for dealing drugs. However, O'Malley has only been able to seize a few of the priest's kilograms of cocaine. O'Malley continues to investigate without support from the Houston Office or the impacted foreign governments. Many stories surround O'Malley. O'Malley impregnated a Mexican police officer. Her brother hit him on the head with a juice bottle. O'Malley's suspected in her killing. In response, the Mex Feds drafted their version of a Provisional arrest warrant for O'Malley.

Moody visualizes the creation of that Mexican Provisional after the Mexican judge signs the purported order; the usual corrupt Mexican notary will unnecessarily stamp it about ten times. See, the document is real.

There is talk. O'Malley is an arsonist. He got drunk and tried to burn down a fruit vendor's cart. Why would he even think about doing that? What is with the fruit rumor? A fruit cart? The best is O'Malley searched an aircraft at the Vatican. Really? An unsuspecting cop on O'Malley's orders strip searched the Pope or something like that. How idiotic. Do they even have an airport there? Where is the Vatican? It does not matter our people can be so stupid.

Moody empathizes with O'Malley's plight. Moody conducted similar cases only to have himself ostracized as a blowhard, hurting too many feelings along the way, an all-around trouble maker and rogue. Moody's eyes squint in the direction of the now empty aircraft. He listens to the ringing on his cellular phone.

"Hey."

"Yeeees...... Moody," O'Malley squirms on his broken chair now dangerously leaning 'far' right and prepares for verbal judo. Moody can be challenging to work with, but who isn't. Plus, Moody is an expert in a second language, cussing. He is famous for completing sentences consisting of nothing but cuss words. What's worse is O'Malley sometimes understands him and replies in kind.

"Mother F..ing sh..t. Here, in a shitty rust bucket. I'm kicking their ass to hell bunch of squirrelly looking bastards."...Moody whispers.

O'Malley interrupts, "I can't follow you on this one."

Moody moves to English, "No, really, bud we're being invaded, it's D-Day, they've unloaded their troops as we speak." Moody smiles as he watches the delegation's pilots drink coffee in the same lobby. The pilots are far enough away from hearing the ensuing sarcasm about to swirl through the two telephones.

"What the hell are you talking about?" O'Malley asks. "Why do I think I am going to get a headache." O'Malley's holding the phone in his left hand and rubs his right hand on his lowered forehead. He looks at the coffee and food stained office Astroturf masquerading as carpet.

"Some holy men were at the airport."

"Hare Krishna's?"

"No, your people, I think looks all, uh, ceremonial, official, but invasion-like. I'm scared." Moody whimpers.

"You mean Catholics?"

"I think so?"

"Fancy plane, people all dressed in white, red and black."

"Hmmm. Penguin-like. However, they are not red. Yeaaaa." It is O'Malley's turn to get sideways.

"You, there?"

"Yes. Do you have an aircraft tail number?"

"Hang on," Moody strains to see the aircraft, "let me get closer to it." Moody walks towards the terminal windows facing the delegation's plane. "XA3097B. Just letting you know. Just jacking with you."

"O.K. got it. It's interesting." O'Malley leans back in his broken chair. "Oh, man. Let me think this out. Oh, how's the girlfriend?"

"It's okay, waiting to vacation with her in the Cayman Islands. You know, do a little diving. Have a few laughs, beverages."

"I know you; you won't be able to stay awake past nine, Ha. Ha."

"You're right, but what are you going to do with this op.?"

"When they deplaned, where did they go?"

"They all left in big SUVs. There was also another guy who left in a Bentley. I was not able to get his plate."

"It's good data, hey, possibly see you later."

"I'll be in the area. I'm waiting for returns on a plate I ran. If you come here, I'll give it to you, cool, out."

O'Malley tracks the same aircraft to Hobby, but what is he going to do?

O'Malley leaves his desk and drives to the airport, that's what he is going to do. Because of his transgressions, his supervisor, John, gave him a pickup truck with at least 100,000 miles. So, what does O'Malley do with it? Of course, he sods his lawn with it. I bet Moody is bored; that is why he called. His way of saying let's do something.

O'Malley's belligerent but revered pod mate, Murphy, is serving his disciplinary suspension. Murphy called

O'Malley at about 1 in the morning babbling that he was about to get into a fight with some guys. Murphy hangs up before O'Malley can talk him out of it. O'Malley reaches out to Murphy's phone, but it is dead of course. Murphy never charges his cellphone. So, O'Malley stays up the night waiting for the jailhouse call, but it never comes. Murphy is learning a lot from his suspension. He'll be a changed man when he returns to the office. Yea, about that.

O'Malley did not complete a written operational plan related to action against the aircraft and accompanying subjects before driving to the airport.

An operational plan requires authorization from two supervisors. Similar to a political supervisor begging for prosecutor case acceptance in search of a 'binky,' the operational plan is another political supervisor administrative 'binky.' The agent details what he/she expects to do, who the subject/s are, where, so on and so forth and finally after 20-30 pages, the subject/s have generally died of old age. If something goes wrong in the approved operational plan, the supervisor can run upstairs to upper management and say, "See, here is our operational plan complete with the caveat "plans can change in the field, blah blah."

Christ, how could a Police Department function if its patrol officers are required to obtain supervisorial written authority before initiating a traffic stop, effecting a domestic violence arrest, pursuing a stolen vehicle and robbery subjects? A police officer traffic 'stop' and 'domestics' are spontaneous dangerous actions that law enforcement consistently conducts. The officers seldom know who is inside the car and residence. Hold up, though; you need an operational plan to stop that person for that expired inspection sticker. Hold up going into that house as screams permeate the street. The prerequisite operational plan is ludicrous. As long as management believes their troops are children, the requirement of an 'operational plan' will remain.

Arriving at Hobby airport, O'Malley meets Moody. Moody repeats that all of the 'penguins' left, but the plane is on the tarmac. He points into the lobby. The pilots are watching television. Of particular note, the female pilot is quite the babe. Look at her in the uniform. Seeing the female pilot in that tight uniform, O'Malley forgets about the aircraft.

While staring at the co-pilot, Seamus O'Malley asks, "Uh. Do you have access to any dogs?"

"Yes."

Glancing at the female pilot, O'Malley speaks to Moody, "Well, can you get a drug dog? Nobody will get hurt, no problems."

"Uh, huh. Do the plane doors have to be open for the dogs to hit on the dope?" asks Moody.

"I do not know; let's ask the dog handler if and when he gets here."

Moody and Seamus decide to get something to eat while the passengers are gone. It's obvious; the pilots are waiting for the passengers to return. They walk to Moody's vehicle. Moody starts the car. Black smoke billows from the exhaust pipe. Heavy, persistent metal on metal knocking noises coming from the engine.

"What the hell is that noise?"

"I think it is an engine lifter. That jack ass 'do nothing' in our group got a brand-new SUV while I'm still driving around in this death trap. Fuck hem."

"The engine is going to blow."

"I know. I was told there are no available replacements. You see unless you are a 'chosen one.'" He looks at Seamus with a brief nod. Moody throws empty power bar wrappers from the edge of Seamus' seat to the back seat.

"Yea, well I got that beauty over there," Seamus points to his truck, "it's about ten years old. Shit, the tailgate fell again."

"What the hell is in the back? Is that sod? Oh, I see that job took about three hours based on the number of empty beer cans in the back."

"Damn, you are good."

Moody accelerates the knocking engine. They make it to a nearby restaurant and return to the FBO. Eat their food from Styrofoam boxes and wait for the return of the priests. Moody explains to O'Malley that he is having nothing but trouble with Customs from the moment he started working at Hobby. A Customs officer, with a narcotic canine, arrives at the FBO. Out of the view of the FBO staff and passengers, the Customs officer meets with Moody and O'Malley. The agents do not want to expose their identities.

Meanwhile, FBO staff shuttle the Mexican delegation pilots to obtain a quick meal. The agents provide the Customs officer a quick brief. The young Customs officer brags that his dog is dual use; it can hit on drugs and track suspects.

Moody, the public relations officer, says, "Who gives a fuck just make sure it hits on the aircraft."

O'Malley says to himself it won't be long until Moody gets transferred to a meth group, this is going to be fun.

The Customs officer's dog sits next to Moody's leg. The Customs officer's mad and says, "The canine's 'positive alert' for detection is to sit next to the contraband, in this case, the canine's third attribute is to detect a terminal disease."

"Fuck you, very funny," Moody walks from the Customs officer.

"Thanks for coming, we will call you," O'Malley laughingly states as he retreats from the furious Customs officer.

O'Malley and Moody go back inside the FBO before the pilots return to establish an 'eye' on the aircraft. The Customs officer returns to his vehicle containing the canine, still out of view of the FBO and waits for a call from the agents advising of the delegation and pilots' arrival.

Shortly, O'Malley and Moody observe the FBO van returning the delegation pilots to the tarmac who open the aircraft door and walk inside. A few minutes later, the Mexican delegation walks through the FBO lobby and towards the plane. O'Malley calls the Customs officer and tells him 'to roll' towards the FBO front entrance. O'Malley, Moody and the United States Customs Service canine handler with a dog in tow approach the aircraft.

"There won't be any dope on that plane, O'Malley." Moody the consummate optimist adds. Moody's battled the administration and they, in turn, him, but for some reason, he is still willing to work. He too is a 'hunter' junkie.

"I know, but maybe money. The computer 'thing' said that the aircraft came from New Jersey. Money, money, south. Drug proceeds always go south. That's all I can think about."

"If the dog alerts to money on that plane. I'm going to ask the passengers for consent to search the plane tactfully. As you know, an alert can still be a false alert. I hope it is a female dog?"

"What?"

"A female dog will always hit on money, just ask my ex-wife."

"Oh, that is wrong on so many levels. I will put that in my memory bank for extortion later on. So, I guess a male dog hits on everything."

"You got that right."

"Well, let's see what happens."

The delegation moves to the stairs of the plane. O'Malley retrieves his badge from his front jeans pocket and shows it to the group placing it back in his pocket. The aircraft tail number matches. That has to be Sanchez, the Black Cat. O'Malley remembers seeing him in a picture on a desk in Matamoras. He has a goatee, now. Jose's photos did not show the Black Cat with a goatee. That's him.

O'Malley, followed by the other two law enforcement officials, including the canine, places his hand into his shirt pocket and pulls out a bullet and a casing sealed in a clear plastic bag marked 'Evidence' for the Black Cat to see. Luckily, the homicide detective mailed it to O'Malley last week. O'Malley crosses the divide that can seal his fate. The NJ TFO already searched the plane.

Simultaneously, O'Malley pulls out a piece of paper from his pocket titled 'Arrest Warrant.' O'Malley holds it in the opposite hand of the evidence bag containing the bullet and casing. The arrest warrant printed on an official document is not complete nor signed by a judge. The agents and officer can see the Black Cat mouth, "Arrest Warrant." The others in the Black Cat's party are trying to assimilate the transpiring events.

If O'Malley fails to rattle the Black Cat, O'Malley will put the evidence bag and the arrest warrant in his pockets and approach the Mexican delegates. Shake their hands, spread good cheer, call the dog off like it is just a big misunderstanding. O'Malley is an expert when it comes to acting dumb and showing signs of early dementia. O'Malley hopes to ambush the Black Cat. Knock him off balance.

O'Malley observed the Black Cat looking directly at his badge, the evidence bag, and the Black Cat drills down on the arrest warrant. The Black Cat then focuses on the canine.

O'Malley says, "I am Agent Seamus O'Malley, a friend of Montreal City Detective MacDougal and the NJ TFO." That's all it took. The Black Cat bolts from the group shocking everybody. The delegates wonder. Did the Black

Cat forget something? Did he have to take a dump? You know the food at the luncheon was terrible. The Black Cat is a clean freak; maybe he does not want to use the plane's facilities. The Black Cat in full regalia with long black coat tails flying runs from the agents.

Oh shit, what does O'Malley do now? He still doesn't have anything; this is bad, chasing a priest through an airport. Oh, yea without a written operational plan.

Moody and the dog handler follow O'Malley taking glances at the group in hopes that the delegates do not ask for their names or remember their faces. The representatives stand motionless and watch in amazement as three overweight men chase Bishop Sanchez to the FBO lobby. The canine jumps at the excitement and almost breaks free from the Customs officer's grip causing the officer to hit the ground. The Customs officer lets out a grunt entangling himself in the dog's leash. Moody leaps over the metal clanging officer shaking his head and asks why didn't he release the dog? Now, we have to chase this guy. Oh, that's right, we are kinder and gentler now. However, even dumber, the canine handler should have used the fall as an excuse to let the dog go. What a fiasco?

This fucking guy, Flaco observes the Black Cat and the agents through the cyclone fence that encircles the FBO. Don Pedro dispatched Flaco to Houston; instead, of Mexico City for the planned 'offload,' anticipating that something could go wrong in Houston and low and behold it is going bad. Flaco locks onto the commotion not realizing if he looks into his rear-view mirror, he will see a whitish determined looking image observing the same incident.

The Black Cat burst into the terminal's lobby, through the hallway straight into a waiting taxi, idling parked parallel to Telephone Road. The Black Cat roars at the cab driver, who stopped his vehicle to wipe food stains from his shirt. The cab driver not looking at the passenger, with a napkin in his right-hand waives at the new passenger and tells him he is 'out of service.'

In a low determined voice, the passenger demands, "Drive. Drive as fast as you can and don't look back." For some reason, the hairs on the driver's arms raise, and he gets goosebumps. The Mexican-American cab driver reaches for a small bible on the vehicle's dashboard cautiously peers into the rear mirror and is shocked to see this priest, his facial bones accentuating his angular face. A face, resembling a Devil directs the cab driver. Foul smell and a sudden surge of heat permeate the vehicle's interior. The cab driver's fingers tremble as he turns a dashboard knob to increase the air conditioner. Horror pervades every part of the cab driver.

"Drive as fast as you can," the deep voice repeats.

As a result of the decree, a cold wind streams from the priest's mouth and frost whirls in the vehicle's interior blanketing the windows. The cabbie slams the accelerator to the floor releases the napkin from his right hand, grasps the bible in his left hand, the steering wheel with his right. The cab enters Telephone Road; its right wheels bounce off the curb. The cab driver loses his grip on the steering wheel. The cabbie's head involuntarily rocks left and right from the bounce.

The vehicle swerves in front of oncoming traffic, causing drivers to slam on their brakes. When it came time for the customary one finger salute and banging of the car horns, the drivers slow their cars below the posted speed limit. Some drive seek cover to the opposite side of temporary concrete street dividers. The cab races at breakneck speed hovering into and out of on-coming traffic. The cabbie's head presses against the headrest — the car steers by itself. A dark shape emerges in the cab's backseat. The driver hears an animal roar before losing consciousness, his arms motionless alongside his body.

"Follow the red car in front of you," the words came from the red car and heard only by the Black Cat.

Unbeknownst to the Black Cat, Flaco occupies the red car. It lures and teases him to follow. The red vehicle taunts the Black Cat. Through his rearview mirror, Flaco looks at the pursuing cab as it groans and swerves tracking him. Flaco waves for the Black Cat to follow. The cab speeds through green, yellow, and red lights. As a result of the cabbie's flight, cars are strewn with abandon leaving Moody and O'Malley a physical map to follow.

O'Malley and Moody fumble for their vehicle keys and jump into their respective cars. The Customs officer rises from the ground with a limp, the canine reduced to occasional barks at unseen culprits. With their heads down, the Customs officer and the canine slowly walk to the FBO lobby. The FBO customers are speechless. They watch as the now bleeding officer and canine enter the restroom. The handler tends to his physical and mental wounds. Shit, that was embarrassing; that Moody guy. What the hell, maybe there is something in the aircraft. He exits the restroom with his canine. The FBO customers conversing with each other as to what they saw, stop in mid-sentence and watch the officer and his dog depart the FBO lobby. Now in his car, he takes a big swig of his big gulp and asks, "Why not seize the dope, before these guys get back and he'll 'stat it.'" Customs could stage a Press Conference without mentioning these guys participation. However, he is scared to act until the agents return. Let them take the heat if nothing is there.

Finally, Moody and O'Malley in pursuit with their undercover cars clip the same FBO parking lot curb as the cabbie. Neither vehicle is equipped with emergency lights and sirens. The State of Texas does not authorize agents to use emergency equipment. One needs to be a Texas Peace Officer to operate an emergency vehicle with lights and sirens. They are not Police Officers. So, they engage their pizza delivery skills. Pizza delivery drivers can move through traffic quicker than police cars with lights and sirens. With the sudden acceleration, Moody's engine loses the first cylinder; it nears its end. Tomorrow, he bicycles to work.

A metal irregular wall, comprised of stationary and smashed cars, is in Moody and O'Malley's path. They drive through metal gaps in the walls. Passengers of parked vehicles and pedestrians point in the direction of the cab's flight. White smoke billows from the taxi as it careens through the streets and enters I-45 freeway, northbound. Moody and O'Malley observe the cab's intermittent brake lights.

The Black Cat is irate. Why had he lost his composure? O'Malley caught him off guard and successfully ambushed him. He wasn't anticipating problems in Houston. He let his guard down. His message from Gaza was not strong enough. The Black Cat had become too confident, too vain, and too complacent in his activities. He consciously ignored numerous warning signs. When shown the evidence bag containing a bullet and a casing and the Arrest Warrant, he lost it. That O'Malley never quits, who the fuck is he? Now the Black Cat demonstrated his guilt. He ran. The taxi speeds north on I-45 towards downtown Houston, the same direction he traveled with the delegation. It is the only direction he knows. The red car leads him. Why? How?

O'Malley and Moody do not transmit on the useless car radios. The radios range are ineffective, and the radio relay sites are constantly undergoing maintenance. An office dispatch system does not exist. By the time O'Malley and Moody contact the 'locals' on the phones, the pursuit will be over when the cab expectably crashes into an innocent citizen. Another issue never addressed.

O'Malley's empty beer cans rise and fall in his truck bed as he accelerates and slows. In drastic turns, beer cans fly from the bed bouncing off citizens cars, and if that was not enough, he finishes them off with globs of broken sod. They are moving fast but careful not to run anyone off the streets. In this town, that is a prescription for retaliation.

Moody already expects lead poisoning from at least one of the drivers. A dirt clod lodges on his windshield a beer can whirls by his driver's window. He laughs; this is crazy. Bam! A second tie rod is out.

Passing a pickup and seeing the driver's rage, O'Malley secures his pistol between the seat cushion and the consul. Not for use against the Black Cat, but for protection against citizens packing their heat.

The Black Cat's taxi is out of sight as it travels over a highway overpass. Moody and O'Malley cannot see it. They accelerate. Based on the wreckage, O'Malley leads, and then Moody will lead. They use their turn signals, making known their intentions.

North of the highway overpass, the red car fades and reappears. Flaco blacks out, convulses involuntarily, and then transforms. No longer in Flaco's control, the red vehicle slows. It positions on the inside emergency lane to the drivers-side of the cab. Trash from the emergency lane flies into the air. In complete disregard of the traffic conditions, the driver of the red car slowly turns its head towards the Black Cat's taxi. She has deep brown piercing eyes and long brown hair. It is the girl assassin killed by the Black Cat in the desert south of Nuevo Laredo. She hypnotically waves at him. She has a devilish smile, and then her smile contorts into a scowl. Her body tenses its muscles readying to pounce from the red car to the Black Cat's. Her stare transfixes on the Black Cat. The twin assassin transposes back to Flaco, who points with one hand a heavy AR-15 rifle through his open passenger window. Flaco intended to lead the Black Cat to a permanent location. Flaco knows it is close to impossible to shoot from a moving car accurately. Secondly, shooting a rifle requires two hands. However, something coerces him into making the shot, now. The gun acquired through a 'straw purchase.' It is still and silent in the cab. Motions slow.

The cabbie awakes and sees the gun. It could have been a cannon for all the cab driver knew. In reality, it is. A flash, without noise, appears from the barrel, then a second flash shattering the driver's side back seat window and penetrating the rear door where the Black Cat sits. The gun hits Flaco's passenger window frame each time he fires. The wind blows into the cab. Glass shards fly throughout the taxi piercing the Black Cat cutting him. It is as if the girl was reenacting her assassination. A third shot, with an accompanying loud bang, follows. The bullets hit their mark.

The cabbie now controls the cab and slams down on the vehicle's brakes. The tires scream. Black smoke rises from the tires. The Black Cat's lifeless body slams into the cab's separation glass. Blood spurts from the Black Cat's carotid spraying the interior glass. The taxi swerves left, hitting the freeway divider, the engine catches fire and explodes.

Flaco avoids the collision with the cab. In front of him, he observes an image of a beautiful young girl holding a young boy's hand. They could be twins. They smile as they rise toward a low cloud. Emotionless, they focus on Flaco and whisper in unison, "You better change your ways."

For the first time in his life, Flaco experiences real fear. He is helpless. He had a similar feeling following the Mexico City earthquake. What should he do? What can he do right now? He's done some horrible things in his life. He throws the gun onto the freeway, what did he care if discovered. The weapon bounces off others and lands in a heap of discarded trash. The twins acknowledge Flaco's act.

The twin assassins lived a hard life. They were born without the tools to survive. Without family or financial support to succeed in this world. The twins were ignored and forgotten by everyone. As bad as they were, in the end within seconds of death, each twin genuinely asked for forgiveness.

The cloud opens to a bright blue sky. As the twins enter the gap, it slowly embraces them. The twins follow the sun's light to heaven.

Traffic stops behind the shooting. Flaco continues north on the 45 freeway, then south on highway 59, disappearing into the fourth largest city.

Three very large freeway lampposts observe the Black Cat's demise and the ascendance of the twins. It is not necessary to report what the heavens already knew.

Vehicle brake lights serve as flares to O'Malley and Moody. They see a plume of smoke resembling the detonation of a vehicular improvised explosive device (VIED). Moody and O'Malley navigate their vehicles on the inside freeway shoulder, discovering the cab on fire. The cabbie jumps from the passenger side door with his hands in the air and paces around the car in a panicky state — Moody's car now with its molten engine rolls to a stop on the inside freeway lane.

O'Malley and Moody approach the cab to find the Black Cat's lifeless body lying partly on the rear seat the remainder on the floorboard. His blood smeared on the separation glass. Shit, what a mess. White smoke snakes to the Black Cat's body, simultaneously O'Malley hears a child's voice. It is the same voice he heard at the burnt car in the Mexican desert. She speaks ancient poetry he somehow understands. Is she his guardian? Did she do this? She's powerful enough.

The fire's heat forces O'Malley and Moody to abandon the vehicle. A brisk wind passes O'Malley and Moody enveloping the cab. A hush fills the air. The fire then roars with extreme intensity throughout the car and suddenly extinguishes. They curiously reflect on the weird event. Of course, neither tells the other that the flames are somewhat suspect, not natural.

Flaco does not want to call Don Pedro, but he reaches out to him, hoping for no answer. Don Pedro does respond and Flaco lazily without providing significant details explains what transpired in Houston. Don Pedro understands. The police will find the narcotics in Houston.

Following the call, Flaco receives a call from the mystery passenger who departed the FBO in the Bentley. Flaco does not answer. Right now, Flaco will take his time returning to Colombia. He decides to remain in western Houston, the home to numerous Colombians residing in low-cost apartments and houses. He saved his money. Now, he will reflect and decide what to do in the future.

A legion of patrol officers descends from both sides of the freeway. Patrol vehicles are present almost a mile from the fire, and the officers are getting mouthfuls from the accident victims. Simultaneously, the police officers' direct wreckers to clear the highway. O'Malley and Moody shrugging their shoulders look at each other, "It is the cabbie's fault. Let him take the heat."

They anticipate management overreaction. Moody calls the Customs officer at the FBO and tells him to delay the departure of the delegation's plane until they arrive. They are going to search the aircraft. The Customs officer acknowledges. After hearing what had happened, the Customs officer is happy not to have entered the pursuit. He gets a 'stat,' without the headaches. Moody and O'Malley remain at the Black Cat scene. You don't just race across Houston through a trail of debris until you provide an accurate account to the first responding patrol officers.

First responders experience everything in their careers. They are quick learners and can grasp enforcement actions differentiating these actions from managers fabricated liability and high drama. By explaining their story to the first responders, O'Malley and Moody also attempt to stop management's inevitable creation of the 'parallel case.' More importantly, they remain at the scene for their protection.

A few pickup drivers are observed working their way through the wreckage to the now smoking cab. These drivers are looking for payback. O'Malley and Moody did not run anyone off the road they merely followed the debris at high speed. However, they are guilty in the pickup drivers' minds. When the pickup drivers arrive at the scene, the police persuade them to leave the scene. The drivers mouthing at Moody and O'Malley from inside their vehicles slowly move from the area. Shame on the next driver who cuts off one of these drivers.

The cab driver suffers a real mental breakdown, not a staged illness to distract the first responders. He is transported to the 'Tub,' Ben Taub hospital, one of the most respected trauma hospitals in the world. So respected, that military doctors train at the facility.

O'Malley finally got the Black Cat. He is sixty percent sure the delegation's plane contains money, twenty percent certain that dope exists, the remaining twenty percent is there is nothing as the Black Cat may have run because he believed there was an arrest warrant. Seamus is not concerned; he's experienced this madness before. It's just a matter of a search. Because of the Black Cat's airport antics, O'Malley and Moody will obtain voluntary consent to search from a delegation member.

Chapter Thirty-Two

As a result of his assistance, the former Mexican Interior Minister Gomez and his family become members of a small select group, Vatican City citizens. Citizenship that inhibits him and his family extradition to other countries; especially, the United States. Of course, O'Malley does not know of this arrangement.

When O'Malley scanned the article about the Minister of Interior's travel to Italy, he did not read the entire article stating that the Interior Minister was acting on behalf of the President of Mexico, obviously to test its viability for the Mexican President.

The Medellin Cartel strikes hard at the Cali Cartel in Colombia. Don Pedro, the Cali Cartel leader, continues to battle the Medellin Cartel. Instead, of retreating to one of his ranches, he decides to hole up in Cartagena, Colombia a purported self-rule, no conflict zone, between traffickers.

Don Pedro and his guards stay at a beautifully renovated Spanish mission now a hotel complete with four-foot thick walls. His men maintain security shifts from the first-floor lush exterior garden to the top floor. His guards possess, a 360-degree view from the top, with sights including the city and the Caribbean Sea. This guard duty is a coveted assignment. As an added incentive, the hotel employs a canine handler to detect explosives.

Daily, Don Pedro frequents the top floor pool and bar. He makes preparations to pay some of the brokers and provides 'product' to others for their losses in the Houston seizure. Don Pedro once again ponders his retirement. As usual, he's occupied in defending himself from numerous threats. The retirement thought passes. Will he go all the way? Attack the Colombian central government itself? He asks, why is Flaco ignoring his calls? Could be a problem.

Although, it seems that Russian General Comstock invested heavily in the now shut down smuggling route. It was not that costly. Approximately 300 kilograms of cocaine and some heroin remain in Gaza for distribution. Because of Comstock's actions, Mexico remains chaotic, and the Americans increased their financial aid to Mexico.

General Comstock remains in good graces with Don Pedro, his Mexican Intelligence contacts and his Colombian government counterparts. Comstock continues to manage various operations. Following the Houston cocaine seizure, Comstock prepares to move his foreign operations to Venezuela. The present regime will give his organization a sanctuary, a base. Essentially, 'base' in Arabic translates to Al Qaeda. Comstock receives a promotion. With the new assignment, his superiors order him to hurt the Americans physically. Accompanying this directive, General Comstock is to ensure that the Americans will share in endless 'Candlelight Vigils.'

Moshe, Medellin Cartel's most prolific hitman, slowly recoils from the public like an alligator sliding on the embankment of a swamp to the concealment of algae and green moss. He has difficulties in moving his partially paralyzed arm that was damaged during the airport battle. Moshe debates as to what transnational criminal group to join or should he remain with Medellin? What group will accept him because of his disability? He is aware that the Cali and Medellin Cartel war has weakened the Colombian Cartels presence in Mexico giving rise to Mexican National psychopaths with no loyalty to anybody or anything. He will not work for the Mexican criminal groups.

O'Malley and Moody receive accolades from the 525-kilogram seizure, but both recognize that they did not get the big boys. O'Malley, Moody and Murphy intend to look for clues leading to those who directed the Black Cat. Management minimizes the Black Cat's death, ecstatic it is not an in-custody death.

The Cardinal gives the agents, O'Malley and Moody the consent to search the delegation's aircraft and allowed entry into the Vatican taped boxes. An interesting note, the canine initially hit on a box with tampered Vatican tape. Secreted in this box, accompanying the cocaine, is antique Middle Eastern jewelry. Seamus O'Malley wonders if a

Middle Eastern terror group sent these antiques to Don Pedro's group, with the intentions of establishing a separate narcotic route.

Seamus can't help in thinking of Moody and his male/female canine theory; was the canine a female? That might explain the canine's positive alert on the jewelry. Man, he has to stay away from Moody. Moody goes to dark places.

In front of both Moody and O'Malley, Cardinal Vazquez genuinely scolds the Mexican delegation for not confiding in him their suspicions of the Black Cat. Cardinal Vazquez also relinquishes ownership of the aircraft to Moody and O'Malley. After all, the Cardinal and his staff do not know who owns it. The Cardinal does not do this to persuade the investigators of his innocence, but to instill to his delegation that until someone provides him a complete overall of the Black Cat's illicit activities, they will walk to Mexico.

The Cardinal confides in O'Malley and Moody that he is suspending Vatican City participation in the Eastern and Russian talks until he assesses the situation. The Cardinal is very much in control of his faculties. As if reversing an old film projector, the Cardinal reviews past events.

The Black Cat was present after the assassination of Cardinal Torres in Culiacan, but he was there as part of his official duties. The Black Cat conducted a commendable job in organizing Cardinal Torres' funeral. However, while in Mexico City, the Black Cat regularly disappeared from the Shrine of Our Lady of Guadalupe making use of a diocese pool car. Why? Sanchez was so attentive to the medical supplies. Personally, loading the boxes in the delegation's plane.

A member of his staff advises him that the Black Cat was involved in a disturbance inside the church at the Shrine before they left. He will investigate that issue. The Cardinal should have realized something was wrong, but

Sanchez, aka the Black Cat, was a Bishop. He should have seen the clues of the Black Cat's guilt, but for some reason, he was exhausted during this period. Now, the Cardinal has renewed energy. He directs the pilots to assist in the Houston investigation. O'Malley will make the pilot debriefings very lengthy. After all, the copilot is comfortable on the eyes. Just kidding; that will be a minefield.

Before the Cardinal departs, O'Malley and Moody meet separately with each delegate priest. Because O'Malley and Moody are steaming about additional management inhibitions related to Source use, they decide to make the priests, Sources. Now, what is management going to say about their use?

Moody and O'Malley instruct the priests to provide their names and numbers to the additional Catholic priest delegates from the other parts of the world also involved with the talks. These new Sources have an income stream, he and Moody will not have to beg the politicals for Source monies. Moody and O'Malley are creating their new world information network which will piss off the establishment. They know it won't be long until their office shuts down this network.

O'Malley makes a mental note to locate the Matamoros 'running' woman that rescued him. She was close then, and he thinks she is still close. He will find her. Will she look for him, no, wishful thinking? For some reason, he believes their worlds will collide again.

After handling the Houston issues, the Cardinal acting on the conversation with the supernatural voice of the Great Mosque in Gaza City, contacts his Saudi Arabian friend. The Cardinal tells his friend that as soon as he resolves a severe problem in his house, he would like to sit down and talk about theirs. The Cardinal details his experiences in Gaza and the associated Gazans' and Israelis' suffering. The IDF encircles the Gazans, but in effect, a small minority of Islamic heretics incarcerate the Gazans more. The Cardinal indicates that these new discussions have to include Israeli's right to defend itself.

The Cardinal reveals that the Gaza Strip is without electricity, fresh water, and food. The Strip is entirely dark at night, and situational reports from the area are decreasing. Maybe, they could come up with some ideas on how to reduce not only this conflict but the constant drumbeat of others that appear to be developing throughout the world. The Iman agrees. The Cardinal makes it known that he will not just stand by. He will do something, anything, even if it is not right.

The Iman is not surprised by the Cardinal's directness. The Iman expected a call such as this. The lack of electricity explains the absence of updates from his people at the Gaza Mosque. The Iman tells the Cardinal he received a similar call from another holy man very close to the Gazan clashes. A sacred man the Iman had assumed was his enemy. This righteous man expressed the same plea.

The Iman replies that the crisis is painful for all. As a result of the conversation, the Iman will first attempt to persuade those referring to the Gazan conflict as 'adventurism' to refrain with such talk. Dark clouds gather throughout the world, he admits. The Iman will meet with this new friend and the Cardinal as soon as they are available. The Cardinal expresses his gratitude in this new-found trust and will send a dispatch to the Vatican advising of the Iman's most generous gesture.

Chapter Thirty-Three

O'Malley's and Moody's Washington Headquarters lit up as a result of the 'big' seizure. Immediately, agents in HQS try to steal the 'stat' to justify their bloated Source budget by saying they had a Source who delivered an aircraft battery and a wheel to the Black Cat's FBO three years ago. Moody ended this nonsense via a harshly stated cuss word sentence.

Meetings then commence solely between Headquarters and the Houston Office. The Houston chain of command knows nothing of the case other than a priest ran from a plane that contained dope. Because none of the coveted and much-touted office wire intercepts picked up intelligence regarding the cocaine seizure, the managers push the narrative that an unidentified suspect killed the independent operating lone smuggler, Bishop Sanchez, in a still-unsolved 'road rage incident.' You know, road rage is a persistent problem in Houston.

The Houston managers advise Headquarters that charges are not filed against the passengers of the Mexican delegation's aircraft. The Prosecutors Office indicated that the passengers were not culpable as they were unaware of the secreted narcotics.

O'Malley's supervisor John jumps on the bandwagon providing the customary incomplete briefs to Headquarters. Field managers/supervisors understand that personal relationships with HQS staff are necessary to get promoted and in acquiring cushy jobs to Disneyland East (DC) when mandatorily transferred. Preferably, a transfer not to a DC office, but a suburban DC office.

John directs O'Malley to present a more thorough PowerPoint detailing the seizure for future briefs. In the PowerPoint, O'Malley explains the Black Cat's purported involvement with the murder of a Mex Fed Colonel in Nuevo Laredo and his association in the death of a Cardinal in Culiacan. As a result of the Cardinal's assassination, the Medellin Cartel and the Mexican government are at war. The Cali Cartel proxy war in Mexico will lead to the rise of large Mexican Cartels.

Continuing his brief, O'Malley advises that the purported Mex Fed liaison, Maria did not commit suicide but was highly likely killed by the Black Cat's organization. O'Malley concludes each brief that Russians are behind the smuggling operation; namely, a Russian identified as Yuri. He believes Yuri resides in Mexico City. Following the Russian reference, O'Malley always observes open mouths, shaking heads and few dozing off, one constant, John, is the first to hit the mattress. The managers that are awake and somewhat interested then ask O'Malley if Yuri's telephone number is known. He says no. O'Malley then sees their hearts drop, and the briefing concludes.

Following each brief, John orders him to update the investigation's Executive Summary. If there are future HQS conferences, John wants to be prepared to tell upper management that his group is actively exploring means to locate subject numbers for an impending wiretap. Ride this wave.

O'Malley realizes all the organizational communication devices have been 'dropped.' Let the overseas professionals exploit the numbers. The two people in Matamoros that saved his life were probably those — intercepting data without having to reveal the means in open court. Why spend months writing a 'go by' telephone intercept affidavit only to write another as the bad guys dropped the phone during the prosecutorial review process.

As a result of this 'target of opportunity case,' meaning just a short investigation, a notation is made by O'Malley's Headquarters that private corporate aircraft might occasionally transport narcotics for rogue traffickers into the United States. Traffickers with no apparent link to the significant Colombian Cartels.

One HQS theory indicates that unidentified traffickers mistakenly placed the narcotics on the wrong aircraft and were unable to retrieve the same.

Another theory surmises that unidentified opportunist traffickers attempted to smuggle the drugs on the plane with the consent of the pilots. The dope to be 'offloaded' at a US refueling point, but law enforcement efforts spook the pilots or ground 'receiving' traffickers from completing the task. This theory concludes that the narcotics were destined for the US nowhere else. The seizure of the 525 kilograms of cocaine is considered an aberration. No one probes directed foreign intervention into Mexico's chaos.

During this period, someone notifies Jose, the priest, and his defense attorney that at the time of law enforcement questioning, Jose was not read his Miranda rights in Spanish. Case dismissed. Out of jail, Jose goes to Harwin Street in Houston. While incarcerated, an inmate advises Jose, the vendors occupying Harwin have access to every kind of counterfeit product on the earth. Jose approaches a vendor and obtains his new identity; he dislikes his newly acquired US name Rice Chicken given to him by the Troopers at the time of his arrest. Jose remains in Houston.

One day while eating at a restaurant in the vicinity of Gessner at Westheimer, Jose notices a serious looking tall, skinny bald Colombian. He listens as the man orders food. The voice is familiar. Could it be Flaco? Jose does not believe in coincidences.

Chapter Thirty-Four

Rebecca, Todd and Socorro's Intelligence boss, discovers another Agent O'Malley report detailing 525 kilograms of dope seized from the Black Cat's aircraft tail number XA3097B. When did O'Malley get the tail number, and when was this seizure, she says to herself? That explains why the delegation's plane has not returned to the Mexico City FBO.

Rebecca continues reading the O'Malley report, and says out loud, "The Black Cat is dead! What the Hell? When are we ever going to share information?" She shakes her head in disbelief and stops reading the file.

Rebecca learns that her HQS, analyzed photographs taken of Yuri and the Black Cat. The pictures Jose forwarded to DEA agent O'Malley. HQS identifies a restaurant in Polanco, a suburb in Mexico City possibly frequented by the Russian, Yuri. Rebecca sends the data to the US 'paras.' The 'paras' concentrate their forces on the Polanco restaurant. Of note, a para previously observes what she believes to be Yuri at their Starbucks surveillance position, but the subject has a full beard and different hair color. However, the paras log the observation only to confirm her sighting and identification when the same subject is seen walking to and from the identified restaurant. The paras follow Yuri determining his secured residence.

They possess a recorded voice exemplar of Yuri talking obtained from Ol' red face's, Netanya's phone. They plan to compare it to Yuri's voice when he frequents the Starbucks. The paras follow Yuri from his residence to the coffee shop. The para who initially observed the bearded Yuri at the Starbucks accompanied by another para confirm Yuri's distinctive Eastern European dialect, one needs to be aware that Starbucks Frappuccino's can be hazardous to your health.

The paras are now set to establish Yuri's pattern of life. Rebecca forwards Yuri's daily movements as observed by the 'paras' to her HQS. Yuri does not meet with known Russian contacts or for that matter, anyone. It is essential to continue the surveillance to identify the Yuri 'cell.' Also, more importantly, if Yuri meets with his boss General Comstock.

However, as time passes the surveillance team concludes Yuri is on a hiatus and or vacation. They have never seen him use a telephone. Yuri is not ignoring surveillance; he is just laying back and enjoying the good life. Surveillance expenses pile up, and all involved in the investigation are aware that numerous hot spots exist in the world and the demands on the paras are extreme.

Surveillance has established Yuri's daily activities. The paras observe Yuri exit his residence as always at approximately 1045 hours, and he then walks to the Starbucks in Polanco, the site of the paras de facto command center. Yuri orders coffee and reads the New York Times on the patio. Finished with his coffee and paper, he leisurely walks on the Polanco sidewalks, window shops, walks to the park and sometimes enters the Ferrari boutique car dealership. Eventually, Yuri frequents one of three restaurants at approximately 1400 to 1430 hours. Following lunch, he returns to his electronically secured residence for a short nap.

Before reaching his apartment, Yuri passes numerous one family, two-story residences, small exclusive jewelry, and upscale clothing shops some under various states of renovation. The developers attempt to keep the exterior walls of the shops in their original form. They spare no expense in making the interiors very fashionable. At times, these structures in various states of construction are empty of the construction workers.

Based on Rebecca's daily reports, HQS reaches a decision. On this date, following a lengthy lunch, surveillance observes Yuri exit Charro restaurant at approximately 1545 hours. Yuri carries a plastic bag most likely containing leftovers. The foot traffic lessens as Yuri walks from the restaurant to a side street.

One structure near Yuri's residence, not occupied by its construction workers for some time, contains two plywood pieces laid horizontally on the ground leaning on carpenter horses. The plywood limits the view into the structure and is placed there only for aesthetic reasons. Nothing of value remains in the building. One can walk between or around the plywood leading to a sizeable low-lit empty room. Exposed electrical wires with unlimited power hang from the ceiling awaiting the electricians care; mortar remnants from demolition litter the floor. Some rolled onto the adjacent sidewalk.

Para 'foot' surveillance shorten their distance to Yuri as he approaches the abandoned structure. These same two members discreetly put heavy clear rubber gloves on their hands. They wear thick rubber 'Duck' style shoes that are for watery and icy environments.

As Yuri nears the front of the structure, the men discreetly push Yuri in his back, causing him to stumble. He loses his traction on the mortar chips leaves the sidewalk and stumbles between the plywood pieces into the low-lit structure's interior. A third and fourth para grab and shove him onto to live electric wires releasing Yuri before he contacts the high voltage wires. A burst of electricity slams into Yuri's body. His body sticks to the voltage and is not released until a breaker engages, creating a loud bang. When the power terminates, his body falls to the ground. His plastic lunch package melts to his hand, and his middle finger explodes revealing the location of the release of the voltage from his body.

The interior paras dressed as construction workers are with a fifth para inside the structure who wears matching clothes as Yuri and has makeup resembling Yuri. The three, walk from the interior onto the adjacent sidewalk. A few pedestrians see Yuri stumble, but within the short time of the kill, the team is already exiting.

The Yuri look alike and the other paras laugh to satisfy the curious. In front of a few remaining pedestrians, the construction team members dust off the look alike. They joke about the incident and get the remaining witnesses to laugh at how clumsy the look-alike is. The Yuri look-alike walks from the area. The remaining team members reenter the structure and take photos and fingerprints of the deceased and casually walk from the building.

Rebecca receives the news of Yuri's death and forwards the information to Headquarters. All thought it was best to keep the Russians guessing about Yuri's death. Scenarios of running Yuri over with a car, poison, a late-night robbery will raise Russian suspicions. Rebecca intends to continue the investigation against Yuri's boss, General Comstock. The case is not over, not by a long shot.

Thousands of miles away, the Israeli Defense Forces (IDF) conduct night patrol in Gaza City. Explosions and small arms gunfire continue throughout the area. To reduce civilian casualties, the IDF moves house to house consciously knowing this action will increase IDF casualties.

IDF troops breach residential metal gates; soldiers run inside to meet hatred, fear, gunfire or an explosion. As the battle intensifies, some civilians remain on the sidewalks and streets watching the events, hypnotized by the pyrotechnics on steroids. Where else can they go?

Some of their residences no longer exist. If habitable, it is an insurgent target to fight from and now a potential IDF target. If slightly damaged, the intense heat inside magnifies with the windows closed and draped. The drapes hide the inhabitant's silhouettes from possible sniper fire and deflect some of the flying glass and debris.

In one section of Gaza City, insurgents armed with RPGs and AK47s run towards the Great Mosque; IDF soldiers in a foot pursuit. The combatants try in vain to open the Mosque's massive doors. As they struggle with the door, the trailing members catch up with their colleagues and all congregate at the exposed mosque entrance.

The insurgents shoot at the lock on the doors. The IDF is now within range, and the insurgents exchange gunfire with the IDF. They breach the door and pour inside through their fatal funnel. One-member falls in the doorway and accidentally discharges his RPG. The rocket flies into a storeroom igniting an insurgent weapons cache destroying the Mosque's western wall. An inhuman groan is heard echoing throughout Gaza City.

The Mosque explosion kills the insurgents and wounds several of the pursuing IDF soldiers. Screams emanate from the IDF soldiers and the remaining inhabitants residing in the adjacent multilevel residences.

A separate IDF foot patrol is walking on the streets their mission also to clear houses occupied by suspected insurgents. Two children kicking a soccer ball between them on the second floor of a multilevel complex, see the approaching soldiers.

Shots come from a window above the children and strike an IDF soldier in the leg. The patrol instinctively crouches and returns superior gunfire to the suspected point of origin (POO). Yelled orders follow and elements of the patrol run towards the stairs leading to the apartment. Others find cover behind rubble in the street and the sidewalk. An IDF attachment goes to the opposite side of the complex. An IDF medic carries the wounded soldier to cover.

The children who were playing soccer, run inside their apartment. Their mother extinguishes the few candles they possess. From inside, they hear the soldiers' shouts. The heavy sounding soldiers' steps come closer and closer. Shots are fired again from an apartment above the children.

A soldier yells, "Is it this apartment? Which house is it? Where?"

Outside the children's door, another soldier yells, "I think it is this one." Pointing at the children's unit.

The children shake, cry, and scream; they are going to kill us. The family runs and then stumble over each other as they fall into the rear bedroom.

"I can hear them inside!" a soldier yells.

Another soldier catches up to two soldiers who stand on opposite sides of the children's door and yells, "Let's hit it!"

A corporal catches up with the soldiers and observes no sign of forced entry (NSFE) to the front door. The drapes are in good condition. The windows contain small cracks. A piece of the window glass is missing from the corner of one of the window frames, but the missing piece of glass is not on the exterior window frames or the walkway.

"Fuck them, let's go in!" yells one of the soldiers.

The children dive underneath their mom's bed. The mother sits on top of it. If the soldiers come in, she will try to divert their attention in some way to save her kids.

"I hear them in there, they are in there," a soldier says.

The corporal tells them to shut up. Calm down. Get your shit together.

The corporal continues his quick scan. Shoes neatly aligned on one side of the front door. One small child's shoe not matching the others is sole up and close to the edge of the walkway.

"Stand down this is not it," the corporal whispers. It is a millisecond decision based on his observations finally completed as he sees the still rolling soccer ball in front of the children's front door. "One more floor," the corporal whispers.

Shots are fired again from one floor above the children's apartment. The corporal radios the Sergeant and advises that the shooter is one floor up from their position. The Sergeant allows the corporal and his team time to close on the shooter. Just before the corporal's team arrived on the third floor, the Sergeant orders the ground forces to fire on the shooter.

The bullets enter the broken windows and pop mark the concrete surrounding the windows. When the Sergeant orders a cease-fire, members of the corporal's team throw grenades into the now glassless windows. A soldier breaches the front door, and the rest passes through their fatal funnel to find the insurgent dead. They hear a noise in the hallway. A woman lays in the hall disoriented from the blast and slowly raises her hand. Two soldiers aim their rifles at the darkened image. Why they did not shoot is not known.

"Are there any more people inside?"

"Yes, my children."

"If you are lying to me, I will kill everyone in here. Do you understand me?"

The soldiers find limited cover within the small unit. "Tell them to come out. With their hands up."

Three children in shock covered in dust stagger from the rear of the hallway. One trips and causes the others to fall on top of her. Startled, the soldiers zero their rifles on the small dark figures.

"Is that all?"

"Yes."

"Who is this guy?" pointing to the dead man near a couch, a soldier asks.

"We do not know. You have to believe us. The guy just barged in, threatened us, and told us to go to the rear the house. Honestly, we do not know who he is. Please, believe us."

The soldiers search the remaining unit and are unable to find new weapons or explosives.

The corporal says, "Let us take a look at the kids."

The IDF provides the family with first aid and rations. A soldier photographs the dead insurgent gets a quick fingerprint, and they descend from the complex and continue the patrol.

Two streets away from the mosque explosion and the recent sniper shooting, a highly trained small company of IDF soldiers on foot patrol under the command of a Sergeant approach a small café. The Sergeant glances at two photographs and instructs his team to form into a crescent as they close on the restaurant. The pictures originated from the southernmost Israeli checkpoint into Gaza.

Mohammad Bin Zarif stands from his seat and points a gun at the approaching IDF company. The IDF company shoot him multiple times. He dies from his wounds. Boris, Yuri's point of contact (POC) in Gaza remains seated and places his hands' palms up on the coffee table. IDF soldiers handcuff Boris and put a hood over his head.

The Sergeant tells Boris that he is to be transported to the Israeli Liaison office. The Sergeant then losses his temper when consecutive nearby explosions nearly knock him to his knees. He glares at Boris and says, "Were you that stupid thinking that we did not know of Mohammad's terrorist activities in Southern Lebanon. His fucked-up co-opting of one of our purported human Sources! You are the prize we have been waiting for!"

"I will be released. Let me take that back. I want to talk to someone."

"Who the fuck do you want to talk to too?"

"The Americans. I have had enough." Boris' covered head slumps.

The Sergeant takes the request seriously. In this mess, nobody will be the wiser to know what happened to this capture. So, they work their way out of the battle and transport Boris to the appropriate authorities.

One member of a three-person American team transmits a microburst. The team secreted itself in the rugged Southern Lebanon terrain for four days and when they located, identified and reconfirmed the designated target, the message containing the strike coordinates is transmitted.

In the darkness, deep within the Mediterranean Sea off the coast of Cyprus, a whir is heard on the sea's surface by distant refugees floating on rafts. The sound disappears. The same whir reaches Southern Lebanon. Muhammed Zarif's team members look up, and the missile vaporizes them.

Zarif's brother perched on an opposite hill sees the carnage. Zarif's brother says to his team that only the US conducts strikes like this. He is tired of fighting the Israelis. He is now more determined than ever to take the fight to the United States. Venezuela will welcome him. He will travel to Venezuela and figure out a way to strike US proper.

When Rebecca's associates at the Tel Aviv Office provided data to Israel revealing Muhammed Zarif's activities, the US and Israel administrations agreed that the US would destroy one of Zarif's teams if the Israelis identify what the US believed is a Russian spy with operations in Lebanon, Syria and believed Gaza.

The Israeli's identify the Russian Boris and Muhammad at the last IDF checkpoint into Gaza. Their photographs, given to the IDF capturing team.

The American assault team remained in the area after the submarine missile strike and observed Zarif's brother's reaction. The US team does not attack. There will be another day and location, and that new platform is Venezuela.

At the same time, Seamus O'Malley is working out in his weight room. The national news is blaring from his living room television.

"Reports are coming in from Quebec along the banks of the St. Lawrence River of an explosion and an engine room fire on a large Panamanian registered freighter. The freighter is in danger of sinking. There are three confirmed crew casualties."

"What! Could it be related to Montreal Detective MacDougal's, Black Cat case?"

Made in the USA
Coppell, TX
23 November 2019

11845026R00203